24

LIBRARIAN

BRIAN FENCE

.

MOON RABBIT PUBLISHING
Librarian
Brian Fence

ISBN: 0989366308
ISBN-13: 978-0-9893663-0-4

To my mother, Karen, who supports me no matter what crazy endeavor I pursue, and to my father, Roger, who taught me I had something worth writing to begin with.

CONTENTS

ACKNOWLEDGMENTS

This novel is the culmination of the talents of countless individuals, and for their help I am eternally grateful.

First of all, my de facto editor and great friend, James Aldous, deserves a gold medal for support; without him, I sincerely doubt *Librarian* would have ever have found its way into the world in its current form. His insights and edits (even the annoying ones about physics) proved invaluable.

My extremely talented Twin Star, Marissa Morris, provided me with the most beautiful artwork for the cover, and the meowtastical Tony Maszeroski contributed helpful technological know-how and happily converted me into a Mac user.

Finally, I'd like to thank my copy-editor Margaret Musselwhite and her brother Doug (who introduced us), the numerous clients of my parents that gave me such encouragement, and the online community. Reddit, in particular, is an unimaginably kind section of the Internet and full of people who genuinely want to read and help indie authors succeed.

CHAPTER ONE

Autumn in Port Hollish was a time of great delight for Lenna; she loved everything from the crisp breeze blowing in from the sea to the even crisper red-gold apples. It was a season of ochre leaves, crackling fireplaces, and the soft rustle of the wind playfully turning the pages of a book placed on a desk beneath an open window. The change in seasons meant the docks and markets, which in the warmer months were crowded with exotic spices and fruits so succulent you didn't mind if their juices dripped down your chin, would begin to quiet, their normal chatter reduced to a soft murmur. Lenna abhorred the humidity that came with the warmer months, when her wavy hair, semi-manageable in cooler times, became a gorse bush of curls.

And so at long last autumn had come to Lenna's beloved city on the sea, and as had been her tradition for some years now she threw open the window to let the tangy morning air into her bedroom. Her father, who shared her sentiments on preferable temperatures, had hours before opened the windows and the kitchen door to the garden on the way to his workshop. The front of their home — a slightly well-to-do, two-storied house in a good neighborhood near Hollish Commons — was devoted to her father's obsession and source of income: timepieces.

In Port Hollish (and some of the closer towns in the nation of Fallowfields) the Faircloth family had an established reputation, passed down from father to son, as craftsmen of highly original and intricate clockworks, despite the fact that both Lenna and her father tinkered with other types of mechanisms on the side. Thane Faircloth's work was truly that of a master clockmaker, but he remained modest and preferred to keep business on the quieter side of things and his clientele even smaller. Lenna knew that underneath his cloak of humility, her father was fervidly proud of his works and, like his daughter, could be an intolerable perfectionist.

Lenna changed out of her nightclothes with a brisk efficiency and folded them atop her quilted bedspread. Slipping her spectacles onto the bridge of her nose, she glanced at the ornately carved wooden clock on her desk: she had woken up earlier than planned thanks to the blare of a steamtrain's horn. The train had come to Port Hollish over two years ago and, though it increased commerce and facilitated travel as far out as Ilya, Lenna, who had always been a light sleeper, had yet to grow accustomed to the noise. Steam power might be the next innovation of civilized society, she thought, but it certainly wasn't a facilitator of a good night's rest.

Hair somewhat tamer than normal, Lenna shrugged into a dark blue, short corduroy jacket and slipped her feet into a pair of leather boots, more practical than stylish. She reckoned she might as well get an early start; there was no chance of getting back to sleep, and the extra hour and cool weather would afford her a walk through Hollish Commons, the expanse of parks and tree-lined paths that constituted a large portion of the city. In addition to Port Hollish's centuries-old ports, the advent of the steamtrain had bolstered the city's industrial growth; still, residents of the city still demanded that the mayor preserve their verdant sanctuary, and so far they had been successful.

Lenna skipped down the stairs to the kitchen, a comfortable — if a bit cluttered — space. The table was usually covered with piles of schematics or a stack of borrowed books since Lenna and her father seldom had the opportunity to share a meal. Thane Faircloth could be found in his workshop from the early hours of the day until mid-morning, when he would open the shop or, should there be a special commission or repair request from a good customer, head out into the city on business. Lenna herself was usually occupied with her own work until the evening, often using it as an excuse to pop into one of the local pubs near her library to buy a pie or a bowl of stew, accompanied by a pint (or more) of lager.

Despite their difference in schedules, though, father and daughter made time for one another nearly every day. Under the subtle light of the gas lamps in her father's workshop, Lenna would sip his homemade cider, becoming increasingly talkative as the potent, tangy liquid worked its magic on her tongue. Now and then her father would ask her to help with a particularly tricky assembly or mechanical configuration, although that was usually before she had too much cider.

Lenna jotted a few sentences to her father on a mostly blank sheet of paper pinned to the corkboard near the workshop door before dipping her fingers into an open jar on the shelf and plucking out a glistening pickled egg. She had an incredible fondness for these little treasures, not only for their pungent, earthy taste but because the lingering vinegary scent on her fingers and breath infuriated her disagreeable supervisor, Senior Librarian Jeffer Scalla.

Under normal circumstances, well-bred young women such as Lenna (or so she told herself) would not be prone to such catty behavior, but Scalla was crotchety, quick to explode in a rage, and — in a terribly old-fashioned way — against the idea of an 'educated woman.' So until the old coot retired or found himself under the sod, Lenna would grimly stick to her regimen of a strong performance at work and a morning ritual of pickled eggs.

The air outside tasted as crisp and juicy-sweet as Lenna had imagined it would. She walked out the shop's main door and stepped under its modest wooden sign — 'Faircloth Timepieces & Mechanical Repairs' — and was greeted by the tingling of cool air against her cheeks. A few other Port Hollish citizens were already going about their day, despite the early hour; they, like Lenna, were taking advantage of the first truly autumnal morning of the year.

The men tilted their heads or removed their caps as they passed her, and several neighbors were busily washing down the cobblestone lane in front of their doors. This section of town was older but comfortable; being this close to the Commons meant most of its residents had been citizens for several generations, since the time of the Unification. Most families in Lenna's neighborhood ran small, well-respected businesses like her father's: florists, cobblers, and tailors whose reputation made them notable in the community, if not terribly wealthy.

Still, being a neighborhood of older construction, it allotted residents sufficient space for gardens, and Lenna found the old-fashioned buildings, constructed of hardy, salty wood, much more charming. In some of the more affluent sections of town, modern constructions of brick and mortar steadily encroached upon Port Hollish, and in the areas around the docks and new train station, life could be quite intense. Lenna preferred her simple, if not so lavish, old home.

She made her way down the lane, toward Hollish Commons. By her reckoning, with the extra hour or so before she was due to clock in at the library, she could take the southern path, where the asters would still be dotting the turf on either side of the road. Lenna would still arrive at work slightly early, but in much better spirits at having been awoken by the howl of a train's horn.

She shuffled down the lane at a delightfully slow pace, murmuring a morning's greeting to some of her neighbors. The road eventually met Lia Street, the grand avenue that ran from the port that surrounded the west and south of the walled city to its main gate. There, it would join the Continental Highway and span the majority of the countryside. While in the past this would have left the wide road a constant source of traders and merchants, bringing their wares from Ilya or the Krevlum Empire to the north, the influx of goods via the new trains had reduced traffic on the main road immensely. Now, it was mostly used for those who traveled by carriage or farmers from the outlying towns coming into the city on business.

In mornings, though, the intersection, granting access to the municipal district, was crowded with a new sort of trader: various public workers eager (or perhaps not so eager) to start their administrative duties or conduct business at one of the embassies. Soon, harried men in their business attire would be determinedly marching off to work while their younger, ambitious counterparts rattled past them on bicycles, the bolder cyclists often evoking curses from passersby.

Across the way, hugging the small decorative archway marking the entrance to Hollish Commons, was the cart of a street vendor run by a good-looking, half-Ilyan man a year or two younger than Lenna. He dealt in strongly spiced Ilyan coffees and teas, and his cart's location varied by day. Lenna grimaced, contemplating heading back the other way, but the merchant had already spotted her and begun waving fiercely in her direction. She sighed, hating to attract public attention, and dutifully crossed the road toward the brightly painted cart and its eye-opening aromas.

"Good morning, Miss Librarian." The grinning vendor's shockingly blonde hair was glaring in the early sunshine. "Might I interest you in a delicious coffee, brought straight from Ilya by my father himself?"

"Morning, Jorian," Lenna answered cautiously. She did not fancy hot drinks in the morning, but she was eager to be on her way. Lenna fished about inside a leather satchel hanging from her belt and withdrew some coin.

Jorian smiled knowingly as he took the money and offered in exchange a paper mug full of steaming, velvety coffee. It was a much more potent blend than Lenna was accustomed to, the Ilyans being known throughout the four nations for their intensely flavored food. Still, Lenna hastily gulped down as much as she could tolerate, thanked Jorian for his service, and set out on her way down the southern path of the Commons before the inevitable happened.

To her back, the coffee seller called, "Keeping any special company these days, Miss Librarian?"

Lenna paused, cringing. She glanced back over her shoulder, cheeks crimson. "No," she said flatly.

The merchant smiled again, merrily. "Well, if you ever want to master a few more Ilyan phrases, I'd be more than happy to teach you." He then rattled off a few sentences in such fast Ilyan that Lenna's head began to swim. While her grasp of the written Ilyan language was fairly strong, her conversational ability left much to be desired. Judging by the lecherous look on Jorian's face, however, Lenna inferred that he wasn't commenting on how lovely the weather was this morning.

"No, thank you," she replied in carefully worded Ilyan, her tongue thick and accent heavy. Switching back to her native language, she coolly bid the young man a good day and marched briskly through the arch and onto the unpaved, dusty path that winded through the southern portion of the Commons.

One encounter with Jorian had been more than enough for Lenna, who now at twenty-two considered herself much more mature, or at the very least more selective, in whom she associated with than she was at seventeen. She had, in theory, only agreed to meet with the young man to practice her Ilyan. Jorian, apparently, had had other ideas as he tried to ply her with beer. It was the first time that Lenna felt remorse for deliberately avoiding local gossip, for if she had listened to even the most uninformed of grandmothers on the other side of town, she'd have known in advance that Jorian was nothing more than a tactless, dull playboy. She felt a fool, like when her classmates in her early years of schooling teased and called the bespectacled girl "Lenses Faceclock."

The encounter had soured Lenna's mood considerably, so much so that she imagined the lovely asters cowering in fear as she stomped down the path in a cloud of dust, splashing raindrops of pungent coffee. It was a great shame, she thought morosely, that her pickled-egg stratagem was not as efficacious on unwanted suitors as it was on Jeffer Scalla.

Lenna arrived at the city center a bit closer to the library's opening hour than she had intended due to an unfortunate incident with a goose. Her temper had not improved much: not only had the mad fowl savagely lunged at her, honking with fury, but her foot had caught on a wayward stone and she had spilled the coffee down the front of her deep red skirt. The stain could be lifted, Lenna believed, but she was not terribly excited about the prospect of smelling like an Ilyan coffeehouse for the rest of the day. According to the small gold timepiece clipped to her jacket, Lenna had just passed the threshold in which she might have been able to return home, change into something clean, and arrive back at work without being late.

Drawing curious glances from others along the road, Lenna crossed Lia Street from the Commons' southern gate and hurried past the town hall. Lenna supposed the building was quite grand in its size and height, and it was true that it was a symbol of Port Hollish's rise to commercial prominence after the treaties of peace were signed between the four nations. Still, she much preferred the library, which was nestled across the way from the town hall and sat in its squat, stony solitude only a few blocks from the bay. It was close enough to the water that Lenna often had time to sneak out to the wharf to eat a boxed lunch and read a few chapters of whatever volume of lore had found its way into her pocket that day.

She darted across the lane that separated the library from the hall and, rather than use the main entrance, headed toward the building's rear door. If luck would have it, she could sneak into the library unnoticed and attempt to salvage her skirt. As she approached the huge library windows, a ginger tabby peeked its head out of the shadows. It saluted her with a mew and a few bumps of its head.

"Good morning to you too, Meow," Lenna said. "I'm afraid I don't have anything for you right now, though. Try again at lunch."

She turned the knob on the door, annoyed to discover that it was still locked. Jeffer refused to give Lenna a key to either of the library's entrances, a testament to his misogyny and inflated sense of self-worth. He had, according to Lenna's knowledge, some gift for the magical arts, but it was so minor that it never constituted a danger to himself or others if untrained. His lack of talent prevented him from being accepted by the Blue Crescent Brotherhood, a scholarly order formed to preserve and cultivate arcane knowledge after a brutal war ages ago. Lenna was well-read enough to analyze Jeffer's insecurity and lofty attitudes as his coping mechanism at being rejected. She was not impressed.

She rapped softly on the oak door, not really expecting an answer. Lenna, who, like Jeffer and all children on the Continent, had in younger years manifested some ability to manipulate magic, fancifully imagined what she would do to the door, Jeffer, and that slimy Jorian had she been properly

11

trained. Something especially painful, and possibly even mutilating. Disfigurement was certainly an option. Lenna contemplated various tortures as she trudged around the side of the building and up the worn stone steps to the library's main entrance.

The double doors opened onto the grand lobby, as Jeffer referred to it, and reflected the library's simplistic design. Constructed after a time of great political and cultural upheaval, it was erected to prevent any further loss of knowledge, not for aesthetics. Over the span of many decades, Port Hollish's library became the nation's primary guardian of knowledge both new and old and now, thanks to the steamtrain, texts could be more quickly imported from other nations, though in recent months rumors of aggressive behavior along the border of the Krevlum Empire had curtailed shipments dramatically.

Jeffer's 'grand lobby' was in actuality an antechamber that served as a reception room for patrons and researchers. Yellow light from the narrow windows spaced evenly along the top of the stone walls gave the chamber an almost desert-like quality, sandy and rustic. In the center sat an unimposing greeting desk as old as the library itself, and behind it a paunchy, sparse-haired man in his middle years.

Jeffer Scalla had worked at this institution for more years than many (except he) cared to remember, though his promotion to senior librarian had occurred only three years ago, about six months after Lenna began working. She had much preferred Jeffer's predecessor, a somewhat eccentric old scholar named Klegg. To this day, Lenna couldn't help but wonder if Klegg's passing was actually a murder orchestrated by her power-hungry, porky egomaniac of a boss.

As if scripted, Jeffer raised his head from a pile of papers — patron logs — and squinted at Lenna as she entered the library. His beady eyes were bloodshot and surrounded by dark rings. They immediately traveled to the wet coffee stain on the junior librarian's skirt. Lenna briefed her superior on the coffee incident, leaving out the damned goose, and then inquired about the senior librarian's health.

He snorted, an act that caused his entire nose — a massive, blood-vessel-coated monster — to shift up toward his receding hairline. "I'm fine, Miss Faircloth," he said, refusing to acknowledge Lenna's title as Junior Librarian. "Moreover, I'm thankful that cooler weather seems to be in store. In the heat, the combination of that Ilyan coffee and those ghastly pickled eggs would be almost too much for a man of my constitution to endure."

Lenna suppressed an urge to roll her eyes and chose instead to shift the discussion toward topics other than her stained skirt. "Is the shipment from Crescent Island still on schedule?" The library was expecting a loaned collection of previously inaccessible texts that predated the God War; historical records such as those were primarily owned by the Brotherhood, who had chosen a rocky, desolate island — aptly named for its shape — a few days northwest by ship.

Scowling, a most natural expression for Jeffer, the librarian shook his head. "The boat was due in this morning, but there has been a delay." He held up a scrap of paper bearing a hastily scrawled message. "An envoy from their embassy delivered this a few minutes before you arrived. Storms or some such nonsense."

It was not in Lenna's best interests to express her disappointment to Jeffer, though truthfully she had been yearning to peruse the new texts since she learned of their existence. In fact, it was because of her connection with an old friend in the Brotherhood that Lenna was able to negotiate the loan at all. It must enrage Jeffer that his inferior had succeeded in an area where he could not; any hitch in the project would indubitably both sickly delight and anger the senior librarian.

"In any case," her superior continued, "the embassy seems to think that the ship should arrive in port sometime this afternoon, leaving us plenty of time to begin on the Back Room."

"By 'us,' I'm assuming you mean 'me,'" Lenna said, groaning inwardly. The "Back Room" was code in the library for the large chamber in the dark recesses of the lower level, where unrecognizable and damaged texts had been stored by librarians and scholars over the centuries. Lenna, allergic to dust and loath to wade through years of moldy paper, had steadfastly avoided the Back Room as often as she could.

"Well, of course I'll need to stay here to monitor and assist our patrons..."

"Of course." Lenna sighed and, cursing the selfish weather gods for delaying the ship, resigned herself to dusty solitude. A breaking storm the night before might have provided Port Hollish with a delicious autumn day, but it had damned Lenna to the dungeon.

After confirming remaining minutiae with Jeffer, Lenna parted ways with the reception desk and threw open the large oak doors at the other end of the lobby. Before her towered her beloved bookshelves: rows upon rows of knowledge ordered, organized, and cataloged. The wide windows on the three walls of the large main floor shed streaks of autumnal light on the leather-bound volumes of history and motes of dust danced in worship of great epics written in vellum.

Lenna's mood lightened considerably, for it was in this one grand space that she could truly let her sense of self float away, awash in an ocean of learning. The library was civilization, community, and comfort: it had been a favorite spot of Lenna's since before she could read. Now, it was a place of solace.

She entered the chamber, closing the doors behind her, and wandered among the stacks that she had come to know so completely. Her fingers lingered on the smooth spines of the books as Lenna walked up and down the aisles, touching the volumes with an intimacy that someone like Jeffer Scalla could never understand. Unconsciously she wandered from section to section like a drunkard come home, clumsily and randomly, but with a familiarity that guided her without mishap. As she had on many occasions before, Lenna suddenly regained her senses as her hand fell on a familiar leather-bound volume darkened by constant human touch.

The book tumbled out into her hand seemingly of its own volition, and Lenna flicked open the cover with a touch of her finger. The title was *The Unification of the Freewomen of Laur*, a work outlining the formation of a united, matriarchal society from various tribes of slaves that had been liberated after the fall of Laur. Though she did not follow their ways, Lenna was half Freewoman by right and her mother had made certain, sometimes against Lenna's will, to properly educate her. Familiar passages, some memorized, leapt out as she idly flipped through the book, and Lenna raised it to her nose, inhaling. Very faintly, beneath the crispy brown smell of the tanned pages, oily leather, and heady earthiness of dust there remained, Lenna imagined, the half-floral, half-astringent scent of her mother, like honey and witch hazel.

She closed the book and started to return it to its rightful place on the shelf before flashing it a brief, conspiratorial smile. If she was doomed to spend her day in the murky depths of the library, why not have some company? Lenna slipped the leather volume into a pocket on the inside of her jacket and gave it an affectionate pat.

"All right, Mom," she said, "let's get this over with." And, having secured a small oil lamp, she opened another door in the room's northwest corner and descended the narrow stairway to the library's lower level.

CHAPTER TWO

As the day drew on, Lenna became increasingly convinced that her nose, assaulted by dust, would rip itself from her face and get lost in the clutter of the Back Room. From the sheer multitude of sneezes that erupted, she knew that her relationship with her nose would never be the same. *Everything has changed*, it seemed to say to her, in a grievous tone. Lenna eventually realized that being alone in a poorly lit storeroom in the corner of a basement of a very old building was not a very good test of one's mental stability. Who converses with their nose?

She did, however, make some headway on sorting a pile of yellowing scrolls formerly neglected by both librarians and time. Not that they were particularly worth saving, in Lenna's opinion; the scrolls, at a glance, were for the most part indecipherable, their lettering having faded. This task was, and Lenna realized this, a revenge designed for her by that big-nosed ninny, Jeffer. She was proud to admit, and had on occasion boasted, that she ignored most of the Port Hollish gossip, but Lenna's ears could not help but perk up when the town began to chatter about the upcoming arrival of the texts from the Blue Crescent Brotherhood.

Acquisitions of this kind, Lenna considered as she unceremoniously dropped a pile of worm-chewed volumes into a rubbish bin, were a rare prospect indeed. Since most ancient documents were destroyed during the God War, the Brotherhood had appointed itself the sole authority of information preservation. Though their order had started for the pure, humanitarian prospect of securing texts and the knowledge of magic for future generations, over the past few centuries, and specifically after the Continent transformed from a series of homesteads and small towns into four great nations, the Brotherhood had become increasingly protective of its archives. Its members shared little and aggressively sought to gain even more.

That Lenna was able to arrange a loan of histories was, in her budding librarian mind, a minor miracle. Her only connection with the Brotherhood itself was her childhood friend, Gilbert Hovey, who was recruited by the Brotherhood to train in the magical arts at the age of twelve. Lenna had been fourteen at the time and was keenly aware of the permanence of his departure. Her ego was slightly pricked: despite

Lenna's natural affinity for magic, stronger than most children's, the Brotherhood was never an option for her. As its name implied, the order was exclusively male.

Not that she had really desired to enter the Brotherhood: Lenna was more concerned with immersing herself in the world of books. She dreamed of heading off to University, where she would presumably read more, and of reading even more afterward while teaching. Though that plan had yet to come to fruition, she convinced herself that life in the library was a happy one. Her imagination was such that even during menial tasks (such as sorting through rank old scrolls, not even fit for toilet tissue), she was capable of wondrous daydreams: fantasies of wild horses running on the beaches of Gallas to the south and adventures in the mysterious floating city, Tel-abol, far to the west, beyond Crescent Island. It was only a myth, but Lenna liked to think that one day, she would prove its existence, organizing a grand expedition out into the dark, uncharted waters that surrounded the Continent.

Over the years, as Lenna's imagination blossomed, her magical gifts faded, as the majority of children's do without proper tutelage. She did keep up a correspondence with Gilbert, however, and would often write him letters in witty prose far into the night by gaslight. Although Gil kept the subject of his education brief, as was required of apprentices in the Brotherhood, he did keep the junior librarian well-informed about any particularly interesting new finds. When he had mentioned the Brotherhood's intention of sending a collection of texts on tour across the Continent, Lenna excitedly wrote him a letter in hasty script proclaiming, "I simply must have these for our Library before anyone else."

For his part, Gilbert had apparently cajoled his former tutor into intervening on the Port Hollish library's behalf. Now, six months later, Lenna stood in the murky depths of the Back Room, waiting for the books' delayed arrival. She worked begrudgingly for some time, and despite her keen interest in literature and historical documents, Lenna's thoughts alternated between speculation about the new volumes and wringing out her coffee-stained skirt on the top of Jeffer Scalla's head. Fewer documents survived the review process than would have were Lenna in a more favorable mood.

By the time the hand on her timepiece breached the midday marker, Lenna was more dust mote than human. She must look absolutely dreadful in the ragged kerchief with which she had tied back her hair. She sighed: despite having woken up early this morning — albeit inadvertently — Lenna had neglected to pack any lunch, presuming she would be sufficiently well-attired to pop into the neighborhood's public house or buy a steaming meat pie from a bakery near the harbor. But now, coffee-stained and dust-coated, she hardly imagined she was presentable.

Lenna untied the knot of the kerchief and shook out her wavy hair, watching speckles of dust dance in the light before fading away into the darkness. She grabbed the lamp and headed out of the chaos of the Back Room and into the more ordered sections of the lower level, which contained some of the less-read books, like technical manuals and censuses. Aside from the Back Room, Lenna didn't particularly mind the lower level; there was something reassuring and safe about the world of engineering and fact-listing. It gave order to lives otherwise filled with angry geese and abrasive Ilyan boys.

Trudging up the stairway, Lenna welcomed the warming light from the library's windows, even if it did demonstrate how dusty she had become. Her stomach gurgled, arousing the attention of several patrons, but she smiled and walked out of the main entranceway toward the desk behind which sat her portly superior. Jeffer was busy conversing with one of the more wealthy patrons of the library, and Lenna knew it would be best not to disturb him. She deftly reached around the rim of the desk and grabbed a clanging ring of keys hanging on a nail, noticing the slight twitch of Jeffer's eyebrow. He wouldn't say anything now, not in front of an important citizen, but Lenna knew he would devise some other form of punishment for her later. Still, she was hungry and irritable, and simply not in the mood to wait.

Off the main lobby, through a rickety door that Jeffer always kept locked, was a hallway that led to the cloakroom, the main librarian's office, a tearoom, and several rooms for storage. The back door through which Lenna had originally intended to enter lie at the end of the long corridor. Jeffer's unyielding need to control of the entire library was a constant source of frustration for Lenna, since if she needed to fetch anything from storage, or even if she wanted to eat her lunch in the tearoom, she required Jeffer's solitary key set. One day, Lenna decided for the eightieth time, she would possess her own set of keys and take delight in arranging situations in which Jeffer was the one locked out. Not that she was particularly vindictive.

Once in the tearoom, Lenna found a tin of biscuits she had stashed some days before in the recesses of the mostly bare cupboard. It looked like the buttery crumb would be her main meal of the afternoon. At least, she thought as she nibbled a biscuit and flipped through the Freewoman book, once she changed after work, she could go out for a warm supper at a public house; if it were something like lamb stew, perhaps she could even encourage her father to leave his workshop for an hour or two.

Thane Faircloth, from what Lenna knew, had always been somewhat reserved; like Lenna, he was an introvert by nature and preferred to wile away his time tinkering with machines than take part in Port Hollish's social circuits. As a young girl Lenna had spent many an hour proudly watching her father repair music boxes and rusted toys in his free time, patiently explaining to his daughter how each gear and spring worked in perfect harmony with the others to produce a particular effect. It was a kind of wizardry of its own, Lenna had always thought, a way for humans to make sense of all the strange rules that governed the universe, without magic.

Every now and then, Lenna's mother Alanna would interrupt the pair and strongly suggest, as only a mother could, that the two hermits in the workshop take some fresh air. The three of them would wander the paths of Hollish Commons, her mother pointing out and subsequently testing Lenna about the different trees and plants they came across. Her father seldom spoke during these times, but as Lenna grew older she became more keenly aware of the secret smiles her parents shared, and the subtle way Thane Faircloth would slip his hand around his wife's and squeeze it affectionately.

Those soft, sunlit memories, scented with grass and gardenia, remained the most valuable treasure in Lenna's life, something steadfast that could be kept locked away inside her mind. After her mother had passed, the walks had stopped; Thane, for days after Alanna's death, spoke no words, and at the funeral — surprisingly not a traditional Freewoman pyre — his ashen hand gripped the ten-year-old's shoulder firmly, as though he were depending on the girl to help him muster the strength to stand. Lenna would never forget the desperate pressure of her father's hand, his fingers pressed deep into her flesh. It had not hurt her, but it kindled within Lenna a stony resolve, a determination to be a pillar that would give her father the courage to keep on standing.

Like all wounds, time helped to heal, or at least numb, the pain of Alanna's death. Though her father seldom left the house unless on business, over the years Lenna had been able, now and then, to forcefully encourage him — much like her mother used to — to get some fresh air and enjoy a dinner at the pub. They would chat amiably about the intricacies of mechanical design or whatever book Lenna happened to be delving into or what she had learned in school. Most of the shopping was done by Lenna, though the two shared other household responsibilities like laundry, cooking, and tidying. At sixteen, Lenna graduated from her college with top marks, but despite her mentors' and father's encouragement, she began apprenticing at the library instead of heading off to University, a decision that, of late, she had come to regret.

Lenna brushed the biscuit crumbs from the table and swept the Freewoman book closed. She hadn't been focusing, anyway. In one swift motion she stood up from her chair and engaged in a lengthy stretch, hardly feeling ready to be sent back to the dungeon. Checking her watch again, like a child waiting for a special parcel to arrive, Lenna wondered if the books had somehow been magicked over to the library during the brief respite with her tin of biscuits. She popped her head into one of the storage rooms and was dismayed to find no new additions. With only one place left to check, she dismally marched down the hall and out into the library lobby.

"Have the volumes from the Brotherhood arrived?" she asked Jeffer, who was busy cramming a tremendous cheese sandwich into his mouth.

His voice was muffled and crumbs flew past his lips, making Lenna cringe as he replied. "Not in the twenty minutes you've been gone," he garbled. "Keys?"

Lenna hastily dropped the ring of Jeffer's keys onto the reception desk, wanting to avoid as much of the cheese storm as possible. They landed with a sharp jangle that cost Lenna a full-on ferocious, chipmunk-cheeked glare from the senior librarian, and, knowing that more than likely she would be harshly reprimanded, she dusted herself off as best she could before heading to the reading room to provide assistance to any patrons who might be there. Even though she was disgruntled and stained, anything was better than being subjected to a messy lecture while enduring that man's tactless chewing and swallowing. Thankfully, Jeffer's mouth was so completely engorged with cheese and bread that by the time he had forced it all down his throat, Lenna was already gone.

The autumn sun fell beneath the western horizon, and the chill of the sea air rolled over the library like a widow's sigh. Lenna shivered and rocked on the balls of her feet as she stood on the stairs before the building's entrance, her corduroy jacket not quite strong enough against the encroaching night air. *And soon enough it will be winter*, she reckoned, and wrapped her arms around herself. The shipment had been delayed once again until the evening, and Jeffer had told her she could wait outside for it; according to him, it was to arrive within a quarter of an hour. Lenna had been shivering for more than twice that amount of time.

She contemplated heading back inside, but ultimately decided that the chill in the air was far more agreeable than Jeffer. He was in a foul mood, precisely because he was forced to wait for the shipment to arrive and was too stubborn to trust Lenna to secure the library on her own. Making a monocle with her thumb and forefinger, Lenna peered up at the rising moon, its silvery fullness like a shining coin waiting to be pocketed. Its solitary journey through the night sky always filled Lenna with a kind of nostalgic loneliness, like a memory plucked out of a past life. She recalled a poem from her youth that her mother had been fond of reciting:

I am a child of the autumn moon,
Few are the children of the autumn moon.
It sings us a silver shadowed tune.

Love you for your mind, child, the moon sings.
Love me with your mind, child, the moon sings.
I'll give you a soul, most precious of things.

But that is a gift that burns like a fire —
Feed it fuel and it burns like a wild fire,
Starve it and soon its flame will expire.

For in this world too many souls are chilled,
Born into this world too many die chilled
Unless we allow their hearts to be filled.

It always had a soft sort of melancholy around the edges, Lenna thought, and as she scanned the lines in her mind she could picture her petite mother singing the poem by the fire when Lenna was a young girl. Her father would be sitting off in the corner, puffing away at his pipe and tinkering with some mechanism or other. Poetry and literature were two of the topics of her mother's Freewoman education that Lenna had not shirked. Knife training, on the other hand...

Lenna's musings were interrupted by a sudden call from a Brotherhood envoy, jogging up the lane. He was young, just out of boyhood, but did not wear the robes that indicated he was an apprentice. Probably he was a family member of someone in the Brotherhood who had no magical affinity but still maintained ties with the order. Lenna skipped briskly down the steps of the library and met the courier as he approached.

"Miss Faircloth?" he asked, panting a little.

"Indeed I am," Lenna replied. "Though a regrettably chilly one. Any word on the books?"

The young man straightened and cast Lenna an apologetic look. "The Brothers are still inspecting them at the embassy. They estimate another hour or so." Seeing the expression on Lenna's face, the page quickly added, "They sent me here with their sincere apologies. The storm was quite intense and they're making sure the volumes took no damage."

Sighing, Lenna gave a resigned shrug. "It can't be helped, I suppose. I'm lucky enough to be receiving the books in the first place." Her hand fished into the leather satchel at her side and plucked out a coin. She tossed it to the boy, whose numb hands fumbled with it a bit before stowing it away in a pocket. "Thank you for letting me know."

The boy nodded and made a polite goodbye before turning around and jogging off in the direction from which he had come. Lenna clasped her hands together and stretched toward the sky, emitting a soft groan of relief as she felt some of the popping of knots in her back and shoulder blades. At the very least, the Brotherhood was polite enough to keep her from waiting outside in the cold.

Jeffer was finishing up his daily routine of reviewing the patron log — all those wishing to use the library must sign in — despite there having been few guests today. Lenna had been confined to the Back Room's dank solitude for a fair part of the afternoon, but from what she had noticed, the head librarian hadn't had much at all to accomplish where his duties were concerned. He stiffened noticeably as Lenna approached the desk.

"Your precious delivery delayed again?" The pockmarked librarian clicked his tongue against the roof of his mouth. "It's high time we closed up for the evening, I think."

"But," she began to protest, "it will only be another hour or so."

The logbook slammed shut with a heavy thud of finality as Jeffer gazed at his subordinate over paunchy cheeks. "I suppose they'll just have to send the shipment in the morning."

"How am I supposed to categorize and index the volumes, let alone ascertain their contents, with only a few hours in the morning?" Lenna felt anger rising up in her.

"That," said the head librarian, "is entirely your concern, Miss Faircloth. This is your project, after all."

As he wobbled off, Lenna decided to curtail any more of his nonsense, once and for all. "Senior Librarian," she called after him. "You do realize that the mayor himself will be in attendance after lunch, don't you?"

Lenna was well aware that Jeffer knew the mayor would be visiting, and that it incensed him greatly. It was one of the reasons he was so bitter toward this project; the mayor had never attended any of Jeffer's functions. After the words had registered in his cauliflower-shaped ears, he stumbled and came to a halt.

"Well," he said curtly, without turning around, "the mayor will just have to be satisfied with whatever you manage to arrange by the meeting."

"You know, as Senior Librarian, I imagine the mayor would expect that any work presented had your thorough supervision and wholehearted support. After all, any presentation or event showcased to the community immediately reflects not only on our institution, but on you, its custodian, as well."

A silence fell, and Lenna gleefully noticed Jeffer's left shoulder twitch as his mind raged. He swiveled around precariously, with all the wobbles of an aspic, and glared at Lenna, red-faced. Every spot on his face looked to Lenna like a great white dollop of marshmallow in a sea of red punch. She desperately tried to suppress a look of revulsion.

"So, you wish me to stay here all night while you work, is that it?" he said acidly.

"I'd love the opportunity to work together on this project," Lenna lied, probably unconvincingly, "but you are busy enough; I can handle this alone."

"You want me to leave you here? Alone!?" Jeffer's eyes nearly popped out of his skull in disbelief.

"I'd need the keys for the evening, I'm afraid," she added. "Of course, if anything happened to them, you'd have the perfect opportunity to find a more responsible Junior Librarian."

Jeffer's eyebrows raised in interest at this. "And if the event is a success…"

"No doubt people would attribute it to your remarkable leadership here at the Port Hollish Library."

Lenna carefully kept her expression passive as Jeffer pretended to consider her proposal; she had absolute faith that his ego would not be able to refuse either prospect. In a few short minutes Lenna quite smugly found herself — after being on the receiving end of an impressive list of instructions, mostly superfluous — in possession of the keys to the library. She heaved a hefty sigh of relief as Jeffer slammed the main door behind him.

A giggle found its way past her lips. She rather felt like a child again, left alone in her father's shop for the first time. Something subtle had changed, as though the mysteries of the building were opening up their hidden truths to her. With the pale moonlight shining through the windows and the gas lamps casting different shadows, the library became uniquely Lenna's at that moment, and she felt an excitement in the pit of her stomach. She spun around, and let her coffee-stained skirt shed more dust in the moody night illumination.

Since there wasn't much left in the way of work and Lenna had absolutely no desire to return to the Back Room at this hour of the day, she sprawled out on the lobby's round desk, gazing up at the domed ceiling of the library. It was by no means as impressive as some of the older architecture on the Continent, but Lenna had loved it since her childhood. After the primary construction of the building, a local artist of no particular renown had been humbled when approached by the architect to paint a mural that spanned the dome.

In shades of gold and vermilion a stylized sun sank below the waves of Bonebreaker Bay, and the artist had delicately created an ombré effect in which the waters of the city's port darkened into the rich indigo of night. Stars of varying sizes, some of which Lenna recognized and some she could no longer seem to find, speckled the sky as it faded into deep darkness, and a lonely moon hung poised directly opposite to its sun. When Lenna was young, she imagined that the moon was the sun's best friend, and some whimsy of fate had forever separated them by the barrier of night and day. Science would prove her wrong in the end, of course, as it usually does the fantasies of little girls.

Still, even after reading a breadth of literature on astronomy, she could still stare at the dome feel the yearning of the moon.

Lenna plucked the small gold watch out of her jacket and let it dangle by its delicate chain, a pendulum against the backdrop of the mural. The watch, crafted by her father, had been given to Lenna as a graduation present and with proper care — not that she had much choice with her father around — the watch was still as unblemished as the day she received it at sixteen, and its hands moved with a graceful, faithful tick. As though she were in a trance, Lenna watched the seconds shuffle along and slip away into eternity.

Six years had passed since her father had embraced and tousled her, at that time, much longer mop of hair and carefully pressed the watch into her palm. She would have already finished her primary studies at University by now, unless she pursued an advanced field of academics. But packing up and attending University would have meant leaving her father alone, and that was not something Lenna could do lightly. As he was reserved by nature, she was certain her father would become a recluse without Lenna there. At least, that was how Lenna rationalized her decision to herself.

She swung her feet down off the reception desk and hopped to the floor with a pleasant clacking of her boots. After another luxuriant stretch and a fair bit of knuckle cracking, Lenna headed off towards the library's main chamber; as long as she was waiting, she might as well occupy her mind with a book rather than brood on the past. Of course, it wouldn't solve any of Lenna's problems or soften her regrets, but a quick trip through a fantastical world or a study of mathematics would occupy her mind until the long-awaited series of books from the embassy arrived.

Just as fingers curled around the bar-shaped doorknob to the library's reading room, Lenna distinctly heard a faint but persistent rapping in the distance. It sounded as though someone was knocking at a door, but not nearly enough time had passed for the envoy to arrive with the books and, in any case, Lenna had deliberately left the library's entrance unlocked to accommodate any messenger or late patron. Frowning in thought, Lenna supposed that the knocking could be coming from some other building in the area.

It persisted steadily, though, and if anything, increased in volume. Whoever was knocking was determined. Albeit unlikely, it wasn't impossible that the courier might use the back entrance, perhaps wishing to avoid any lingering patrons. The more she listened, head crooked to the side, the more convinced Lenna became that the source of the knocking was the rear exit. Her hand slipped away from the doorknob and she strode purposefully toward the side door of the lobby. At least, Lenna thought twistedly, it would be an excuse to use

Jeffer's keys. She would wear them down to metal nubs if it would prove a point.

When the door to the corridor opened, it was evident that the source of the knocking could be nothing other than the back door. Lenna continued down the hallway, shrugging off any self-doubt or logical thinking about how unwise it was for a young woman, on her own, to open a door to a mysterious caller in the evening hours. After all, however well-read, a bored librarian can be tempted to throw caution to the wind. She called out to the knocker in a stern voice and flicked aside the top bolt. Jeffer's key, obviously handled with care, slid smoothly into the bottom lock and turned with a satisfying click.

The heavy wooden portal swung outward, letting a gush of briny sea air into the musty corridor. Standing on the ledge were not one but two couriers, both dressed in the livery of the Blue Crescent Brotherhood, though their uniforms varied slightly. The shorter of the two young men wore a conservative short robe belted over a plain blouse, modest trousers, and scuffed brown leather boots. Everything was deliberately unadorned, from the grey-blue cotton of his clothing to the cropped, neatly combed dark hair on his head. From Lenna's knowledge, this young man — barely eighteen, he seemed — was dressed as an apprentice of the arts.

His companion, on the other hand, wore the well-tailored, longer robes of a full-initiated Brother.

Even the sleeves were longer, ending in large, embroidered scallops, and the neck was fastened with an ivory clasp that showed the magician's rank within the Brotherhood's confusing hierarchy. Both men looked pensive, as if they were in a hurry to enter the library, but the higher-ranking Brother's expression lightened as his gaze fell on Lenna.

She looked at the older man, puzzled, and took in his features: sandy hair in a perpetual state of disarray and a fiercely determined cowlick, green eyes speckled with hazel, and a lopsided grin. Lenna had not laid eyes on this face for more than eight years, yet she recognized it at once. The Brotherhood had taken her childhood friend at the age of twelve and had since produced a tall, solidly built version of the young boy who used to crunch apples and read books with Lenna underneath the shade of maple trees in Hollish Commons.

"Gilbert," she said.

The lopsided grin widened with relief and the tension in the mage's forehead relaxed. He took the stunned librarian's hand in both of his own and clasped it tightly. "Special delivery for a Miss Faircloth. Care to receive it?"

Both Lenna and the younger apprentice simultaneously rolled their eyes at Gilbert's casual confidence. Stepping back and extending her arm in an over-exaggerated gesture of welcome, Lenna ushered one old friend and one complete stranger into her library.

CHAPTER THREE

True to her nature, Lenna was full of questions, the most pressing of those why her friend was at the doorstep of her library with no notice and, unless he had magicked them into some deep pocket of his robes, without the rare volumes she had been expecting all day. Gilbert deftly deferred all questions until Lenna could procure them some chairs and something to wet their "travel-parched throats." As she escorted them down the hall in the direction of the tearoom, Lenna thanked any number of lucky stars that Jeffer had already gone home.

Gilbert did, at least, introduce the apprentice accompanying him; he was Luc Tural and, according to the older mage, an apprentice of considerable potential and ingenuity. As Lenna was introduced, Luc's eyes seemed to focus directly on the stain covering Lenna's skirt, and his nose wrinkled in a look of what Lenna interpreted as disdain. Mentally shrugging it off, she simply led the way to the small room where she had, earlier in the day, enjoyed a few moments of peaceful solitude and some biscuits. She wondered if she was socially bound to offer Luc the Prat some of her stash.

A silence had fallen over the group as they sat down. Lenna was able to provide Gilbert and his companion with some cold tea; the fire had earlier in the day settled down to embers and Lenna had not rekindled it. They each sat in silence, not drinking the brew and waiting uncomfortably for someone to break the silence. As they had been wont to do as children, Lenna and Gilbert both began speaking at the same time, interrupting each other.

"You've gotten taller," she said.

"Your hair is shorter," Gilbert said.

They both laughed as Luc stared, unmoved, at the porcelain teacup in his thin, well-manicured hands. Lenna could understand his awkwardness, but without really knowing why he had come, she could do little to ease his discomfort. She turned to Gilbert and pushed her spectacles up the bridge of her nose, assuming an expression of expectation. Hands folded over his crossed legs, Gilbert tentatively grinned again, and Lenna could see a nervous crease in his forehead that he hadn't possessed in his youth.

"I don't imagine you came here to personally deliver the books," Lenna inferred. "Have you received leave to visit your hometown?"

"You could say I experienced a sudden longing to see an old acquaintance," he replied jokingly. "But don't worry: your books are on their way, though I'm afraid their arrival is a tad delayed."

"Delayed again?" she asked incredulously. "The embassy is down the street; I could just *walk* there and fetch them myself! I needed those books this morning, to catalog them properly."

Gilbert shared a conspiratorial look with Luc, who smirked and swirled the tea around in his mug as though it were a fine wine. The blonde mage smiled apologetically at Lenna. "I'm afraid they'll be arriving tomorrow morning instead of tonight; they were a bit bulky for Luc and me to carry ourselves. We arranged for that messenger to tell you they were coming so we could be certain you'd still be here."

Subterfuge wasn't a tactic Gilbert had ever employed in Lenna's recollection. To her, he appeared just a larger version of the joyful youth who, demonstrating exceptional magical talent, had been accepted by the Blue Crescent Brotherhood. He was twelve when he boarded the Brotherhood's chartered cruiser to carry him across Bonebreaker Bay to the reclusive island the Brotherhood had colonized after the God War. Most Brothers, to Lenna's knowledge, seldom left the confines of the

Brotherhood unless on official business; apprentices, she was certain, never did. Lenna turned her gaze from her friend and caught Luc's attention. His eyes looked defiant and proud.

"Actually," Gilbert continued, drawing Lenna's attention back to him. He took a swig from his teacup, grimacing a little at the clammy liquid inside. "Luc and I are here on a mission for the Brotherhood."

"A mission," Lenna repeated.

"Yes," Gilbert said solemnly, "one of great importance for the future of the unified nations!"

Lenna burst out laughing, the peal of her great guffaw echoing off the whitewashed walls of the tearoom. "Say something *really* cryptic, Gil." She had to have a sip of the tepid tea to help calm her giggles.

Much to her surprise, Luc paled and his eyes flashed with anger. "How dare you speak to him like that, woman?"

Taken aback, Lenna could do nothing but stare at the enraged young man with the dark hair. In the moment it took her to process Luc's words Gilbert uttered a sharp reprimand on her behalf. She had an idea of what they were taught to think about the other sex in the Brotherhood, but at least Gilbert seemed to remember to behave like a cultured individual.

Abashed, Luc muttered something that could have been "I'm sorry" or "sod off" for all its clarity, but Gilbert seemed pleased with this response and turned back to Lenna. "Yes, it does sound melodramatic, but it also happens to be the truth. I'm sorry I can't say much more, but you know how it is." He put one finger to his lips, as if this should convince Lenna of the need for secrecy.

"So you're on a mission," Lenna played along, "and you've come to visit me."

"Actually, I've come here to ask for a favor."

"A favor? What on earth could I possibly do for a Brother from your order? I'm a librarian."

"Yes," Gilbert said cautiously. "It's not a big favor at all, really. Do you think you could put us up for a few hours, discreetly? If I recall correctly, you and your father still live in the house near North Gate, right?"

Perplexed, she answered tentatively. "Yes, but wouldn't you just stay at your embassy?"

Gilbert spread his hands, as though showing a hand of trumps. "The fewer eyes that see us, the better, even within our own order. I've arranged it so that a courier will deliver your books early tomorrow morning, but I would prefer it — if you are asked, mind you — that you say you received them tonight and were up until all hours poring over their revelatory insights."

Lenna immediately grew suspicious. It was widely accepted throughout the four nations that the Brotherhood engaged in clandestine activities, and the rumors of increased militaristic activity from the Empire up north — rumors of new, advanced technology and magics — had everyone a bit on edge as of late. Still, as Lenna drummed her fingers against the wooden table, Gilbert looking at her expectantly, she could not help but think a formidable organization like the Blue Crescent Brotherhood would have more reliable assets than a twenty-year-old mage, an apprentice, and their librarian chum.

"The books are just a ruse, aren't they?"

The blonde mage shrugged. "They're real and one of a kind — definitely what you're expecting."

"But it's no coincidence that they're coming here, to my library, and that you're back in Port Hollish."

"I suppose you could say that," Gilbert admitted.

"Are you getting me mixed up in something nasty?"

"Would I do that to my oldest friend?"

One finger on the bridge of her glasses, Lenna fixed her gaze on Gilbert and considered. They had always been truthful to one another. She recalled vividly a steamy, drizzly day in the rain. The summer heat melted the droplets and mist from the sea and blanketed Port Hollish with a deep, grey fog that stuck around her feet. Lenna's father had gripped her shoulder tightly as her mother's ebony casket was gently lowered into the tide, on pulleys. She wanted to throw her bouquet of flowers, a bundle of white roses that were her mother's favorite, onto the casket, but the young Lenna couldn't move. Her father was relying on her, and she was frozen.

Gilbert, though he was only eight at the time, seemed to understand Lenna's intent. That day, dressed in his most formal attire, he pushed through the small gathering of people, past his parents and neighbors, and strode up to stand by Lenna as she silently endured Alanna Faircloth's funeral. The small boy, with hair so blonde it would shine white in the sunshine, gently pried the flowers from Lenna's stiff, cold hands and, leaning over the dock, let the bouquet fall to rest on the coffin as it at last crested the rolling waters of the bay. Afterward, when the two children were alone, they had made a promise: if one of them was ever in trouble, the other would help, no matter what the request or circumstances. Gilbert had even made the sullen Lenna laugh by choosing a ridiculous password to invoke their new pact.

"Say the password," Lenna said.

Gilbert looked at Luc and then returned his gaze to Lenna. "You're really going to make me say it?"

She nodded, while Luc looked on, exasperated, and took a dainty sip from his mug.

"Fine," he said. "Sparkle ponies."

There was a sputtering sound as the collected apprentice choked on his tea, spraying some of the liquid on the table. Lenna raised her eyebrows queryingly in his direction as he hastily produced a handkerchief and wiped up the dribble. Meanwhile,

Gilbert's face turned a shade of red so intense that
Lenna was instantly reminded of Jeffer. She wanted
to laugh at the whole ridiculousness of her
adventures with geese and dark rooms and waiting
for books and not waiting for books. What a day!
Lenna's stomach was signaling it was dinner
o'clock, and her best friend had mysteriously
appeared and needed her help. He had invoked the
password. Sighing, she pushed back her chair with
her feet, the rungs grating across the floor, and
stood before the two magicians.

"All right," she said rather unceremoniously.
"Sparkle ponies it is. Let's go."

Gilbert beamed; Luc shrugged; and so Lenna
emptied their teacups, locked up the various parts
of the library as per the senior librarian's detailed
instructions, and led her two guests out into the
clammy sea night of Port Hollish. She made sure to
stash the keys where Jeffer had indicated, lest she
incur his wrath come morning. Lenna wanted
nothing in the world to interfere with her enjoyment
of the rare texts Gilbert had promised would be
hers, albeit temporarily, tomorrow.

It was still early enough in the evening that there
would be plenty of passersby on the streets,
especially in this area, the administrative district of
Port Hollish. Though most people by now would
have finished their various jobs, those who stayed
late or fancied a bit of supper from a pub would yet

be lingering around the main roads. The temperature, having dipped considerably after the setting of the sun, would keep most people from the damp pathways of the Commons, though, so Lenna decided the group's best chance at avoiding attention would be to take a slightly circuitous road to her house.

The southern path, where Lenna had been so annoyingly assaulted by the goose earlier that day, was thankfully deserted save for a fine mist that danced a ghostly waltz a few inches above the ground. Gilbert, for his part, remarked quietly but amiably about how he had missed the damp fog of Port Hollish; Crescent Island, he lamented, was rainy and fog-laden as well, but lacked Port Hollish's charm. Apparently, there was not much time for leisure, and the island itself was dull and craggy. It was, in Gilbert's words, a paradise, so long as your hobby was collecting piles and piles of grey stones.

Lenna kept up a steady but not overtly brisk pace; while some of her neighbors were prone to taking evening constitutionals, Lenna was not known for jogging at any hour of the day, let alone on misty evenings. Her primary concern was that, if by chance anyone from her neighborhood saw them, the mages' robes would give them away as members of the Brotherhood or, worse, some of the local residents might recognize Gilbert. If someone spotted them, town gossip ensured that the news would spread of Gilbert Hovey's return to Port Hollish as a full-fledged magician.

As they crept into the light of a street lamp, their feet squishing along the muddy path, Lenna frowned. A quick glance at her timepiece alerted her to the fact that a steamtrain was due to arrive shortly, meaning Train Way, a road of new construction (and dubiously named in one librarian's opinion) designed to facilitate traffic to and from the station, would be inundated with travelers. Lenna quietly cursed her timing. Raising one hand, she signaled her companions to halt.

"What's the matter, Lenna?" asked Gilbert, his breath coming out in delicate white puffs.

"We really should keep going," Luc added.

"Gil, can't you do something about those robes? They're a dead giveaway. Couldn't you have changed?"

Gilbert and Luc both looked down at their attire curiously, as though the thought of wearing anything else had never occurred to them. Frowning, Gilbert scratched his chin, and Lenna was surprised to see a faint blonde stubble blanketing it like down on a baby chick. It seemed strange that he could be a twenty year-old man who shaved, she thought. Luc continued looking at Gilbert, and when his gaze was returned, both nodded. Gilbert placed a hand gently on Luc's shoulder and shut his eyes in concentration. All around their feet the mist gathered and the light of the streetlight seemed to pull away, letting the shadows cloak the two mages. Lenna detected the faint scent of the sea on the air.

She shook her head and blinked at the two mages, adjusting her glasses. "What did you do?"

"There's no such thing as true invisibility," Gilbert explained. "At least, if there is, it's not within our power. Still, we can make ourselves a little less noticeable."

Lenna was impressed. Her friend was correct: neither Gilbert nor Luc was invisible, but they had somehow become more *subtle*, and if Lenna had not known they were standing before her, she would have probably just ignored them altogether. Staring at them now was like trying to read without her spectacles: their edges were blurry, out of focus. All in all, Lenna thought it was rather elegant.

"Is that better?" Gilbert asked.

"How did you do that?"

"Magic." He smiled. "I'll show you someday."

"Gil!" cried Luc indignantly. "You can't!"

The elder magician ruffled Luc's hair, which, from Lenna's perspective, was dizzying from the effects of the spell. "Always the devout pupil, eh?"

"Right," said Lenna. "Let's keep on. No sense standing outside." A few droplets of rain had fallen onto her head and shoulder with a plop as wisps of cloud had moved in to obscure the night sky.

She led the group along the tree-lined path, furtively casting glances from side to side as Gilbert and Luc walked in tandem behind her. Gilbert's commentary had stopped, as though he had suddenly become aware of the gravity of being discovered. Apparently, Lenna thought morosely, Gilbert wasn't much better at covert operations than she was. Luc remained taciturn and probably still wore a sour expression on his face, though with his cloak of shadows it would be hardly noticeable.

The main path branched off into a narrower, less-kept trail that winded through denser foliage to the north. Continuing in the group's current direction would ultimately bring them out of the Commons where Lenna had entered this morning: at the intersection of one of the busier roads in town, where there were sure to be crowds coming and going and, knowing Lenna's luck, an annoying Ilyan suitor. Instead, she took the narrow trail, grimacing as she felt her boots sink into the wetter earth.

As the group progressed, the brambles and bushes grew thicker than Lenna had expected. She hadn't taken this trail much this past summer as it was usually a getaway for young couples seeking some privacy, and stumbling over two people rolling around in the undergrowth usually had unfortunate results. Gorse nagged at her skirt and uneven, squelchy ground significantly hampered their speed. More droplets fell from the night sky as clouds quickly moved in, hiding the moonlight, and away from the streetlights the road before them quickly became dark.

Gingerly, Lenna led Gilbert and Luc down the darkening path, wondering what she had gotten herself into by agreeing to help the two mages. Out of nowhere, a root conspired to grab her foot and Lenna stumbled forward with a lurching feeling in the pit of her stomach. Gilbert moved silently but quickly, and before Lenna plummeted into the mud his embrace, with more muscle than his robes displayed, enveloped her. In that brief instance, as Lenna's body was wrapped in her friend's arms, the path before them, angry root and all, was illuminated by a pale blue flash of light, and both Lenna and Gilbert seemed to hum with a subtle vibration.

It lasted but a moment, and Gilbert pulled Lenna back up to her feet, swiveling her around to face him. In the darkness, she could just barely make out the incredulous look on his face, and she imagined her own expression was, if anything, more shocked than his. Though the queer sensation had stopped, Lenna's body still retained a memory of the vibration, making her skin tingle. She could only assume that some kind of magic had just happened.

"What the hell was that?" asked Luc from somewhere behind Gilbert.

"I agree," said Lenna, hating the shakiness in her voice. She gulped down her nerves. "What just happened, Gil?"

"I'm not sure," he said distantly. "But let's hurry; if memory serves, we aren't far from your house."

Nodding, Lenna continued leading them along the path as the droplets turned into a persistent, if light, drizzle of rain. The temperature was rapidly dropping too, causing the group to shiver. Perversely, Lenna mused that her entire outfit would have to be taken in for proper cleaning at this rate. She wondered if the Brotherhood would reimburse her the fee.

Before long, they trooped out of the more vicious of the undergrowth as the path joined a larger walkway running along the base of Neap Hill. Streetlights dotted the landscape like evenly spaced trees, showcasing a bedraggled librarian and two nondescript figures. A few passersby gazed at Lenna oddly, but that was probably because most people would not go tramping along an ill-kept trail at night in miserable weather. Lenna shrugged it off: she was used to overhearing stories about the strange girl who worked at the library.

Following the proper path took them to a smaller gate that let out into Lenna's neighborhood. The weather, in this case, at least provided a boon: in nicer conditions, it was highly likely that some of the local gossipers would be lingering around here, enjoying the autumn evening. In this misty drizzle the gate was deserted. With a mock hurrah, Lenna escorted Gilbert and Luc out into the fog-draped Port Hollish street.

"Ah," said Gilbert. "I remember now." He strode confidently down the road, toward where it forked into three separate lanes. Once he rounded the corner to take the northeast branch, he would practically be on Lenna's doorstep.

"Gil, wait up," Luc and Lenna both called at the same time. Luc shot her a withering glance and then shuffled up to Gilbert. Shaking her head, Lenna followed suit.

At the intersection, Gilbert paused. As Lenna approached she stared in the direction he was looking, and noticed that the fog was unusually thick compared to how it was on other roads; it was so dense and gaining such height that it completely veiled the road and houses behind it in a screen of white. Gilbert extended his arms, barring Lenna and Luc from advancing any further into the mist.

"I'm assuming weather patterns in Port Hollish haven't changed to accommodate large, deliberate masses of fog in the past eight years?" Gilbert asked flatly.

"Oh, yes," said Lenna, paling at the sight of the cloudy pillar rolling on its misty axis. "It also snows ice cream and rainbows grow in the meadows."

"Sparkle ponies must love that."

"Look," Luc said.

From the midst of the fog a dark, humanoid shadow approached them. Lenna heard a sharp intake of breath from Gilbert as the figure stepped out of the cloud pillar, wearing the same blue-grey robes as him. He was an older man, his brown hair greying at his temples, but only a little taller than

Lenna. An expression of impatience lined his pale face.

"Brother Jaron," Gilbert said.

"Brother Gilbert, Apprentice Luc," the man named Jaron replied. "And someone else? Who is your disheveled companion? Your Port Hollish tour guide?"

"An old acquaintance of mine, Brother," said Gilbert. "My being in town gave us the opportunity to see some old sights and catch up."

"Cloaking yourselves, too? So as to not be seen?" Brother Jaron waved a hand in a simple gesture of dismissal, and both Gilbert and Luc came sharply into focus beside Lenna, their spells of disguise discarded like playthings. "You know you need permission to leave the confines of the embassy."

Jaron caressed a tendril of fog with his fingers, causing it to swirl about him like a grotesque snake. Gathering a fair amount, he lifted his palm and let a steady trickle of mist fall to the ground where it began to pool, piling up on itself and taking on a more substantial appearance. As Lenna watched with horrified fascination, a pale shimmering overtook her and her companions for a moment, slightly muffling the noise of the town around them. Before she could ask what had happened, Jaron had shaped the bits of cloud into a roiling, dog-like phantom.

"Surrender, Brother Gilbert," Jaron said. "The Brotherhood knows of your treachery."

"No," Gilbert said.

"Treachery?" asked Lenna.

"I'm sure you know how the Brotherhood deals with traitors." A second phantom took form beside the mage, and both creatures leaned on their illusionary haunches as though poised to strike.

"Lenna," Gilbert said softly. "Stay behind me. And Luc, you know where our priorities lie."

Luc nodded, and without warning Gilbert thrust both arms forward sharply. Drawing on the mist frothing at their feet, he formed the fog into two devastatingly sharp spears that launched toward Jaron's phantoms. The missiles pierced both dogs at precisely the same time, and a faint, mournful howl echoed on the wind as the weapons and creatures melted away into the air.

Smirking, Jaron took a step forward, and suddenly a crackle of thunder and a spark of light flashed above Gilbert's head. It reeked of ozone. One after another, similar strikes roughly crashed against a shimmering wall in front of the three of them, and Lenna realized that Gilbert was magically shielding them against the assault. When she glanced to the side, she noticed Luc's hand on Gilbert's left shoulder, with a look of concentration on his face; Luc must have been helping Gilbert with the shield.

Despite the assistance, Jaron was slowly gaining ground, and Lenna surmised that a sort of magical tug-of-war was occurring. Jaron was on the offensive and throwing more and more raw power against Gilbert's shield, hoping to weaken it; Gilbert just desired to hold out until the older magician was too exhausted to continue the struggle. Lenna wished desperately that she could help, but the magical gifts of her youth had long since expired, and even if they hadn't, she simply wouldn't know what to do with them.

Gilbert's brow was spotted with beads of sweat, and with each consecutive strike, the bolts of energy seemed to crackle longer and harder against the glimmer of his magical barrier. Though the combat had started off almost elegantly with the summoning of the fog creatures, it was very clear that now it was brute force that would make the difference in this fight.

Wanting to encourage him, Lenna placed one hand on Gilbert's shoulder, as Luc had done. At once the tingling sensation she had experienced before began again, traveling down her arm and up into her shoulder. With each blast from Jaron the buzzing intensified, as if a swarm of wraith-like wasps had been released into her veins. When she winced, she noticed Gilbert wincing as well. He glanced her way with an indecipherable expression on his face, and then back at Jaron, who, puzzled, had halted his advance.

The next blast fizzled out above Lenna's head, barely fazing the shield. Gilbert stood more confidently and Lenna could feel, through him, his power growing and pulsating. His shoulder blades tensed as he drew back his arms, and then heaved forward with a massive shout in Jaron's direction. A clap of azure thunder blinded Lenna and the force of the wave knocked her to the ground. Her ears rang, and her nose detected some faint, floral scent cutting through the distinctive tang of ozone.

Suddenly two hands were on her shoulders, shaking her roughly. Lenna's vision began to clear, and as the ringing stopped words regained their meanings. In one strong move, Gilbert hoisted Lenna to her feet as if she were nothing more than a child. Still stunned, she looked toward the middle of the intersection, where the fog was gradually dispersing back into an even layer. Jaron lay on the ground, motionless.

"Is he dead?" Lenna asked distantly. Her voice sounded strange.

Luc, who was hovering over Jaron's prone body, shook his head. "He's alive, but breathing shallowly. He should be all right. The Brotherhood will be here any moment; there's no way they could have missed *that*."

"Luc's right," said Gilbert as he looked off into the distance, frowning. He returned his attention to Lenna. "Lenna, are you all right?"

"I have no idea how to answer that question," she replied airily.

"Good enough for me." Gilbert jerked his head toward Luc and the apprentice hurried to his side.

"Lenna, we have to go, and we have to go fast. Can you get us some supplies, and then to North Gate?"

"Sparkle ponies?" she asked.

"Bloody *huge* sparkle ponies," Gilbert said.

Lenna nodded, and they ran up the street toward her house.

CHAPTER FOUR

The rain continued to fall as Lenna hustled Gilbert and Luc up the street toward her house. Her thoughts were steadily growing into a tangled briar patch, and the burning, acrid sting of the ozone had blistered her nose. Of all things Lenna had expected to experience today, a magical clash between two members of the Brotherhood was not one of them.

Gilbert and Luc, for their parts, remained silent and kept a few paces behind their guide. The shock of the confrontation must weigh more heavily on them than it did on Lenna, which was why, she reckoned, she felt an overwhelming sense of responsibility for her friend. Sparkle ponies or no, she knew she would get the two young mages out of Port Hollish through its northern gate.

Within moments Lenna's two-story home came into view. At this hour, the front door would be shut and bolted, the large front room serving as a showcase for Thane Faircloth's exquisitely engineered clockwork, so Lenna scurried down the narrow pathway that led around the side of the house, Gilbert and Luc in tow. She could hear tightly bitten-off curses from both mages as they tripped over loose cobblestones, and Lenna told herself for the umpteenth time to remind her father to patch up the walkway. She reached the back door, framed on either side by healthy curtains of ivy that, on inspection, were in desperate need of pruning. Living reclusive lives, it seemed, had left both father and daughter laughably unprepared to entertain visitors.

But I'm not entertaining visitors, Lenna thought. *I'm escorting two — what, magical fugitives? — out of the city.* The librarian shook her head, wondering how the sudden appearance of her childhood friend and his even more pressing need to vanish again would be received by her father. Exhaling, she turned the brass knob of the backdoor that opened into the lovingly cluttered Faircloth kitchen.

Uncharacteristically, her father was seated at the table, taking a long pull at a tumbler of brandy, instead of off tinkering in his workshop. His eyes smiled at Lenna as she stood on the threshold but widened into two intense, blue discs as Gilbert and Luc shuffled up behind his daughter, shedding droplets of rain from their hair and robes.

"Hi, papa," Lenna said cautiously.

Thane Faircloth swirled the amber liquid in the tumbler around, its strong legs lingering on the sides of the glass. Lenna could smell the potent aroma from across room. After what seemed a gratuitously long period of brandy aeration, her father finally put the glass to his lips and took another palpable, heavy drink before setting the beverage on the mahogany table.

"When I said that you should be out in society and consorting with men your age, rather than your own father," he said, "I thought you'd do it one at a time. Bringing home two handsome young men at this hour? You have more of your mother in you than I thought."

Lenna surprised herself by flushing in indignation, but collected herself quickly. Somehow her father's words had diffused a cloud of tension that had been weighing on her shoulders since the encounter with the Brotherhood magician. At home, in the warm kitchen with its rosy fire, surrounded by memories, her father's little jab at her rekindled a sense of calm and normality.

She remembered her companions and inched away from the doorway, allowing Luc and Gilbert to properly enter the kitchen. As they did, Lenna's father's eyes were immediately drawn to the distinctive clothing of the Blue Crescent Brotherhood. Much of Thane's face was unreadable; he kept his expression so schooled that the soft lines around his mouth and on his brow barely even moved. If there was a reaction under his mop of unruly, gingery hair, even Lenna would have been hard-pressed to guess what it was.

"Good evening, Master Faircloth," Gilbert said tentatively, and Luc stiffly followed suit, though he added a formal, practiced half-bow that, to Lenna, betrayed his origins as some nobleman's son. Her father's eyebrows rose, surprising the librarian, and he smiled softly as he recognized the man who had once been his daughter's greatest childhood friend.

"Gilbert Hovey," he said more mildly than Lenna could ever hope to emulate. "It's been so many years; you've become a man."

Gilbert looked abashed. "Not feeling quite as mature as I look, admittedly. You look well, Master Faircloth. I'm sorry to intrude so suddenly."

"You are always welcome here, though I agree that this is all rather sudden." Thane nodded at the unoccupied chairs surrounding the kitchen table, and Gilbert and Luc obligingly sat down, looking to Lenna like two children who had just been caught stealing biscuits from the larder. As Lenna started toward the last remaining chair, her father shook his head.

"Lenna, I'll see to our guests for the moment. Fetch two more tumblers, and then go and change into something less... disheveled." All three men looked at Lenna, who in turn looked down at the state of her attire. She was caked in mud and still had a presumptuously large splotch of coffee on her skirt, and she could only imagine the bird's nest her hair must be. Her spectacles were so blurry from the rain she was surprised she had not walked into a wall yet.

But correct as Thane was about his daughter's appearance, Lenna knew a dismissal when she heard one. Rather than argue, she simply plopped two more glasses on the table and excused herself upstairs to her bedroom. The subtle tone in her father's command suggested that Gilbert and Luc were in for a rare, but merciless, questioning from Thane Faircloth.

The door closed quietly behind Lenna with a satisfying click. She was half-tempted to leave it open, just a smidgen, to hear snippets of the conversation downstairs, but decided against it. Her father had an uncanny ability of knowing when Lenna was up to mischief. In several swift movements she shed her clothes and threw the wadded lot of them into a wicker hamper at the bottom of her closet. Lenna would have to take them to a cleaner — or a bonfire, she thought grimly. She had fancied the skirt in particular, and unfortunately, making her own garments was a skill Lenna, unlike some other young ladies her age, neither possessed nor desired.

She filled a large, porcelain washbasin, formerly her mother's, to the brim with a bucket of icy water that she had left near the window, too lazy and pressed for time to worry about drawing a bath.

Having set her spectacles aside on the table, Lenna stared at the water as though through sheer force of will, she could heat it to a more pleasant temperature. But if magic were that easy, she thought, she would have been a wizard ages ago. Sucking in a good lungful of air, Lenna plunged her face directly into the cold basin, water sloshing over the sides and onto her wooden bureau.

After an eternity or two, she pulled her face from the water, gasping. Her entire head tingled and felt tighter; her mind, too, felt as if it had been shocked back into working order. Lenna blindly grasped for the soft down towel near the basin before she could spread puddles of icy water around her bedroom. As she toweled off her face, Lenna could feel her pulse beating between her ears and clarity — specifically in regard to the absurdity of today's events — presented itself before her like an unwelcome, drunken relation suddenly appearing at the front door. She collapsed on her bed, chortling quietly to herself.

"I'm going mad," she said out loud. Sadly, however, Lenna realized that as long as one had the capacity to question one's sanity, one probably wasn't mad at all. A shame. What Lenna really needed was a beer, and she cursed herself for not even having the forethought to nip a bit of her father's brandy on the way up to her room.

Lenna recovered herself enough to continue her toilet, and took a few minutes to clean the rest of her body before clothing herself in a new white blouse and a stiffer, heartier deep blue skirt that fell to her knees. Her hair, still damp from her chilling bath, she pulled back and tied with a bit of string, though as usual a few curly tendrils escaped her grasp and wound up framing her face and neck.

It was during the process of slipping on a new pair of stockings that Lenna realized that her only truly comfortable boots sat caked in a neat layer of mud from her jog through the meadows. She rummaged around the bottom of her wardrobe — a place where many a useful item ventured but few returned — and after a minute of grunting, swearing, and lots of grabbing, resurfaced with a bristly brush and a canister of cleaning powder.

She had just brushed off the last flake of dirt when she was roused by a knocking at her door. It had been years since anyone had knocked on it, its once-smooth surface marred with crude but fantastical shapes imagined by a much younger Lenna. Startled, she remained squatted on the floor of her bedroom as she granted the knocker permission to enter. When her father appeared behind the opening door, she was awash with surprise; Thane Faircloth had not ventured upstairs in his house since his wife passed away. Lenna leapt to her feet, brush and boot clattering to the floor.

"Papa," she said.

Thane nodded as he glanced around the room, as though he still expected it to be blanketed with bits of papers, clumsily drawn dragons, and half-finished stories written in a shaky hand. Lenna still had some writings and the like, but she prided herself on keeping them (slightly) more organized and written with what she hoped was a steadier command of the pen. Without all the clutter, her father must be seeing her bedroom floor for the first time in twenty years.

He gingerly sat on the foot of Lenna's bed, his tenseness suggesting he was ready to sprint out at a moment's notice. Curious, Lenna sat beside him and at first waited for him to speak. For him to even seek her out here indicated something grave was weighing on his mind.

After a minute had passed, Lenna took the initiative. "Have you finished your talk with Gil and Luc?"

"Yes," her father said. "I've asked them to have a look at my workshop; both of them seem interested in some recent advances I've made." He shook his head. "But that isn't the point. Lenna, what do you mean by throwing your lot in with these two?"

Lenna blinked and adjusted her spectacles. That was a bit more blunt than she had come to expect from her delicately tempered father. "I haven't exactly 'thrown my lot in.' My best friend just appeared before me and asked me for help. I'm showing them to North Gate, and that's it."

Her father locked his eyes, blue-grey as a melancholy sea, on Lenna's own and fixed her with a stony gaze. "They told me about the run-in with the other magician."

Ideally, Lenna had hoped to keep that detail to herself, especially since a part of her mind was currently (and very deliberately) ignoring the implications of the battle between Gilbert and the other Brother. Still, there was no point avoiding the topic now that her friend had apparently already filled her father in on the evening's various events. After a moment's pause, she replied, "Well, I imagine we won't be running into him again this evening."

Red-faced, Thane stood up angrily from the bed. "Lenna, how can you be so damned flippant about this? They are *mages*, members of the Blue Crescent Brotherhood. They're dangerous."

This was new. Though the Brotherhood wasn't universally loved, most people, as far as Lenna had experienced and read, did not hold a particularly negative opinion of it. Her father had certainly never indicated that he distrusted the mages before. "I realize that, but it's Gilbert. I had to help, and the sooner I get them to North Gate, the sooner this day will finally be over."

The throw rug, made by Lenna's mother years before had suddenly become a path for Thane Faircloth's pacing. He was in such a state that Lenna was unable to predict his responses, which was a highly unusual phenomenon. Out of the blue, he exclaimed, "I should have been there more often after your mother died. Look how disconnected from reality you've become."

It was true that Lenna often felt detached from and unconcerned with some of the more practical aspects of life, but she did not believe that was in any way a hindrance. If anything, it allowed her to immerse herself in daydreams, great literature, and study without worrying about trivial concerns. But she didn't think she was particularly disconnected from reality.

"They will easily find out who you are, Lenna," her father continued. "Even without relying on any of their usual methods, there's only one girl who fits your description remotely — correction, there's *only one girl*, period — affiliated with the library. Do you think they'll just ignore your involvement?"

"But I haven't done anything wrong or illegal," Lenna said slowly.

Her father spun toward her and ran his hand through his greying red hair. He looked suddenly very old and tired. "Do you think that matters in their eyes? Do you think that will prevent them from coming to question you? Lenna, a member of the Brotherhood attempted to kill Gilbert — and subsequently you — because by your friend's own admission, he and the apprentice are fugitives from the order because they've taken something of great value without permission."

So what the older magician had said had had some truth behind it after all. Lenna frowned and tugged at her ponytail, deep in thought. "But I haven't taken anything. I can answer a few questions." How could she explain to her father the sense of obligation she felt toward Gilbert from the strength he had given Lenna on the day they sent her mother's body out to sea? Of course she had to help him.

Thane's voice rumbled low in his throat, like a growl. "You are as stubborn and as *thick* as your mother. You're an accomplice, Lenna. They're not just going to overlook that."

"An accomplice," she repeated.

"You have to get out of town for a few days — let me deal with the Brotherhood. Then you can come back and we'll put this all behind us."

Lenna was aghast. "Leave town? And go where? And what about my job at the library?"

"Damn your job with that fat idiot!" Thane exclaimed. He shook his head and regained composure. "Lenna, I'm sorry, but you have to go. Head out with the two mages, but split up as soon as you can. I'll make sure you're supplied; visit your mother's people, or go to Ilya — but you must leave, and immediately."

"What is going on? I don't want to leave. This is absolute madness, Papa."

"I agree," Lenna's father said. "But sometimes, that's a part of life — sudden events, meetings, and partings. I would not have you leave unless it was absolutely necessary, because, honestly, you're the one thing that keeps me grounded and sane in this world."

Silence hung in the air for a few moments, and father and daughter stared into each other's eyes as though, for the first time, each was acknowledging his or her own sadness since Lenna's mother had passed. They relied on each other; they had kept moving and established normalcy because of each other. Both of them had been running from life, unable to move past Alanna Faircloth's death and stuck in a perpetual cycle of waking, working, eating.

"A sudden adventure is a bit of an exhausted trope, if you ask me," Lenna said. "This sort of thing should only happen in works of fantasy."

Thane looked at his daughter dubiously before replying, "You read too much. Sometimes, a little adventure can lead to moments of great pleasure. How do you think I met your mother?"

With a look as dubious as her father's, Lenna allowed herself to be escorted down the stairs, calling for Gilbert and Luc as she went. She was careful to school her expression as she descended; after all, she wasn't just honoring a childhood promise so she could have a quick tumble in the meadow with some mage.

With the efficiency of a military commander, Lenna's father issued concise, curt instructions to the two mages and his daughter. They shuffled about the kitchen, reaching into cabinets and stuffing linen rucksacks with a few loaves of hard bread and a couple of mild-smelling cheeses. Gilbert sorted his items with a practiced calm while Luc and Lenna awkwardly tried to cram various items into their bags; the backpacks were quickly starting to resemble lumpy potatoes.

Gilbert, sighing like a patient father, quietly unpacked and demonstrated to Luc the proper way to store the provisions and carefully tie the cords. Lenna was watching with a dazed fascination when suddenly, from behind, her father spirited away the sausage she had forgotten she was clutching in her hand. Startled, Lenna watched her father put the sausage down on the counter and adjust some of her kit so it was slightly less potato-like. Tying it off, Thane gave the rucksack a quick pat on the side, as though it were a horse, and then walked out of the kitchen and into his workshop. Lenna and Gilbert peered curiously after him, though neither had the courage to follow.

When he returned, his face was clouded with emotions Lenna did not recognize, and he held his shoulders with a grim resolution. "Take this," he said succinctly, and thrust a small cloth bundle into his daughter's hand.

Unwrapping the pale, thready cloth, Lenna stared at the item clutched in her hand. She knew the ornate gold leaf pattern on the burgundy sheath; her fingers remembered well the smooth mother-of-pearl pommel. "This is Mother's knife. I can't take this with me."

"Nonsense. She wanted you to have it in any case, and considering the current circumstances..." Her father quirked an eyebrow at the sausage he had liberated from Lenna's hand. "I fancy something a bit sharper than a homemade sausage will probably be needed."

Lenna pursed her lips. Her first thoughts — despite the violence earlier in the evening — had been speedy flight and provisions; she had not considered a weapon for herself. It seemed unnecessary, for even though Gilbert was younger than she, he was a magician. Surely his magic would be more effective than her knife, especially when she recalled the details of the recent incident with the mage. Still, when Lenna slipped the knife a few inches from its sheath and let the silvery blade catch the light of the fire, she recalled her mother's deceivingly demure form, sitting in her chair with a whetstone, keeping the edge regularly honed.

"Promise me," her mother had said to her when Lenna was a young girl, "that if something should happen to me, you'll take care of the knife."

Despite her mother's insistence on basic training, young Lenna at the time had had no interest in learning the art of war: her passion lay in academic pursuits and tinkering with her father's clocks. She saw no need for a knife and said as much. Looking back, Lenna grimaced at her precocious remark, recalling all too well the disappointment on her mother's face when her only daughter suggested that the knife go to her father instead.

And so it had done, when Lenna's mother passed away twelve years ago. Since then Lenna had scarcely thought of it. But now, as she let firelight dance along the length of the blade, a lingering melancholy she hadn't known existed melted away, like the weariness of a long journey after a soak in the bath. Lenna slid the blade back into its sheath and inquired where her father kept its whetstone.

"You'll take it, then?" Her father's brow rose.

"Only a fool refuses a gift twice," Lenna responded and began to buckle the weapon to her belt, fumbling quite plainly.

Sighing, her father showed Lenna twice how to fasten and unfasten the sheath and then made her demonstrate the procedure until he was convinced she could do it on her own. "Your mother was much better at teaching this sort of thing than I am," he apologized.

"If the biggest problem I run into is strapping on a knife, I'll consider myself blessed. Now," Lenna said, "give me back that sausage and we'll get on our way."

"Are you sure you want to do this, Len?" Gilbert asked, frowning at the knife.

A cool, briny breeze crept in through the open kitchen door and tousled Gilbert's hair. He had recognized the knife too. Luc, ever taciturn, glanced up from knotting the rucksack strings. With all eyes on the librarian, she glanced down at the blade strapped to her side. When was the last time she had even worn a knife?

She thought for a moment. "It's just a knife, Gil. It's better than going out unarmed."

Gilbert considered Lenna a moment, then nodded. "If you're certain it's a good idea, then I suppose we're all prepared." He gave a formal bow to her father, and Luc followed suit.

Lenna was surprised when Luc said, "Master Faircloth, thank you for your hospitality and infallible grace." It was one of the longest sentences she had heard the boy speak; his voice was delicate and his words beautifully enunciated. With his looks, she thought Luc would be better suited to theater, not magecraft.

Thane Faircloth nodded at both Gilbert and Luc, the crease in his brow and tightness around his eyes demonstrating his displeasure. "Go quickly, and make sure my daughter comes to no harm." He turned once more to his daughter. "Lenna, you know how to reach your mother's settlement?"

She nodded tersely, her feet kicking the ground with irritation. Her memory conjured up an image of her mother teaching a much younger version of Lenna a series of stretches and exercises to loosen one's muscles for combat. The autumn leaves had already fallen in the garden, and every step the girl made rewarded her with a satisfying crackle. Her mother shook her head and repeated the motions, making no sound even when her foot happened to land on the brittle, ochre leaves.

"Place your heel gently down and roll the foot forward," her mother said. "This is the key to being silent — swift, decisive movement and balance."

"But I don't intend on being a fighter."

"You never know when these kinds of skills might be useful, Lenna," her mother chided. "What if you get into trouble?"

"If I get into trouble, I'm supposed to find your people's village."

Lenna's mother smiled, and the adult Lenna realized that there had been a small measure of sadness or resignation in the woman's features. *At least she's learning something,* the look said to Lenna. Banishing the image from her mind, Lenna smiled meekly at her father.

"I think Mother drilled the directions into my head often enough that it would be impossible for me to forget," she said.

Thane Faircloth took Lenna's hand and pressed into it another small pouch; Lenna could feel the weight and shape of the coin in the purse. "This should allow you to get a horse from one of the villages or homesteads along the way. That'll make your journey to Granemere Settlement go much quicker, especially since your friends Luc and Gilbert will be parting ways with you after you head north."

Lenna shot Gilbert a look. He at least had the grace to look a bit sheepish: he had obviously shared more of his plan with her father than he had with her. When she looked back at her father, Lenna was startled to see his eyes damp with tears. Coming home to this house, with its sharp metallic scents from her father's instruments and the lingering hint of apple from homemade cider, was like crawling into bed with a thick blanket: full of warmth and comfort. Now Lenna would flee it in the night like a fugitive.

"I'll sort out the Brotherhood here in town," her father said cryptically. "Until then, be safe, and wait to hear from me before coming home. The Continent is a wide place and may seem devoid of dangers, but in its vast emptiness are things that aren't meant for even the smartest of librarians to see. Don't try to outthink everything."

She nodded, surprised at how her throat and tongue became thick with emotion. Tentatively, Lenna reached out and put her arms around her father for an awkward but meaningful embrace. "You stay safe too, Papa."

"Right," said Gilbert, slinging a rucksack over his shoulder. "Would the lady do me the honor of escorting us to North Gate?"

Lenna grabbed the ruddy sausage from the kitchen table, where her father had previously placed it, and stuffed it into her pack. It was an awkward fit, and the rest of her gear would no doubt reek for days, but adventure or no, Lenna would be damned if all she was eating for the next day or so was bread and cheese. Adjusting the straps on her shoulders, she nodded to her father, took another longing glance at the warm kitchen, and marched toward the door.

"Come on, then," she said over her shoulder to Gilbert. "Follow the one with the sausage."

Shrouded by the misty night, Lenna was not privy to the mixture of mirth and horror on the three men's faces as she left them behind.

CHAPTER FIVE

Lenna had consigned the sausage to her rucksack, but she still assumed the role of guide; after all, she thought, though Gilbert had grown up in Port Hollish, he had not been back since the arrival of the railway, and since then the town had changed greatly. What was once a narrow, tree-lined avenue that skirted the walls of the seaside town had been widened and laid with pavement, sadly at the expense of some of the smaller, older residences. Train Way was the vein that connected the railway station at the north of the city to the main street.

Lenna quickly navigated a few of the hazy pathways between the wooden houses, hopping over a broken step here, avoiding a stray dog there, until the trio popped out onto the paved street. Despite the deepening dark of evening, the neighborhood still hummed softly with the bustle of traders and passengers, some on horseback or with carts and some in the purring, steam-powered motorcars of recent Imperial invention. Before she let the mages out onto Train Way, Lenna insisted that they summon whatever disguising magics they had used earlier in the evening; the Brotherhood's robes were still far too conspicuous for her liking. Tired but functional, Gilbert and Luc instantly shrank back into the shadows, their silhouettes softening around the edges.

"I'm not sure I'll get used to that," Lenna commented. Even though she could make out Gilbert's sheepish smile and Luc's face, blank as ever, the distracting effect of their guise left her queasy.

The citizens of Port Hollish had insisted that safe lanes be installed and barricaded along the roadway so that pedestrian use might still continue. This and the condition that Hollish Commons remain untouched were the stipulations that the city council had demanded of the mayor when the establishment of the railway became more of an imposing reality than the four nations' pipe dream. Thanks to the council's tenacity, Lenna could briskly escort Gilbert and Luc up the thoroughfare with a minimum amount of worry; at this hour, the train having arrived and departed already, the pedestrian walkways were mostly empty.

But Lenna still could not help glancing from side to side, as though at any moment agents of the

Brotherhood would materialize out of rising fog. Despite this one concern, she grew more convinced with every pace that there was really no true need for her to flee the city. But since her father so seldom bore a strong opinion regarding anything, she felt she had no choice but to comply. Her only regret, she supposed, would be not being able to see the rare texts Gilbert had initially promised, though Lenna could grill him about them later. For now, Lenna's priority was to get them all out of the city.

Even though North Gate was closer to the railway station, citizens and travelers used it far less often than its counterpart to the east. The main highway into the countryside, which was the most direct route to Junction, the central crossroads of Fallowfields, started at East Gate. Lenna hoped to avoid the hustle and bustle of the highway and escape through the outlying Hollish villages and farms, thinking the Brotherhood would almost certainly be keeping watch on the most obvious routes.

A chill had descended on the night, and Luc's breath came out as puffs of steam. His brow was peppered with droplets of dew or sweat — Lenna could not distinguish which — and his delicate lips were pursed in effort. Every so often, his concentration would slip, and his conspicuous robes shifted jarringly in and out of sight. Gilbert, noticing his younger companion's struggles, placed one hand gently on Luc's shoulder. There was, at that moment, a subtle vibration around the two mages, and into Lenna's nostrils glided the scent of the sea, despite the harbor being across town. The stuttering illusion around Luc at once ceased its flickering, and the young mage was once again rendered a shade.

Lenna maintained a steady pace toward North Gate but could not help but being curious. "What did you just do?"

Surprisingly, Luc was the one to respond. "Gilbert helped to reinforce my spell. I'm a bit tired and distracted."

"So he transferred you some of his magic?"

"Transfer is a crude word," Luc said. "But I suppose it works well enough for you to understand it that way."

Luckily for Luc, Lenna was a few paces ahead: he could not see her roll her eyes. Gilbert chimed in, chiding his companion. "Luc, there's no need to be condescending; Lenna's better-read than most of the Brothers back home."

Luc snorted audibly, and Lenna ignored it; she had little patience for petulant children, and even less for adults who acted like them. She waited for Gilbert to continue.

"Every person has an inherent defense mechanism — a barrier, one might say — that surrounds their will, which is where we draw our power to perform magic from. It strengthens as we mature and transition from child to adult." Gilbert hopped over a loose cobblestone. "It's possible for a magician to lower that barrier and have someone else bolster his magic. That's what I did for Luc. So, in effect, it is a form of transfer, I suppose."

Luc scoffed. "What is this, magecraft for beginners?"

Lenna spun around on her heels, her ponytail whipping through the air. A look of genuine surprise flashed across Luc's face. "Listen, you little brat," she said. "As I see it, you lot have gotten me tangled up in some sort of magical escapade, so I have a right to ask some questions. And while you might not know me well, Gilbert does: I'm very, very good at getting answers to my questions. Since we're all in a hurry, I suggest you start acting like the man your age dictates you should be, and put the wisecracks aside."

Stunned into silence, Luc blinked several times in rapid succession before anger slowly washed over his face like a red tide. Clearly, the young mage was not accustomed to being rebuked, and certainly not by strange female librarians. Gilbert, standing to Luc's right, gave a soft whistle and winked cheekily at Lenna. He ran his fingers through the longer strands of blonde hair at the back of his head.

After a moment of silence — during which Lenna imagined Luc's face would grow so red he might burst into flames — Gilbert skipped forward a few steps to face his two companions, who were currently engaged in a sort of staring contest, with pride as the ante and dominance as the reward.

"Luc, I wouldn't encourage a tongue-lashing from Lenna. I imagine she's made many a grown man cry. And Lenna, let's talk more about your magic later."

Lenna blinked. What did Gilbert mean by "her" magic? Her curiosity grew exponentially, but stopping in the middle of the pavement on the street was a surefire way to attract unwanted attention, even if two of them were covered by magical shrouds. She could ask all the questions she wanted after they were safely outside of the city walls; once in the farmland to the north of Port Hollish, they would find a stable or a reasonable farmer who might sell Lenna a horse or help her arrange for other transportation.

North Gate itself was merely a pair of sturdy oak doors set into the stone wall that both protected and helped organize trade routes in Port Hollish. During the day it was cast open, doors bolted to the thick walls, so that citizens or farmers from outlying homesteads could enter freely. Recently, however, the growing aggression from the neighboring Krevlum Empire had encouraged the city council to secure and guard the doors after dusk. Since autumn had come, the number of hours the doors remained open was growing smaller. Lenna was not surprised to find them shut and being watched by two guards, wearing the gold-and-green uniforms of lower-ranking members of the Port Hollish city watch.

As the group approached, both guards peered at them curiously. One of them, a scruffy character with an undulating paunch, eyed the three companions. Lenna did not recognize these guards, but then again it was extremely rare that she would venture outside the city walls at this time of night anyway. The paunchy man looked a bit more approachable than his companion, who was a clean-cut, muscular man the height of a roof.

"Good evening," Lenna said. "I'm on business from the library and need to head into the villages to make some inquiries."

"So you're the girl from the library, eh?" said Paunch. "Kinda late for library business, isn't it?"

The muscular giant cut in, snickering. "You know that old coot, Jeffer, don't you? It's no surprise that dodgy bastard is sending his junior out at all hours."

Thankful, Lenna confirmed that she was indeed tasked by the eccentric and vindictive head librarian to head out on such a dismal night. The guards seemed persuaded by this, especially since her employment at the library was something of a curiosity for most townsfolk. Lenna disliked the attention but did not have qualms about using it to serve her purposes when necessary. Muscle-man peered curiously at Gilbert and Luc, a frown beginning to line his face.

"Who are these strange fellows?" He rubbed his eyes. "They're standing right there, but then the instant I turn my head, I just kind of forget about them."

The paunchy guard looked startled, casting a furtive glance at Lenna's allies before shaking his head, as if trying to clear it of the image of two nondescript young men. The magics were obviously befuddling the guards, but if the group lingered, they might begin to ask questions about Gilbert and Luc's strange lack of presence. As both men kept silent, Lenna took the initiative.

"Two new assistants, helping me with the archives," Lenna hastily explained. "They're also serving as bodyguards, I'm afraid. They didn't want to leave a young lady defenseless, considering the recent unrest with the Empire and whatnot."

Muscles and Paunch nodded and dismissed Gilbert and Luc's strange, forgettable appearances; servants were beneath their notice. Comforted by the fact that so young and polite a lady, Port Hollish's own female librarian, would be protected on the road, Paunch yanked a jangling set of keys from his belt and set about unlocking and unbolting the tall door that led to Luc and Gilbert's freedom. Now that the adrenaline from the evening's events and sudden flight had worn off, Lenna was finally overcome with a sense of pursuit. The niggling feeling made an unsavory combination with the growing list of questions that pulsed in her head, the most important of which repeated itself in punctuated tones: "What the hell am I doing?"

Once the door was open (after a bit of fumbling on Paunch's part), Lenna, Gilbert, and Luc bid the two guards a hasty farewell and set out along the wheel-rutted road beyond. The mist and rain made for a muddy path, but for once Lenna was unconcerned about the condition of her shoes. Leaving Port Hollish for the first time in what felt like ages was liberating, despite her confusion and suspicion.

Gilbert and Luc walked, side by side, a few paces apart from Lenna. Their steps were light on the soft ground, as though they feared sinking into the soggy road. Lenna wondered, amused, if Brothers of the Blue Crescent never had to worry about muddy lanes. Probably not, considering how Gilbert and Luc were dressed; a Brother's uniform was not designed for rough-and-tumble travel.

The wall surrounding Port Hollish was a relatively new construction and served to protect it to the north and east; for years after the city's founding, when it was only a collection of villages and common rooms nestled on the shore of Bonebreaker Bay, there had been no need for any defenses. After the Unification of the four countries and the fall of the slave nation of Laur, a group of elders — who became the first city councillors — decided to erect the stone wall, effectively making a border between Port Hollish and the outside world. Still, for several miles outside the wall, smaller settlements had remained: villages and hamlets dotted the countryside, providing Port Hollish with a fair share of its produce. It was to one of these that Lenna intended to take the two mages and then part ways.

After about twenty minutes of traipsing down the deserted lane in silence, the trio came upon the somewhat famous Seaways Tavern, a two-storied wooden establishment that stood as a milepost to travelers heading to Port Hollish from the north. According to legend, the Seaways had survived two fires, immeasurable flooding, and countless hurricanes, making it a true-to-life "port in the storm" to travelers on their way to the docks. Its walls were battered green planks and the windows were shuttered in a color that was probably once gold, to reflect the colors of Lenna's city. The current proprietor, it seemed, had fallen behind in the tavern's upkeep.

"Lenna," Gilbert said as the three approached the Seaways, "what do you think the chances are that the Brotherhood would choose North Gate as a way out of the city?"

"Well," she replied, "you'd know the Brotherhood's way of doing things better than I would, but unless they're intimately acquainted with Port Hollish, I doubt they'd choose this route." Lenna held out her arms, indicating the sparse countryside around them. "Over the past few years, most foot traffic and travel has been routed through East Gate, since it's the fastest way to the highway."

Gilbert rubbed his chin, considering their options, while Luc stood off to the side, glumly looking at his mud-caked boots like a man about to drown a kitten. "I certainly wouldn't object to getting out of this mud," he said mournfully.

"You'll have more than mud to worry about if the Brotherhood catches up with us," Gilbert said. "But we did make a quick departure, and it's doubtful Brother Jaron is very coherent yet. We hit him pretty hard." He sighed and looked at the dubious establishment before him, firelight pouring out of its battered windows, and then nodded to himself. "Let's at least have some dinner; no sense digging into our supplies if there's a hot meal to be had."

Matters decided, the group walked past the corral where patrons could tether their horses; most country folk would never be able to afford automated means of transportation. Lenna noticed that only two horses, a dappled brown and woeful red mare, were present, meaning the Seaways didn't have a large crowd tonight. For their purposes, that was welcome news indeed.

Gilbert pushed open the wooden door, wincing as it creaked with years of neglect. The Seaways Tavern was nothing more than a large pub, with the second story overhanging the first, connected by a rickety staircase in the corner. The doorway to the kitchen hid behind a heavy burlap curtain, and traces of something warming and spicy immediately tickled Lenna's nostrils. Two patrons, one dark-haired and one bald, probably local farmers, sat on low-backed chairs surrounding the inviting fire in the tavern's hearth.

The proprietor, a plump but melancholy individual with greying temples half-heartedly welcomed the group and ushered them to a small table a few meters away from the fireplace. It granted them enough space to talk without being overheard while still enjoying some of the warmth from the fire. Lenna settled into a rough-looking chair — it was missing a rung or two — as Gilbert followed the proprietor to the bar. Luc pulled back a chair with reluctance and sat down at the table, directly across from Lenna, but with his gaze locked on the knotted old wooden surface.

The silence, which under normal circumstances Lenna preferred, began to grate on her nerves. The librarian could handle quiet, and indeed her job required a certain quantity of it, but Lenna could not accept that Luc was merely taciturn. There was something about his direct refusal to acknowledge her, or his outright expressions of dismay, that irritated her to no end. She sighed resignedly, amused at how a wisp of hair that had escaped from her ponytail bounced on the traces of her breath.

"Luc," Lenna began. "How old are you?"

"Eighteen."

"It seems odd to me that the Brotherhood would allow an apprentice, someone not even of age by its standards, out on what is obviously a dangerous mission. Why are you here?"

Luc's head whipped up and he stared directly at Lenna. His eyes were strangely deep, almost lilac in color, and they forced Lenna to blink at the severity of his gaze. What might have been a frown traced his mouth, and Luc said, "Because I couldn't let Gilbert do this alone. Isn't that why you're here?"

Lenna hesitated a moment before nodding. She was uncertain what kind of response would be appropriate or could possibly convey the sense of debt she felt toward Gilbert. Luc, who had only known her for a few hours, would never be able to understand the strength Lenna had received from Gilbert after her mother died. In fact, Lenna thought, he might even resent it: something about his gaze spoke of some kind of protectiveness or even possessiveness in regard to Gilbert.

As if on cue, Gilbert arrived at the table, awkwardly balancing three mugs full of frothy, cinnamon-scented ale. He shot Lenna a grateful look as she stood up and relieved him of the most precarious-looking vessel. Albeit a bit delayed, Luc followed suit and grasped one of the mugs before it spilled onto the surface of the oak table. The barkeep, melancholy aside, was a generous pour indeed.

"I took the liberty of ordering us three portions from the carvery; the beers are cheaper that way." He smiled almost, but not quite, apologetically. In salute, Gilbert raised his mug and toasted his two companions. "To an eventful, if strange, day."

"But why are you running from the Brotherhood? They're your people," Lenna blurted out, and then quickly lowered her voice as a scullery maid suddenly appeared, brandishing three steaming plates of roast pork. After the girl was out of earshot, Lenna leaned over the table, close enough to Gilbert and Luc that a stray strand of her hair dangled precariously over Gil's beer. "What's this all about, then?"

Luc coughed with the subtle discomfort of those gently born, and Lenna wondered for the second time if the young mage had been raised as a member of the aristocracy. Gilbert, looking thoughtful, remembered to chew his food and swallow it down in one loud, audible gulp. Lenna could not stifle a laugh and Gilbert, characteristically, smiled like a child caught pinching a gingersnap from a market stall. Time changes many things, thought Lenna, but not all.

"Luc," Gilbert remarked, his knife and fork now tastefully placed at the side of his plate, "Lenna deserves as much of an explanation as we can give her, since it's our fault she's tangled up in this mess."

After a curt nod that signaled Luc's acquiescence, Gilbert's hands searched the folds of his robes and brought forth a shining globular jewel, a lighter shade of blue than sapphire, suspended by a lustrous silver chain. The core of the gem flickered as if it caught the firelight, though Gilbert's back clearly shadowed the blaze. The sparkling reminded Lenna of a growing storm on the horizon, and she longed to stretch out her hand like a child and caress the smooth, perfectly round stone. Gilbert quickly stashed the jewel back into the hidden pockets of his clothing.

"Is that what you took from the Brotherhood?" asked Lenna.

"Yes," Gilbert said, picking up his fork and poking around at some roasted cauliflower. "It's an artifact of immense magical power — so strong that, in the right hands, it could change the balance of power in the Continent."

"And you don't want your Brotherhood, where you've lived for almost a decade, to be in control of that?"

Luc frowned and said, "The jewel wasn't public knowledge in the Brotherhood, which violates some of our tenets. A small group of high-ranking mages were trying to keep it a secret to themselves, but recently the jewel's existence came to light before the entire Brotherhood."

Flummoxing exhaustion was starting to set in, and Lenna removed her spectacles and began rubbing her eyes. "This is a little bit trite for me," she commented. "I may just be a librarian, and a junior one at that, but do you realize how much of this sounds like absolute rubbish?"

Luc grew crimson and Gilbert chortled, his mouth full of meat. He swallowed, thankfully, before he replied. "It is a bit fantastical. A magic treasure, stolen away by a young Brother and an apprentice — maybe you could make a book out of it, Len."

Lenna glared in response and replaced her glasses.

"But, really," Gil continued, "the question of what to do with this stone has divided the Brotherhood into factions…"

"Let me guess," Lenna filled in the gaps. "One side wants to use it to strengthen the Brotherhood, and one side thinks such ancient, mystical powers are best left undisturbed?"

Gilbert threw a bit of potato at her. "You really love taking the wind out of my sails, don't you?"

Something of a polite society food fight followed, which came to an abrupt halt only when Luc looked at Gilbert and Lenna with a face of utter horror and outrage. A strip of roast pork had landed on his shoulder. Naturally, the only fitting response to this was a bout of relentless giggles that left the two old friends doubled over and squealing. Luc sighed and plucked the meat delicately from his shoulder, setting it to the side of his mostly untouched plate.

After their laughter had subsided, Lenna sat back up and wiped the streaming tears from her eyes with a handkerchief. In retrospect, it was the only natural response to the ridiculous day Lenna had

had, first an angry goose and now a magical amulet of doom that had caused civil war in one of the oldest establishments of modern civilization. She briefly snickered, wondering if, as in some of those popular adventure novels, Lenna would be swept off her feet by a dashing airship pilot next.

"But really, Lenna," Gilbert said. "We're serious. My former teacher heads the faction that believes this gem would lead us to war. Our side wants to remove it from play."

Lenna said, "Not to sound uncertain of your abilities, Gil, but if you've only just joined the ranks of full-fledged Brothers, aren't there other... er, candidates for such a mission?"

"Gil is well-thought of and very highly skilled!" Luc cried incredulously.

"It's true I don't have much political sway," Gilbert admitted. "But that's also a benefit. What newcomer like me would dare pluck something so important right out from under the elder Brothers' noses?"

"So why is he here?" Lenna pointed at Luc.

"Moral support?" Gilbert offered.

Luc knuckled Gilbert in the shoulder, offended. Laughing, Gil reached out and ruffled the younger man's hair with a crumb-coated hand. "Like my master trusts me, I trust Luc. He's one of the most important people in the world to me."

Surprisingly, Luc looked down at his plate and blushed. So there was a touch of jealousy after all,

Lenna thought, amused. "Surely, there has to be another reason for you to be the one... oh," Lenna said with sudden realization. The letters Gilbert had sent her, which mentioned the rare texts. Lenna had responded with utmost zeal, practically begging him to allow her library to host the collection of books. Not once had she questioned how easily the Brotherhood had acquiesced to such an arrangement; normally the Brotherhood would never agree to such a request, especially when the requester was a female, twenty-two-year-old junior librarian.

The thought must have plainly registered on her face, because Gilbert immediately held up both hands in supplication. "It's not like that, Len," he said hastily. "I really did manage to get the books for you. My former master just thought it would be a perfect excuse to get me to Port Hollish, so we jumped on the opportunity."

"There must have been a traitor on our ship or someone already informed at the embassy," Luc added darkly. "We were sure we wouldn't be followed. It should have just been a matter of popping through the town and setting out east on the Continental Highway to meet Gilbert's old teacher."

"But you realized you were being pursued?" Lenna asked.

Gilbert nodded. "There was something strange about the storm that delayed the ship; it came out of nowhere, and it seemed centered on our vessel. That's why we snuck out as soon as we could, without the texts or any supplies, hoping you'd be able to smuggle us out of town along a more unnoticed path."

"We see how well that worked out for you," Lenna commented dryly. "So now what? I'm part of this great political scheme?"

Shaking his head, Gilbert said, "No, the Brotherhood will have no interest in you; only me and Luc. And your father has more influence in Port Hollish than you realize, Lenna. I don't think there will be any action against you. Just lie low for a few days, like Thane suggested."

Lenna sighed. Roughing it with the Freewomen of Laur was not something she had ever planned on doing. And to think the only book she brought was about them! Lenna supposed she could always practice her knife skills, but that seemed a bit brutish and unnecessary. Still, Gilbert had invoked the sparkle ponies clause, and there was no way she could avoid going to the settlement now. Resignation rapidly filled the gaps that adrenaline had formerly occupied.

"Where will you go?" she asked.

"We probably shouldn't tell you that," Luc said in what Lenna took as a condescending tone.

"When do we leave?"

"I imagine once Gilbert finishes stuffing that face of his."

In between mouthfuls of pork and gulps of ale, Gilbert grinned fiendishly. "Before we set out, there's something I want to try."

Lenna grimaced outright at Gilbert's slurred, heavy speech; Luc had the good breeding to look away from the powerful chewing of the older mage's jaw. Gilbert choked down his food and drowned the subsequent coughing fit with the remaining beer in his mug. He leaned back, both hands behind his head, contented.

"Aren't you going to ask what I want to try?" Gilbert asked.

"I think we're both afraid to," Luc replied, his eyes connecting with Lenna in one brief but poignant moment of pure camaraderie. Lenna smiled and nodded in return.

"Well, then, I'll just blurt it out. I want to see how potent that magic of Lenna's is before we set out."

Both Lenna and Luc sat in silence, stunned.

"I know," Gilbert said. "Shocking, right? Now, if we're all finished, shall we gather our things and pop outside for a spell or two?"

Luc's outrage and protests practically paved the group's exit into the brisk autumn air, now much cooler in the deepening night. It was well-known that members of the Brotherhood were terrific misogynists and believed that the "art" of magecraft belonged solely to men. Providing magical tutelage to a female would violate one of the primary tenets of the Brotherhood. Luc continued to expound, his voice becoming shriller and shriller, that Gilbert's experiment was absolute treachery as they made their way across the stubbles of crunchy grass to a clearing across the way from the tavern.

"You'd think Gilbert suggested we slice open the horses and use them for sacrifice," Lenna said, amused.

"Actually, sacrifice used to be practiced by the Brotherhood, though in the past century or so it's gone out of fashion," Gilbert said, bringing the group to a halt. He spaced Luc and Lenna apart evenly so that the three formed a human triangle underneath the cloudy night sky. The rain had stopped, but by now the mists from Port Hollish had spread out into the air, filtering the moonlight and transforming Gilbert and Luc into pale, zombified versions of themselves.

"I'm just stating, for the record," Luc said, his arms folded either in indignation or in protection from the night's chill, "that I object to teaching any female the art of magecraft."

"We've already broken several of the Brotherhood's tenets," Gilbert said cheerfully. "What's one more?"

Thankfully, Luc held his tongue and let Gilbert proceed. Magic was a gift that presented itself naturally to most of the population at an early age, though the amount or strength of an individual's magic varied greatly. New parents often feared extremely gifted two-year-olds more than bandits on the highway. A selfish whim could cause just as much destruction as a typhoon blowing in from the ocean. Though she barely recalled them, Lenna's father had often teased her about numerous catastrophes she had caused as a small child.

"Now, Len," Gilbert started. "As I'm sure you know, without proper training even children with the potential to become amazing mages lose their ability to access their magic well before their bodies even begin to develop into adults."

"Right," said Lenna, her breath forming puffs of mist in the night air. "According to Father, I stopped causing all the clocks in his workshop to keep different times when I was about seven years old."

"Well," he said, "I'm not so sure that's the case. Back when we confronted Brother Jaron, I'm fairly certain you raised some magic of your own against him, and it felt pretty potent to me. I can sense it even now. Luc?"

Begrudgingly, Luc nodded. "Yes, I agree."

"How can you 'sense' it?" Lenna asked. Any book she read on magic never went into great detail on the subject.

Gilbert placed his hand on his chin, rubbing it thoughtfully. "It's hard to explain, but it's almost like another sense of smell. It's fleeting, like a butterfly landing on the tip of your nose and fluttering off into the distance. And everyone's scent is unique."

"How poetic. I always knew you were a romantic, Gil."

"Quiet, pupil," he chided. "Here, take my hand."

As instructed, Lenna put her cold hand into Gilbert's. It enveloped hers completely and shockingly reminded Lenna that, though he still acted like her childhood friend, Gilbert was now a tall, proper man. It was a strange, stirring feeling, coupled with a sadness at the realization that the simple times of their youth were locked in the past, never to be repeated. Lenna began to question which of the two — pupil or teacher — was the real romantic.

"Now, Lenna," Gilbert continued. "You probably don't remember how to draw on the source of your magic, since it comes so naturally to children, but I want you to close your eyes and imagine a warmth in your chest, rising up from your center of gravity. It could be a tiny ball of light, a soaring zeppelin, or a gentle tide coming in. And think, if you can, of a simple desire, the purest of wishes, as if you were a little girl again."

The thought of so juvenile an action caused Lenna to shuffle about awkwardly, and she felt her palm grow clammy with sweat. Still, to this day she enjoyed using her imagination, and as she closed her eyes, Lenna tried to ignore the thought of Luc's prying eyes watching her every move. Gilbert, sensing her hesitancy, gave her hand a reassuring squeeze.

In her mind's eye, Lenna examined her own body and searched for its center of gravity. Of their own volition, her feet rearranged themselves to provide a steadier sense of balance, and suddenly a memory, unwanted and intrusive, came to her mind. Something tightened in Lenna's chest. She was watching Alanna Faircloth weave her plaited hair into a crown around her head, and Lenna faintly caught the smell of that small leather volume, the history of the Freewomen of Laur. Her mother's soft but unwavering voice recited its pages. Like a book itself, something inside Lenna opened, unfurling its pages and spreading a breezy, gentle warmness throughout her body. She ceased feeling the chill of autumn around her, and for a brief moment the strength of the summer sun and a faint dusting of lavender lingered on her skin.

Gilbert gave a low whistle, and Lenna slowly opened her eyes. Her body felt light and she tingled all over, as though she had just been massaged or taken a long bath, but soon enough the brisk wind returned and she shivered. Gilbert let go of her hand and clapped cheekily, while Luc stood off to the side, doing his damnedest not to look nonplussed. All things considered, Lenna supposed she'd done as Gilbert had asked.

"Congratulations, Lenna! You've just consciously tapped into the source of your power. It takes most of our apprentices a year to get that far." Luc snorted, and Gilbert quickly amended his words.

"Though there are some far more prodigious than others, like our lovely Luc here, and they come to the island already knowing how to draw on their power."

"So aside from feeling all sunshiny and perfumed," Lenna asked, "what am I supposed to do next? Wiggle my fingers?"

"Funny you should mention that," Gilbert said. "Luc, care to demonstrate something sunshiny for Lenna?"

"No," Luc said. "I told you where I stand."

Gilbert sighed. "All right; it was worth a try. Lenna, watch me." Gilbert bent over and nonchalantly swept up a stick from the ground, brandishing it before him. Although almost unnoticeable, Lenna saw Gilbert squint his eyes to focus on the tip of the stick; then two quick sparks shot up from it like miniature flares, and the wood began to gently burn like a small torch.

"This is one of the most basic applications of power," Gilbert said. He blew out the tiny flame like he would a candle. "Drawing on your innate strength, concentrating it on a specific area, and applying enough of your will — as raw energy — to an object to achieve a result. The great mages of old were said to be able to melt the rocks themselves."

"Can *you* melt rocks?"

"Alas, no," Gilbert chuckled. "Magic isn't what it once was. But do let's be an attentive student, shall we?" He stepped forward, the grass and leaves crunching beneath him in a most satisfying, autumnal way, and forcefully pressed the stick into Luc's hand. "All right, Apprentice Tural, hold out your arm, and let's see if Apprentice Faircloth can't set that branch a-blazing."

Luc looked as though he had just taken a sip of soured milk, but did as he was told, stiffly holding the branch a few paces from Lenna. The librarian looked between the piece of kindling and her smiling teacher, unsure of how to proceed. Gilbert had said that it was a matter of focusing one's energy on an object, so Lenna delved back into that warm place, opening the dense volume and plucking out swatches of magic as though she were tearing out pages. The power rose into her chest, she squinted hard at the stick, urging it to catch flame.

After a minute or so of intense concentration, her nose started to tickle, and it felt as though someone had submerged her head in a tub of cheap perfume. Lenna sneezed violently, causing a whinny of surprise from the nearby horses, and two puny puffs of smoke rose from the tip of the stick. Gilbert laughed heartily, his voice carrying out into the night, and even Luc, that patronizing prat, had a smirk creeping about the corners of his lips. Lenna grew red with frustration.

"Lenna, my goodness!" Gilbert said, still laughing. "Must you always look so angry when you concentrate? You'd make a perfect old schoolmarm at this rate."

Frowning, Lenna pushed her glasses up the bridge of her nose. "What did I do wrong?"

"You didn't shape the energy correctly," Luc said matter-of-factly.

Failure and fatigue were swiftly making Lenna irritable, and the expression on her face pronounced an unfortunate fate for Luc.

"Now, now, children," Gilbert chimed in. "Are we going to start throwing rocks and pulling each other's hair as well?" Gilbert placed one hand gently on Lenna's shoulder. "I deliberately didn't tell you *how* to do it because I was curious to see what you'd come up with. Now, this time, I'm going to help you shape the power, so start drawing on your magic again."

As Lenna once again flipped through the pages of her power, she felt a strong force brushing up against her; it reminded her of the waves beating up against the jagged rocks of the harbor of Port Hollish, and she could practically taste and smell the briny sea on the wind. *This is Gilbert's magic*, she thought. Dismissing the curious sensation as best she could, Lenna reached for her power and urged its warmth up into her chest. She could feel Gilbert's power encourage hers along and out of her body, like a tide rolling out. At first, it was the merest of trickles, but suddenly it seemed that Gilbert had thrown open a floodgate and a torrent of energy roared out of Lenna, raging toward the stick in Luc's hand.

There was a flash of bright light and Luc cried out, biting off a surprisingly inelegant swear word. Gilbert squeezed Lenna's shoulder, and his presence enveloped hers, damming the tome of her magic. Lenna panted heavily as the sense of Gilbert's presence subsided, and all that remained was an annoying vibration in her head, as if a bee had flown into her ear. The stick that Luc had been holding was a smoldering heap of cinders on the dark autumn landscape. Sucking on his finger, Luc targeted Lenna with the most piercing of glares.

"Well, that was unexpected," Gilbert said airily. "I suppose we'd better move you up to healing next."

Lenna was genuinely surprised Luc didn't clock Gil in the face, right then and there.

CHAPTER SIX

The night was growing late and, pursuit or not, Lenna's fatigue was rapidly seeping into the marrow of her bones. The Seaways Tavern was just too close to Port Hollish for there to be any safety in spending the night there, so Gilbert proposed that the three of them walk a few more miles into the nearest village, which had no proper name, as it was really just a small collection of fields and farmland with workers who regularly delivered goods to the city. Hopefully, in exchange for a bit of coin or early morning labor, they would be able to convince a local farmer to grant them some rest in his hayloft.

Luc lagged a few paces behind Lenna and Gilbert, still silently fuming. Though Gilbert was quick to magically heal the minor burn from Lenna's unexpected gout of flame, no incantation or direction of mystical energies (or whatever Gilbert wanted to call it) could mend the young apprentice's pride. Not only was he embarrassed by Lenna's sudden success but he appeared to still hold a great deal of resentment at the fact that Lenna had been taught any sort of magic at all.

Not that any of this really concerned her. Lenna was more cognizant of the fact that her feet were beginning to ache and her hair was getting dusty. Still, underneath all of those complaints, Lenna's mind gleefully reminded her that *she had performed magic*. To the librarian's knowledge, almost all innate talent becomes inaccessible if left untrained by puberty; it was inconceivable that now, over a decade later, Lenna could reach inside herself and summon fire. Wickedly, she wondered what Jeffer would do if she decided to demonstrate her newfound abilities near the classics section of the library, even though she'd never have the audacity to destroy a book.

The majority of the countryside was barren; since the War of Unification, people had flocked to the various cities where newer technologies were being developed, drastically increasing the production of food and clothing. Now, Port Hollish's outskirts were a piecemeal series of homesteads, some neighboring each other and some miles apart. The only thing that linked them all together was their proximity to the Continental Highway, the great road that joined the four nations on the Continent. Initially, the Krevlum Empire had wanted the railway to pave over the highway, but that would have left travelers without the means to purchase tickets no way of easily navigating the Continent.

The nation of Fallowfields, with Port Hollish nestled against the shores in the Continent's western crook, was expansive but largely undeveloped, save for a few Freewoman settlements and the homesteads surrounding the city. Most of its prosperity came from providing access to the Brotherhood, or circumnavigating the dangerous, rocky waters surrounding the land. Before the steamtrain had come, trade with the other nations, despite their physical proximity, had been difficult. Krevlum, or rather the Krevlum Empire, had long been separated from society by treacherous cliffs that practically walled the country off except for a few passages in the rock. The south faced a similar problem; Gallas was (according to the books Lenna read) a beautiful place but uneven and equally plagued with mountains. Even the train would have difficultly plotting a course there, so recently airships had been deployed from Ilya, which hugged the eastern coast of the Continent.

For an hour or so Luc led the team, having conjured a small, pale blue globe of illumination, aptly named magelight. They soon came upon a dwelling, and Lenna instantly recognized the splintering, faded whitewash of the fence: it was the Meekses' farm. Once a great supplier of apples, particularly cider apples, to Port Hollish, the Meeks family fell on hard times, like many other families, with the arrival of the steamtrain and the goods it brought. As a child, Lenna had often accompanied her mother on a visit to Mistress Meeks, and while the two young mothers chatted about the affairs of the world, a young, curly-headed Lenna would run with the Meeks children throughout the orchards, darting between rows of healthy apple trees. As autumn approached, the children were often gifted with the ripest, sweetly tart apples of the crop, eating two or three before filling their pockets with extras for later.

But recent years had been truly unkind to the Meeks. As Luc, Lenna, and Gilbert climbed over a fallen plank of the fence, Lenna noticed that the orchards and fields were besieged with weeds and untended, overgrown roots. From what she could tell from the pale incandescence of Luc's magelight, the trees were spotted with shriveling apples, devastated by blight and pests. The ground was littered with the rotting remains of fallen fruit. Lenna put her handkerchief over her nose, attempting to mask the fetid smell of decomposition as best she could.

Gilbert made something of a choking noise. "What the hell happened here?" he said nasally. "I remember coming here as a child."

"Let's head to the house," Lenna said.

Luc dimmed his magelight so that it flickered like a firefly. "There is a light ahead."

Peering off into the distance, toward the Meekses' house, Lenna could make out the glow of a lantern or small fire. Despite being very poorly tended, the farm appeared, at least, to not be completely abandoned. Nodding, mostly to herself, Lenna began to carefully make her way toward the farmhouse, tiptoeing around squishy, putrid apples, some of them writhing with creatures unidentifiable in the darkness. She reckoned she would not be touching the ration of apples in her rucksack for some time.

Once they drew close enough to the farmhouse — a centuries-old, several-storied establishment of the same whitewashed wood as the fence, and in a similar state of disrepair — Luc completely extinguished his magelight. Even through the thickening clouds, the moonlight bathed the trio in enough illumination to make out the shape of a humanoid figure, hunched over and sitting on the dilapidated steps up to the farmhouse's wide, open porch. The firelight, streaming out of the open door, silhouetted the figure in a cloak of shadow. The group halted.

"Who do you think that is?" Gilbert nudged Lenna, speaking in what could best be described as a stage whisper.

"Hush," Lenna said much more quietly, and raised her arm in front of Gilbert and Luc to bar their progress further. She did not want the two uniformed men to startle whoever sat before them.

Careful to avoid stepping on any of the fallen leaves, Lenna inched toward the porch of the Meekses' home: something about the shadowed figure rekindled a memory from childhood. As she approached, Lenna noticed a slight trembling in the hands of a woman who, upon closer inspection, looked far older than her years. Her hair, which had once been a spectacular shade of honey, had faded into a grey, yellowish color, and wisps of it fell about her lined face. It was Mistress Meeks, whom Lenna remembered as a tall, spritely woman who could leap alarmingly from branch to branch, shaking down apples from the trees by the bushel.

What sat before Lenna, as she kneeled down and placed a hand on the woman's knee, was the shriveled husk of a woman who should only be in her forties or fifties at most. Her skin was sagging and pallid, and the skirt, blouse, and shawl all appeared to be the same color as her complexion. What could have happened in the past fifteen years to have aged her so? In her deep-set, rheumy eyes, Lenna saw no glimmer of recognition.

"Mistress Meeks?" she asked. "Do you remember me? Lenna Faircloth — Thane and Alanna's daughter."

The frail woman tilted her head in Lenna's general direction but gave no sign that she had understood the girl's words. Lenna frowned, and wondered if the woman had gone deaf, or, worse, become mentally ill. With her hand on Mistress

Meeks's knee, however, some of the trembling in the matron's body seemed to have calmed. Lenna gave the knee a light squeeze, unsure of how to proceed.

Silently, Gilbert appeared at Lenna's side, kneeling as well. There was a puzzled look on his face, something between concern and intrigue. He waved one hand, the sleeve of his blue robe trailing behind him, before the confused woman's face, and muttered something under his breath. Lenna couldn't be quite certain, but she thought her nose once again detected that faint, briny scent of the sea.

"Lenna, may I?" asked Gilbert.

She nodded and shifted to the side, assuming an awkward seat on a step below Mistress Meeks. Gilbert, still in a kneeling position, shifted directly in front of the woman, and with the utmost care, as though he were picking up a fallen bird's nest, he cupped Mistress Meeks's chin in both of his hands. The woman attempted to avert his gaze, which was the most movement Lenna had seen thus far, but Gilbert held firm and started reciting a soothing chant that Lenna couldn't quite make out. Suddenly the ocean roared in Lenna's ears, and the damp musk of seaweed and salty air flooded her nostrils. A flicker of light played in Mistress Meeks's eyes before she screamed and then began to seize.

Instantly, Luc was by Gilbert's side and both mages struggled to hold down the violently shaking woman. Gilbert mouthed something at Luc, who nodded in understanding, and both of them immediately began to speak a series of quick, liquid utterances. Lenna fell back onto the dusty path before the porch, aghast and helpless. Her first instinct after the shock was to summon a doctor, but with a seizure this serious, Lenna knew that even if she had a horse she would never make it to the nearest physician in time.

But as quickly as the violent episode had begun, it ended. By whatever miracle Gilbert and Luc had performed, Mistress Meeks's body calmed, and she lay back against the steps of the porch, her eyes closed and her breathing slow but steady. A droplet of sweat ran down Gilbert's nose and fell to the ground as he stood up, nodding grimly to Luc. The younger man, with a distant look in his eyes, gave a curt nod in return and walked off into the darkness of the apple orchards.

"Where is he going?" Lenna asked in a voice barely above a whisper. She managed to get to her feet and dusted herself off.

Gilbert's voice was strange, as if his mind was somewhere else. "Let him have a few moments, Len. That was not an easy thing for him to see."

"What happened?"

Before Gilbert could provide Lenna with an adequate response, a loud cry reverberated from somewhere inside the ramshackle house and the light from the door was suddenly obscured by the figure of a young man, pointing what was quite obviously an old flintlock pistol straight in the direction of Gilbert's head. Gilbert immediately grabbed Lenna roughly by the arm and pulled her close, and she felt the tingling sensation of Gilbert raising a magical barrier around them both.

"You lot there," called an accented voice, the kind that was once prominent in the region but gradually faded out as Port Hollish became more commercial. "You all get the hell away from my ma."

"We mean your mother no harm," Gilbert said slowly and deliberately, one hand raised in a gesture of peace. "I was trying to help her."

"Ain't nothing you magicking freak can help with." The young man stepped forward, the shadows falling from him. Like most farmers in the area, he was dressed simply in linen trousers and a shirt, though he wore no shoes. He had long, shaggy flaxen hair, and a sprinkling of freckles around his nose. Lenna had a burst of recognition.

"Devlin! Devlin Meeks!" she called, surprised. "Is that you?" The last time she had seen Devlin, he had been barely more than a toddler who took pride in throwing rotten apples at his parents' guests. Even though he was a man now, Lenna recognized the pattern of freckles, the manner of speech, and the resemblance to his once-beautiful mother.

"Aye, that's me, all right," the man replied warily. "But who are you folks?"

"Lenna Faircloth. Do you remember me? My mother — Alanna — used to be very good friends with your mother. And this is my friend, Gilbert."

Suspicion and relief mingled on Devlin's face, and it appeared to Lenna that he relaxed his grip on the gun. There might be hope after all, and she nudged Gilbert in the ribs, trying to get him to lower his shield. He shifted his stance and seemed as though he was prepared to do so when, from beside the porch, a shimmering whorl of force ripped through the air and pummeled into Devlin before he could even raise a cry. The blast knocked him off his feet and slammed him into the doorframe, causing him to drop the pistol in the process. Devlin slumped to the floor, joining his mother in unconsciousness.

Lenna felt Gilbert's shield evaporate away into fleeting particles, and both she and her friend turned their gazes to Luc, who, from the corner of the porch looked as confused as Lenna looked cross. Gilbert quickly vaulted the stairs and checked Devlin's condition. Breathing a sigh of relief, he nodded at Lenna to indicate that the young man was fine, all things considered.

"What did you do that for?" Lenna asked Luc accusingly.

"He was pointing a pistol at you," Luc said calmly, as though Lenna had asked him to pass the salt.

Lenna sighed heavily. "Let's just get him inside — both of them, actually — and try to get them comfortable. They're old family friends."

The house's inside was as dilapidated as its exterior. The wooden floorboards creaked with lack of care, and various pieces of furniture, covered in white tarps, were pushed up against the walls. The only functional pieces that remained were a wood-burning stove, a fireplace, and an old-fashioned wooden rocking chair, one Lenna recognized as the seat where Old Granny Meeks used to peel and core apples for pies and other treats. The entire place smelled of dust and mildew.

While Luc and Gilbert lugged Devlin's prone body into the house, Lenna began unceremoniously ripping off the tarps from pieces resembling sofas or more comfortable chairs. She raised furious clouds of dust in this endeavor and had to cover her mouth and nose with a handkerchief lest she choke. Luckily, she quickly discovered a discolored, ripped lounge chair and small sofa. She helped her friends install one Meeks in each.

"Now," Lenna said, her voice slightly muffled by the handkerchief, "would one of you gentlemen care to explain what the hell just happened to Mistress Meeks? I'm fairly certain I have an accurate grasp of what happened to her son." She shot Luc a glare of daggers, which he nimbly avoided.

Gilbert reached his arms over his head, hands intertwined, and stretched on his tiptoes until his back emitted several loud popping noises. Luc grimaced. The older mage scooted Granny Meeks's rocking chair from its place near the fire up to the sofa, before the softly breathing body of Mistress Meeks. At first Lenna thought he might have brought it for her, but Gilbert plunked himself down into the chair and began to creakily rock back and forth, his hands knitted behind his head.

"This woman has suffered from a kind of magical shock," said Luc quietly, standing off to the side of the fire. "When someone with immense potential isn't trained and the magic lingers, it can destroy the body from within."

"You mean, if someone — like your Brotherhood — had recognized her powers when she was a child, this wouldn't have happened?"

"The Brotherhood does not accept women," Luc said stonily.

"Then shame on your damned Brotherhood!" said Lenna with much more heat than she had intended.

Luc gave Lenna an icy glare and without a word swept out of the farmhouse, his blue robes kicking up more dust as he passed Gilbert and Lenna. Lenna raised her eyebrows in a curious glance at Gilbert, who merely shook his head in dismissal. She shrugged; let Luc have his tantrums. To Lenna, there were more pressing issues at hand, and she encouraged Gil to continue the explanation.

"There are other outlets for magical tutelage, Len," Gilbert said, not unkindly. "Your mother's people, the Freewomen of Laur, teach magic, although their methods differ from ours greatly. The

Ilyan nation to the east and the Empire to the north also train and utilize mages, though I will admit without much bragging — well, maybe a little — that with steam power so popular nowadays, and magic not being as necessary, the Brotherhood is the best place for training."

"So what happens to people, like Mistress Meeks, who have potential but aren't trained? Do they all end up like this?"

Gilbert rocked forward and leaned his elbows on his knees. "This kind of situation is exceedingly rare, which is why most people aren't even aware of it. At the Brotherhood we're taught certain skills to treat some of the symptoms of these cases, but at this point that's about all we can do. But there's something extremely odd about this, Lenna."

"What's that?"

"As we discussed about earlier, our ability to handle magic, without training, starts to fade as we grow. If she was that powerful, and untrained, this trauma would have destroyed her mind when she was still a girl. But we both know she was a well, capable woman until very recently."

Lenna frowned at this, and her brain was starting to make connections that were far less than agreeable. Here was a woman who suddenly suffered a case of magical trauma, and now Lenna, who should not have been able to access her magic at all, was being trained to draw on that power as though she were a ten-year-old girl. What had been the natural order of the world for several hundred years was being turned on its head.

"Something is changing, isn't it? About magic?" she asked Gilbert, who said nothing in response. He did, after a moment, notice Lenna staring at the pocket in his robes where she knew he had been storing the strange gemstone.

"I should know better than to keep information from you, you nosy ninny," Gilbert began.

Devlin began to groan and slowly opened one eye, peering warily at Lenna and Gilbert. As he strained to sit up, Lenna rushed to his side, encouraging him to sit back and let the stunning effect of Luc's spell wear off before trying to move too much. At first, Devlin was incoherent, but after a moment or so his tongue began to piece together syllables into understandable, if somewhat slurred, words.

Gilbert apologized profusely for Luc's attack on Devlin and explained that they meant no harm to Mistress Meeks. For her part, Lenna told Devlin that if he wanted revenge, as far as she was concerned Luc was fair game, and she would even help load the pistol. Although Devlin laughed and his mood lightened considerably at this, a rare scowl of anger from Gilbert curtailed Lenna's mirth. She supposed she should cut back, just a little, on her jabs at the young mage.

"Ma's been sick for weeks now," Devlin offered. "I know the farm looks a right mess; I'd been out lookin' for work in other homesteads, even out so far as Junction. A neighboring estate sent word Ma was sick. I can't make any sense out of what she says, when she speaks at all."

Lenna looked around the dirty farmhouse. "How are you supporting yourself, Devlin?"

"I made enough money, Lenna — been trading with some local folk for some supplies. I can get Ma to take cheese and bread and some water most days. But for the past few, she's been wantin' just to sit there on the porch, like she was waitin' for somethin'."

Gilbert leaned forward and spoke as gently as he could. "I don't think there's much we can do for your mother, Devlin. If you can take her to relatives or back with you, and keep her comfortable, that would be the best option."

Devlin nodded, as though he expected such an answer. "T'be honest, Master Mage, sir — and sorry 'bout that language of mine before — I'd've taken her back with me already if she weren't so damned insistent on staying here."

It was at that moment that Mistress Meeks's eyes fluttered open, and she sat up so rapidly Lenna was worried she would hurt herself. She turned her head back and forth, surveying her son, Gilbert, and Lenna, and then nodded. Lenna noticed a clarity in her eyes that was not present before, a brief moment of lucidity. Mistress Meeks pointed one bony finger toward the ceiling of her house.

"A mighty chill is coming, Lenna," she croaked, as though her voice were unfamiliar with speech. "Best to get ahead of it, before you three all get stuck."

Devlin slid down to his knees, despite Gilbert's protests, and grasped his mother's hand. "Ma, what do you mean? What's coming?"

"An early winter," she said, voice barely above a whisper.

A whoosh of wind and the creak of the farmhouse door startled Lenna, and both she and Gil turned around to see Luc standing there, looking slightly damp and startled. A bit of white substance clung to his boots. Mistress Meeks merely nodded.

"Gilbert, Lenna," Luc said, out of breath. "It's begun to snow."

Lenna and Gilbert blinked incredulously. Autumn had come quickly to the Continent, but snow at this time of year was completely unheard of and, in Lenna's recollection, had never before occurred. Even Devlin, concerned with his mother, rushed to his feet and followed Lenna and Gilbert to the door. Luc shuffled to the side, revealing an overcast night sky beginning to be crowded with delicate petals of snow. Holding out one hand, almost in shock, Lenna began to collect a small pile of the substance in her hand and stared, mystified, as it melted into chilly water in her palm.

The ground itself was barely covered, and Luc's hurried return to the house suggested he feared this snow was unnatural. Gilbert, his brow furrowed, left the porch and knelt down on the earth. He scooped up a small handful of dirt, lightly sprinkled with snowflakes, and poked at it as though it were some laboratory experiment. After a moment or two of observation, the blonde mage dropped the pile to the ground and rose to his feet, dusting off his knees.

"It's snow, all right," he deadpanned.

Lenna resisted kicking Gilbert in the shins.

"It doesn't snow this early, Lenna," whispered Devlin from behind her left shoulder. Lenna resisted kicking him, too.

"It just started a few moments ago," Luc explained. "The night has been gradually getting cloudier, but suddenly it was like the clouds converged over this farm, and it just began snowing. Even the temperature feels like it's only just dropped."

Gilbert, done with his tomfoolery, nodded at the apprentice. "It's certainly magical in nature; I've been through some strange weather in my time, but the only time I've seen results like this has been when the Brothers focused on weather-working. Considering the storm that delayed our ship, I would say that this is definitely their style."

"They've caught up with us already?" Lenna asked wearily.

Luc shook his head and Devlin stood about uselessly, so Gilbert continued. "I doubt it — a curse with this kind of potency can't be cast at a distance without some immense power. Luc or I must have been targeted by someone at the embassy, and the effects are just beginning now. It's meant to slow our escape. We'll need to outrun it; it will be strongest here, at its epicenter."

"All this effort, for us?" Lenna asked.

Gilbert and Luc exchanged knowing looks but remained silent and conspiratorial. Lenna's patience for immature men and their secrets had just about come to an end. She swiveled about on the balls of her feet and pushed Devlin back toward the porch and up into the house. In shock at so bold an action — from a librarian, no less! — Devlin offered little resistance and within a moment he stood in the dusty threshold of his family home.

"Devlin," she said imperiously, "I imagine this snow isn't going to get better any time soon. How much food, water, and lumber do you have to hand?"

"Not sure we got that much, Lenna." He sounded even more dubious than normal.

"Do you have a wagon and a horse?"

He nodded quickly.

"Okay, then we need to get you and your mother out of here, as quickly as possible. Head where the snow seems lightest; if you have family or friends you can stay with, stop there if it's safe. Otherwise, get as far away as you can from the weather. You don't have the supplies to outlive a snowstorm."

He nodded again and started toward the door, before hesitating and looking back toward his mother. Lenna sighed in frustration and pushed her glasses up into her hair, rubbing her eyes. She had always known Devlin to be a tad simple, but maybe the thrashing he took from Luc and his mother's sudden premonition of the snowstorm had stunned the poor boy into shock. He needed firm direction.

"Luc, Gilbert," Lenna called out the door. "Go hitch the wagon, and fit in any supplies from the storage shed you can. Make sure to leave room for Mistress Meeks to rest comfortably."

Gilbert nodded and headed off, but Luc hesitated. "What is it?" Lenna asked.

"I've... never hitched a wagon before," he said softly.

Definitely aristocracy. "Okay, Devlin, go with Gilbert and help him with the horse and wagon, and the supplies. Luc, come here and help me with Mistress Meeks."

Devlin obediently scurried off and Luc shuffled in, a touch of red coloring the sides of his face. Lenna had the distinct impression that very rarely had he been asked to perform a task of which he was incapable. The librarian could work with that later; for now, as she gazed out the open doorway, feeling a wintery chill creep in and watching the flakes fall in heavy white sheets, her primary concern was to get the Meekses, who deserved all the kindness they could offer, moved, and then the three of them would head on their way as swiftly as possible.

Within minutes, Luc and Lenna had managed to bundle up Mistress Meeks as best they could with the materials lying about the room; Luc found a warm patchwork quilt that was reasonably clean, and they used it as a base around which they formed a sort of cocoon with the least dusty of the furniture coverings. Luc, stronger than he looked, supported Mistress Meeks and somehow managed to walk her out the door where, at the bottom of the porch, Gilbert and Devlin were waiting with the horse and wagon.

A quick glance out the door informed a frowning Lenna that the wagon was ill-supplied. She noticed a bag or two of apples, hopefully healthier than the ones she and her companions had trampled earlier, but nothing else. Around the stove sat a few cabinets, in which Lenna found a lump of hard, potent-smelling cheese and a basket of eggs that she hoped were still fit to eat. She put both into a larger wicker basket, which had been woefully empty, and then, resignedly, she walked over to her rucksack — dumped onto the least dusty of the furniture — relieved it of its sausage, and with a silent farewell, placed the meat in the wicker basket along with the other goods.

"Gil or Luc, can you do something about the fireplace? We can't leave it burning," she called over her shoulder as she tucked the basket snugly into the back of the wagon. Devlin had already taken up his position in the driver's seat and was looking down at Lenna gratefully. He had, Lenna noticed, thrown on a wool coat and tucked his feet into a pair of worn, but sturdy, boots.

"I remember I used to throw apples at you," he said mournfully. "I'm sorry for that."

Lenna smiled up at the nice-looking lad. "I'll get you back for it, one day. Now drive quickly, before the snow makes it too difficult for the horse to pull the wagon."

Devlin nodded and clicked his tongue, flicking the reins against the horse's broad flank. It snorted out a whorl of steam in the cold but begrudgingly began a steady gait down the main path of the Meekses' farm. At this rate, Lenna had faith that mother and son would outrun the brunt of the snowstorm, though as she stood in the falling snow, shivering, she began to question whether she and her two companions would.

A moment later Gilbert and Luc, obviously having used some kind of magic to extinguish the blaze, hopped the steps and joined Lenna outside, their breath, like the horse's, steaming in the increasingly chilly weather. To Lenna's surprise and dismay, both young men looked at her as though she should decide their next course of action. She grew flustered and kicked a bit of dirt off the ground. She might be capable of organizing a quick getaway, even if it required the sacrifice of a decent sausage, but dealing with magical snowstorms wasn't exactly her specialty.

"Well?" she said, impatient. "What now?" She shivered in the cold, and for the first time Gilbert seemed to realize Lenna wasn't dressed nearly as warmly as he and Luc in their robes.

"Luc, magelight, please." Luc summoned another small, bright sphere of energy that made the falling snow almost festive. Gilbert, meanwhile, reached into his robes, pulled out a silver flask, and, after unscrewing its cap, passed it to Lenna.

She eyed it dubiously. "What's this?"

"Portable fireplace."

"Isn't there something magical you could do?"

"Probably, but this is quicker." Gilbert's expression was downright impish, and Lenna, resigned, put the flask to her lips and took a good, long pull from it. A fiery liquid — whiskey, she imagined — filled her mouth and seared its way down her throat. She coughed a little at the strength of the drink, but she did feel a bit of toasty warmth starting to build in her stomach.

Gilbert looked up at the sky, considering the steady snowfall and the movement of the clouds. He snagged the flask from Lenna and took a mighty swig himself. "The clouds are fast, spreading in all directions. Unless we want to get snowed in here, we're going to have to move swiftly and find a place to wait it out."

"Is waiting really an option? It doesn't seem like the Brotherhood is pulling any punches in pursuing you," Lenna commented.

Gilbert took another drink from the flask before gesturing at Luc. Understanding it to be an unspoken command, the younger mage pulled a rolled sheaf of parchment out from a pocket of his robes, causing Lenna to wonder just how many hidden compartments the Brotherhood's uniforms contained. Luc unfurled the parchment, and peering through the snow, Lenna saw it was a map centered on their location, the Meekses' apple farm.

With a nod from his superior, Luc pinched two fingers together and pressed them at the center of their location, and then slid them down the page. Lenna watched in amazement as the farm slowly shrank and more of the countryside became visible; the map had widened its view of their current position to show them the surrounding land. Out of all the magecraft she had witnessed thus far, this map was by far the most intriguing to Lenna.

"After we realized our plan had been compromised, we intended on heading a bit north, to avoid the highway, the most obvious of paths out of Port Hollish," said Luc, sliding his finger along their intended path. "But the Brotherhood obviously intended to make sure we were slowed, no matter what path we took."

"Judging by the clouds, the snow is just going to get heavier," said Gilbert.

Teeth chattering, Lenna borrowed Gilbert's flask for a second time and washed away some of her chill with the potent liquor. "So what do we do?"

"We're simply not equipped to travel in the snow like this," Gilbert replied. "We need to find shelter until this blows over. The Brotherhood doesn't have the resources to keep it up forever, but we also don't want to freeze to death."

Lenna scooted closer to Luc and practically squealed with joy when she discovered that she could manipulate the magic map at a touch of her finger as well. She urged it to expand its view a bit more and thought about their options. Port Hollish would not be a safe place to return to, and if what Luc had said was true, there would no doubt be more Brotherhood mages headed east along the highway. Lenna's finger stopped on a small town about halfway between their current location and the highway, not impossibly far to the south.

"Brest," she said.

"I beg your pardon?" asked Luc, affronted.

"No, the village of Brest. It's a small town, and not too far from here. It will be hit by the snow too, but as much as this storm hampers our travel, it will hamper anyone pursuing us as well, right?"

Gilbert grinned. "That's my Len." He gently knocked her on the forehead. "With our considerable lead, and since they probably expect us to be farther along the highway, Brest seems like a safe enough destination for us to seek some shelter."

Nodding, Luc rolled up the map and checked the straps of his rucksack. Lenna felt she could hold up for a few more hours, especially with the solid fortification of Gilbert's flask, though as she looked dismally down at her boots, currently amassing their own piles of snow, she wondered if her footwear would survive. She supposed it was time for new boots anyway.

Gilbert summoned his own ball of magelight, making it appear as simple as snapping his fingers. Luc rather vocally disapproved for the first hour or so while Gilbert explained to Lenna the basics for making the light appear and maintaining it, but as the snowfall grew heavier and the wind picked up, his voice was gradually drowned out. In fact, all conversation came to a halt, and the worried furrow on Gilbert's brow deepened as the snow piled up at their feet. Walking became progressively more difficult, and Lenna wondered if they'd make it to Brest before dawn — or freeze to death.

"Gil," Lenna shouted over the wind. "What's wrong, besides the obvious?"

"This is a pretty strong working," he shouted back. "It's widespread; it's powerful. Sorry, Len," he added, "to get you mixed up in this."

"You should be," she shouted back, and linked one of her arms with his. Luc stumbled up through the mounds of snow to latch onto Gilbert's other arm. The three of them dotted the solitary white landscape: three figures, arm in arm, softly illuminated by magelight in a blinding curtain of snow.

CHAPTER SEVEN

Covered in snow and bones rendered brittle by frost, Lenna, Gilbert, and Luc trudged exhaustedly toward the mark on the map that indicated the village of Brest. Before long Gilbert's flask ran out, and the three huddled against the wind and stinging precipitation. Gilbert nearly exhausted his magical reserves, using a type of shielding to keep the group warm. Though a boon, its maintenance slowed their progress even further, but by some divine grace, the mage kept them safe until they arrived at the small village. They collapsed on the threshold of the public house.

Drained of energy but not lacking tenacity, Gilbert spent the next two days wrapped in a blanket before a fire, steadfastly employing himself in teaching Lenna the basics of magical shielding. It was a skill for which she had little aptitude. Still, Gil was a patient instructor, using their free time to, at the very least, instill in his pupil an understanding of the initial concepts.

"You're quite a natural at directing energy away from you," he explained, "but you seem to have some difficulties in holding onto any power for yourself."

Lenna heard Luc sigh despondently off in the corner of the room. She didn't exactly blame him; for almost forty-eight hours, the boy had been shut in an inn with someone for whom he very obviously had little patience, particularly considering his opinions regarding the teaching of magic to females. Lenna was just thankful that the small village had an inn that could accommodate three people, even though they were forced to share a room.

Considering the circumstances and the town's size, the accommodations were more than adequate. The innkeeper, an elderly woman by the name of Joranne, had run the Tawny Apple since time immemorial. The inn stood proudly in the corner of the village of Brest albeit, like its proprietress, a bit hunched, and it was a hale stone landmark of survival against harsh changes in the nation's economy. Only two floors, the Apple also boasted a common room — which in more obliging weather also served as the village pub — with a roaring fire and rich, slow-cooked stews. Despite a lack of visitors in recent years, Joranne still kept a clean inn, ready to host travelers at a moment's notice.

Their room was spacious and contained two large, soft beds, a luxury for the exhausted companions. Gilbert and Lenna sat on two wooden stools near the rosy embers of the hearth while Luc, brooding, sat at a small breakfast table in the middle of the room, playing a one-man trumps game he had learned on Crescent Island. Despite the fire and the boarded window, Lenna could still feel winter's chill creep into the room.

"Try again." Gilbert's soft insistence roused Lenna out of her musings. She sighed, hooking a loose hank of hair over her right ear and pushing her glasses back up the bridge of her nose.

"It's late, Gil."

"You'll never get better with that attitude," he replied, folding his arms. "Now, give it another go."

"You sound like my mother." Couldn't she just borrow a book from Joranne and curl up under the plush covers of the bed?

A soft but caustic voice carried across the room. "Give it a rest, Gil. It's a lost cause."

Lenna immensely disliked being told what people thought she couldn't do. She shot Luc a dark look through her glasses, hoping the magnification of her spectacles and pursing of her lips would tell the jet-haired youth exactly what she thought of his snide remark. Succeeding in Gilbert's test had just become personal.

Gilbert, his eyes ever fixed on Lenna, put his hand on her shoulder. "Easy. One of the first things we learn as novices is that anger is a good source for a quick burst of power, but it isn't sustainable, and it's very hard to shape correctly. A proper shield is going to require concentration." He turned his cowlicked head toward his comrade at the table. "And Luc, you've made your misgivings about me teaching a woman — about me teaching Lenna — clear numerous times. I'd like for you to remember, once again, that I outrank you, and that it's not your place to question me."

There was a sharp intake of breath from Luc as Gilbert finished. For a moment, Lenna thought she recognized a flash of hurt on the boy's face, but any trace of pain was gone as he very deliberately stood up from his place at the table, cleaned up his cards, and marched out of the room. Both Lenna and Gilbert let out simultaneous sighs as the door silently shut.

"Luc is young and very opinionated," Gilbert said cautiously, his brow furrowed in thought. "But he really is very kind."

Lenna rubbed the back of her tangled head with one arm, quirking an eyebrow at her old friend. "I can tell he's brilliant, but 'kind' isn't the second, third, or thirtieth adjective that comes to mind when thinking of words to describe Luc."

Turning once more to the fire, Gilbert absently scratched at his scruffy chin. "I'm surprised at you, Len. Growing up, I thought you were one of the most sensitive people I knew. I remember, when I

134

was chosen to join the Brothers, how you took on the responsibility of my chores and comforted my parents. Where's that Lenna now?"

Gilbert thought a moment. "Your mother, Alanna, was a wonderful woman, and I know better than anyone how her death affected you. But loss can change people in far different ways than it did you, Lenna, and Luc has had his fair share of suffering."

Lenna said nothing. Gilbert waved one hand at the dying flames and with a thought coaxed the embers back to crackling life.

"This isn't my story to tell, but if it helps you understand Luc even a little bit, I consider it worth breaking his confidence.

"Luc's family is from an estate in southwest Krevlum, and it has a long tradition of producing powerful members of the Brotherhood. Their blood runs back since before the Unification, and their ties to my order are strong. It's almost expected that the youngest son will be an exceptional talent and join the ranks of adepts, bringing honor to both the Brotherhood and the Empire. Luc doesn't disappoint in that regard; from what I understand, he exhibited tremendous magical potential from an early age — not unlike you, if the stories I remember about you growing up are true."

Lenna rested her chin on one hand and stared idly at the rekindled flames. Those stories were true indeed; she had often heard of incidents that occurred around her as a child, and she could even remember certain times in her youth when she could produce certain desirable effects if the need arose. Still, she found it hard to believe that Luc was such a wonderful magician when working with him — and his attitude — would be so awkward and clunky, almost abrasive. Working with Gilbert, on the other hand, seemed so natural, like breathing or walking.

"In any case, Luc wasn't alone in his magical gifts. He was born with a twin sister by the name of Clarie, and from what I understand, her aptitude for magic exceeded Luc's by far. If I'm any judge of such things, Clarie's power levels would have rivaled those of the top members of the council."

Lenna frowned in thought. The Blue Crescent Brotherhood shunned women and forbade they use any magic. The Freewomen of Laur offered training for all, but if Luc's family was tied to the Brotherhood as strongly as Gilbert was suggesting, Lenna doubted Clarie would have been allowed to seek outside training. Did they train her in secret at the Brotherhood, then? After all, from what Lenna had witnessed with Mistress Meeks, untrained power of the level Gilbert was described could turn disastrous.

Gilbert nodded as though he had heard her thoughts. "Like I said, Luc is from an extremely old and noble family, and there are rules there that don't apply to us. Like me, Luc joined the

Brotherhood as an apprentice when he turned twelve, but Clarie was left at home at the family's estate, her magical gifts ignored and untrained — despite their being other options, like the Freewomen of Laur or in her own nation of Krevlum. Shortly afterward, just as Clarie was crossing the threshold into womanhood, her control slipped.

"She spiraled into madness, issuing portents and visions that doomed those around her to horrible fates. Where she walked, flowers and trees would die or twist into horrible shapes. Less than a year passed before she died, and on her deathbed she screamed for Luc and damned him at the same time for receiving the control she needed as much as he."

"So he blames himself for her death," Lenna said quietly. "Even though there was nothing he could do about it. And thus he hates the idea of women using magic."

"It's more than that," Gilbert said, placing one hand on Lenna's shoulder and turning to face her once again. "Luc knows how strong you are, that your innate strength rivals ours."

"He doesn't understand why I'm alive and his twin sister isn't," Lenna finished. "Why I'm receiving the training she was denied."

After a silent moment, Gilbert nodded. "That's how I see it. It's irrational, I know — but life can't always be rationalized and filed away into neat sections, like your library."

Lenna slowly rose to her feet and walked to the dressing table near her bed. On it lay the mother-of-pearl-handled knife that was once her mother's. By right, Lenna had a place with the Freewomen, and she knew it had been her mother's wish that she claim it. Lenna had shirked that duty actively, denying her heritage and her mother's wishes. And yet here she was: taking up the very blade that she had rejected all these years. And resenting it. Was she so dissimilar from Luc? Was she giving him any more of a chance than he was giving her?

Sighing, Lenna dropped onto her bed and raised one hand toward the ceiling, making a monocle with her thumb and forefinger. Gilbert remained motionless by the fire, watching her.

"Get me some wine, Gil, and let's practice that damn shielding a bit longer," she said.

Their last breakfast at the Tawny Apple Inn was truly resplendent, Joranne apparently being in possession of mildly spiced honey that sweetened the heady tea she served with crispy, flaky pastries filled with savory game fowl and rich with clove. Sweeter pastries filled with apples and cinnamon followed. It was a great injustice to Lenna, then, that she could not appreciate any of the glorious food because of a gut-churning hangover. She groaned as Joranne firmly plopped a mug full of steaming liquid before her.

"Drink this," Joranne said with a cheerfulness that Lenna thought bordered on malevolence. The woman was too chipper for her own bloody good.

Lenna sluggishly eyed both mug and innkeeper, her head lying on the smooth oak table. "What is it?"

"My husband's recipe," the innkeeper replied. "It'll have you feeling right as rain in no time, or at least well enough to take your head off my table."

Gilbert, seated across from Lenna, interjected, "Was your husband fond of the local wine, ma'am?"

"No," she replied, casting the young mage a dubious glance. "I'm the one fond of the wine." And she imperiously swept out of the dining room and back into the kitchen, no doubt to supply their spread with even more sumptuous treats.

"Drink up," Gilbert said.

Affronted, Lenna raised her head from the table and winced every time the hangover struck her brain like a mallet. The liquid in the mug was an opaque carmine concoction that smelled strongly of juniper and some unique chemical scent Lenna couldn't place. Her stomach lurched at the mere thought of guzzling anything down, let alone some backwoods innkeeper's mysterious hangover remedy.

"Do I have to?" a plaintive Lenna asked.

"Yes," replied Gilbert, who made no effort to conceal his amusement at his friend's dire straits.

"If this comes back up, I'm aiming for you."

"I expect nothing less."

Lenna lifted the mug midway to her mouth and gave another tentative sniff. Was there a magical cure for a hangover? She supposed not, or the Brotherhood would never get anything productive done. Pinching her nose shut with the thumb and forefinger of her left hand, a very desperate Lenna took a deep breath to steel her rebellious stomach before bringing the mug to her lips. The cure-all left a bittersweet, metallic tang on her tongue as it plunged down her gullet and into the raging maelstrom that was her empty stomach. Lenna groaned and put her head back on the blessedly cool table.

"That wasn't so hard, was it?" Gil asked.

"I am going to die," she pronounced from under a curtain of hair.

"Undoubtedly, once Joranne sees your head on her nice table with your curls in the jam. Oh, morning, Luc."

The young man, moping a bit, deposited himself in a chair next to his elder, diagonally opposed to the miserable wretch of a librarian. Lenna tilted her head and peeked at Luc with one red-rimmed eye; contrary to Gilbert, who devoured the innkeeper's fare with relish, specks of pastry crumbing his lips and chin, Luc broke his fast mechanically, like one of the clocks her father constructed. It seemed a shame that such a bountiful meal would be wasted on a sullen automaton and a near-comatose lady.

A silence descended upon the dining room, punctuated only by the intermittent crunch of flaky pastry yielding to Gilbert's teeth. Lenna was glad of it: Joranne's drink had yet to prove itself efficacious and even Gil's nibbles drove the point home that wine, not the forces that pursued them, was her enemy. She enjoyed the silence she was allotted before Luc cleared his throat in a manner that Lenna could only find exceedingly annoying.

"From the look of things outside," the youth began, "the snowstorm has abated and any accumulation is beginning to melt. It should be safe to set out again."

Gilbert frowned and a worry line creased his forehead. "I agree we shouldn't linger here for too long, but I wish I had the means to contact Master Sebastien and ask for new instructions."

Lenna began to inquire as to Master Sebastien's identity, but Luc was first to speak, his glassy eyes flashing in the morning light. "Who cares what he has to say? *He's* not here, running for his life for the sake of some shiny rock. I say stuff him. We set our own rules."

"Apprentice," Gil commanded, "know your place." Luc stiffened in his seat, another expression of pain flickering across his face for an instant. The older wizard softened his tone a bit and gently placed a hand on Luc's arm. "Trust me, okay?"

Meanwhile, Lenna had managed to haul her body up into something vaguely resembling a sitting position, the churning in her stomach and fogginess in her head abating a little.

"Hello, team," she said. Gilbert removed his hand from Luc's arm and both young mages turned to regard their hungover companion.

"I believe I've been rather fair about not pestering for details," Lenna began, starting to feel a bit giddy. "Tell me more about this Sebastien character. Call me a crazy librarian, avid reader, drunken harlot — but is a little exposition too much to ask for?"

Surprisingly, it was Luc who smirked in amusement and Gilbert who adopted a somber disposition; Lenna had assumed it would be the other way around. Not that it mattered much to her; whatever Joranne had put in that strange-smelling panacea, it was not only clearing her head but rousing in her a delicious, fiery sort of courage.

Gilbert cast an eye toward the door to the kitchen, as though the elderly proprietress might be a spy. "Master Sebastien was my instructor when I was an apprentice. He holds a lot of influence within the order, and it's he who arranged the theft of the jewel."

"So why are you the one on the run with it instead of him, then?"

"My teacher isn't just powerfully gifted; he's well-known in a good number of political circles. Besides being a nobleman from Gallas, he's been involved in delegations all over the Continent."

"Ah," said Lenna. "So the lesser-known pupil is doing the grunt work."

Much to Lenna's surprise, Gilbert blushed. It was highly unusual for her childhood friend's carefree confidence to falter. "It isn't quite like that, Lenna."

"To begin with," Luc added curtly, "since Gilbert is no longer an apprentice, Sebastien isn't technically his 'master' anymore."

Gil shot Luc a piercing glare. "While that is true, I still respect him as a teacher. He's a wise and great man, and loyalty to one's teacher is something to be praised."

"Well, I chose a different kind of loyalty," Luc replied caustically.

Gilbert blanched and said, mollified, "Yes, I know."

Though she had an inkling about to what — or to whom — Luc freely gave his loyalty, Lenna decided not to pursue the topic in the awkward silence that followed. Whether she felt the stillness fall over the three companions or merely had impeccable timing, Joranne chose that moment to grandly march out of the kitchen with another mug of her mysterious beverage and a plate bearing an impossibly tall stack of bacon. She placed both before Lenna without much ceremony, though she did leave with a stern look on her face that very plainly said *you'd better eat all this, young lady*. She could be heard muttering to herself as she strode out of the inn to begin sweeping the backyard clear of snow.

Plucking a piece of bacon off the plate, Gilbert continued, unfazed. His former instructor, Sebastien, who feared the Brotherhood's growing interest in the gem and its power, arranged for its extraction. Sebastien would have fled with the gem itself, taking it to a "safe place" away from the Brotherhood's steadily growing military movement and the already powerful Krevlum Empire, had not Gilbert intervened and offered to take it himself. With his master's help, the young magician, through a mix of magic and subterfuge, successfully escaped from Crescent Island on a ship bound for his childhood home, Port Hollish.

"You actually volunteered to betray your order?" Lenna asked.

Her friend shrugged as though to say he did not consider his actions a betrayal. "In any case, our original plan was to take the Continental Highway east to Junction, and then head south, to Gallas, to Sebastien's hometown. But considering the trouble we've run into, I'm not sure it's safe to take the planned route as our information appears to have been compromised. That's why I wish I could speak with him."

In between sips of Joranne's elixir, which Lenna suspected contained a highly potent alcohol, the librarian said, "Can he contact you?"

"He has his methods," Gilbert answered vaguely, causing Lenna to snort with impatience and Luc to roll his eyes.

"The gem's magic can supposedly cross great lengths of time and space," Luc said. "Why don't we try reaching out to Master Sebastien ourselves?"

"Mmm," agreed Lenna, her mouth full of bacon and buttery toast.

Reaching into a pocket in his vest, Gilbert slowly withdrew an object wrapped in a cloth, handling it with care not unlike that which Lenna's father would give to an expensive pocket watch or clock he created. As Gilbert placed the bundle on the table, the delicate grey material fell away, revealing the impossibly shiny gemstone. Its presence filled the Tawny Apple's public room, exerting a subtle yet undeniable pressure against the consciousness of those gathered at the table. Lenna much preferred the throbbing of her head to this invasive, otherworldly force.

"Sebastien didn't prohibit me from using it to try to contact him," Gilbert admitted, "but I've never used such a potent artifact before."

"It's literally seeping energy," said Luc. "If I close my eyes, I can almost see it rolling off the surface of the stone, in steady waves."

Lenna was quite certain that closing her eyes would set her world spinning. "Let's hurry up, Gil," she said. "The jewel gives me the most peculiar feelings."

He nodded and held his hand aloft, parallel to the surface of the oak table. Lenna felt a slight vibration, as though a tuning fork was resonating in her head, and the stone began to emit a pale blue light. Gilbert's face was void of all expression, as if manipulating the vast magical resources of a mysterious artifact was no larger a task than passing the butter.

The librarian leaned forward and whispered to Luc, "Is it really all right that he uses this thing out here?"

"A bit late for concern now, isn't it?" he hissed back. "And he's a full-fledged Brother; it's his decision. Not," he added, "that it matters much, seeing how we're on the run."

Gilbert sighed and the light slowly faded from the jewel. He opened his eyes and said, "I don't think that did much. I tried using it to amplify a standard spell of communication, but it didn't seem to have any effect."

"Well, it looked like it was doing something," Lenna said speculatively.

"I just accessed the energy, that's all. I couldn't even shape it, though I suppose I'll be helpful if the Tawny Apple runs out of candles." Gilbert smiled.

"Well, now what?" Luc asked.

The door to the kitchen swung open as Joranne dashed into the room. Her expression was one of stony determination but she wrung her hands, as though hesitant to be the bearer of bad tidings. She loomed ominously over the head of the table.

"Is everything all right, madam?" Gilbert addressed her, one hand nonchalantly maneuvering the stone off the table and into the pocket of his trousers.

"The sky," she said, her voice tinged with frailty. "The sky to the west, it's darkened quicker than I've ever seen. I've been through many a storm in my day, but the sky has never changed in an instant."

Gilbert and Luc exchanged a knowing glance and leaped up out of their chairs. Grabbing her spectacles from beside her place setting, a wobbly Lenna followed the two young men out the main door of the inn, Joranne trailing in her wake. Luc had been correct: the inclement weather of the other day had cleared up considerably, and the sky directly above them was a pale blue with only a few patches of cloud scattered about indecorously. From the northwest, a steady current of dense black cloud advanced, an army of fog that moved too quickly to be natural.

"Shit," said Gilbert.

"What is it, Gil?" Lenna asked.

The young man remained calm, his voice unwavering as he turned to Joranne and very briefly thanked for her hospitality. Pressing on her a handful of coins worth far more than the innkeeper would see the rest of the year, Gilbert encouraged her to return to her cooking and not venture out until the storm had passed. It wouldn't be long, he promised.

Luc, meanwhile, had already entered the inn and reappeared with some of their provisions, unceremoniously dropping them to the ground at Lenna and Gilbert's feet before popping back inside for more of their effects. Immediately, Lenna and Gilbert squatted down and began stuffing their rucksacks with their sparse equipment.

"I'm glad I taught you some shielding," Gilbert said abruptly.

"Gil, what's going on?"

"It was a mistake to attempt to use the jewel. I should have realized that someone would be looking for signs of its power; I probably just lit up Brest like a bonfire on a mountaintop."

Lenna finished packing her bag and checked the leather straps binding her mother's dagger to her side. Confident that it was secure, she stood back up as Luc shuffled out of the inn with a bag crammed full of apples and a cheese. "What is that hugely terrifying cloud, Gil?"

Gilbert stood and turned to face Lenna. "It's a massive working. We need to get moving."

Luc started, "The amount of power..."

"Yes," he replied, eerily calm. "And it looks like this one isn't keen on just delivering more snow, and the stone must be its target. We can't be here when that storm breaks, or we'll put the kind people of Brest in danger. We head back to the fields."

Luc gingerly grasped Gilbert's wrist. It was the single most intimate, human gesture Lenna had witnessed from the apprentice. "No showing off, all right? Promise?"

Gilbert feigned innocence and bumped his forehead against Luc's, causing the younger man's cheeks to color. "You'll get no grandstanding from me, young sir. But we'd best be on our way."

Luc nodded, appeased. He spared a quick glance toward the darkening heavens and indicated that he was ready to go. All three shrugged their rucksacks onto their shoulders, and oriented themselves toward bluer skies. The plains were only a few miles off, and a rise in temperature had melted some of the snow, especially along the road out of town. Why exactly they would head toward a several mile-wide expanse of nothingness puzzled Lenna; if the storm broke over them when they had no shelter or cover, they would be extremely vulnerable.

Gilbert seemed to sense Lenna's hesitation. Glancing in her direction, he said, "Lenna, that shoulder strap looks loose." He had been standing between her and Luc, and he reached over to Lenna's right shoulder, his face drawn closer to hers in the process. He fumbled a bit with the strap, attempting to tighten it. "Do you trust me?"

"Yes," she said.

"Good, I trust you too." He dropped his voice to a soft whisper that tickled her ear. "Promise you'll watch over Luc for me, all right?" Unsure of how to respond, Lenna gave the faintest of nods as Luc was standing only a few paces away. Gilbert added, in normal tones, "There. That should hold much longer now."

Gilbert rushed a few strides forward before turning around to face Lenna and Luc. He grinned and said, "All right, children! Off we go! Don't want to get caught in a storm again." He turned and began briskly down the road to the east. Lenna and Luc exchanged a look of mutual understanding: whatever carefree attitude Gilbert was assuming at the moment did little to cover the sadness in his deep green eyes. Lenna shook her head, to herself mostly, and in her mind repeated Luc's words. *No showing off, all right?*

At a brisk pace the three departed Brest, their temporary port in the storm, as the encroaching darkness closed the distance at a speed Lenna preferred not to calculate.

Lenna was obviously not in the same physical shape as her two companions; until now, she had been leading a very peaceful — if somewhat sedentary — life poring over encyclopedias and great works of literature. While Gilbert and Luc were tapping into mystical energies and scampering about their island like some sort of military regiment, Lenna had probably been hidden away in some crevice of her library, reading up on the Ilyan language or the War of Unification. She was indeed thankful for her fast metabolism, but her legs whined at her in protest, and whatever hangover-buffering effect Joranne's steamy beverage had provided Lenna apparently stayed behind in Brest.

Thankfully, Gilbert kept back with his friend, though it was evident from the pursing of Luc's lips that the he was displeased with their speed. Without pause they had been alternately running and jogging from the village, the roiling black clouds in the sky behind them giving chase like a hunter after his quarry. Lenna worried that her slower gait would ultimately be the group's downfall. She panted heavily and sweat dripped onto her spectacles, blurring her vision.

Gilbert brought them to a halt, and Lenna was relieved to see she wasn't the only one drenched in perspiration. Luc, on the other hand, bounced lightly on his feet back and forth, as though he impatiently awaited the start of another three-mile sprint. They had successfully made some headway into the plains, an expanse of flat terrain with pathetic-looking foliage and a particularly aggressive species of squirrel. Though the highway cut through the emptiness of the area as one of the primary means of travel for those who couldn't afford the pricier steamtrain running to its north, the time of year and sudden shift in weather meant there would be few travelers on the road. Brest, the last Fallowfields village until the outpost of Junction, would also be the last source of humans the group would encounter for some time.

"How far do we intend on going?" Lenna panted.

"As far as it takes," Luc snapped. "It's not as though we had time to arrange a wagon."

Lenna knew a challenge when she heard one. "Excuse me, but I didn't ask to come along on this mission in the first place…"

"Quiet, both of you." Gilbert's voice was low, but it cut through the heavy air and the bickering like a plowshare through a crop of wheat. He reached into a pocket in his vest and pulled out a poorly folded sheet of paper that, when opened, revealed the magical map Luc had used a few days before. "I know everyone is familiar with the local geography, but we're here right now." He pointed to a spot just north of the highway, not far from Brest. "That sending," he nodded toward the west, "we need to try to outrun it; the greater the distance that foul creation has to travel, the weaker it will get."

"I thought that kind of magic had to be locally targeted?" asked Lenna. "Could a member of the Brotherhood have followed us to Brest?"

Luc inhaled sharply through his teeth and Gilbert assumed a ponderous expression. "It's possible, but it's hard to imagine they had the foresight to know their previous snowstorm would drive us to Brest. And to use this kind of offensive magic against the three of us — especially considering the treaties we have against large-scale workings in other nations — it would be considered an act of war."

"Then who else could have cast it?"

Gilbert shrugged. "Who can be certain? In any case, we'll head north, where the steamtrain runs. I can't guarantee we'll be able to pay our way on or even stowaway on the sodding thing, but I don't believe the sending is powerful enough to follow us so far a distance."

"What's to stop whoever trailed us from sending another?"

He shook is head. "Apprentice, care to explain?"

Luc rolled his eyes. "If a spell like that could have targeted us from a distance, it would have done so days ago; like the last weather-working, someone nearby would have had to cast it. Someone at our embassy probably cursed Gil or me, and that's how the snow found us. Now it seems that someone or something near Brest was waiting for a sign that the jewel was being activated, and then unleashed that thing on Gilbert's magical aura. That means the party behind it doesn't know who we are; it just knows *someone* nearby activated the jewel." He pointed to the rolling dark clouds.

"Like locking onto a target," Lenna said. "And unlike the Brotherhood's, this one isn't just snow; you think it's set to kill."

Gilbert nodded. "If we get far enough north, ahead of the spread, we should be safe. We're not too far from Granemere Forest, and that's Freewoman territory. I'd rather we not get caught up in politics, but we can get Lenna safely there on the way to the train."

The Freewomen of Laur, thought Lenna. Her mother's people. Their zigzagging path had actually brought them closer to the settlement than she had realized, though she had expected to arrive alone. She was also vaguely aware of the mutual distrust the Freewomen and the Brotherhood shared and understood Gil's desire to avoid any delay because of a political entanglement. According to him, if they cut north now, at good speed, they would most likely be able to outrun the chaotic clouds nipping at their ankles. The three nodded in agreement, and after Lenna gulped down a refreshing splash of water from her waterskin, she steeled herself for more gut-wrenching running.

They journeyed farther at their hurried pace for the better part of an hour, with Luc several meters ahead and Gilbert obligingly staying back with Lenna. She looked back from time to time, and luck seemed to be on their side: the group appeared to be gaining ground against the rumbling darkness. Inwardly Lenna breathed a sigh of relief. If she could convince Gilbert and Luc to let her accompany them to the steamtrain, then just perhaps she might be able to arrange for transport back to Port Hollish and get herself out of this sudden adventure, avoiding the Freewoman settlement altogether.

As they pressed on, it became increasingly difficult to tell the time of day; the sun fell behind grey clouds and Lenna's only timepiece, she was frustrated to see, had stopped sometime during the morning. She would have to wait until they arrived in a populated area to reset it. Over the course of what seemed like a few hours, after the group had put a fair amount of distance between themselves and the darkness, the natural clouds that had moved in began to sprinkle the ground with powdery flakes of snow.

"The weather was so clear this morning..." Gilbert murmured as the three companions stopped to look up.

"Not again," groaned Luc.

Still they continued, the once-clear sky now their enemy as well. Their pace became painfully slow as the snowfall grew heavier and heavier; already the stretch of plains before them was buried under a soft white blanket. At the rate it was precipitating, this would prove to be quite the storm, and none of the group was prepared to brave such wintry conditions. Worse yet, as their progress stalled, the great ebony clouds drew nearer, and off in their direction Lenna could hear what sounded like a faint howling.

Gilbert made no effort to veil the look of concern on his face; he had heard the beastly noise echo across the darkening sky too. "Lenna," he asked, looking her straight in the eyes. "Do you remember enough from last night? Do you think you can shield yourself?"

"I'll try," she said honestly.

"Luc, whatever comes, help reinforce Lenna's shielding. I'll do what I can as well."

The dark-haired youth nodded silently.

The snow continued to fall at a steady rate, obscuring Lenna's vision. As the wind picked up, it became increasingly difficult to maintain any amount of speed, and the group found themselves huddled close together against a blinding curtain of whiteness. Any light that managed to seep through the thick veil of clouds began to fade as the darkness encroached upon the plains. Lenna pressed near Gilbert, who walked in between herself and Luc, as a sudden gale tore at their clothes, causing Lenna's hair to fly into discord. Sidling up against her friend, Lenna could feel a subtle vibration through his pocket, one similar to the humming from this morning when Gilbert attempted to use the jewel to communicate with his former master, Sebastien.

"Gil, is that the gem?"

"Yes," he replied darkly, "it's been doing that for some time now. I can't seem to get it to stop."

More howling pierced the night, closer now than before. Between the snow and impending nightfall, it had become impossible to track the location of whatever magical sending pursued them; the darkness had become one under the snow. Suddenly, the hairs on Lenna's arm began to rise and within a moment's time the ground a few meters before them exploded in a blast of snow, earth, and light, the force causing Gilbert and Luc to stumble and Lenna to fall onto her backside. The stench of ozone and burning sullied the crisp, cold air.

Gilbert quickly assumed a defensive posture and stood in front of Lenna. As he did, she noticed a brief shimmer in the air around her, and the wind sounded as though it were filtered through a piece of gauze; he was shielding them both. Another burst of lightning, a few meters to the north of the previous strike, tore through the sky, and the air near Luc crackled with sparks and a faint shining. He had invoked a magical barrier as well.

"Stand up, Lenna," breathed Gilbert. "Open your mind; let me help you get up a shield, and then we need to start moving around. We can't stay in one place or the lightning will find us."

The librarian hastily complied, scrambling to her feet and taking deep breaths, trying to recall Gilbert's teachings from the night before. She calmly looked for the source of her power, her magic, and once she found that glowing softness, she let down her guard. Her trust for Gil was complete, and she could soon feel his strong presence, his magic, pressing against hers. With an invisible caress, Gilbert's arcane self took some of Lenna's magic and wound it around her physical form, weaving an intricate net of magical strands into a globe surrounding her. It took but a moment, but when Gilbert's presence faded from her mind, Lenna could still feel a tightly knit blanket of her own power creating a shield around her.

At that moment, both she and Gilbert instinctively jumped apart, a jagged bolt of energy roaring down to char the place they had been standing. Lenna felt a strange electrical buzz and shivered as some of the shock's residual energy crackled against her shield. She darted left and right, feeling decidedly foolish; it was only a matter of time before a bolt found her, and she wondered if the shield she tentatively grasped in her mind's eye, the shield that felt as fragile as a child's balloon, would hold against such a potent attack. She was not alone in her running pattern, however: both Luc and Gilbert ran jagged paths through the snow, zigging and zagging and leaving wide swathes of powder in their wake. A few thunderbolts crashed into the plains around them, but no strikes were as close in proximity as were the first few.

It was then that Lenna heard the growling. The dark cloud that had loomed after them, a vast pool of writhing blackness, was directly overhead, visible now in the night as it flashed with pockets of electrically yellow light. Like tar oozing down a wall, great globs of the cloud, five as Lenna counted, slowly descended from it, leaving long, viscous trails that severed only when the blobs made landfall. Pulsating with energy, the masses of dark, fluid matter whirled about into helices before each bubbled and formed a crude dog-like shape with eyes of piercing topaz. Someone let out a high-pitched scream that was soon swallowed in the roaring and howling of the dogs; Lenna realized the source of the shriek was herself.

"Gil, hellhounds!" Luc exclaimed.

"Luc, reinforce the shielding, please."

The hounds began to circle, surrounding them. Luc and Gilbert strategically placed themselves around Lenna, their shields overlapping and Luc's energy buffering them. Lenna thought she could feel their shield pulse in time with Luc's heartbeat. The first of the hounds growled gutturally and crouched on its haunches, preparing to leap. As it sprang into motion, Gilbert's hands blurred, gesticulating wildly, and in a flash of light and peal of thunder, the hound disappeared. Its former companions, wary, fell back a few paces.

"Keep up the barrier, Luc," said Gilbert, and he began a furious sequence of unsummoning spells that warped the reality around the conjured hellhounds, returning them to the ether. Within moments three more had been dispatched by Gilbert's magic.

Lenna inwardly breathed a sigh of relief as the remaining hellhound shuffled back a few more paces, its snarling muzzle visible despite the darkness. Above it, the black cloud, diminished in strength from the creation of the hellhounds, churned angrily. A crackling arc of electricity erupted from its interior, but Luc's buffered shielding held. Gilbert struck out with renewed confidence at the final hound, his hands cutting a deft arc through the air. All that was left was the dark cloud hovering in the snow-filled night.

"Is it safe?" Lenna asked.

The blonde mage nodded and stepped some paces away from Luc and Lenna, out of the extra shielding, and looked thoughtfully up toward the cloud. Despite being considerably smaller than it was before, its evil presence still flashed with potent arcane energy. Confident that danger had passed, Luc slowly relinquished his enhanced shielding; Lenna shivered as his power slid away and her senses acclimated to her environment. The sensation left her feeling naked and exposed.

"Now to take care of that." Gilbert began to mutter under his breath, contemplating his options. The cloud still bubbled about fervently but showed no indication of moving, and Lenna felt strangely calm; she trusted Gil and Luc would dismantle it as easily as they had managed the hellhounds. She slid her spectacles off her nose and wiped them dry on her skirt, a difficult task in all of the snow.

"Lenna!" Gilbert suddenly called out, and the librarian hastily restored her glasses to her brow. The entire mass of writhing cloud spun perilously toward her, shaped into a solid bolt of darkness. With sickening slowness, she realized that she had allowed her own shielding to lapse and, paralyzed with dread, Lenna could not form a new barrier in time.

In desperation, Gilbert flung his arms toward his friend, his legs struggling to propel him forward through the crunching snow. Lenna sensed a rush of energy as Gilbert futilely tried to funnel his own shielding toward her, to cover her in a cage of magical force. But it was a crude shaping; without the time or concentration Gil could do naught but extend his own protections over her, and the result was barely a veil, flimsy as tissue.

Lenna knew it would not hold against the pillar of blackness plummeting toward her. She wanted to run, but her feet refused to comply. Thoughts of her father and his slow, steady hands making timepieces in front of her as a little girl flooded her mind. Being chastised by Jeffer. Her mother demonstrating a new knife technique. The cloud drew closer, piercing the air with a shriek, and then it was over in a sickening crash and cry from Luc.

Gilbert fell forward in a cacophony of magic and light and rolled across the snowy ground several yards away from Lenna, struck in the back by the ominous missile of darkness. His body steamed in the wintry air, and as the last of his ill-shaped charms shimmered away into nothingness, he groaned quietly into the night. To protect Lenna, Gilbert had flung himself before her and used his body, not magic, as a shield instead.

Lenna and Luc sprinted across the powdered ground, panting as they arrived at Gilbert's side. Noticing his ashen face and slow breathing, Lenna was uncertain much healing could be done — magical or not — and hung back a few feet, allowing Luc to examine Gilbert's injuries.

The dark-haired youth dropped to his knees in the snow beside Gilbert and gently clasped his wounded companion's face in his hand. "Gil, Gil," he stammered. "I'm not sure I can heal this."

Gilbert looked up at Luc and smiled grimly. "Ask Lenna to help."

Lenna quirked an eyebrow at this; Luc had been downright opposed to working with the her before, insisting that all of Gilbert's magical teaching was both wasted on her and degrading to the Brotherhood. From her experience with the mage thus far, she knew he would not choose to work a healing with her unless he had no other option.

Gently falling snow framed Luc's dark expression as he gazed intently at Lenna. His mouth twisted as he formed words to which he had never been accustomed. "Lenna," he began, "I need you to help me heal Gil."

"So much for pride, eh?" coughed Gilbert.

Lenna nodded a quick assent and knelt next to Gilbert in the snow, opposite Luc. Without uttering a word, she offered her hand to Luc.

"Like you did with Gil before, accept my presence, and feed me your magic. I'll 'shape' it, as you say."

At once began the queer sensation Lenna experienced whenever she accessed her magic, a lightheadedness in which the edges of her world began to blur. Immediately she felt Luc's presence brushing up against her own: it was a soft, feathery presence, even gentler than Gilbert's. Where Lenna had expected rigid control and icy power, Luc's magic caressed her like a mother's light tickling of a newborn babe. Lenna opened her mind and let whatever strength she possessed flow into the young man gripping her hand. His magic smelled of lilies.

Luc's hair quickly grew damp with sweat, and whether his mouth uttered incantations, prayers, or curses, Lenna couldn't tell. After what seemed like eternity his pull on her magical reserves stopped, and Lenna opened her eyes and looked down at her childhood friend. Gilbert's breathing seemed a bit more controlled and his expression was painless, but his face was still void of all color.

"It didn't take," Luc told him, letting go of Lenna's hand and gripping Gilbert's in both of his. "I couldn't repair all the damage."

"I know," Gilbert said softly. "It's all right."

Lenna twitched at the sound of a hound — or something very much like a hound — in the distance. Standing up and brushing the snow off her skirt, she scanned the horizon. Though she could see nothing, something inside her told her another sending was rapidly approaching.

She turned back to Gilbert and Luc. "They're coming. Luc, we'll have to carry Gil…"

"No, Lenna." Gilbert's voice was low and firm, and though he addressed her, Lenna noticed that Gilbert's eyes were fixed firmly on Luc. "Leave me."

"Lenna's right; we can move you, and I can heal again." Tears carved canyons in the caked dirt on Luc's face.

"Luc, between the two of us, we should be able to manage," Lenna said.

Smiling, Gilbert shook his head and, reaching up, very gingerly caressed Luc's cheek. "Lenna."

Lenna knelt down once more next to Gilbert as he turned his head to her. Coughing, he removed a shining object from his pocket and thrust it into Lenna's hands. She gasped.

"The stone? Gil, I can't."

"It responds to you. Take it. Take it and leave me, please."

"You can't be serious. There's no way I'm going to just leave you here to die in the snow. Not now, not after we just got started on this insane adventure of yours. There's so much you were going to teach me."

"Sparkle ponies," Gilbert said, his voice quiet.

"Damn the bloody sparkle ponies!"

A howl pierced the silence of the falling snow and Gilbert's eyes desperately pleaded with Lenna. His stare was penetrating, and he held the librarian's gaze for a moment before turning his eyes once more to the weeping Luc. *Protect him*, his eyes said. *Please*. Contrary emotions were waging war in Lenna's heart; logically, she was not confident she and Luc would get far towing Gilbert. But she could not fathom abandoning him here, her best friend and secret source of strength; not alone in the snow.

"Gilbert," cried Luc softly.

An eerie light from the gem reflecting off the snow painted Gilbert's calm face as one much younger, and Lenna recalled him as a boy, doing what she couldn't: leave her mother behind. With determination had Gilbert pried the flowers from Lenna's clenched fist and thrown them atop the casket, simply because he wanted to be strong for Lenna. And now, he was asking her to repay the favor.

With a grim expression Lenna nodded at Gilbert and stuffed the pendant into the satchel hanging at her side. The relief on Gilbert's face was evident as she leaned forward and kissed him on the cheek, stifling her urge to cry. Her face twitched as she stood up and straightened her skirts.

"You were always such a bossy kid," she said quietly.

Luc desperately clung to Gilbert's hand and shook his head, his tears and runny nose dripping onto the snow. "Gil!"

"For once, shut up." Gilbert reached one hand around the back of Luc's neck and roughly pulled his face down against his own. Their faces remained pressed for a moment, and Luc whispered something into Gilbert's ear before pulling away.

"Same here," Gilbert murmured, smiling. Lenna watched as a remarkably beautiful snowflake, a silver crystal in the night, fluttered down and landed gently on the brow of her childhood friend.

No grandstanding, indeed, she thought. Trust Gil to find the most remarkably dramatic way to die.

CHAPTER EIGHT

An almost human cry pierced the snow-laden night air and Luc's muffled whimpering. Frowning into the distance, Lenna knew that a second sending would be upon them before long. If they didn't move, and quickly, there would be two more corpses to join Gilbert's.

"Luc," Lenna said, placing her hand on his shoulder. "We have to go."

"You go," he muttered.

"We go together; come on. Let's go." Lenna leaned over and attempted to pull Luc to his feet. "Something's coming."

"Leave me the hell alone!" In his anger and desperation, Luc lashed out with uncharacteristic force, shoving Lenna. The snow let out a crunchy whiffle as the librarian fell backward onto her rump.

"Leave me!" Luc repeated.

Lenna scrambled to her knees before Luc and shook his shoulder. "He's gone, Luc. Gilbert's dead. But we're not, and if we want to stay not-dead, which is what he would want, we have to move."

"You unfeeling bitch," Luc said.

The night air rang out with a resounding smack as Lenna's hand collided against Luc's cheek with such force that the boy was nearly knocked prone. Lenna stood up angrily and spoke in quick, terse words.

"Do you think you're the only one who knows what loss is? Do you think you're the first to stand over the body of a loved one?" She would regret these words, and striking Luc, but for now anger flooded her veins, lit her up like blue-hot fire against the night sky. She held up the gem above Gilbert's body.

"I see why he didn't give this to you," she continued. Luc's eyes stared at the sparkling jewel and his lips twisted painfully. Lenna knew that what she was about to say could never be taken back, that it would destroy a part of Luc and probably herself, but she knew a beast was coming and could focus on nothing but her angry determination not to let Gilbert's death be wasted. Sparkle ponies.

"Go ahead and stay here if you want," she spat, stuffing the blue stone back into her satchel. "You'll just prove what I've been thinking since the moment I met you. You were never worthy of Gil's love."

Lenna quickly turned and marched in the direction of a copse of trees a few hundred meters to the northeast. She was silently thankful that all she heard was a sharp intake of breath from Luc; she did not want to witness the pain on his face or the tears welling in his eyes. She hated herself for what she said, not only because it was a lie but because, at any other time, Lenna would rather help him grieve, not force him to ignore his pain.

She kept her pace deliberate, silent, though Lenna knew her thoughts should be focused on speed and speed alone. She was certain her cutting, calculated words would register. He would come. Whether he spoke to her ever again, or spat in her face, Lenna knew Luc would follow her. And probably hate her all the while.

The boundary of the copse slowly drew closer under the curtain of falling snow. It was a smallish ring of trees, almost like a fairy circle, especially in its random positioning in the mostly barren fields. It dotted the landscape like a dimple on the face of winter. Perhaps it was her acquisition of the gem or the reawakening of her magic, but Lenna intrinsically understood that this small cluster of firs offered the best chance of survival on this pale, death-wrought night.

Lenna clambered into the copse exhaling white puffs of breath, all the while thinking sardonically that, of late, she had been engaged in far more flight than any librarian should ever have to be. Then the immediacy of Gil's death crept into her thoughts, and at a more somber pace she pushed away branches of fir and moved toward the center of the trees.

The branches gave way to a small clearing, which in the spring would no doubt be a pleasant meadow. Though the sky was still plainly visible, the forest floor was covered in only a very small blanket of snow, with patches of completely dry ground available near the line of trees. Lenna's eyes widened in mild surprise — mostly curiosity — as she examined the ring of firs that surrounded her. Though when viewed from the outside the clearing seemed sparse and almost inadequate for any means of protection, from her current vantage point the arboreal wall seemed dense and fortified. She knew she would be safe here for tonight, though with the implication that now either Lenna or Luc had become the target of more vicious magic, she dared not linger much more than a few hours.

Settling down in the crook between two of the older-looking trees on the eastern side of the clearing, Lenna had very little to do except replay the events of the past few minutes over and over in her head. Her hurried escape had not taken so long but Gil's death felt like ages ago. Such a bitter, bookish trope! She should be bursting with grief at losing her friend, but all Lenna really wanted to do was sleep. Shock, she thought rather morosely, was not nearly as romantic as fiction made it seem.

That Gil chose her over Luc to take the gem was at the moment a niggling thought in the back of her brain. The feelings between that couple aside, Luc was a magician, an initiate of the same society in which Gil had been so recently promoted. Lenna had picked up a few things in the last few days and was willing to admit she was clever, but her heart and mind simply couldn't come up with any sort of actual reason for her to be the new bearer of this damn jewel.

She slipped it out of her satchel and gauged its weight in one hand. It was heavier than her knife — much more like the gold paperweight Jeffer used — and felt denser than its size suggested, not that she was very knowledgeable in gemology. Lenna could at least say with certainty that this jewel was no sapphire; it was about the size of a large marble, but so perfectly spherical and smooth that it seemed unnatural. No skill or technology or magic with which Lenna was familiar could have crafted so flawless a specimen. Or caused it to cast pale, eerie blue shadows.

Lenna dangled it by its length of silver chain. Turning it around, she noticed for the first time a series of intricate carvings, a mix of vertical and circular markings, engraved into the silver links that held the stone. An acute and familiar peculiarity, a sense of nostalgia, flickered across Lenna's mind for an instant. She wondered if Gil or Luc was able to read the markings.

Interesting foreign script aside, Lenna mused, it would still be a cumbersome and unflattering piece of jewelry to wear. She grimaced and stuffed her ill-gotten gains back into the pouch at her side. Though she was curious about its origin, and particularly its strange markings, for tonight Lenna knew that she would have to accept having no answer. If Gil had any knowledge of the jewel's secrets, he had carried it away with him to whatever waited beyond the veil of death.

Lenna had begun abandoning her thoughts and letting her lids slowly droop down when she heard a rustling in the trees opposite her position. Starting, she let one hand slip down around the knife buckled to her side, even though she was certain the source of the sound was Luc catching up with her. After a moment or so, a curtain of fir branches on the western side of the clearing parted and Luc, ghostly pale and lips pursed, entered the copse. His eyes lingered on Lenna for a scant moment before he lowered himself to the ground, pulling his legs up close to his body and burying his face in his knees.

The instant their eyes had locked Lenna noticed the bitterness in his. It was not undeserved, though Lenna secretly hoped that one day, whether he forgave her for her harsh words or not, Luc would understand the reason behind her actions. She sighed. Like it or not, Gil had forced her into becoming responsible for Luc. He was clearly in no position to be on his own, especially when she considered that a very nasty something-or-other was pursuing them aggressively. Travel come day would be easier, but would Luc follow her, and at what speed?

Lenna knew any words she offered would fall on deaf ears. Luc could probably barely register anything other than his own fatigue. Across the clearing, his breathing was slow and shallow; he had not even bothered to brush off any snow lingering on his person. The shock of her words after Gilbert's death had made him angry enough to heed her once, but Lenna honestly did not believe that, even if she was capable of spouting such venom again, her remarks would motivate him to move any further.

Lenna scrambled to her feet and headed to the center of the clearing, where there was evidence of a small fire pit. Someone had once lit a fire here and, pursuers be damned, it was cold enough to warrant one again. She gathered up what few branches and twigs she could find and threw them together into a rather pathetic pile of kindling. Even if she had flint and steel, the damp wood would probably never catch, but Gilbert had taught her to produce flame. Weary but confident, Lenna crouched beside the pile of wood and cupped her hands over it.

Just as she began to draw forth her magical reserves, she became acutely aware of someone's gaze on her back: Lenna had subconsciously positioned herself with her back to Luc. Would he be bitter about Lenna using magic, especially considering that the one who taught her, despite Luc's protests, was his lover? Suddenly Lenna realized that she could not steal any more of her departed friend from Luc, and that a demonstration of any skill from her — especially since the joint healing between Luc and Lenna had failed so devastatingly — might damage him far more than her angry words had done.

At least I can give him this, Lenna thought, and focused just the tiniest bit of energy toward the little pile of kindling. She had to be careful not to feed it too much power, or the kindling would catch, but after a moment or two of intense concentration Lenna produced a single spark and a faint wisp of smoke. *Good*, she thought with an inward smile. For the next few minutes, sighing deliberately ever so often, she consistently produced small puffs of smoke, a flicker of light here and there, but never a proper flame. Shortly thereafter she began to shiver and stood up, ignoring both kindling and Luc, and marched back to her rucksack on the eastern side of the copse. She hoped her gut about Luc would be right and that she wouldn't spend the next few hours alone with her chattering teeth.

Several moments passed and despite the chill in the air Lenna's eyelids once again began to grow heavy. Only when the sensation of light and heat wafted across her did she open her eyes to see a small fire burning steadily in the center of the clearing and Luc settling back down directly opposite her. Lenna hated to think about his grief in terms so calculated, but his lighting of the fire, be it out of spite, the cold, or compassion, told her that Luc, the mage, was still present.

When she woke a few hours later, Luc's fire was nothing more than a drifting trail of smoke against the backdrop of the approaching dawn. Stiffly, Lenna climbed to her feet and scanned the area; Luc wasn't present in the clearing, but the sound of snapping twigs to her south indicated he hadn't gone far. Lenna quickly checked over her belongings: knife and jewel were still present, and in the rucksack slung over her shoulder she had a small hunk of cheese, some apples, a waterskin, and her Freewoman book. The encounter with the sending had driven them far from the road and some of her kit had fallen out on the way.

Lenna silently cursed her own folly last night. Grief and fear had driven her to seek flight and protection, ignoring the fact that Gilbert was carrying his own rations and — more importantly — the magic map. The thought of going back for his corpse, assuming she could find it, was not a pleasant one. Still, she had no alternative: without directions, Lenna would never be able to find the highway or her people's settlement, or even the route back to Brest.

A muted thunk startled Lenna, and she blinked at the knapsack that had landed on the clearing floor a foot in front of her. She recognized it immediately as Gilbert's, and when she brought her gaze up Lenna found herself looking into the stony expression of Luc, rigidly standing a few feet from her. Lenna's eyes betrayed her pity; she could not bear to imagine Luc returning to the body of his beloved and, like a grave robber, looting his corpse. She should have been the one to undertake that responsibility.

"The map is still in there," Luc said. "Take it, and let's go."

Lenna tentatively picked up the knapsack. "Don't you want to carry this?"

"No." His response was businesslike.

Nodding, Lenna removed the neatly folded map from Gilbert's knapsack. Opening the bag released the soft scent of Gil's magic, the salty tang of the sea that she now associated with the howling of wraiths and shouting as Gilbert waged war with Brother Jaron. Lenna at once understood why Luc could not bear to claim the knapsack for his own; she barely wanted it for herself. Still, Lenna could not bring herself to leave it behind in the clearing. Grimacing, she continued to transfer the bag's contents to her own before finally folding up the fabric and tucking it into her bag as well. She held onto the map, though, and unfolded it carefully.

"There is a village called Uppridge about twenty miles from here, to the northeast," Lenna said. "It's our closest shot for the steamtrain, without backtracking. We should go toward it circuitously; I think it's best we stay away from our... previously planned route." She did not put words to her fear of more sendings awaiting them, or the more alarming thought that Gilbert's clandestine mission had been completely compromised.

Luc nodded once, crisply, before turning on his heels like a resigned soldier and marching northeasterly toward the line of trees. Before reaching them, however, he cocked his head back and stared intently at Lenna's disheveled hair and grief-stricken face.

"Last night, you deliberately didn't light the fire."

Words failing her, Lenna merely shook her head.

Luc nodded once before disappearing into the line of firs.

The journey forward was silent, save for the crunchy sounds of their footprints as they traveled away from the copse and the scene of Gilbert's death. As she was the one holding the map, Lenna became the de facto guide and took the lead; Luc followed several paces behind, seemingly oblivious to the cold and falling snow. Lenna understood his current state, but — selfishly, she realized — she wished for some conversation to take her mind off her own grief.

According to the map, the journey to Uppridge would have been easy were it not for the snow, which was steadily accumulating with the advent of a new wave of precipitation. It made for exceedingly slow going, and neither Luc nor Lenna was properly dressed for such a long winter trek.

After hours of travel, exhaustion was beginning to set in, and Lenna suddenly noticed with some alarm that the jewel in her pouch began to throb, producing a highly uncomfortable sensation where it rested against her thigh. It seemed as though the farther she walked the stronger the stone pulsed. She wanted to ask Luc what it might mean, but she dared not. Instead she pushed onward, her calfskin boots keeping out most but not all of the white mush she tramped through. Wearily eyeing the sky, Lenna knew that, at their current rate, they would not survive the day.

"Lenna," Luc said softly. "What is that ahead? Through the snow."

Although surprised by the sudden conversation, Lenna squinted and tried to focus on whatever Luc was seeing in the blaze of white. She could barely make it out, but there, off in the distance, was a dark line besmirching the horizon. It was a line of trees, Lenna realized. A forest. In haste Lenna scrambled to unfold the map, almost dropping it to the ground. The wind tore at the page, but from what she could tell in the lingering daylight, Lenna had not been as good a guide as she had thought. Confusion in the ever-white surroundings had led them off her planned path toward Uppridge by several miles, and now they drew close to Granemere Forest.

Last night, trees had provided the respite they had needed. The copse that had sheltered them, though, had been special: Lenna was sure of that. Granemere Forest, on the other hand, had a reputation for neither good nor evil; it was merely home to the Freewoman settlement where her mother had been born. Lenna's well-read brain and the hints dropped by Gilbert suggested that mages from the Blue Crescent Brotherhood were not exactly welcome in Freewoman territory without going through the proper political channels; would her young mage be safer there?

Glancing back, Luc was standing some several paces apart from Lenna, shivering. Exhaustion plagued his face, and Lenna knew at once that he needed rest and succor. Though she wasn't entirely confident that the Freewomen would protect him, getting Luc out of the dense snowfall was her top priority.

"We head for the cover of the trees," she called across the wind. "We'll worry about the rest once we get there."

Luc spoke a reply that was lost on the rising gales, but he began to follow Lenna more closely as she set off in the direction of the forest. The storm was progressing rapidly, and Lenna began to doubt they would even reach the edge of the woods before it was too late.

As she slogged through the snow, the humming of the jewel against Lenna's leg grew stronger and more uncomfortable as she neared the line of trees. She gripped it tightly through the satchel and felt its vibrations travel up her arm. Lenna silently willed the jewel to be still, but the more she focused her energy on it the more intense the rumbling within the gem's core became.

Desperately, Lenna realized that by merely willing the stone to cease its tremors she had subconsciously begun to send her magic toward it. She tried to sever the link, but to no avail; Lenna let out a gurgled cry as she sank to her knees, clutching at the pouch that contained the leech sucking away her essence. There was nothing but the throbbing from the jewel, invading her brain and pulling everything from her.

Suddenly Luc was crouched before Lenna, his hands gripping her shoulders fiercely. His lips moved as though he were speaking, forming words, but Lenna heard nothing but the steady beat of the jewel.

Blue light poured out of the seams of her satchel, and both Lenna and Luc pressed their hands over its leather bindings as though they were trying to smother the jewel's glow. The eerie paleness of the light cast Luc as a ghost, and his eyes went wild as he too began to feel the throbbing reverberate through his body.

Intensity beyond belief, the scent of lily and lavender, and a myriad of images washed over Lenna. Her father tinkering with a clock, her mother whetting the knife. A group of men dressed in blue robes argued around a table and Gilbert and Luc ran through alleyways toward her library. Gilbert's death; a craven expression on Luc's face shifted into an image of people unknown to her: a curly-haired youth and a running figure with ginger hair; a dashing man and an airship. The woods were still so far ahead and her head so pressured by these images that all Lenna wanted was release. She stopped fighting the constant tug from the jewel and instead pushed against it, throwing the entire weight of her magical being against the oppressive strength of the stone.

Luc might have shouted something, but Lenna did not hear: a violent, almost orgasmic rush left her body as the gem pulsed molten blue against the harsh white of the storm. A peal of thunder crackled in the sky and one last flare of light swept the area before vanishing them into the nothingness of the winter sky, leaving only a small patch of scorched earth and the scent of burnt lavender behind.

Lenna awoke to the sounds of rustling somewhere close by. There was a mild but steady throbbing in her head, and she groaned as she hauled herself up to a sitting position. That she was in the woods was obvious: a few meters from the snowy edge of the plains, Lenna lay amidst the crackling undergrowth of Granemere Forest. Dried twigs annoyingly poked her in the sides.

The trees above her were sparse enough to show that the snow had ceased and that the time was almost noon. Lenna frowned and wondered how long she had been out. Luc was lying face up to her right, still unconscious. She scrambled to her feet and walked over to the young mage.

He's not dead, Lenna thought as she leaned over him and placed two fingers against his neck. Whatever brought them here — which Lenna supposed she should figure out eventually — didn't kill them.

A soft moan escaped Luc's lips as he sat up, cradling his head with one hand. At second glance Lenna saw the beginnings of several nasty bruises on his cheeks and jaw; perhaps whatever had brought the two of them from the fields to their current position had not been as gentle with Luc as it had been with Lenna.

"What happened?" Luc asked as he surveyed his surroundings.

"I don't know," Lenna responded, offering a hand to help her companion to his feet.

Luc ignored her and stood up on his own. "We've obviously been teleported — but no one's been able to work that kind of magic for centuries. It's just too complex. Unless…"

"The stone? Yes, that must be it." Lenna fumbled about for a moment with the pouch sashed to her waist before producing the calm, faintly warm stone that had pulsed so mightily before the incident.

"It shouldn't be able to react like that," Luc said. "Give it here."

Though Lenna did not quite appreciate Luc's authoritative tone, she did recognize that, compared to her, he was the expert here. Cupping the jewel in one hand, she reached out and offered it to the fledging mage. "What do you think caused it?"

Luc extended his hand to take the gem, and as he did a harsh cry pierced the air. With a rush of wind, a group of five whooping, weapon-brandishing women clad in an assortment of outfits, even hide armor, surrounded them. Lenna became acutely aware of two crossbows, a blunderbuss, and two very nastily curved blades pointed in their direction.

She immediately dropped to her knees, bowed her head, and held up both hands as a sign of supplication. Lenna hoped intently that Luc recognized and understood who these women were and how to respond to this situation. As her head was bowed, she had no idea what Luc was doing; a moment later, though, Lenna's fears were confirmed when she heard a slightly accented voice address Luc.

"Lower those hands, boy," the voice commanded. "Your clothes show your rank plain as day. Even if you think to attack, my bullet will pierce your belly long before your magic strikes me."

Lenna heard a soft rustling that she decided was Luc shifting his stance to one less aggressive. She breathed a silent sigh of relief. Her companion obviously didn't realize that these were the Freewomen of Laur; for countless ages, these women's ancestors had been enslaved, and after much sorrow and strife, a number of them had rebelled and won their freedom. They were thus fiercely independent and understandably suspicious of certain groups.

Fortunately, for once Luc had enough brain to lower his arms and stand down. His antagonist was a shortish girl who, if Lenna was any judge of such things, was probably at the most eighteen. She was dressed simply in leather trousers and a white muslin shirt; were it not for the blunderbuss she carried with a most alarming familiarity, Lenna would have thought the girl, with her short, curly brown hair and smattering of freckles, could have been from any village on the outskirts of Fallowfields.

The girl was steadily frowning in Luc's direction. "Novice, even you should be aware that large-scale magical nonsense by your order is prohibited on our lands."

Luc quirked an eyebrow. "I'm certain I have no idea what you're talking about."

"Freewomen of Laur are not raised to be idiots," the girl continued. "I had always heard that the Blue Crescent Brotherhood was full of pigs, but at least you're supposed to be educated pigs. I guess I was wrong."

The other four young women around the girl snickered and Luc's ears grew red. In better circumstances Lenna might have giggled in spite of herself at the expression on the young mage's face. Her reaction was not as guarded as she had hoped, however, because the short-haired girl, having recovered her composure, turned to face Lenna. Lowering the blunderbuss, she regarded Lenna coolly.

"You at least seem to know a little about our ways. I'm Pim Hartnell; I'm going to have to ask you to come with me." The girl spoke tersely, as though this measure was merely perfunctory and there was better prey worth quarrying. Luc grunted, a sort of muffled outrage, as one of the girl's companions, a tall redheaded woman with innumerable intricate plaits in her hair, retrieved a length of rope from her backpack and began to bind Luc's hands. Pim looked at Lenna apologetically.

"Sorry 'bout the precaution with your friend. The number of suspicious types around these parts has been shooting up lately, what with the unrest from the Empire. And," she added, "however low-ranking he may be, a member of the Brotherhood needs to be conducted to our mayor. The law's the law. Do you have any other weapons than his magical hands?"

As Luc seethed, Lenna stood back up and removed her mother's knife from its sheath. Pim's eyes went wide as she took in the blade.

"Chickens and snakes, where the hell did you get this?" she asked.

"It was my mother's."

A sudden quiet fell over Pim's band of scouts. Luc and Lenna said nothing, their expressions curious and, in Lenna's case, more than a little confused.

After a moment or so, Pim, having regained her composure, coughed and said, "Well, at any rate, off to the village, err...?"

"Lenna," the librarian responded, adjusting her rucksack. "And this is my friend and traveling companion, Luc." The young mage snorted.

"All right, Lenna and Luc. Follow me! I'm eager to hear your stories." Pim slung the strap of her blunderbuss over her shoulder, briskly pirouetted to the tune of crackling forest leaves, and began trekking deeper into the forest.

And so it was that Lenna and Luc — whether they were prisoners or guests was anyone's guess — were conducted to Granemere Settlement, a bastion of the Freewomen of Laur, a community protected by leaf and bough and strength of will.

CHAPTER NINE

After being met at the gate of the settlement, the party of Laurian huntresses, save Pim, disbanded and headed off in different directions about town. Lenna marveled at its size, for up until this point she had always imagined a Freewoman village as just a smattering of cottages hidden deep in the woods or damp caves nestled in the foothills of mountain ranges. Instead, what she found was a thriving community with a much larger population than most country villages would ever boast.

A properly maintained country road led through the gate of a sturdy oak fence and progressed directly toward the center of town. The dense trees in the outer regions of the village were impeccably maintained, trimmed and tended well enough to act as storefronts for merchants and skilled workers. Neatly built cottages along the road were meant to provide services, Lenna noted; there was a forge, a bakery, a tailor, and a cobbler, and the people going about their daily tasks quite deliberately paused to ogle two strangers as Pim guided them toward what was presumably the town square.

Residences began to spring up among the commercial buildings, and Lenna saw at once that these amazingly constructed cottages were proof of the Freewomen's perseverance. Port Hollish, despite its vast resources and income from the influx of trading, could never hope to match this kind of intricately planned construction. Homes were flawlessly thatched and, though not modern brick and mortar, were so detailed and smooth that only the most oblivious of people could ignore the craftsmanship.

The Freewomen of Laur, after their liberation, had vowed to provide for themselves, and their vow resulted in a society that, rather than rely on the assets of other nations, was determined — even honor-bound — to produce the most sturdy of creations. It might not be fine art or the latest style of architecture, but everywhere Lenna looked, she could see the same kind of love and craftsmanship that she noticed when her father doted on his clocks.

More often than not, Pim would point out whose-family-built-what or this-lot-live-there, but Lenna knew this was mostly for dramatic effect. Pim was obviously young and overconfident and wanted the entire village to know she was escorting

two foreigners to the mayor. The incident with
Lenna's knife was somewhat perplexing to the
librarian; she knew that it was her mother's, and
thus of Freewoman origin, but she was gobsmacked
by the hunting party's reaction to it. Despite how
many times she had read that damn book, Lenna
obviously had a lot to learn about her heritage.

The trees surrounding them eventually thinned
as the street led to evenly spaced rows of cottages,
the living quarters of the Freewomen of Laur.
Freewomen culture was a tricky thing to explain to
outsiders, Laur itself being an extremely violent,
misogynist society that built its dominance by
abusing the ruined nations after the God War. From
what had formerly been a small collection of
fiefdoms, Laur conquered and collected the women
and their daughters: the men were slaughtered and
the land raped for supplies. The women and their
female descendants were, for two hundred years,
slaves.

But tenacity prevailed. As other nations unified
to halt the spread of Laurian power, the headstrong
women captives began an underground escape
route, funneling slaves one by one, when they
could, out into the countryside. By the time the
united, peace-loving nations broke Laur down, the
Freewomen — as they came to be called — had
dispersed their strongest, their leaders, to the
corners of the Continent. Once Laur was
disestablished, the remaining slaves were freed, and

they spread across the land, joining up with their escaped comrades.

It became a matriarchal society, though men and boys were welcome, and it spread across the land in patches. The Freewomen were everywhere — settled in different villages, cities, commons — but they all expressed and believed in the same philosophy: no one shall be oppressed, and all men, women, and children will know how to protect themselves. A tight network of communication linked the various Freewoman homesteads, and, despite possessing little in terms of property, they became a unified and potent political force.

Lenna had learned that much from her mother, but her stubbornness as a young girl had prevented her from ever exploring her lineage. So many times her mother had commanded, implored, and reasoned with Lenna to visit this homestead, and so many times Lenna had resisted. She had no desire to become a warrior woman, and said as much. After all, if her Freewoman kin were so important to her, why did Alanna never visit them herself?

The Faircloths were clockmakers, mechanists; what use would Lenna have for learning to fight with a knife? Port Hollish was an epicenter of civilization and culture; Lenna believed the brutish ways of tribes had no use in educated society. Lenna embraced the order her father's mechanical clocks provided, and she applied that organization to her library: whatever complaints Jeffer might have about Lenna, he could never fault her work ethic.

But now that she saw the Freewoman settlement, she realized how organized it was. It wasn't modernized like Port Hollish, as there was very little steam power here, but it was artfully crafted. What was once a bunch of tents and thatched roofs became, after the liberation, a proper town. It was a great misconception of society that the Freewomen were wild; in fact, their delicately maintained spaces were a marvel of town planning. Lenna was shocked, and that shock made her blush with embarrassment when she thought of how she had rejected her mother's heritage.

At the center of town stood the largest and best-maintained structure in the entire village. Pim informed Lenna and Luc that this was the assembly hall and administrative building, where Mayor Northen received visitors, assembled the townsfolk for important meetings, and conducted day-to-day governing of Granemere Settlement. Compared to the town hall in Port Hollish, this building was unadorned and unpretentious; although Lenna was fond of her hometown, she could not help but think that the hall back home was positively garish compared to the Freewomen's. Pim, a haughty skip in her step, ushered the travelers toward the simple wooden door, before which a woman stood with a bemused expression on her face.

Jaice Northen performed her role as mayor more out of a sense of duty than desire. A woman about the age of Thane Faircloth, she greeted Lenna and Luc with resignation; if she was displeased at the arrival of two travelers, she made no mention, though neither did she attempt to exchange in pleasantries beyond what she referred to as standard protocol. After receiving Pim's report and Lenna's dagger, she briefly, and without much heat, chastised Lenna and Luc's young guide for dillydallying before subsequently dismissing her. Scowling, Pim stamped off, not bothering to hide her thoughts on being sent away from the most exciting development the village had seen in weeks.

As far as mayors were concerned, Lenna was immediately impressed with Jaice's no-nonsense personality and appearance. Port Hollish's current mayor was an older man, and greedy and lazy, characteristics manifesting in his tremendous gut and discernible lack of concern for any citizen who didn't possess a certain "financial" character. In contrast, Jaice was smartly dressed, and underneath the simple muslin blouse the mayor was thin but well-muscled, and taller than both Lenna and Luc. She kept her hair pulled back in a haphazard way Lenna could never hope to emulate, and the stress of being a leader of the Freewomen rewarded Jaice over time with a steady increase in worry lines and streaks of grey in her brown hair.

"My apologies for Pim's eagerness," the mayor said after Lenna and Luc introduced themselves. "She's young, and determined to prove her value in

Freewoman society. She'll soon grow out of it. For now, come with me."

Jaice beckoned the two companions not into the town hall, but around the side of the planked building. Not noticeable from the street, a small pavilion with an annexed cottage connected to the larger structure. Rather than commanding an authoritative air like the town hall, this diminutive place resembled a person's home. It was framed in a dark cherry wood and walled with white oak, giving it a cheery, homely sense of comfort that Lenna found quite welcome after recent events.

The mayor led them through the unlocked door and into a tidy, sparsely decorated sitting room. Inside, a humble table and four chairs claimed most of the space, though there were several bookshelves crammed with books, a stack of papers and writing implements on an ornately carved desk in the corner, and a cozy, crackling fire nestled in the fireplace. From atop the mantle Jaice took a kettle, sloshing with water, and set it on the flame.

"So," she said without preamble. "I've brought you to my own home instead of interrogating you in the assembly hall as Freewoman custom would normally demand. It would also require that I report this to my peers in other settlements, which for various reasons could complicate matters. Luckily, the citizens of this village are loyal and trust my judgment: there will be no talk of my 'personal' affairs."

Lenna settled herself into one of the chairs, curious. What reason could the mayor of a Freewoman community have for hiding her and Luc from other leaders? Her hand instinctively fell to her side, where the leather satchel was buckled to her waist; the stone was giving off a gentle and barely noticeable vibration against her leg. She was certain recent events had been observed and reported, and from what she had pieced together, the Brotherhood wasn't the only group vying for possession of the jewel.

Luc tersely explained to the mayor that he was a scholar from the Blue Crescent Brotherhood who had hired Lenna, a local Port Hollish girl, to act as guide and stenographer as he journeyed to Ilya to research airship technology. During the sudden snowstorms, he said, the pair had become quite lost and, looking for shelter, had more or less stumbled upon the forest, where the Freewoman hunting party had found them. Lenna was impressed with the cool delivery and quick thinking, though she supposed both Luc and Gilbert had planned for occasions when they might be questioned.

The mayor considered for a moment, then took the whistling kettle of the heat and poured its contents over a tea strainer and into a pot to steep. "I see. So an apprentice from the Brotherhood has received special dispensation from his order to travel alone through other nations in order to conduct research. Of course, such a person would possess the proper documentation to cross borders, specifically since certain bodies, like the Freewomen of Laur, are very particular about whom they allow on their land. Please present your papers, Apprentice."

Luc flushed and appeared to lose his composure for a moment, and Lenna took the opportunity to interject. "Had we known this was Granemere Forest, we certainly wouldn't have entered without going through proper channels —"

"Of course. That's why I'm willing to overlook the transgression, and the young mage's attempt at magic against my people, if you produce the proper documents." Jaice poured Luc and Lenna a cup of tea each before serving herself and taking a seat in one of the empty chairs, crossing her legs and folding her hands over her knees expectantly.

With Luc still at an apparent loss for words, Lenna said honestly, "We don't have any."

"Lenna!" Luc, red-faced, burst out. Anger rolled off him in waves, and Lenna could sense magic building within the young mage.

Abruptly, the sensation vanished, though Luc's anger did not. He looked at Jaice, aghast. The mayor's face was as blank as fresh canvas; during her years of ruling this village, she had obviously learned to maintain a steady composure that no Brotherhood novice could hope to challenge. Lenna, a tad sheepish, looked between the mayor and the mage, curious as to what had just transpired.

"Two things," Jaice began. "First, whatever the misogynist Brotherhood might teach you about women, and Freewomen of Laur in particular, know that you do not own a monopoly on magic, boy." She paused briefly to shift her gaze from the glaring Luc to Lenna. "Second, I would appreciate honesty from the start. I have little time and even less patience, and so trite games of true-or-false serve no purpose except to irritate me further." She calmly sipped her tea.

Lenna, abashed, murmured some kind of apology while Luc silently seethed in the seat next to her. She saw no way to explain to the mayor how the two ended up on Freewoman land without delving into a deep explanation of the gem, their flight from Port Hollish, and Gilbert's death — a topic too near to both her and Luc for her to describe with any sort of cool-headedness.

The porcelain teacup chinked as Jaice placed it gingerly on the saucer in front of her. "Now. As I've just established we're going to be upfront with each other, let me begin. The Freewoman information network is vast, and in some ways superior to that of even the Krevlum Empire, specifically because of the nature of our society. Being neutral and having settlements all throughout the Continent, we have a more well-rounded intelligence base than most countries.

"Knowing that, it will come as no surprise that I received word a few days ago that the Brotherhood was astir with internal strife. It seems a small group of mages, for motives unknown, smuggled a very powerful artifact off the island and left Port Hollish, presumed to be heading east."

Both Luc and Lenna blanched. The very fact that the nation had been created and had survived all these years was a testament to the strong wills of its founders and subsequent leaders, but that the Freewomen had access to such secret information was shocking news. From what Lenna understood of the ways of the Brotherhood, they protected knowledge — specifically knowledge about their internal workings — like a mother guards her child. If the Freewomen had acquired this information, it stood to reason that any number of nations or factions might be pursuing Lenna and Luc as well.

Breaking the silence, Jaice continued, pausing once to sip at her tea. "And now I find a Brotherhood apprentice and his 'guide' from Port Hollish on my doorstep. Not at the border crossing, as protocol demands, but instead unconscious, having broken through several layers of magical protection. What conclusion would you draw, if you were in my position?"

Lenna knew a rhetorical question when she heard one, and Luc thankfully held his tongue. The gem at her side suddenly felt like a heavier burden than before. Its weight pulled Lenna down, toward some great, oppressive darkness that spread below her like a gaping maw. The terrible pitch cloud, writhing like a living creature, threatened to swallow her, and all around her enemies and friends, and friends who could be enemies, jeered. Lenna was falling, and as she fell she heard Gilbert's voice call out to her.

A brief crack of power sent a jarring vibration up her arm and through her body, and Lenna snapped back to reality. She blinked rapidly and looked at Jaice, whose hand gripped Lenna's shoulder tightly. Worry creased her forehead. Even Luc's eyes had widened. Lenna's head tingled slightly, as if it was being pricked by tiny needles. Although not painful, it was not a particularly enjoyable sensation and she shook her head, trying to clear it.

Jaice's grip on her shoulder lessened slightly, but was still firm. "You have the gem, don't you?"

Still a bit dazed, Lenna nodded and said simply, "Yes."

There was little doubt in her mind that Luc considered this a betrayal of the secret that had ultimately destroyed Gilbert, and his rage was palpable. His knuckles turned white where he gripped the lip of the mayor's simple wooden table, and his eyes shone with pure fury as he glared at Lenna. Jaice gave him a curious expression before settling back down in her chair.

"I thought as much. There's no way you two could possibly breach our defenses without the power of a Godjewel."

"It's called a Godjewel?" asked Lenna.

"Yes," the mayor responded. "It's a relic of such immense magical power, it can make a person stronger than a team of mages working together. The Godjewels were supposedly lost long ago, though most rulers have always suspected one of them to be in the possession of the Brotherhood."

"You mean, there's more than one?"

Jaice frowned and considered Lenna a moment before answering. "There are supposedly three in total, and another has been recently found, yes. It's in Ilya – Tranum to be precise – in the hands of a prominent merchant family who built their fortune pioneering the airship innovation."

Lenna heard a sharp intake of breath from Luc, and she found herself staring gravely at Jaice. Unless Gilbert had been withholding facts from both of them, he too had been unaware that a second, powerful article lay across the border in Ilya. Though she did not care to think of Gilbert using her as a pawn or, worse, keeping such a secret, Lenna understood the need for his silence: if one jewel alone could wreak havoc, a pair would surely create an almost unstoppable force.

As if reading her mind, Jaice responded to Lenna's thoughts. "You can see why, then, the acquisition of these jewels has become a matter of priority for certain parties. When one activates its magic, it is possible to sense the location of the source, or even another jewel, since they are somehow connected to each other. And of course, large bursts of magic released through them would be noticed by anyone sensitive to magic."

A horrible thought crossed Lenna's mind. "So then, anyone who uses the jewel can be... tracked?"

"So I have inferred."

By that logic, Gilbert's death, then, was indeed a result of using the gem. His attempt at using the Godjewel to bolster his communication spell alerted whoever was tracking the trio. And Lenna, just now, had inadvertently activated its power. Despite herself, she covered her mouth with her hand, feeling slightly numb with shock. Had Luc known this?

"Don't worry," said Jaice. "The Freewomen of Laur have special protections. The outburst just now won't be detected by anyone or anything."

Luc silently rose to his feet, politely replacing his chair. His face twisted like a child trying desperately not to cry, though Lenna thought she saw a single tear flitter off into the air as, after a nod from Jaice, the young man swiftly turned and marched out of the mayor's home, quietly shutting the door behind him. Lenna understood his feelings; she felt sick to her stomach thinking that, if Jaice was correct, Gilbert might still be alive had the party successfully found a place like this in time. It must be devastating for the boy to hear. She rose to go after Luc.

"Let him be," Jaice interjected. "I can see the boy is grieving."

Lenna explained the suffering the group had been through since leaving Port Hollish as succinctly as possible, not wanting to relive painful moments. Jaice nodded from time to time, her brow furrowed in thought or consternation. When Lenna finished, the mayor sighed and placed her hand atop Lenna's own, which rested on the table. The familiar, motherly gesture startled the librarian.

"Lenna Faircloth," Jaice mused to herself before addressing the young woman across the table. "Lenna, would you mind explaining to me how you came to possess this weapon?" She lifted Lenna's knife from where it had been sheathed in her belt. Its mother-of-pearl pommel and well-polished blade caught the flickering firelight and cast rays about the room. It was truly a masterwork.

"It was my mother's. It was left to me when she passed away."

The lines on Jaice's forehead curved upward in an arc. "I thought as much. The resemblance is too strong, and I'd know this blade anywhere."

"What do you mean? I know I'm a Freewoman on my mother's side, but I've never followed your ways. She left this settlement and never returned."

"Your mother and I served as mercenaries together in the south. Alanna saved my life, which made her my sister as true as any blood, by our ways. That means, Lenna, that you and I are kin."

Lenna blinked and attempted to process this highly unlikely coincidence in addition to swallowing the concept of having a pseudo-aunt. A battle-aunt? War-aunt? In any event, Lenna was baffled that her mother would fail to mention the fact that her sister by Freewoman law was living in a village that, under normal travel circumstances, was not at all far from Port Hollish. Jaice seemed to accept this quite readily, but for Lenna, her mother's reticence about her past yet desire for Lenna to embrace it left a bitter taste in her mouth.

"I knew of your existence, of course," Jaice continued. "We Freewomen, as I'm sure you know, often meet men while doing hired work or while serving as diplomats, and if we fall with child we usually return to our villages to raise them, be they boy or girl. The men sometimes come back as well, and we accept them, provided they adhere to our ways. Some women, however," she said with a slight trace of displeasure, "choose to follow a man or woman and become a wife somewhere else, abandoning Freewoman society.

"I was deeply saddened when your mother chose that mechanist over her heritage, but I am glad that my niece has returned, at least for a visit, whatever the circumstances may be. It has been a long time since I've had family in these parts, and knowing a Freewoman is guarding one of the jewels is a great comfort."

Lenna was not at all comforted by the fact that she was the one guarding the jewel. The only thing Lenna felt she was qualified to protect was books.

All of these strange occurrences seemed to have herself or her family at the crux, and for a girl who liked nothing more than to be left alone to her musings, it was quickly becoming more of a burden than she was willing to bear. Her body ached and her heart was heavy.

The mayor, now her aunt, seemed sympathetic to Lenna's situation and actually made a great fuss of her niece. Jaice guided Lenna outside and handed her off to a solidly built Freewoman with dark skin and hair full of tiny braids, plaited with beadwork. Moods were considerably lightened when it was discovered that Lenna was a Freewoman by birth, and her guide chatted amiably about the village as she commanded Lenna to eat and drink.

Though she had no appetite, the librarian heeded her companion's instructions to take nourishment and idly hoped that Luc was doing the same. According to her guide, Chait, Luc had ventured out for a walk in the woods, but Lenna shouldn't worry because the Freewomen "have scouts with sharper spectacles than even yours" and they would keep an eye on him. By the end of the meal, fatigue rolled over Lenna like a steamtrain carrying a car full of iron ingots. Her brain was overloaded by the utter destruction of what was once a relatively peaceful life.

Ultimately, after Lenna dozed through dinner with a little wine for encouragement, she allowed Chait to escort her off to bed in a cabin reserved for guests. Lenna had little memory of undressing and getting under the covers, but that night she dreamed of her mother, the Godjewels, and Jaice sipping at a tumbler of brandy before her fireplace, shedding tears as silent as the snow that blanketed the plains.

A sudden outcry and the sound of a wooden door colliding against the wall of the cottage awoke Lenna from what should have been her first restful night of sleep in days. She sat up quickly, her eyes barely adjusting to the gloom. After a quick scramble for her spectacles and a moment to focus, she noticed the shape of Pim standing outlined by sunlight in the open doorway.

"Come quickly," she said. "Jaice needs to see you."

Lenna hopped out of bed and hurriedly began dressing, ignoring her tousled hair. "What's happened?"

"The gem is gone. And so is your friend, the mage."

The librarian dropped one of the boots she was holding. Her brain had become accustomed in the past few days to processing certain bits of shocking information, or rather, compartmentalizing it into a tidy room in the back of her brain to deal with later, after the immediate details were addressed. Pim was red-faced and out of breath, making her look particularly freckled. Her mouth was screwed up into a position that suggested that she would not offer any more exposition until Lenna was dressed and standing before the village leader.

Wisps of fog curled around the cleared forest floor, wafting up from the nearby riverbank like the tentacles of some great sea creature, their mist leaving droplets of water in Lenna's hair and on her spectacles as she walked toward Jaice's cottage. Most of the town was still asleep, unaware of the jewel's existence in the first place, let alone its disappearance. The few awake were the scouts and hunters, readying themselves to take to the woods and bring back game for meals and trade. Lenna envied their ignorance.

Lenna exhaled a puff of wintry breath, her arms folded in front of her, as Pim knocked at the door of the town hall. Even though the village was protected by the dense trees of the forest, the cold still found a way to chill deeply, and the damp mist made it bite all the worse. Despite her teeth chattering, though, Lenna's mind raced with the gravity of what Pim — however briefly — had told her. Both Luc and the gem, gone; could whatever force that had hunted them and killed Gilbert have found them, despite the wards the Freewomen of Laur maintained? Or worse, and she mentally grimaced at this idea, could Luc have claimed the gem for himself?

Time for conjecture was abruptly cut short as the door swung open, revealing not Jaice as Lenna had expected, but a grizzled man, well-muscled and in possession of glassy green eyes. He regarded Pim and Lenna coolly. "Good timing. She's just finished reducing a full-grown woman to tears and should be warmed up for you lot."

Pim rolled her eyes and said, "Thanks for the warning, Bahl." She swept past him and into the room.

Lenna stood where she was, not quite so bold as to push past the man. Noticing her hesitation, Bahl smirked and turned inward in a gesture of mock beckoning. "Welcome to the town hall; proceed to the mayor, Freewoman Jaice Northen."

Beyond the door was a spacious chamber, furnished sparsely save for two matching rows of benches lined up against the walls under some windows; it confirmed Lenna's theory about this building functioning as a meeting hall. A door at the opposite end of the hall, she supposed, must lead to the mayor's cottage, which left one other smallish door off to the right, on the southern wall, toward which Pim was heading. Lenna dutifully marched after her with Bahl in tow.

"Come in," came Jaice's voice from beyond the gnarled wooden door. Pim opened it and revealed the older woman pacing in front of a crackling fire. The room was tiny but meticulously organized; the small fireplace warmed the simple mahogany desk in front of it. That desk, Lenna noticed, was currently being assaulted most indelicately by a horde of papers, maps, and a few books. Whatever problem Jaice was tackling at the moment had shattered her normal sense of organization.

Jaice herself was, in appearance at least, not the slightest bit disheveled, though her brow was furrowed. She ceased pacing and sat down on the array of scattered papers on her desk as the group entered her study.

"There you are. I was beginning to think Pim had taken it upon herself to pursue our missing mage." She smirked defiantly at her attempt at frivolous alliteration. "But let's get to the matter at hand."

"What happened?" Lenna walked into the center of the room before Pim or Bahl could speak up. "Did Luc really steal the gem and run off?"

"By all accounts, yes," the Freewoman replied as she massaged her temple with one knuckle. "And 'by all accounts,' I mean according to Melia, the scout I secretly had surveilling your friend's cottage. And yes," she added, looking sharply at Bahl, "I have already given her quite a reprimand, even though it appears Luc used some magic to fool her in his escape, sneak into Lenna's cottage, and remove the gem from her possession. I apologize for such a violation. We all should have been more vigilant."

Pim inhaled sharply. "That's a crime!"

A wave of one hand silenced the girl. "It is, and by our agreement with the Brotherhood we're allowed to pursue him for such an act of aggression. But that's really the least of our worries at the moment. I knew the boy was grieving, but I should have tasked one of our own magic-users to guard him."

Guilt assaulted Lenna; she knew that her carelessness and trusting of Luc had facilitated his stealing the stone, right from under her nose. Even if he had used magic against her and the guards of the village, the librarian should have been more wary of what Luc was capable of in such a perturbed state of mind.

"We already know that the Brotherhood is searching for the jewel and seems willing to go to great lengths to get it back. The Brotherhood is also seeking the remaining jewels. The gems separately are powerful enough; according to all of the knowledge passed down through the Freewomen — the little of it that was recorded, that is —" Jaice said as she waved one arm over her cluttered desk, "even two of the gems would create a worse imbalance of power."

Lenna clicked her tongue and stroked her chin in thought. "And I'm guessing that yesterday you left some information out, about what party might be in possession of the last jewel."

"I'm not in the habit of divulging sensitive information — and this is critically sensitive — in front of outsiders, especially those from the Brotherhood." Jaice stood up. "But yes, Lenna, you're right. As I said before, we have recently come to know that a gem is in the possession of an Ilyan merchant, and though none of us have had concrete information regarding the location of the third, Imperial forces have been seen along the borders of Ilya, to the northeast."

Bahl, arms folded, added: "Our trackers found signs that the mage headed towards the steamtrain, and unless he plans on heading back to Port Hollish and his Brotherhood, I reckon he'll be catching the next one to Tranum, in Ilya."

Lenna considered this new information. She wasn't particularly surprised that Jaice had been withholding information from her, especially considering the Freewomen's attitudes toward the Brotherhood, but what would they gain in telling her now? Luc was headed toward Ilya, the nation of travelers whose innovations in airships and steam power had changed commerce and transportation throughout the entire Continent. While Lenna believed he desired revenge for Gil's death, the stony calm in the young mage's eyes had not relayed any immediate desperation, any indication that Luc would head out on a suicide mission against those who would be seeking the other jewel. And, unless her judgment was more impaired than Lenna thought, the only information Luc knew was that another jewel lay in Ilyan hands.

"They aren't referred to as the Godjewels without good cause," Jaice said, her gaze fixed on Lenna. "She — or he — who possessed them would have an unforeseeable amount of control over the forces of nature. One might even hope to gain access to power over life and death. The stones are ancient, primal magic."

An image of Gilbert falling backward into the snow flickered briefly into Lenna's mind despite her desire to suppress it. How funny for it to seem so long ago. She cringed as the sound of her hand against Luc's cheek rang inside her head, at the shock and misery in his eyes as he looked up at her. His escape wasn't about revenge, it was about controlling life and death. Get the jewels, and he thought that all he had lost, his lover and, years before, his sister, could be brought back. Could they be? Lenna believed Luc might just have enough reason to pursue it.

"So, what are we waiting for?" Pim chirped. "Let's cut the chatter and get on with the tracking. I could find that boy in my sleep with a sausage up my nose."

Jaice waved a hand in abject dismissal, a gesture carrying enough weight, apparently to silence Pim on the spot. "I appreciate both your enthusiasm and your interesting turn of phrase, Pim. But my partner, Bahl, will be tracking down Luc for us."

Without a word, he nodded, turned around with an almost militaristic crispness, and walked out of the room. He would waste no time in beginning his hunt for the rogue magician. Pim scrunched up her face in obvious displeasure, and Lenna, though she had no desire to pursue her one-time companion as if he were a criminal, felt her stomach lurch at the thought of Bahl confronting Luc.

But Jaice was not yet finished outlining her plan. She sifted through a few of the shorter stacks of papers on her desk, producing two almost identical sheets. With economy she signed her name and placed the seal of her village on each before rolling them up and binding them. "These papers designate those bearing the names written on them as my personal representatives. While my connections aren't as far-reaching as the Emperor's or the Brotherhood's, they should help get you through any sort of bureaucratic problems. Provided the officials are friendly, that is."

Lenna took the scrolls from Jaice's outstretched hand. "I take it that Pim and I are being assigned a task as well, then?"

"Bahl will be able to track the boy much more quickly — no offense to your skills, Pim — but I'll need you both on your way to Ilya to meet up with him. From what little knowledge our clan possesses of the jewels, it appears they can sometimes attune to an individual." Jaice nodded at Lenna. "From what you've told me, and from what I've seen firsthand, that jewel and your own magic are intertwined at the moment. Until we sort that out, Luc — or whoever else possesses the stone — will have a hard time masking its energy."

In other words, Lenna thought, she was needed to be a smokescreen. Gilbert had given her the jewel, after all; was it possible he was aware that it would attune to her? And if what Jaice said was true, while the jewel and her magic were bonded, the longer Lenna spent away from it, the more difficult its signature would be to hide. It would leak arcane energy and become a beacon to anyone — anything — that could sense magic. The Empire and the Brotherhood would be drawn right to it; suddenly the idea of Bahl finding Luc was, to Lenna, a much better idea.

"If this weren't so delicate an issue, I'd spare more scouts to join you, but since the Brotherhood and, I suspect, the Empire are both actively seeking the jewel, haste and secrecy are our best allies. I can only surmise that Luc is heading for the Ilyan Godjewel in Tranum — which means that it is possible for two of the stones to be in the same city at the same time. It's too attractive an opportunity for interested parties to miss. Lenna, as they're no doubt aware of you as well, and two women traveling alone will attract much more attention…"

Lenna glanced down at the numerous writs the mayor had been preparing. The names on the documents were definitely those of the other gender. "You can't be serious." Jaice was expressionless.

And so it came to be that Lenna and Pim assumed the disguises of two brothers, sons of Freewomen, headed to Ilya to seek their fortunes. As Jaice, with a businesslike demeanor, ran through a list of preparations to make before the girls-become-boys departed and then ushered them brusquely out of her office, Lenna remained silent.

Pim, on the other hand, was bouncing excitedly on the balls of her feet at the prospect of this mission. Any distrust or concerns she might have had about having Lenna as a partner did nothing to diminish her bubbling enthusiasm.

CHAPTER TEN

Much to Lenna's surprise, Pim was a more than amiable traveling companion. Perhaps Lenna was just comparing her company to the experiences she suffered with Luc, or maybe it was her desire to ignore processing Gilbert's death; Lenna could not tell the difference. As they left the safety and much-missed warmth of Granemere Settlement and trudged dutifully across the snowy plains toward the nation of Ilya, the librarian was overcome with an impending sense of dread. The white expanse before them served only as a canvas to illustrate the worst of Lenna's recent memories and her darkest fears, and the cold seemed to dig its claws into her flesh more deeply than it had before.

Despite the weather, Pim chattered on quite merrily. At first, Lenna was confused at the girl's sudden change in demeanor. A few hours into the trip, after Lenna had very genuinely inquired why Jaice couldn't lend them a pair of donkeys to lug the cumbersome, thick sheepskins they would need for warmth, Pim had snippishly told her that sons of Freewomen (as they were pretending to be) would never deprive their village of resources that weren't necessary. After that, Lenna held her tongue and resigned herself to the comfort of her own unpleasant thoughts, but over the course of the next few hours Pim seemed to accept the librarian's presence.

"After all," she had said, "you can't choose your family; that'd be like trying to choose the color of a baby cow before it was born!"

It appeared that the revelation of Lenna's Freewoman heritage had helped soften the young huntress's perception of her. Lenna made it a point to hide her eager denial of her heritage, lest she enrage her companion. She also neglected to mention the fact that, according to the most current books concerning science, one could very much choose the color of a baby cow if one paid attention to the breeding stock; Pim, it seemed, peppered her speech with colorful, if rustic, figures of speech.

As the rosy light of dusk fell upon them, Pim called their progress to a halt, for which Lenna was most grateful. She knew that they hadn't covered as much distance as they should have, but Luc would certainly not be as prepared as they were, and fresh legs would get them further in the morning. The young Freewoman proved herself to be as capable as she had boasted; despite the bleakness of the pair's surroundings, shortly after the decision to stop for the night, Pim began moving lithely through the snow, digging out small patches with the butt of her blunderbuss and her foot.

Once she was pleased with the depth and shape of the clearing, with piles of white mounded around the circular hollow like a barricade, she showed Lenna how to spread the sheepskins like a tarp to help insulate themselves from the snow. To make herself useful, Lenna applied herself to finding her flint and tinder amid the heavy folds and added pockets of the wolf-pelt cloak Jaice had provided her; she and Pim had been gathering what kindling they could find during the latter part of their journey today.

Pim raised her eyebrows in evident surprise. "Can't you just use magic to light us a fire?"

"I didn't really think about it," Lenna answered, before adding more honestly: "And it didn't feel appropriate, for some reason."

"You think the Freewomen of Laur are against magic?"

It was more than that, though Lenna was loath to explain. Her magic seemed uncontrollable and forced, and in light of Gilbert's death and the new information concerning the jewel — one which, she was told, quite probably had linked to her in some mystifying and frightening way — Lenna had decided that keeping herself away from magic was the most optimal strategy.

"That's like refusing to eat a bull because you might grow horns."

Apparently Pim is full of bovine anecdotes today, thought Lenna, as the girl squatted down beside her. The heavy winter clothing and its mannish cut — the same wolfskin cloak as Lenna's, a woolen tunic, thick grey cotton trousers, and short calf-hide boots — suited Pim much better than Lenna. The girl seemed as much at home in this skin as her own, though in Lenna's experience Pim already dressed on the tomboy side. She really did appear to be a boy a year or two before the start of manhood.

"Magic is a tool, same as any other." Pim picked up her gun and gestured with it nonchalantly. "Like Old Burt here. On its own it can't really do anything to hurt you; it's the user that decides what happens."

Lenna frowned. "But magic is more of a force — if I don't shape it correctly, it can go wild, deadly. It isn't inanimate, it's — it's a thunderstorm." She clutched at the air, trying to explain her fear, but saw nothing but Gilbert's death and could even now recall that sickening stench of ozone.

"But I hear that science-minded people in the Krevlum Empire are able to draw down lightning using tools they made, and that they tame it for their own purposes. To make it into a tool."

"It's not the same thing at all."

"I guess not, huh?" Pim screwed her mouth up to one side. "Well, listen, Lenna. Answer me a question about magic, then. Let's say you actually did want to use it to start us a fire — how would you do it?"

Lenna had no problem discussing the technical aspect of her informal arcane education. "I'd focus myself, find the power source within me that is my connection to magic, and direct it out in a small but concentrated ray of energy until the wood heated enough to ignite."

"Huh!" exclaimed Pim, unimpressed. "Is that what they tell those boys in the Brotherhood? That's like trying to use a chunk of cheese to whack a mouse to death rather than lead it to a trap."

"What's that supposed to mean?" Lenna asked, affronted.

Nudging the kindling with the butt of her blunderbuss, Pim continued: "It's such a thuggish way of trying it. It's brute force. Why should it have to work like that? I'm tiny compared to most men, but I could take more than a fair share of them in a fight, if you ask me."

"How would you start the fire, then?"

"Same way I'd fight someone bigger than me: I'd use their energy against them. Do you think if I were to punch a big brute in the stomach with my fist, I'd hurt him much?"

"Probably not," Lenna conceded.

"Right. Sure, I could train and train and train 'til I was stronger, and I could punch a lot of guys in the stomach, but I might not ever be strong enough to really hurt that one guy if he's solid. If you focused your energy on a rock, could you set it on fire?"

"Of course not."

Pim nodded. "But wood *wants* to burn, Lenna. It's made that way. And the big dolt I want to punch? His body wants to move about. Instead of attacking him with my own strength, if I encourage him to direct his movement toward me..." She dropped the blunderbuss to the ground and stood up, mimicking someone punching. "I just scoot about a little, grab ahold, and use his momentum to take him down." Almost a blur, Pim mimed a quick dodge and grab, using the heel of her foot to slam her imaginary opponent into the snowy mush on the ground. "Then I kick him in the head." She shrugged.

"So you're saying that rather than putting my energy into directly heating the wood, I should *encourage* it to burn instead?"

Pim picked Old Burt off the ground and affectionately dusted off a few lingering clumps of snow before shrugging once again. "How should I know? That's how they told us the Freewomen did magic so that's how I've always believed it was done, but unlike somebody here I was never very good at paying attention to my lessons. Anyway," she continued, plunking herself back on the ground and beginning to root through her pack. "Preaching over. I'm hungry and I don't feel like waiting for the fire to get up; I'm going to munch on some delightfully dreadful but energy-packed dried meat."

Contemplative, Lenna only nodded in response. It didn't surprise her that the Freewomen had a different way of thinking than the Brotherhood when it came to the application of magic (though Lenna was a bit surprised that to Pim it seemed like trivial knowledge). It certainly was a much more subtle approach, one that suited Lenna's admittedly nonconfrontational attitude. So much of what Gilbert had taught her seemed forced, almost aggressively masculine, to the librarian that Lenna briefly wondered, if she had been taught by the Freewomen, she would have been able to heal him. If, instead of pumping energy out and letting Luc direct it, she had just used that energy to surround Gil and encourage his body to *live*, like it wanted to do...

"Oh, and Lenna," Pim added quietly, rolling up one arm of her tunic. "I know what it's like to be scared of something that's just supposed to be a tool." The bare skin the young huntress revealed had white and pink gnarled scar tissue from the wrist almost to the crook of the elbow. "When I was ten and learning how to use my first gun, I got impatient and incorrectly loaded the thing. It backfired and damn near exploded; I was lucky it only got my arm, and not my face. It was hard getting the courage to pull that trigger again, and it took me a while, but I did it. Why? Because I knew it wasn't the gun's fault; it was mine. For being reckless. For not learning how to control it." She rolled her sleeve back down. "War usually comes to Freewomen, whatever village they're from. I decided I wanted to be prepared to control that tool for good if it came to it, and not be controlled by my fear of it." She resumed rummaging through her provisions, seemingly oblivious to the world around her.

Pim had barely finished peeling half a potato in the time it took Lenna to light the fire, the flint and tinder haphazardly discarded in a mound of snow behind them.

The following day's journey progressed much more smoothly as Lenna and Pim traveled farther away from the heaviest snow. Within a few hours the air warmed noticeably, and Pim led them to a small copse of trees in the plains that, like the one Lenna had used for shelter the night of Gilbert's death, seemed untouched by most of the elements around it. It radiated an air of calm and protection, and Lenna mentioned as much.

Pim nodded as they drew closer. "These are outposts for us Freewomen; they've been around since before the Unification. Some kind of powerful magic draws us to them and keeps them going, though nobody nowadays knows how to make them anymore."

She shrugged down the hood of her heavy cloak, revealing her cap of tight brown curls, and ushered Lenna inside the safety of the trees. According to Pim, little groves like this had once peppered the entire Continent during the time the Freewomen were still an ethnicity bound in servitude to Laur. Over a few centuries the number of these copses, waypoints for women who managed to escape the bonds of slavery and flee, had greatly diminished, but the Freewomen did what they could to preserve and protect all that remained.

"They're good for a quick bit of shelter on the run," Pim added, "but we primarily use them to store supplies."

To Lenna, at least Pim's explanation — with the knowledge that her own mother was a Freewoman — gave her some insight as to why she had been drawn to the protective trees a few nights ago. Still, all of the magic in the air the past few days unnerved Lenna, and her brain required logical explanation as a baby needs milk. Madly, the reasoning that a physical birthright could bestow tree-finding capabilities seemed far less ridiculous than a mysterious blue gemstone with the power of a demigod randomly bonding with her. That she was trying to rationalize this at all was an exercise in futility, so Lenna shook her head and tried to let her meandering mind rest.

Pim had already removed her wolfskin cloak, folded it neatly, and placed it on the ground at her feet. She gestured impatiently for Lenna to do the same. In short time, the girls had removed their winter kit — the cloaks, heavy boots, and thick cotton leggings and tunics; Lenna was particularly grateful that she would no longer have to drag about a heavy, slightly smelly sheepskin. From a cache well-camouflaged under the gnarls of a tree Pim had produced two similar bundles and simple calfskin short boots.

"All right," she said, "time to complete the look. From here on out we should be warm enough."

Pim might not be modest, but Lenna was in no mood to stand about in a small grove of trees in nothing but her undergarments. She eagerly took the offered bundle, undid its leather bindings, and began to dress. The brown trousers were of a lighter cotton than the previous pair and had a much looser feel about the legs, mimicking the popular Ilyan style favored by young men lately. They were paired with an equally baggy, long-sleeved tunic that looked entirely homespun and hung upon her in billowing folds that helped disguise her waist and hips. Pim deftly instructed Lenna how to belt the tunic as a young man would, loosely about the hips, creating a slightly more masculine appearance.

"Okay," Pim said after she herself had dressed in an outfit very similar to her normal attire in the village, albeit less formfitting: deep brown leather pants and an off-white tunic belted similarly to Lenna's. She swung the blunderbuss over her shoulder. "We need to do something about that hair of yours, and that chest."

Lenna blinked and, much to her own disgust, blushed. Her hair was almost to her shoulders, a mass of loose dirty blonde curls; she knew it was almost certain to give her away as female. "But what am I supposed to do about my chest?"

"You don't have to be so prim about it." Pim rifled through the contents of the cache, almost disappearing into the cavity of the tree. In due course she emerged with a length of gauzelike cotton swathed around her. "This is normally used to bandage injuries, but I think it's time to be creative."

After twenty minutes of struggling, grunting from both parties, and a string of swear words from Lenna so colorful even Pim paled, the girls decided on a compromise. The makeshift bindings held, but not as tightly as Pim would have liked; Lenna, inwardly pleased at having won the battle of her bosom, mollified her companion as best she could by donning an oversized suede jerkin over her shirt. Although it hung on her body in the oddest way and made it seem like she had no shape whatsoever, Lenna hoped it would help her pass at least a cursory assessment of her gender. As for her hair, several minutes of fussing with some hairpins and a good amount of tucking into a russet felt cap hid most of it, save for a few rogue locks that popped out from the brim to dapple her forehead with curls.

It was nearly midday before a satisfied Pim led them out of the small grove and back onto the plains, where the snow had tapered down into a mixture of greyish, brittle grit that cracked like fireworks under an unsuspecting foot. Without the environment to inhibit their advance, the pair's progress increased, and as the sun rose toward afternoon, Lenna could glance back along their path and find no trace of the trees of the great forest or the secret Freewomen shelter.

The plains eventually yielded to more prosperous growth; verdant blades of grass punctuated the dusty soil like pygmy spears and, eventually, the brambly overgrowth of the plains gave way to tamer brush. Though chilly, it was warm enough that the last traces of autumn still lingered in the air here and whetted Lenna's imagination. Unimpeded memories of a crackling fire, dying down to rosy embers, the crisp leaves of a book borrowed from her library, and her father's cider sloshing about in a ceramic mug took shape in Lenna's mind; but these memories she was quick to banish, focusing on the journey ahead.

Pim informed her that they were attempting to make it to the Continental Highway by nightfall, where they would take accommodations for the evening. The highway, as its name implied, was a vast expanse of road that linked Lenna's own harbor town of Port Hollish to towns and cities across the Continent. If they could arrange passage to

225

Uppridge, where they might catch the steamtrain, they would save miles of walking toward Tranum, the large trading city that straddled both Fallowfieldian and Imperial borders. With their disguises and an exercise in prudence, they would hopefully be able to enter Ilya quickly, and most importantly, inconspicuously. Lenna wondered if she could convincingly play the part of a young man and if Pim, prone to energetic outbursts, could contain herself long enough for the two of them to pass through unnoticed.

Indeed, as they drew closer to the highway that afternoon the ground beneath their feet became noticeably more worn with travel, and occasionally signs of grazing cattle, wagon tracks, and human rubbish speckled the countryside. The place to which they were headed, Pim said, was not exactly a town, more of a throughway of traders, soldiers, and farmers hoping for a bit of beer or some supplies during their travels to the various towns and cities that the highway connected. From Junction, as it had come to be called, roads extended in all directions, though with recent militaristic turmoil from the Krevlum Empire travel to the far north was being widely avoided.

"They're pretty harmless people, at Junction," she said. "Most of the time, anyway."

Lenna and Pim came upon the highway a bit more to the west of Junction than originally planned. The road itself, usually in decent repair, surprised Lenna: near Junction and further on toward Ilya, the highway was normally kept well-cobbled and free of debris, as it was by far the most popular route for conventional trade and hired hands who could not afford passage on the steamtrains. Now, chipped bits of pavement lay scattered across the road, with whole sections of stone cracked viciously. Splintered wagon wheels, refuse, and the broken, useless remnants of tools lined the sides, and the sickly sweet scent of death wafted through the air.

"This is wrong," Pim commented, appropriately wary. "I came along the Continental Highway less than four days ago."

"Let's hurry on to Junction," Lenna suggested as a bubble of uneasiness began to well up in the pit of her stomach. She had been to Junction a few times before, with her father and once with Jeffer to receive a shipment of rare Ilyan historical texts; by her best estimate the outpost couldn't be more than a mile from their current location.

Pim ceased poking at a pile of rubble and nodded. She swung her blunderbuss off her shoulder and knelt down on the road, propping the firearm up while rifling through a small satchel at her hip. Within moments, Pim had expertly loaded her gun; she poured a blackish powder into its muzzle, followed by a lead shot and stuffed it with a ramrod. After carefully sprinkling gunpowder into the flashpan, she closed the lid and stood back up, this time with her weapon at the ready. Lenna, having never seen anyone load an old-fashioned firearm so nonchalantly, was impressed.

"If I were you," Pim said tartly, "I'd think about readying that pretty little knife of yours."

Lenna grimaced. Pim was right, of course; considering recent events and the state of the immediate vicinity, a bit of forethought couldn't hurt, though the idea of using her blade against someone, shredding flesh, gave Lenna pause. She reached into an inner pocket of her floppy vest, where the knife had been concealed, and slid its gleaming blade out to greet the sunlight. It felt at once awkward and reassuring in her hand: despite Lenna's protests, her mother had managed to impart a few basic techniques. The way the cool hilt rested against her palm reminded Lenna of the calm patience on her mother's face. She shook her head to disperse the image of the woman from her mind.

Weapons at the ready, Lenna and Pim began the tense walk up the litter-lined highway toward the outpost of Junction. As they drew closer, the stench of death became even more oppressive, clogging their nostrils with its fumes. Lenna covered her mouth with a handkerchief; Pim merely grimaced. Before long the source of the stench revealed itself: in piles along the cracked road were a dozen or so corpses, speckled with the white eggs of flies and serving up a delectable feast for carrion eaters. Some of the bodies were already too desecrated to be recognizable as male or female; dead for several days and nearly picked clean by the scavengers, some were nothing more than scattered entrails and savaged limbs. Pim, with a rigid composure Lenna would remember in the months that followed, performed a cursory search on one of the fresher-looking specimens, one only slightly purple and as yet wholly untouched by animals. As she nimbly frisked the corpse and searched the pockets of its torn clothing, the smell of rot, urine, and feces washed over the two of them.

Unable to suppress a gag, Lenna choked from behind her handkerchief, "What are you looking for?"

Pim stood and grimly wiped her hands on her trousers before walking back toward Lenna, taking care to avoid the pools of blood draining from some of the corpses. "How these people died, mostly." She jerked her head back in the direction of the body she searched moments ago. "Pockets were emptier than a henhouse with a fox in town. Junction is a place for merchants and travelers; odds are if you're here you've got some kind of coin on you."

"So someone looted the corpse. Corpses." By deliberately focusing on Pim, Lenna found that she could glaze over the morbid scenery around her.

"But this one's more recent than the others. He's been stabbed and left here as an afterthought."

"So what does that mean?" Lenna wondered what connections Pim had made.

"That whatever got these people in the first place isn't the same thing as what stabbed and robbed this man."

Lenna allowed herself a quick glance at the man Pim had inspected. True enough, even without employing Pim's hands-on method, Lenna could tell that a lot of time had elapsed between when death claimed the majority of the corpses and when it took the more recent specimen. She became acutely aware of her own sweaty palm tightening its grip on the hilt of her knife, and Pim's gaze darted off at something in the distance, behind Lenna. As Lenna started to turn around the words "stay behind me" whispered a faint warning.

While the two girls had been examining the destruction around them, a trio of men had advanced toward them from the direction of Junction. They had been clever, using the natural curvature of the road and objects such as overturned merchant wagons to obfuscate their approach. By the time Lenna and Pim noticed them, it was too late to hide; the men, if they chose aggression, could likely close the distance between the two parties within moments, and there was no shelter in the immediate vicinity for the travelers to take.

As the three men drew closer, Lenna observed Pim holding her blunderbuss in a nonaggressive manner, but with her thumb subtly close to the flintlock. She, too, held her knife in what she hoped was a non-threatening stance and stood her ground.

Soon the men were practically upon them, and it afforded Lenna and Pim a better assessment of their appearance. All were dressed in simple attire — by Port Hollish standards, indicating a certain level of poverty — though the immense-bellied, brutish one to the left wore a surprisingly well-polished pair of leather boots that seemed incongruous with the oafish look on his face. The other two men were dressed nondescriptly; the solidly-built man on the right, grizzled and mean, had with a long scar running from his left ear down his cheek, ending just where his neck began. All three had crudely wrought dirks buckled to their belts.

Oddly enough, thought Lenna, the most alarming-looking of the three men was the short one in the middle. He was barely as tall as Pim, gaunt like a skeleton, and seemed to possess only an eighth of her muscle. His eyes, though, were striking; glassy and bordering, it seemed to Lenna, on lunacy. It wasn't until he greeted them, extending his hand and curling back his lips in a gummy smile, that she saw he had two rows of discolored, misshapen teeth.

"Hail, friends," the little man said, his voice tinged with a lisp. "What are two young lads such as yourselves doing out and about? It's not exactly a lively place at the moment." He sneered as he gestured to the piles of corpses strewn about.

Pim responded coolly. "We're heading to Ilya; my pa said the highway was clear."

"Ilya, is it? That's a bit of a hike for little boys like you to make from here. Where are we coming from?" The man inched toward Pim and Lenna and was met with the muzzle of Pim's blunderbuss. He backed off a few paces, snickering.

The greying man to the right laughed heartily, one hand placed dramatically on his forehead in disbelief. "Oh, Lanzo! This be rich! Boy's balls've probably barely dropped yet but he's holdin' a gun like he'd stroke his own shaft!"

The short man, Lanzo, cut off the subsequent guffaw from the stoutest of the three as Pim flushed, dumbfounded. "Now, now. Let's mind our language, shall we? Don't want to shock the poor lads. You in the back." Lanzo jerked his sharp chin toward Lenna. "Don't you have a pretty face? Tell me where you and your little brother hail from."

Lenna blanched, wondering what to say. Pim's features and mannerisms might help her pass as a boy of thirteen, but if Lenna spoke, there would be no mistaking her sex. She tightened the grip on her knife and coughed, searching for words in a voice that wouldn't betray her.

"He don't speak much, do he?" asked the fat man.

"My brother is slow," Pim responded warily.

Lanzo deliberately stroked his dirk with a dirty, long-nailed finger. After a moment's thought he shook his head. "The taller one isn't his brother, Hodge. It's his sister."

Despite their preparation, it appeared that Lenna's disguise did not hold up to thorough inspection. She fell back a pace as Pim protectively wedged herself directly between Lanzo and the librarian. "We don't want any trouble."

Lanzo leered toothily. "And we don't want to give you any, do we, boys? Not like he got." Lanzo gave a nod to the corpse Pim had searched earlier. "Junction's a ghost town, and folks that come through it are easy pickings for men like us."

Lenna asked, angrily, "You murdered him, and for what? A pair of boots?" She gesticulated at the oaf's obviously new shoes with her knife.

"She speaks!" exclaimed Lanzo with false surprise.

"Oh, Lanzo, Lanzo, I wants to keep her for me pet. She's feisty, she is!" Lenna quickly forgot her ire when she noticed the hungry expression on the grizzled man's face.

Pim cut the salivating thug off. "When the Junction watchmen get here and see this mess..."

"Junction watchmen?" Lanzo laughed. "Weren't you listening, boy? Junction's dead — two days ago a band of Imperial soldiers and their damned arcanists rolled through the town with one of their lightning-making machines. What's left of Junction and the highway — after the soldiers got through with any stragglers — made easy pickings for a few chaps on the road needing some coin and new kit." He grinned his skeletal grin at Pim. "That gun you're holding looks like it might fetch me a fair treat. There's always a market for a classic."

Pim shifted to a blur in an instant, uncoiling into action; in one swift motion, her arms slid down the barrel of the blunderbuss, transforming it into a cudgel. Using her momentum as the source of her power, Pim drove the butt of the firearm directly into Lanzo's navel. Winded and visibly surprised by his small opponent's initiative, the bony man doubled over as Pim, with an elegantly minimal amount of movement, continued her assault.

Like a dance, she deftly floated back a step, sliding her arms to a higher grip on the gun's muzzle. She transitioned her movements into an arcing swing, rewarding the stunned onlookers with a resounding thud as the heavy wooden grip of the blunderbuss connected with the flesh between Lanzo's neck and right shoulder. Witnessing their leader as motionless and prone as the corpses that sullied the landscape left Hodge and the grizzled man in a moment of startled silence. Lenna exhaled, realizing the whole event had happened in seconds.

Pim assumed a firing stance, aiming the barrel of her blunderbuss alternately between the two standing thugs. "Right. One of you donkeys will be able to trot your way over to me before I can reload, but the other one will be nice and exploded like an overripe pumpkin. Just tell me which one of you wants to die and I'll let my sister, who happens to be a witch, take care of the other one."

The grey-haired man, obviously the veteran of the two, opened his mouth to speak but shut it quickly, settling on a withering scowl. Hodge looked between Pim's diminutive figure and his companion's expression pleadingly. If circumstances were drastically different, Lenna might have found this interchange much more amusing; for the present, she decided to focus on more important things such as preventing herself from revisiting lunch.

"Well?"

"What should we do, Poln?" Hodge asked.

After a moment, the angry man attempted to soften his face. "All right, boy. You've done me in right well. Never did think Lanzo much of a leader, anyways. We'll just be on our way, then."

"You can't expect us to just let you go off and attack more innocent people," interjected Lenna, Pim nodding in agreement.

"Well, then, my pet," Poln said, "it looks like ye'll have to put all three of us out of our misery." He began to draw his cutlass.

As long as they believed she was a witch, Lenna had no problem taking some creative liberties. "I've got a better idea," she retorted, pushing her glasses up her nose and fixing a gutting glare upon the two criminals. "Unless you want to bear the full brunt of my magic, you'll start giving these corpses decent burials while you wait for the loyal soldiers of Fallowfields — who are no doubt almost here if the

events in Junction happened the way you said —
and then you'll let them take you off to prison in
Port Hollish."

Hodge looked blankly at the librarian while Poln
gave a laugh straight from his belly. "That's rich,
pet! How about you magic yourself out of those
boy's trappings and let old Poln break you in
instead?"

Lenna frowned — threateningly, she hoped —
and dramatically extended her hands toward Poln.
In retrospect, Lenna realized she had very little
notion of what she intended, but Pim's discussion of
magical theory last night had imparted to her some
kind of mystical epiphany. As she reached into the
recesses of her mind, there was a sudden sense of
disconnection; Lenna could sense the environs
through her physical body, but her magic, her
energy, created a feeling of herself completely free
of any human limitations. Feeling wispish, almost a
ghost, the librarian could with great clarity divine
not just the motion of the breeze but its desired
direction. Like Pim had said about wood wanting to
burn, the air yearned, for whatever purpose, to head
in one direction.

So Lenna gave it a nudge. She allowed her
magical self to encourage and subtly change the
course of the wind. *You want to*, she thought at the
air, and though at first it resisted, Lenna felt her
energy gently brush against the physical presence of
the breeze around her. She guided it toward and

had it envelop Hodge and Poln, until the breeze whirled around them, siphoned from the direction of the corpses. With a thought, she increased the air's ability to latch onto the stench of decay and blood and waste, concentrating all that putrescence on the two villains. The bits of wind suddenly vocalized the cries of the dead, and the air's increasingly swift movement mimicked lost voices and shrieks of expiring life. Lenna aimed these wails and scents of death directly at her targets. Soon, Hodge and Poln stumbled to their knees, unbalanced by the strength of Lenna's gale and ravaged by the sounds and stench of hell.

"By all that's sacred, Lenna," Pim said, putting one hand on the librarian's rigid shoulder. "That's enough."

Lenna slowly came back to herself, blinking. Where she had gone just now had felt like a place removed from time; in truth, only moments had passed. Hodge and Poln were only yards before her, cowering. The grizzled warrior who only a few minutes earlier had threatened Lenna now wept uncontrollably. She might have felt a pang of guilt, briefly, but a glance at the corpses around her and the memory of the now-unconscious Lanzo's callousness pulled a solid sheet of iron over Lenna's emotions.

She looked directly at Hodge. "Now bury these people or I swear those horrors will visit you every single night of your life, until it renders you mad."

The big man nodded feebly and Lenna turned to Pim with a look that implored her to move on. The two began to walk toward Junction, completely certain that the brutes would do as Lenna commanded. After a few paces Pim called back over her shoulder, "And give that man back his shoes, fat-man!" Lenna was glad they were moving, because she did not want anyone to see how terribly her hands were shaking.

The remains of Junction consisted of piles of shattered, strewn-about wood and ebony scorch marks marring the surface of the once well-kept road. What was but a few days ago a small respite for weary travelers, Lenna observed, was now a desecration caused by the Krevlum Empire's military technology. Where an inn and public house once stood was a still-smoldering pile of rubbish; any people or items that might have been inside reduced to cinders along with its walls.

A lone old man with a horse-led cart, clearly a farmer, stood before a collection of rubble that, if Lenna's memory served, was once Junction's small but well-stocked general store, offering an eclectic mix of items and foodstuffs from the four nations. It had also served as a depot for the exchange of parcels between various cities, a hub of trade.

The farmer, wringing his leathery hands, noticed the two silent companions approaching and gave them a cursory nod. His cart contained nothing remarkable from Lenna's immediate perspective: a few burlap sacks containing smaller-than-average potatoes; some shabbily made wooden crates loaded with a mishmash of carrots and parsnips. If this was all the farmer could bring to Junction, he would be hard-pressed to garner enough coin to buy any essential items for the upcoming winter. That is, Lenna thought, if there was still a merchant in Junction with whom to trade.

Pim, having shouldered her blunderbuss, greeted the farmer warmly, as though she had not, but thirty minutes ago, physically assaulted a bandit on the highway. All in a day's work for a warrior of Laur, Lenna supposed. The man, called Kenta, was indeed a farmer, hailing from a small farmstead several leagues to the south, toward the nation of Gallas. As he had done every year for the past fifty or so, Kenta had set out for Junction a few days ago to sell some of his finer produce, keeping what remained for his wife and some of their relations in his village. There was no way for him to have known of the outpost's destruction during his journey, though he supposed himself lucky to have arrived after the tragedy that transpired here.

"What d'you s'pose did all this?" Kenta asked dourly.

"The Empire," Lenna responded, not caring if her voice betrayed her disguise. "They've certainly been more aggressive lately, but to send a force all the way to Junction... it's too brazen, too soon."

"They say they have devices — machines — that produce lightning that the soldiers can aim at things, like a gun." Pim crouched low to the ground and ran a finger against one of the numerous scorch marks. She held it up for inspection; the tip was covered with a fine soot and smelled of char.

"Machines that make lightning?" The farmer shook his head wearily. "That's all too much for an old man."

"Judging from the damage, I'd say Pi — my brother is right," Lenna said, hastily correcting herself. "From what I've read and heard recently, the Empire's unearthed an old technology that combines machinery with magic. None of the steam power we have now could cause so much thorough destruction on its own, at least not so quickly, and I doubt the Krevlum Empire could have sent enough mages into Fallowfields without being noticed."

"It's a right waste," the man commented. "What am I going to do with this veg now?"

"We could buy some of it," Lenna offered, though the girls did not need more rations.

"No offense, lass, but you don't look like you're going to be hauling sacks of potatoes very far, and your younger brother here looks scrappy, but whatever your purpose is I doubt it involves lugging produce for miles."

"He's right... sis," said Pim. "And I don't want to be caught with an armful of carrots if bandits or the Empire's forces pop up again."

Lenna considered for a moment and decided the elderly farmer was trustworthy. "We're headed toward the Ilyan border. We were going to arrange for transport to Uppridge from Junction, along the highway, but..." She let her voice trail off.

"Highway's not too safe anymore, eh?" Kenta scratched his scruffy chin. "And Uppridge is miles up the highway to the north."

The librarian nodded. Two very modestly dressed young adults riding the train alone would certainly draw suspicion, but they were running a race against the hourglass and starting to lag terribly behind. The only problem, Lenna thought, was that the journey to Uppridge would take them considerable time without transport, and that it was to the north, toward the Empire. Were they to encounter any unsavory characters on the road, Lenna and Pim would almost certainly be stopped and questioned at the very least.

"What if," Lenna suggested, "we paid you to take us to Uppridge? A farmer and his grandchildren, heading to market in Uppridge since Junction's not an option? Surely that's far less likely to draw any attention."

"Hmm. I agree with you, lass, that it would be the safest way to get you there, and I won't deny times, being what they are, I could use the coin. And to sell the veg at Uppridge on top of that, it's an offer hard to refuse. Boy," he addressed Pim, "you any good with that gun there?"

"Could shoot the comb off a cock, blindfolded and drunk. But let's hope I don't have to prove it."

Kenta nodded, seemingly assured by the young gunner's response. "All right, then, hop in the back there. I don't mind doing a profitable favor for a Freewoman of Laur and her little brother."

Lenna and Pim simultaneously blinked in surprise. "How could you tell?" Lenna asked as she and her companion clambered into the back of Kenta's cart, settling as comfortably as possible among the potatoes and crates of root veg.

"You're not the first Freewoman to pass through Junction, lass." He clicked his tongue and wagged the reins, moving his surprisingly well-muscled horses into a healthy gait. "Not many ladies dress like you."

The wagon moved briskly through the remains of Junction, leaving behind the scent of burning on the air and crumbled remnants of the outpost's livelihood. Lenna yearned to feel a greater sense of sympathy and loss for the people caught up in this terrible act of destruction, but all that was within her was a sense of relief at leaving behind so much death. The past week felt like an eternity, and the steady rocking of Kenta's cart brought upon Lenna a sudden and oppressive drowsiness.

"Psst." Pim's elbow jostled Lenna from her twilit musings. "Why does everyone immediately see through your disguise? Why didn't Kenta realize *I* was the proper Freewoman?"

"You've got no tits," Kenta called from the driver's seat. "And you walk like a farmhand with saddle sores. Nothin' girlish there."

Apparently the farmer's hearing was not at all impaired despite his age or the clatter of horses' hooves against the highway. Pim was seemingly at a loss for words, her expression grim. Next to her, Lenna felt the tension lift like a rising fog, and she wholeheartedly guffawed, laughing like a deranged woman until hot tears streamed down her sooty face. It was her first laugh since Gilbert's death.

"I do *not* walk like a farmhand," Pim said determinedly, her arms crossed.

Lenna chortled, arms wrapped around her achy sides, until a sweet fatigue claimed her and she fell asleep in the company of carrots. Kenta drove the horses on through the evening, ushering the two young bandit-thwarters ever closer to Ilya and hopefully, to Luc.

CHAPTER ELEVEN

Kenta was true to his word, and when Lenna and Pim awoke the next morning, a tad sore and slightly bruised due to excessive parsnip abuse, they were only about a mile outside of Uppridge. The night had passed without further troubles from bandits or malevolent magecraft, and without any surliness from Pim, who was apparently as tired as Lenna and snored with an even greater gusto. The sun was just peeking over the crest of the hills as the old farmer led his cart down its stoned path, every now and then muttering words of encouragement to his horses. They soon overtook other travelers heading to and from the town.

Uppridge, barely a quarter of the size of Port Hollish, had been nothing more than a hamlet until the steamtrain rolled through town and transformed it from a spot of no interest into a bustling center of travel. It could, in its own right, be referred to as a new Junction, since modern transport was swiftly assuming responsibility for the shipment of most supplies. Around the new station, several markets and inns and two public houses, all built with lumber transported from the east and so fresh that it had barely any time to blister under the sun's rays, had practically sprouted overnight. Lenna marveled, leaning precariously over Kenta's sturdy wooden cart, at how Uppridge was already brimming with travelers and custom. While she was accustomed to this kind of liveliness in her hometown, this far out in the middle of nowhere it struck her as out of place.

Kenta drove the wagon toward the town square, where in due course the markets would open and fresh produce would be bought and transported or purchased by the pubs. As they drew closer, traffic in the street, which was not wide enough to accommodate the increased number of people in Uppridge, brought their progress to a halt. The elderly farmer, quite hale, slipped down from the driver's seat and patted one of the horses on its flank.

"Looks like the end of the line, ladies," Kenta said. "They'll have me lead the horses and cart off to the side now, to make way."

Lenna nodded and thanked the man, hurriedly pressing the promised coin into his hand before he could refuse. Kenta muttered and grumbled but, as

Lenna knew, he and his family needed the money; with Junction all but destroyed, trade most likely would not be restored to its former glory for several years, if at all. At Pim's insistence and under the strict supervision of a matronly woman of considerable girth, Lenna and Pim helped Kenta guide the horses and wagon to a ramshackle unloading space on the outskirts of the square.

"You two be careful now," the farmer said, looking both of them squarely in the eyes one at a time. Much to Lenna's surprise, he patted Pim on the head and grinned, mumbling something like "couldn't resist" before he turned smartly and began to unload his cart. Pim, aghast at the old man's sudden display of grandfatherly affection, stood stiff as a board.

Chuckling, Lenna grabbed Pim's hand, no doubt further traumatizing her, and pulled her off toward the square. "Come on, Pim; we've a train to make." Pim obligingly followed.

The square was a proper mix of travelers, local merchants, and villagers. Some haggled over wares at various stalls, commenting on the expense of goods from the Empire. Others, mercenaries by their appearance, accosted some of the younger townswomen, who in the mercenaries' defense, seemed generally pleased with the idea of being accosted. Lenna marched Pim briskly through the crowds with an ease only one familiar with bustling marketplaces could manage; as a child she had spent many a morning with her mother at the docks in Port Hollish, the brusque woman matter-of-factly conducting business, trading for goods, or acquiring the latest news from sailors.

Pim, on the other hand, was obviously not accustomed to such a large, raucous crowd. Despite an intense warrior's physical training and a proper education at the hands of Freewoman teachers, children raised in settlements led quiet, peaceful lives, albeit lives with guns and pointed objects in their care. This was probably the most people Pim had ever seen in one place, and she very noticeably gawked at individuals and merchant stalls as Lenna tugged her through the crowd.

"Lenna, who's that?" Pim asked, indicating a tidy-looking woman with a satchel slung over her shoulder, going from door to door.

"Most likely the postmistress, Pim. She sorts the letters and parcels that arrive via the train and delivers them to their intended recipients. Do you not have the post back home?"

"Who would I write to? Jaice sends out a rider if we need to communicate village concerns or someone else sends a rider to us."

"Well, after this mess is all tidied up, you can have the mayor start up the post and you can write to me in Port Hollish," Lenna said.

"Huh," Pim replied, and Lenna couldn't quite extrapolate if Pim was pleased or unsettled by the proposition of a penpal.

"In any case, let's inquire about the next train to Ilya and then reward ourselves with a proper breakfast. Fried tomatoes, sausages..."

The station, situated at the north of town, was smaller than Port Hollish's and looked, to Lenna, even more out of place. It was squished into the landscape, only a stone's throw from the mayor's old house. Its simple one-story waiting room and ticket office, which led to two platforms, was painted a rather distasteful yellow, like an underripe lemon. Patches of forest still remained, decorously dotting the train tracks on either side of the station, though most of the woodlands surrounding Uppridge had been crudely torn down during the railway's construction. Lenna checked her timepiece, which was thankfully wound and kept the proper time once again; the morning passenger train out of Port Hollish would be leaving within an hour, which meant the two of them would have ample time for breakfast after they purchased their tickets.

Pim fidgeted as they queued up behind a rotund man in an ill-fitted waistcoat. He persistently argued with the clerk, a pale, delicate-looking young man around Lenna's age, in an attempt to barter the price down. Lenna sighed and resigned herself to a few minutes' wait while the inept clerk struggled to placate his patron. Beside her, Pim had different ideas: she coughed, shuffled her feet, and then began to comment loudly on the delay.

Appalled, Lenna tried to shush her companion, but Pim vehemently gesticulated and complained directly to the round man. He turned, diverting his attention from the harried ticket vendor to Pim, eyes rounding when they fell on the blunderbuss strapped to the small girl's back. People were beginning to stare.

Desperately, Lenna fished into her pack and pulled out the signed document that they had received from Jaice. Pushing past Pim and the man and spouting gibberish about "official Freewoman business" and "hurried diplomatic missions," Lenna practically flung Jaice's writ at the startled clerk. The sudden action on Lenna's part drew Pim's and the man's attention and unfortunately that of the passersby as well. She felt her face go warm and red; so much for not drawing attention to themselves.

The clerk, thankfully too flustered to verify Lenna and Pim's boys' names, adjusted his spectacles and glanced at the document before him. "According to this, you're entitled to a discounted fare." This statement had the undesired effect of setting the man off again, and he launched into an impressive tirade swear words that made Pim pale and Lenna want to giggle. She hurriedly handed over a few notes and swayed on the balls of her feet as the clerk quickly processed the payment and gave Lenna two fare vouchers. "Train leaves at a quarter past the hour," he added as his eyes darted between Lenna and the angry man.

"Thank you," she said quickly and, grabbing Pim by the arm, led her off toward the town square, leaving the unfortunate clerk to continue being berated by the cranky patron. Lenna admonished Pim, in amazingly colored language, for causing such a scene, and wondered, oddly, if this was what it was like to be an embarrassed mother. A mother who spouted some excellently phrased obscenities.

The young Freewoman, while surprised at Lenna's tongue, offered no apology. "A lot of people think Freewomen are outspoken man-haters," she explained. "Even though we have male partners and sons and all, they think we're some sort of angry warrior woman commune." Pim casually slipped out of Lenna's arm but continued walking in pace with her. "So a Freewoman's son who gets impatient at a man is far more forgettable than a Freewoman's son skulking about on 'official business.'"

"Huh," said Lenna.

"Exactly. Now, about that breakfast. I'm hungrier than a fat baby on market day!"

The warmth of a hearty breakfast lightened Lenna's mood, though under normal circumstances she would never be able to stomach this much food immediately after waking up. In addition to the fried tomatoes and sausages she salivated over, the pub they chose, the Lamp Post, served lamb kidneys, toasted bread studded with seeds and nuts and smeared with honey and fresh butter, and even Lenna's compulsory pickled eggs (though they were nowhere near as delightful as the ones made by her father). Pim was deliciously pleased to discover that the Lamp Post also offered what she called "breakfast wine," which was apparently a tradition rooted in Laurian culture. Pim ordered two pints of the stuff, which turned out to be a mulled red wine mixed with a little water and fruit.

"I normally don't drink with breakfast," Lenna commented drily after a few sips, "but I might make this a habit if life continues in this manner. My books never try to kill me. Most of the time."

"Breakfast wine eases the mind and body. It makes one the master of dispatch and accuracy!" Pim's freckled face was already an interesting shade of mauve after having downed the first half of her pint.

Lenna crunched into warm toast, letting the honey trickle over her tongue. Between the wine and the heavy fare, all she wanted was her bed with its fluffy, goose-down pillows and warm quilt. She realized, as she started to drift into the realm of daydreams, that she had not had an uninterrupted night of sleep since the day before that damned train woke her up an hour early. Her slumber, recently, seemed altogether too reliant on the train schedule. Even removing her cap and letting her hair tumble down to her shoulders felt like a night's respite, and she ruffled her locks about with one hand.

"Hey," Pim said, summoning Lenna back to reality. "Don't turn around, but there's a group of Imperial soldiers on the other side of the pub shooting us some strange looks."

The girls had taken their breakfast at a small table on the northern wall of the dark, smoky pub; Lenna's back was to the common room and bar, leaving Pim with the only vantage point. Most people having already had their breakfast, there were only a few other patrons when they arrived, so the soldiers must have come in after them. Lenna wondered if, contrary to Pim's statements, the row at the station had attracted unwanted attention. Recalling a maneuver she had once read in some popular fiction, Lenna nonchalantly moved her elbow up as she pretended to reach for more toast, knocking her knife to the wooden floor in a soft clatter. She then stooped down to fetch it, tilting her head to peer across the room through her hair, as if embarrassed.

"Very subtle," Pim's voice said cheerily.

Lenna quickly sat upright in her chair, knife in hand. She thought she had executed her bit of subterfuge quite smoothly. Whether she had botched it or not, however, Lenna did catch a glimpse of three Imperial soldiers seated on stools at the bar about ten yards away. Like all the Krevlum Empire's military, the three men were dressed in stark, spotless white long jackets and flat-topped caps in the same color, with alabaster buttons running down the length of the coat. What they were discussing was indiscernible from the soft murmur of the pub.

"You're not going to antagonize them, are you?" asked Lenna.

Pim took a long pull of her breakfast wine and then pointed the mug at Lenna, its contents sloshing about threateningly. "I never antagonize anyone, cousin."

"You're antagonizing me now."

"That's just because you like —" Pim's words were cut off by the approach of one of the soldiers; he had crept up to their table unnoticed as the girls quibbled.

"Excuse me," he said cordially, his speech sounding clipped with his heavy accent. "Pardon the intrusion." The soldier turned on his heel and looked at Lenna directly. "Is this boy offending you, miss?"

The look on Pim's face was so utterly priceless to Lenna that she erupted into a most unladylike stream of laughter. The poor soldier stepped back, uncertainty and embarrassment plain on his face, and Pim fumed and boiled so fiercely that it appeared as though the freckles might launch from her face and pierce everyone in the pub like bullets.

Lenna removed her spectacles and pretended to clean them with a cloth napkin to keep from laughing. "Yes, he's bothering me," she managed to say to the soldier. "But it's fine. He's my brother."

"Ah, yes. The resemblance is striking. My apologies for disturbing you." The soldier hastily withdrew to the mocking cheers of his brothers, ears crimson with embarrassment. With the enemy gone, Lenna immediately fell into a fit of giggles while Pim downed the rest of her pint in one enormous gulp before slamming the cup down.

The soldiers made a sullen exit, and Lenna calmed down enough to breathe normally. In an effort to mollify Pim, she bought two more pints of breakfast wine and attempted to get the affronted tomboy moderately intoxicated in the twenty or so minutes remaining before they had to leave for the station. Luckily for Lenna, Pim couldn't outdrink a kitten, and a little more wine coupled with talk of the upcoming train ride cheered Pim considerably. When the urge struck her, Lenna was genteel enough to hide any gurgles of laughter with her napkin.

It was Pim's first time on a steamtrain, and she bounced from window to window as the train began to pick up speed and leave the Uppridge station behind. Bemused, Lenna silently said a goodbye to Junction and Uppridge, the Freewomen, and her home in Port Hollish; the next time she stepped outside the train, she would be in Ilya, nation of traders, explorers, and aeronauts.

Pim and Lenna had been frightfully lucky; despite the Empire's increased presence in

Uppridge and their difficulties in securing tickets without arousing suspicion, the train itself was largely uncrowded. In fact, they had somehow managed to claim an entire box for themselves, for which Lenna was grateful: up until now, the only other thing that had gone right was Kenta getting an opportunity to sell his vegetables. And while she had been able to get some sleep in the old farmer's cart as it wobbled down the highway to Uppridge, the cushioned seats of the modern train were infinitely more comfortable; Lenna could already feel the velvety softness beneath her and the steady chug of the engine lulling her into a misty dreamland.

Sleep was not to be, however, as Lenna was almost immediately roused by Pim's incessant chattering. "Is it safe to move? What if we suddenly stop? Look, Lenna, a cow!"

Lenna opened one eye and squinted at Pim, whose youthful exuberance was a stark contrast to the girl who was prepared to explode a bandit with her blunderbuss. Pim hadn't spoken much about her childhood, but Lenna sensed that something other than the training of the Freewomen of Laur had hardened the curly-haired girl; Lenna's own life, mostly shut up in a library, didn't exactly make her an expert on judging people, but every so often, underneath Pim's usually composed exterior, she glimpsed a kind of sadness, a crease in her forehead or slight frown on her lips. Something about Pim's grim determination and levelheadedness weighed heavily on Lenna's mind.

"How long will it take us to get to the Ilyan border?"

"According to the stationmaster, about two hours," Lenna said.

Pim gazed out the window at the cascading landscape. "I'm going to go explore the rest of the train," she announced.

"Try to be inconspicuous!" Lenna called after her, but Pim, nimble as ever, had already exited their compartment and slid the door shut. At least, Lenna noticed, the girl had left her gun behind, safely stashed under their kits on a wobbly metal rack above their seats. Pim had wanted to keep the explosive weapon by her side for the duration of the voyage, but Lenna told her it would do naught but draw unwanted eyes to the two girls (or rather, one boy and one girl); besides, though she was loath to mention it, as far as weapons were concerned Lenna appeared to have controllable magic at her disposal.

Alone in the wobbling compartment, Lenna took a moment to gaze out of the window, hands against the sill, though she did not spot any of Pim's cows. The steamtrain had brought modernity to people in even the remotest of places, but at what cost? Local farmers like Kenta simply couldn't compete with the trainloads of produce and meat that this new innovation guaranteed, and the dots on the map where the train made its stops certainly grew in size and prospered, but not all train-towns were as lucky as Port Hollish, which had been used to being a center of trade for centuries because of its port and its ability to circumnavigate the Continent. Many of the smaller villages, unfortunate enough to lie in the path of the ever-expanding railway line, would be either demolished or, even worse, transformed into hubs of travelers, tradesmen, and the brothels and public houses that came with them.

The squeak of the compartment door sliding on its casters tore Lenna from her mental exploration of technology. She turned her head, starting to comment on the speed at which Pim had returned, only to quickly clamp her mouth closed when she realized that another passenger, a male one at that, was the one who had opened the door. He was tall enough that his carefully coiffed shanks of hair, artfully framing his angular face, brushed the top of the doorway as he entered the smallish compartment.

"Excuse me," he said casually. "May I join you?"

Lenna stared. This man was shockingly beautiful — not just handsome, but so luminescent he reminded Lenna of the heroes in the cheap romance pamphlets young girls and gossipy wives read. She was convinced that his presence would cause women of more delicate constitutions to swoon, and despite herself Lenna could not help but drink in his deep, jade eyes, his chestnut hair, and a slightly amorous scent of clove and citrus that he exuded.

People like this should not exist, thought Lenna, and with a minimal amount of stammering managed to grant him permission to enter. The man slid effortlessly into the seat directly across from Lenna and flashed her a subtle smile. She gulped, and despite the logical side of her brain raging against her hormones, Lenna's stomach began to flutter as though she were fourteen again. She and Pim had both freshened up before boarding the train, and Lenna had removed her cap and bulky coat, but the librarian suddenly felt slovenly. She desperately wished Pim would hurry back.

Across the way, the man folded his hands over his knee, drawing attention to his impeccably pressed cotton trousers. His outfit was similar to Lenna's, designed for ease of travel, but his garments were of such quality tailoring that they hugged him in a languorous, effortless fashion. From his left ear, on a silver chain, hung a glistening stone: a sapphire, if Lenna was any judge of such things. This stranger was one of substance, and she silently questioned why a passenger who could afford a more luxurious compartment on the train would choose to ride with those who could not.

"It's not often I encounter Freewomen of Laur on the steamtrain," the man said languidly, looking Lenna in the eyes. "Is this your first time?"

When he spoke, the hairs on Lenna's arms rose to attention and she shivered as his pungent aroma permeated her body; she could taste it on her tongue and feel it like a caress on her skin. Though most of her mind and all of her stomach were aflutter, there was one part in Lenna that turned to rage. It all felt unnatural, a violation. Her intellect sensed an oily presence coating the man's allure, and her will rebelled. Against her body's volition Lenna drew on that anger, using it to bring up, like a roaring tide, a surge of magical energy. Gilbert had been right — she could not shape this kind of power — and so Lenna released that silently seething rage in a burst, driving away the man's presence.

In seconds, Lenna's mind cleared, like it would after a drug had run its course or a fever had broken. There was no trace of the man's smell in the air, just a very faint lingering of lavender. Blinking, Lenna stared at the man sitting across from her. He was attractive, with well-kept brown hair, but his cheekbones were a little too pronounced for Lenna's taste, and the slightly sour expression mingled with surprise made his face look decidedly pinched.

"You used magic on me," she said sharply.

Whatever initial shock the man had felt melted away from his face, and he leaned back in his seat and said simply, as though it were the most common thing in world, "It was a glamour."

"And do you just go around bewitching all the women you see?" Lenna found that she was still quite livid and that the power within her was rising once more.

"Don't be crass," he said flatly. "And let go of that anger: you caught me once by surprise, but it won't happen again."

As Gilbert had taught her, Lenna reached out with her mind, tentatively prodding at the magician. She felt nothing; her magical self had collided with an invisible barrier. "How did you do that? Who are you?"

The man tilted his head and fiddled casually with the jewel dangling from his ear. "The Brotherhood doesn't give out its secrets, Miss Faircloth. I'd ask you to respect that, but it seems like you've already acquired a few of our tricks. Tell me, what are you willing to give as payment for them?"

Lenna felt her anger harden into a stony sullenness. "You were testing me?"

"Not exactly. From what I understood, Gilbert had taught you some basics, but I didn't think you had any real potential. And the glamour was to facilitate communication, so to speak."

"But who are you?"

"My name is Sebastien Branford; I am one of the higher-ranking magicians in the Brotherhood of the Blue Crescent."

A silence fell on the train compartment, and for a moment all that could be heard was the steady chugging on the tracks and the sharp, sudden intake of breath through Lenna's front teeth. Her memory yanked her back to the breakfast table at the Tawny

Apple, where she overheard with hungover ears Gilbert and Luc discussing "Master Sebastien." Images of Gilbert's prone body sinking into the snow, thoughts of Luc running off to Ilya on his own, madly determined by grief and hope, and the resounding smack of her hand against Luc's face in the wintry night all flashed before Lenna's eyes with phantasmagorical realness.

Voice tight, she asked, "Do you know about Gilbert?"

Though it hardly seemed possible, Sebastien's face became more expressionless than before. "Yes."

Another palpable pause. Lenna stared blindly ahead at the mage; he couldn't be much older than she, thirty at the most, yet to be so detached and clinical about the death of one's pupil? When Gilbert had described Master Sebastien and his plan to smuggle the stone off Crescent Island, Lenna had pictured a wise mentor, a font of wisdom and confidence. This young man certainly reeked of the latter, but it was the wrong kind of confidence. She wondered why Gilbert would trust this man so implicitly.

"I am grieving for Gilbert," he said so suddenly that Lenna started, wondering how Sebastien knew what she was thinking. "And no, I'm not reading your mind. You should really learn to school your emotions better. Your face is an open book."

Only her pride kept Lenna from issuing a huge harrumph; instead, she kept her face neutral as the wizard continued. "It was my intention to contact him much sooner, and if I had been able to, Gilbert might still be alive. But there are many forces at work, and I did not expect our plans to be discovered so quickly."

The train chugged along, maintaining its steady pace. Lenna's eyes darted toward the door again, wondering when Pim would be coming back. "That 'sending,' as Gil and Luc called it," she said, trying to form a question she wasn't sure she wanted the answer to. "Who, or what, sent it?"

Sebastien smiled ruefully. "That was, as you might have suspected, a large-scale working of my order. Those who sent it did so at great cost to themselves, and it is something of a perplexing miracle that you and Luc survived a second sending after Gilbert's death. I can only assume the jewel somehow protected you."

"Why would the Brotherhood want to attack two of its own initiates?" Lenna did not like the direction her brain was taking her, that perhaps the second sending was targeting herself.

"To the order's eyes, Gilbert was a traitor, as is Luc, and as am I. We conspired to steal a powerful magical artifact, and succeeded."

"And traitors are put to death?"

"Miss Faircloth, I'm not sure how much you've managed to piece together for yourself, but even Luc's knowledge in this matter did not run very deep. What do you know of the God War?"

Though most records that survived from that time were housed in archives owned by Sebastien's Brotherhood, Lenna had read as much as she could. More than five hundred years ago, a fanatical king, thinking himself a messiah, turned his nation into a land of religious zealots; the people of Zeist revered their God King, Ytra, who supposedly had the power to summon miracles or devastate blasphemers.

Yearning to spread his message across the land and become the one true ruler, Ytra brought instead the greatest war the Continent had ever known. The destruction from massive war machines and devastating magical attacks was ultimate: entire nations fell, and civilization plunged into a dark age. A few surviving scholars banded together to preserve magic and knowledge from falling into obscurity; today, they were known as the Blue Crescent Brotherhood.

"What even the books in your library don't tell you, Miss Faircloth, is that God King Ytra's power came from possession of three ancient artifacts. And war escalated as other nations wanted them for their own purposes."

"The gems…"

"Hence the name, Godjewels."

And now, thought Lenna, all three of the insanely powerful gems had resurfaced: one said to be currently in Ilya, one likely with the Krevlum Empire, and the last in the hands of a frightened young apprentice grieving for his lover. The order would be pursuing him for his crime of treason and, if Jaice was correct, the Krevlum Empire would be after him as well. As Lenna had witnessed firsthand, the potential of these gems individually was immense; with all of them, she could only imagine the great havoc one could wreak.

"Since you're telling me all of this, tell me why you betrayed your people," Lenna asserted, her hands held wide in an expression of frustration. "Wouldn't it have been safer to keep the jewel on the Brotherhood's island, where it was protected? It's now in the hands of one deeply hurt, unstable boy who is aiming to get another from Ilya. And the third one is probably already in the hands of the Krevlum Empire, whose soldiers are probably on their way as well."

"The 'third' you're referring to is believed to have been found some time ago," Sebastien said. "The Empire — or, I should say, the Emperor — does indeed possess it. How and where he came across it, no one knows, but the instant he bonded with it, the gem in the Brotherhood's possession reacted. Most of the Brothers are unaware of the jewels' existence; it is only the high council that is privy to such information. However, once it was activated, anyone sensitive to magic — so anyone on our island — would be able to detect its presence. It became public."

"When was this?" Lenna asked.

"About half a year ago. When our intelligence reported that it was the Krevlum Emperor who possessed a Godjewel, and that he was employing new technology in the military, the Brotherhood decided it would take action to acquire all three. A committee was formed, and I was chosen to serve on it. But I do not believe the Brotherhood should be in possession of one of them, let alone three: they're too dangerous, and they invite war. With all three, my order would literally become the greatest force in the world."

"So you stole it?"

"Yes."

Well, Lenna thought, at least his answer was direct. "And what were you planning on doing with it? Were you going to just bury it somewhere and forget about it?"

"Bury it? Quite possibly. Forget about it? Never. Miss Faircloth, why are you headed to Ilya?"

Lenna blinked at the change of topic. "I thought that much was obvious: I'm going after Luc."

"Is that your only motivation?"

She did not want to reveal that Jaice had explained to Lenna about the Godjewel bonding with her, or how she could nebulously sense its magic, like a fine tendril, spanning the miles. Lenna knew she could close her eyes and walk straight to the gem if need be. But Sebastien was correct: Lenna was not just going to find Luc. There was much she wanted absolution from, including Gilbert's death and the denial of her own heritage as a Freewoman; if she could somehow make things right, perhaps the cacophony of feelings surging against the ironclad dam she erected in her mind would for once be quiet.

"You smell of the gem," Sebastien continued, apparently extrapolating whatever information he sought from the librarian's silence, "and I know you can sense it. When one of the Godjewels binds itself to a host, it is like a flare of magic exploding in the sky. The other Godjewels react. The very creation of your magical bond with the stone signaled as to the exact location of the last jewel — in Ilya — much like the Emperor's bonding awoke ours. They function as a trinity, but their purpose is one, Miss Faircloth: to create one holy host. And while proper skill can allow one to manipulate their powers, the gems' wills can never bend; only certain people have a natural affinity for them. However unlikely or unfortunate, you are one of the chosen, and the forces that be know it. Consider well whom you take as an ally."

And, as though unaware of the impact of his sudden exposition, Sebastien stood, his right hand grabbing the bar above his head to steady himself and the blue earring sparkling like a tiny version of the blue Godjewel in the sunlight from the window. Lenna considered Sebastien and his motives for a moment before asking the reason for this conversation.

"You are free to think of me however you like. My original intention was to extract what little information you had and move on, but I've changed my mind. Gilbert was a promising young mage and, more importantly, my friend. I think he would expect me to pass on what information I could, so that you do not enter the playing field completely unaware of the game."

"But you're not being exactly genuine, are you?"

Sebastien's mouth curled in what might have been his attempt at a smile; to Lenna, it appeared to be a smirk. "Indeed. Enjoy the ride, Miss Faircloth; I'm sure I'll see you in Ilya."

With that, the wizard, seemingly unaffected by the swaying of the train cabin, slid the compartment door open and swept out magnanimously. Lenna's head pounded with possibilities, anger, and a fair amount of trepidation. She had no reason to trust Sebastien Branford other than Gilbert's testimony to his good character and her own instincts: still, he provided convincing information that pointed out glaring omissions in what Jaice had told her of the jewels' history. Could the leader of Granemere Settlement be misleading Lenna for her own gain? Were the Freewomen after the Godjewels as well? Thoughts spun faster than the whirling landscape to her right, and Lenna was still deep inside her head when Pim wobbled in, holding two mugs and clumsily trying to shut the compartment door behind her.

"They have beer," she announced proudly, as though she herself had brewed it. After a shaky time of settling into her seat without spilling, the girl thrust the mug forward at Lenna. The librarian silently took it and continued to stare out at the scenery. From time to time Lenna sipped mechanically, tasting nothing as she wandered the recesses of her mind and pondered everything Gilbert, Jaice, and Sebastien had told her. Pim eventually gave up attempts at conversation and sullenly took to staring out at the scenery, realizing that no amount of beer or chatter could rouse Lenna out of her current musings.

CHAPTER TWELVE

As the train chugged slowly into the bustling city of Tranum, Lenna breathed a quiet sigh of relief. Her reticence was both a blessing and a curse; while she was in no mood to endure Pim's prattling, the somber silence of the train compartment forced the librarian to dwell on numerous issues for which she had no solution. The more she delved into her thoughts, in fact, the more Lenna realized how grossly foolhardy her entire situation was. Who was she, a librarian of twenty-two who lived with her father, to become involved in political and explicitly dangerous affairs? With grim reflection, Lenna realized how lonely her life as a librarian had been, and though she craved the comforts of home more than ever, she knew that this sudden adventure was her mind's way of drastically rebelling against the cowardice that had prevented her from changing her situation. It was a rash decision to get involved, but it could hardly be undone now.

Pim had been snoring peacefully for some time, the combination of breakfast wine, beer, and swaying of the steamtrain having lulled her to sleep. She was ever the warrior; a light tap on the shoulder from Lenna revived the girl immediately and, blinking, she stared out at the slowing landscape. It was no longer the fields and groves of Fallowfields; after the train crossed the wide, swift Callca River — its bridge for the steam-powered locomotive a daring bit of engineering that left Lenna a bit breathless — the land briefly gave way to rolling hills blanketed in patches of yellow rapeseed. Since before the God War Ilya had been renowned as a place of temperate weather, with a slight penchant for rain, and famed for its abundant crops; rape in particular was currently used by the Ilyans to lubricate various mechanisms and motors.

Despite its natural beauty, technology such as the steamtrain and the airship had brought rapid modernization to the nation. The city of Tranum experienced this growth more than any other urban area of Ilya as it straddled the borders of Fallowfields and the Krevlum Empire. Connections to a train station and an airship port made Tranum thrive as the primary source of dispatched goods throughout the Continent. Ships that arrived in Port Hollish transported their wares here via train rather than wagon, and Ilyan merchants either peddled them in the busy trading district or shipped them to more distant locales on other trains, or even farther by way of the skies. As such, Tranum was in all ways a metropolis, and as Lenna and Pim stared out the window the grassy view gradually transformed into clusters of storied buildings built densely together. The tracks ran on an elevated platform overlooking several of the city streets, which brimmed with the daily activities of merchants, artisans, and officials.

Pim whistled in appreciation. "I've never seen so many people."

"They say Tranum is the most frequently visited city on the Continent," Lenna remarked, a bit alarmed herself at the sheer volume of humanity. "It's my first time here, too."

The pair remained silent as the steam-powered engine gradually slowed and halted, the last of the train's momentum pulling the cars into the elegant station. It was larger than Port Hollish's by far, and everything was fashioned in smooth mahogany and trimmed with brass and gold accessories. The platforms, flanked by gaslight lampposts in neat intervals, were no escape from the city's crowds. Dozens of people, resplendent in finery, eagerly boarded a neighboring train, and others queued up in designated areas, awaiting the disembarkation of the passengers on arriving trains. Even Lenna, who had grown somewhat accustomed to the changes the train brought, was startled.

They hurriedly grabbed their kits from the shelving above their seats and prepared to exit the train. Pim, in a manner unlike anything Lenna had witnessed from the girl yet, became surprisingly timid and clutched her blunderbuss to her chest awkwardly. When asked, the freckled girl blushed fiercely with embarrassment and murmured, "Everyone out there is dressed so differently."

Lenna peeked out the window. Comparatively, both she and Pim were dressed like country bumpkins; the people flocking to the train platforms were in varied fashions, mostly Ilyan in origin, though of considerable quality with materials in silk and gleaming patent leather. Since Tranum was a city of commerce, however, a large number of foreigners were present in the crowds as well; many folk were dressed in the finery of Fallowfields, ladies wearing long skirts and blouses with elegant pins, their hair tidily piled upon their heads in great swathes, and gentlemen sporting canes and brimmed hats.

"I thought Freewomen dressed for utility, not style?" Lenna asked genuinely. She grabbed Pim by the hand and tugged her down the corridor of the train, past numerous other compartments, one of which had no doubt been occupied by Sebastien.

"We do, of course, but..." Pim stammered and blindly allowed her companion to guide her.

"But what?" Lenna asked, her voice rising against the indecipherable hum of the crowd on the platform. She stepped down off the train and began to weave Pim toward the station entrance, careful to avoid people rushing to join the queue for the next departure.

"I don't feel very pretty!" Pim shouted back.

Lenna abruptly stopped and laughed in spite of herself, and Pim collided into her, nearly knocking her into an oncoming patron. Briefly apologizing, Lenna contained her giggles and pulled Pim to the side. Amidst all the chaos, not only the stampeding people surrounding them but the raging turmoil in her brain, Lenna had ceased to notice the effect the journey was having on so young a girl. Despite her upbringing as a Freewoman of Laur, which afforded Pim the opportunity to become educated and experienced at fighting, she was not used to cities, fashion, or large crowds. After comparing her attire to the other women's elegant frocks — and after having repeatedly been told she looked like a young man — the eighteen-year-old understandably felt self-conscious. Lenna suddenly felt far, far older than her companion, despite having been eighteen herself only four years ago.

So she apologized for her negligence, in particular for laughing so intensely and so often at Pim's expense. Lenna also assured her that in Tranum, it being such a cosmopolitan city, citizens were accustomed to seeing people in all manner of dress, including that of the Freewomen. Despite this, Pim still looked skeptical and a touch defeated.

"And," continued Lenna, "since you forced me into this clothing and tried to strap down my bosom, I promise that once this is over, I will subject you to all of the horrors that are involved in wearing a proper lady's dress."

"Really? I've never worn a proper dress before," Pim said, mollified.

Lenna reaffirmed this, and with her friend displaying an elevated level of confidence, she marched toward the office of the station's customs official, where their papers would be inspected and verified. Hopefully, the documents that Jaice provided would be impressive enough to not only grant them safe passage into the nation of Ilya but also obfuscate their real identities and purpose for being in the city of Tranum. After that, it would be a matter of merely navigating the helter-skelter streets to locate Luc before the Empire, Brotherhood, or any other unsavory party did. *How bloody simple*, thought Lenna, and she joined the line to clear immigration, chagrined. She tucked her hair back into her russet cap as best she could and was content to let Pim use her androgynous looks and attitude to get them through customs passably as boys.

Outside the station, the streets of Tranum were, although to Lenna and Pim it hardly seemed possible, even more crowded. People from all across the Continent scrambled about, participating in a delicate dance of almost, but not quite, bumping into passersby while hastening to numerous stores, eateries, and chemists. To add to the two girls' confusion, vendors pulling carts, some even motorized and equipped with blaring horns, pushed through packs of nimble locals and awestruck foreigners, ignoring any pedestrian in their way. The noise was fantastically loud.

"What now?" called Pim over the din.

"I thought you were supposed to be my guide."

"Not in the city," came a terse reply.

Pim was correct in desiring an immediate plan of action, Lenna realized. Freewomen usually exuded a calm confidence and a sense of purpose; right now, the people on the street saw two young Freewoman citizens, wide-eyed and stunned, standing at the bottom of the wide stone steps leading up to the train station, one of them clutching a firearm. They were beginning to draw some strange looks. Naively, Lenna had just assumed things would fall into place as soon as they arrived in Ilya, and much of her opportunity to plan since leaving Granemere Settlement had been spent in selfish reflection and brooding. Sebastien was out in the crowd, presumably tracking Luc, and Bahl, much less prohibited in travel than Lenna and Pim, was more than likely closing in as well. It wouldn't do to stand around, addlepated.

"Let's at least find somewhere quieter," Lenna practically shouted.

Gawking at the crowds, Pim nodded and followed her companion as they attempted to navigate their way through the masses, hoping to find a side street or square where Lenna could pause and get her bearings. People to the left and right jostled them, which at least set off Pim's temper enough to make her less shy and reserved, and eventually they were able to duck into a less-occupied wide alley that cut a curvy path north of the frantic road and its scampering travelers. Here Lenna and Pim could walk side by side and avoid collisions with other passersby.

People still flitted about, some looking at menus written in curving Ilyan script, others seated at cloth-covered tables in front of dining rooms from which rich and exotic smells wafted out into the city air. By accident, Lenna and Pim had found a street dedicated to food, and its tantalizing scents provoked their stomachs into fierce growls.

"Do we have money for lunch?" asked Pim. "I'm hungrier than a horse at a hay festival."

Lenna was instantly glad that, save for the Krevlum Empire, the rest of the Continent had adopted a common currency to facilitate trading; ten years ago, the coins she had in her satchel would have been Fallowfieldian and she would have had to exchange them for the Ilyan graat just to purchase a pint of ale. She fished inside her leather pouch and did a quick assessment of their current funds. The prices were bound to be higher than back in Port

Hollish or Uppridge, and the girls should hasten to find Luc, but a full stomach was sure to aid them in their search, or at least give them a bit of respite during which they could formulate a plan of attack.

Fifteen minutes later, after Lenna ordered in carefully-worded Ilyan that received a response in perfect Continental tongue, two earthenware bowls filled with steaming broth, root vegetables, and tender chunks of braised meat made their way to the girls' table. Both Pim and Lenna tucked in with relish, the relief of being off the crowded streets invigorating their appetites. For the first few moments, no words passed between the two as they sopped up the subtly spiced liquid with thick, nutty slices of brown artisan bread.

"Can't you use your link to the jewel to track Luc?" Pim asked in a muffled voice, her mouth full of parsnip. She swallowed and pointed her spoon at Lenna. "Jaice said the gem and you are connected."

Lenna's spectacles, fogged and blurry from the steam, slid down her nose. She fished out a handkerchief and began to wipe them. "Yes, if I close my eyes, I can tenuously feel it. It's hard to explain, but it's like a tickle in the back of my throat, or the feeling when your ears get stuffy because you've climbed up a mountain. It's easy to ignore."

"Well, what if you stopped ignoring it?"

Glasses replaced, Lenna considered Pim's proposal. In truth, finding Luc via her link to the Godjewel was what Jaice had intended when she sent Lenna and Pim on this dangerous mission to Ilya. Without its bonded individual near it, the gem leaked waves of magic as some kind of arcane signal for its partner to track. Unfortunately, anyone sensitive to magic would notice these mystical reactions and be able to locate the jewel as well. Lenna knew the consequences of that: the Brotherhood, the Ilyan who possessed the third jewel, Sebastien, and the Empire were all in swift pursuit of the young mage. And the Emperor was already in possession of one of the deadly artifacts; were he to obtain a second, let alone all three, it could be a harbinger of another Zeist, the religious cult that swept over the Continent and brought the destruction of civilization. Could Lenna allow her own discomfort and reticence be the cause of another tyrannous nation's attempt at domination?

"I suppose we don't have any other options," she decided.

"Let's finish lunch first though, eh? You gonna eat that?" Pim leaned over the table and scooped up a cube of meat, plopping the bite into her mouth before returning to her seat. "This meat is so tasty! We don't have anything like this back in Granemere Settlement. What is it?"

"Horse tongue."

"What?"

"I said, horse tongue. Horse is a delicacy here in Ilya; that tangy flavor in the broth is from the blood, I think."

Pim spent the rest of the meal poking her spoon at the remaining parsnips in her bowl, apparently full enough for once.

Despite her assertions that she was dying because horse was poisonous to Freewomen of Laur, Pim managed to keep pace with Lenna as she hurried down the restaurant-lined side street toward a small, unoccupied pavilion with a few trees and benches. The owner of the establishment at which they enjoyed lunch (or at least Lenna enjoyed it) had kindly given Lenna directions when she inquired if there was a quiet place nearby. Most likely, she thought, the owner assumed that the cacophony of the city was too much for out-of-touch country folk and Lenna and Pim needed such a place to relax and gather their wits.

That's probably true, Lenna thought. *Though I doubt I'll be doing much relaxing.* She'd be doing just the opposite: tracking down the source of a whole heap of trouble, with her only defense being her untrained magical skills and Pim's martial abilities. She supposed she could add Bahl to her list of allies, assuming they managed to find him. Sighing, Lenna mentally checked off each of the different directions as she remembered them, and without error guided them through a labyrinth of curving, high-walled alleyways and eerie side streets where a tunneling effect caused the wind to whip up their hair and whistle loudly. Lenna was glad of her cap now.

Thankfully, the owner's directions proved to be entirely accurate. About halfway down a clean but empty alley, surrounded by flats and shadowed by a net of clotheslines and undergarments, a narrow space between two buildings opened up into a cramped but well-kept residential garden. The ground was not cobbled like the streets; instead, the pavilion was blanketed with patches of grass and dandelions, springing up out of the earth to catch the sunlight that filtered down between the residences. Benches nestled against the three walls enclosing the space, flanking a modest fountain that barely reached Pim's height. Lenna instantly recalled some of the older, quieter areas of Port Hollish and felt a pang of heartache for her hometown.

The quietness of the space seemed to be a great comfort for Pim as well. She immediately scurried to the fountain and began flicking the sputtering jet of water with her hand like a three-year-old. Lenna settled down on the bench on the far wall, watching Pim's youthful innocence with a mixture of envy and trepidation.

No, she's not quite innocent; she's naive. For Pim, this was her first big mission, a special assignment from the mayor of the village in which she grew up. The girl had yet to experience any of the real hardships Lenna had faced, except for the incident with the bandits, and Lenna herself had yet to tell her the truth about what happened before she and

Luc arrived at the Freewoman settlement. In less than a week Lenna's ideal, if simple, existence had been drastically changed and she was forced to look at the world through the eyes of an adult. To think that until Gilbert and Luc barged into her library she was just hiding from real life, living in her father's home and burying her daily life in daydreams and books — Lenna was disgusted with herself.

Gilbert, Sebastien, Jaice, even Luc — these were people who saw the direction of the world and tried to change it. They all realized the grave consequences of a powerful force obtaining the gems and they acted to preserve the wavering peace of the Continent. Whenever something bad occurred in Lenna's life, she merely found a new book, took a bath, and had some wine or ale. Like when she was too scared to accept a position at the University in Gallas, or when her mother wasted away to a shell of her former self and faded into nothingness, leaving Lenna and her father behind.

Even now, Lenna was delaying the inevitable, getting trapped inside the net of thoughts in her brain. She refused to acknowledge her grief for Gilbert and she delayed moving forward toward finding Luc because she was a coward. Lenna did not want, or need, any more pain. When had she last been as mirthful as Pim? When she was nine? Ten? Though she thought herself bright and personable, Lenna lacked the confidence in herself to let go, at least not while she had a security blanket such as her job at the library or a home to return to.

But there was no one here but Pim to protect Lenna now, and the reflective librarian did not want to force the girl to sacrifice her youthful exuberance because Lenna refused to take responsibility. No, she resolved; Gilbert died protecting her, and she repaid that sacrifice with cruelty toward his lover. Had she really slapped Luc to motivate him to move, or was that just a convenient excuse? Could her own inability to prevent Gilbert's death and her resentment toward Luc have been the real reasons behind that blow? Lenna bowed her head forward, resting it on her hands.

She had only one choice if she wanted to move forward and become the Lenna she wanted to be. The fear would not go away — but that was all right, for a lack of fear was just stupidity, she told herself — and although there was nothing she would rather do than crawl under her bedspread with a good book, Lenna closed her eyes and let her mind wander toward the source of her magic, the small bright flame pulsing inside her.

Once she found it, Lenna imagined a tendril of light-blue energy leading from it; this was her connection, the chain that bound her to the Godjewel. There was a constant sense of its presence on the outskirts of her mind, and now all Lenna had to do was follow the thread back to its source. Slowly and deliberately, her mind traversed the cord that joined her magic and the jewel's, and through her lidded eyes Lenna had a sense of the architecture and people around the invisible thread over the distance it traveled. A careful process, it felt as though it took ages, though in reality mere seconds had passed. By the time she opened her eyes again and looked resolutely at Pim, still playfully batting at the waterspout, Lenna had ascertained the location of the stolen Godjewel. As fate would have it, it was much closer than she would have believed, and Lenna knew that she could unfalteringly navigate her way to it.

Her jaw was set in determination as she rose from the bench and tucked a stray lock into her cap. Pim stopped her game and looked querulously in her direction.

"You look like you're about to head off to war," Pim commented.

Lenna nodded. "That's exactly what I intend to do. I can feel it, Pim; it's close."

"Then what are we waiting for? Let's find that little mage friend of yours."

The librarian would hardly describe Luc as her friend, but her stomach lurched with an unwanted responsibility for him. It was time: within a few minutes, she would be able to hopefully convince the brash youth to relinquish the jewel and return to Fallowfields with her. Lenna briskly guided Pim from the pavilion and down the empty path, crossing over to interconnected alleyways and up small steps carved precisely into the stonework of the city. As their boots rapped against the pavement, Lenna felt the urgency in her gut grow oppressive and she quickly became lightheaded.

"You look pale," Pim called. "Do you need to slow down?"

"No," she panted. "It's just —"

And then, as though a great dirigible were exploding, the tightness in her stomach released in one frantic, massive rush. Unconsciously, her mind's eye registered a brilliant aura of energy directly ahead of them. It was invisible to Pim, but to Lenna it was an eruption, blue and brilliant. Her hand whipped out to the side, barring Pim and halting her progress. The pent-up sensation she had experienced was a reaction to the drawing of power from the Godjewel. Once the power was released, the queer sensation ceased.

"Someone's used the jewel; any mage in Ilya will have noticed it," she said, and they ran.

Pim, a trained warrior, was without a doubt Lenna's superior when it came to running and soon outpaced her. After all, what use had the librarian, whose normal exercise routine consisted of angrily walking away from lecherous suitors, for running? Lenna schooled herself to ignore the digging stitch in her side and to breathe evenly between her shouted directions to Pim. The Freewoman raised her hand in mock salute, acknowledging Lenna, and blazed down the alley, her blunderbuss clanking against her shoulder. She quickly disappeared around the corner, several lengths ahead of the out-of-shape librarian.

When Lenna turned the corner into the wider lane, she only managed not to collide into her companion because of Pim's keen awareness of her environs. Not a curl out of place, she deftly sidestepped the barreling librarian with a fighter's unconscious grace. But why had Pim stopped in the first place? Lenna, winded and white-faced, managed to stop and regain her balance, flecks of sweat pockmarking her spectacles.

It was then that her eyes, widening, processed the scene before them. Though this lane was not as lively as the main stretch in front of the Tranum steamtrain station, it still experienced a fair amount of human and cart traffic compared to the deserted alleyways through which the girls had just run. Now, however, the pedestrians and market goers, primarily Ilyan, were hushed and stood in a tight crowd that spanned the breadth of the road. Between the silent onlookers and the new arrivals, Luc Tural loomed over a man who appeared to have collapsed. The mage wore a dazed expression, his eyes slightly glazed over, and clutched the shimmering blue Godjewel in his right hand.

Lenna's eyes traveled down to the figure on the ground. His face was badly burned, one-half of it covered with oozing crimson and pink blisters. The wounds spread down to completely cover his neck, and a fair portion of his shirt had been seared away, leaving behind a nasty, whip-like lash of charred flesh crossing his chest diagonally. The stench of burning hair, human skin, and ozone was obscene, and Lenna barely managed to stifle a gag.

Pim's voice shredded the heavy silence and she threw herself down onto her knees before the still man. "Bahl!"

Upon a painful second glance at the unscathed half of the man's face, Lenna realized with horror that he was indeed the Freewoman's best hunter and Jaice's partner. His good eye was closed, and though he was quite obviously unconscious, the subtle rise and fall of his stomach showed Lenna that Bahl was breathing, albeit shallowly. He would not, however, survive long without proper care; at this point, Lenna was certain he would need a mage trained in healing arts to pull through at all.

"His body's gone into shock," Pim said, assessing his wounds. All Freewomen were trained in basic medical techniques. "He's going to need healing, and quickly."

Lenna's gaze rose and latched onto Luc's glassy eyes. "Luc," she uttered in a voice barely louder than a whisper, "what have you done?"

For a brief moment, the young man's eyes came into focus and met Lenna's, boring into her like a drill into soft earth. She glimpsed a flicker of recognition before Luc recoiled, taking a step back away from Bahl and brushing up against the wall of citizens behind him. Swearing desperately, he dropped the gem to the ground, revealing a bubbled, bleeding burn on his hand. As the crowd began to close in, he pushed his way into the throng of people and slipped out of sight.

"Pim," Lenna started.

"Go after him; I'll stay with Bahl."

A young Ilyan man in bright clothing, probably Pim's age, assured Lenna and Pim in heavily accented Continental that he would hasten to find a magical healer or, failing that, arrange to take the burned hunter to a medical facility. He faded into the background before Lenna had a chance to utter a word of thanks, the crowd parting to help him make his way. Lenna briefly bent down and scooped up the jewel, its weight and presence reassuring in her hand. She felt strength and vigor rise up into her chest.

With a quick nod to Pim and a fretful glance at Bahl, Lenna launched into action. The crowd parted for her as it did for the helpful young man, and she sprinted past them, grimly resolved to intercept the rogue who had struck down one of her comrades.

Renewed by the gem's energy and a sense of purpose, Lenna nimbly weaved between pedestrians as she pursued Luc across the busy streets of Tranum. She could not see the mage with her eyes; he was several years her junior and certainly more vigorous, so even with her newfound source of vitality Lenna could never hope to match his speed. But that was irrelevant: with the gemstone clutched tightly in her hand, slightly warm and pulsing, Lenna could feel Luc's residual presence even as he darted down alleyways, in between pavilions, buildings, and various stalls. He was headed toward the Landing, the famous aeroport in Tranum around which had been organically built a market so exotic and bustling it made Port Hollish look like Junction in comparison.

Heads turned and various oaths — some of impressive potency — followed Lenna as she sprinted across the cobbled and paved Ilyan roads, which, due to the city's recent commercial success, were in excellent condition. Lenna had never run this fast and a corner of her mind was devoted to the concern that she was relying on the jewel's power too much to propel her, but her need to find Luc was great, and the pale coral buildings, typical of Ilyan architecture, blurred as her leather boots steadily padded against the ground. For now her dominating thought was, and must be, Luc, and so Lenna actively ignored the sweat dampening her hair, the aching in her legs, her shortness of breath, and anything that was not an immediate obstacle, like an old woman with a goat.

Tranum was originally a smaller city, the streets and buildings blossoming after construction of the aeroport, and as such, rather than having any defined structure or planning, the layout of the city was haphazard. There were intersecting alleyways, secret paths, and stairways leading to dead ends spreading out from the Landing in jagged and curving arteries. The widest of the roads, though, always led to the aeroport at the heart of Tranum and could be expected to be brimming with tourists and merchants. A native of the city would know how to navigate the complex labyrinth of passages that fed into the main streets, ostensibly cutting the journey time in half. Lenna was no local, but by tuning into the Godjewel and gazing with her mind's eye she suddenly became cognizant of how the intricate streets came together. After nearly colliding with another young man, Lenna darted off the main road and took great strides, two steps at a time, down a short stone stairway that descended into a winding alley.

Lenna was not certain what would have caused Luc to attack Bahl other than sheer desperation, and she was perversely thankful that the young mage had exhibited no proper control over the jewel, or the devastation might have been greater. From what, though, was he running? The walls of the alley, some decoratively vandalized, slid past the librarian as she took a sharp curve and the path began to incline. She inwardly pulled on more of the jewel's power, urging her legs to grind up the slope despite their wickedly loud protests. She drew closer to the market and could once again hear the hubbub of the city proper. Up ahead, like the sun streaming into the mouth of a steamtrain tunnel, the alley opened up to the core of Tranum, the Landing.

Deliberately slowing her pace, Lenna approached the edge of the entrance, peeking out from the shady mouth of the alleyway and into the sunlight of the Landing. People infested the area like an insect swarm, walking between the makeshift stalls that decorated the vast circular port. The breadth of the area made Lenna's own Port Hollish seem vastly insignificant, as though her entire town could fit within this one marketplace. It was a wide field outfitted with rigging and ropes to which were docked four great airships, though from Lenna's reading she knew the aeroport was capable of harboring up to ten of these large mechanical marvels.

Airships were still a new invention, and the only pilots and crafters of the devices were Ilyan, though rumor had it the Krevlum Empire was preparing its own fleet. In design, the massive vehicles were not unlike the ships that would dock at Port Hollish; the large hulls of the newest models gleamed, being constructed of shiny metal alloys designed to be sturdy but lightweight. Even the older ones, albeit made of wood, sparkled in the high afternoon sun with varnish.

Nowadays it was commonplace for airships to be fitted with any number of parts to achieve flight, from simple gas-filled envelopes to powerful propellers that, with the advancement of Ilyan craftsmanship, were capable of achieving the magic of flight on their own. The vessels were primarily used for the transport of goods and exploration; it was possible for some wealthier citizens to bargain with the Ilyan traders who piloted the ships and arrange passage, though such citizens might very well end up sharing their pleasure cruises with boxes of spices or stinking salt cod.

Lenna was awestruck by the daunting number of people going about their business here in the Landing, the sheer volume making her head spin. Moreover, whatever electric sense of excitement the jewel had given her during her race after Luc was wearing thin. As that feeling of vitality slowly faded, all of Lenna's previous exhaustion and muscle pain began to seep in. It also meant that her innate understanding of Luc's position was waning, drifting away from her subconscious like one forgets a dream upon waking. How would she track her former companion now, amidst this unfathomably dense cluster of people?

Entering the fray seemed like an elaborate game of skip rope. If she timed it correctly, Lenna would be able to dip her foot into the whirl of people — merchants and patrons alike — moving from stall to stall, browsing. A misstep, however, would sweep her along with the unruly waves of tourists. Luc, if his primary function was to lose Lenna in a crowd, succeeded; between all the foreigners and native Ilyans, finding one boy would be nearly impossible.

Taking a deep breath, a tremendously fatigued Lenna took one step toward the surging masses. All of her earlier grace and confidence left her, and within seconds Lenna found herself moving in the same direction as the people around her, driven like cattle. Sensing her confusion, a well-muscled woman of considerable age grabbed Lenna with both arms and hoisted her up like a sack of beans. The woman placed her down to the side gently, within her protection, and guided Lenna along in the confusion.

"New to the Landing, eh?" she said over the din. She continued ushering Lenna forward until they mystically arrived before a pile of open crates, filled to the brim with white peaches.

"Is it that obvious?" Lenna shouted back. "I'm trying to get to the aeroport."

"You picked a right fine time to do it! The *Trilyala's* just landed and they're bringing down the wares; all us traders are scrambling to get the best pick."

A rakish trader, prying the lid off a crate in the back of the lot, greeted the old woman and said something in Ilyan that Lenna couldn't parse. His hair was very blonde, almost white, and tied back behind his head loosely, and he possessed the light blue eyes common among Ilyans. Dressed in loose-fitting, deep purple trousers and a white ruffled shirt belted at the waist with a gold buckle, the young man gave a grin that, despite the small white scar above it, betrayed how absolutely confident he was in himself.

"Cheeky," the woman said in Continental before replying in Ilyan. What the trader wanted was beyond Lenna, but she was on a mission to find Luc; Lenna had no time to be dillydallying over a box of peaches, no matter how sweet and fruity they might smell.

As the two Ilyans picked up their banter, Lenna spun around and impatiently scanned the crowd, tapping her foot in frustration. There was no sign of Luc, and anxiety swelled in her bosom as she feared she might lose him. She idly fingered the gem that she still held in her hand, its smooth surface slightly warm to the touch and oddly comforting. If she drew on its power again, perhaps her strength and ability to track Luc would return.

Lenna withdrew into her mind, finding not just her own magic but also a force pressing against the rigid wall between the edge of her being and the powerful, urgent will of the Godjewel. It increasingly encroached upon her awareness, and this time she allowed it access; she lowered her defenses, closed her eyes, and prepared to let the power in the jewel wash over her consciousness. The jewel grew warmer, and even with her lids pressed shut Lenna could feel the warmth of its sapphire light beat against her face.

Moments later an arm grabbed hers fiercely, disrupting Lenna's concentration and severing her connection to the gem. She opened her eyes and practically growled at the young trader, who had leaped over the crate of produce to interrupt Lenna. The look on his face was more concerned than angry, though for Lenna's part, she was more than a little annoyed at the brash Ilyan.

"No," he said in deliberately slow Ilyan. "Don't use."

Like I'm a baby, thought Lenna, though it was probably necessary, as Lenna's Ilyan fluency was lacking, to say the least. She wanted to say as much but found herself at a loss for words, either Ilyan or her native Continental.

"Don't use that," repeated the trader in Lenna's tongue. "It's not safe; others are looking for it."

Lenna blinked in surprise. Not only did this brash young trader know that Lenna was being pursued, he also possessed knowledge of the Godjewel. She hastily tucked the jewel into the leather pouch at her belt and took a step back. The older woman, glancing between the two younger figures, silently retreated into the crowd. Though Lenna didn't even know the woman's name, she wished she hadn't been left alone.

"Who are you?" she asked.

"I'm Raif, a trader from family Vandever. Just off the *Trilyala*." He jerked his head toward one of the airships currently docked in the aeroport.

"How do you know anything about what I'm doing?"

Raif raised his eyebrows in an emotion Lenna couldn't quite place. "I was going to ask you the same question. Mainly, where did you get that stone?"

"That's not your concern. Now, if you'll excuse me..." she said rudely, and began to walk away, but his arm held her tight.

"It is my concern," he said haughtily. "The Krevlum Empire and the Blue Crescent Brotherhood will have seen the recent bursts of magic from the jewel; I've been noticing them for the past twenty minutes. They'll be on top of this place in no time."

Lenna was aghast. "How do you know anything about any of this?"

"Because," Raif replied, smiling, "my family is currently in possession of what you foreigners think of as the third and last Godjewel."

CHAPTER THIRTEEN

"There are a few too many coincidences lately," Lenna admonished. "What are the odds that, out of all the people here in Tranum, I conveniently come across you?"

"It's not a coincidence at all." Raif had yet to let go of her arm. "The woman who escorted you to me was a cousin of mine, trained in the magical arts; my relatives all over the city have been looking for the one spewing power from the Godjewel, though I see my original information was inaccurate. I wasn't expecting a woman."

So much for her disguise; somewhere along her run Lenna must have lost her cap, though she doubted it made much of a difference. She tried to shrug off Raif's grasp to no avail and resigned herself to momentary captivity. Her eyes danced around the Landing, searching for any hint of Luc, but they unsurprisingly found no trace among the writhing monster of the crowd. Wondering how much distance the young mage could have covered, Lenna's mind tossed about calculations as a child plays with a ball. If she could gather a rough idea of how far he had gotten, she could try to use the jewel's power — but in a more constrained way, hopefully attracting less unwanted attention.

The rakish trader uttered a mild curse in Ilyan before switching back to his very natural Continental. "Don't even think about using that stone. Your face is easier to read than a Krevlum soldier's at a brothel." Still, Raif released his tight grip on Lenna.

Massaging her tingling arm, Lenna asked, "What do you intend on doing with me?" She was prepared to defend herself if necessary, having newfound confidence in her innate abilities, but since there were so many bystanders about, Lenna was unsure if she could control her magic enough to avoid doing them harm.

Raif tilted his head and made a few quick gestures to one of the workers hovering nearby. The worker acknowledged and replaced the lid on the crate of peaches, ready to dispatch the goods to some market or whatever warehouse the trader's family used for storage. Orders given, Raif returned his attention to the frowning librarian, beaming at her with another of his irritatingly smug grins that made Lenna want to clock him in the face.

"I suppose asking you to give up the gem would be pointless?"

"One friend died for it, and another man is now devastatingly wounded. I'm going to use it to find Luc, and then go throw it in the ocean."

The smile on Raif's face contorted itself into an expression of horror. "You're serious, aren't you? Do you have any idea how valuable these things are?"

Lenna shrugged and adjusted her spectacles. As much good as the jewels could do, she realized she wanted no association with them. Let this trader's family and the Empire sort out what to do with the remaining two; Lenna's current objective, which hardened her resolve like a wall of stone, was finding Luc. Once she had him, the Godjewel would be pitched into the sea and Gilbert's mission would be accomplished.

Either Lenna was just as obvious as Raif had earlier suggested, or he was a masterful judge of people. "This friend who died for it, I assume he was from the Brotherhood. Only a member of their order would have any chance of smuggling it off Crescent Island."

Lenna pursed her lips, not sure whether she should confirm or deny Raif's claims. Strange characters were coming out of the woodwork for this gem, but oddly enough they never tried to take it by force. Were they scared of its power, or Lenna's? Surely a magician worth his salt would notice at first glance that Lenna had no training and very little experience using her skills.

"If this friend's mission was to get rid of that Godjewel you carry, why didn't he just drop it overboard into the ocean himself? Then you presumably wouldn't be involved in this, and he'd still be alive." Raif paused for a moment. "Well, his order probably would have executed him, but the gem would be gone forever."

She hadn't thought about that until now. If Gilbert, and she supposed Sebastien, really desired that the jewel be lost forever, why would they not dispose of it from the start? Instead, they chose to enter a dangerous political game of cat and mouse as players from all over the Continent made their moves for the gems. Although it pained her, and the image of Gilbert's final moments on that wintry night still haunted her, Lenna briefly considered the possibility that her childhood friend might have had ulterior motives.

"What's your name?" Raif asked, interrupting Lenna's musings.

"Lenna."

"All right, Lenna, I want you to turn your head toward the airship dock and tell me what you see. Do it as casually as possible."

Stealth was not one of the librarian's stronger points, and being asked to perform a subtle maneuver almost guaranteed failure. Still, as nonchalantly as she could manage, Lenna craned her head back over her shoulder and used one hand to brush her hair back in what she hoped was a smooth, non-awkward manner. The bustling crowd seemed to be parting, some distance away from Lenna and Raif, and through the opening she glimpsed several ivory uniforms.

"Imperial soldiers," she breathed.

"Lenna," Raif said in a flat tone, "by now, the Empire has probably received the description of a bespectacled Freewoman of Laur and a certain artifact of power. I suggest we relocate."

Raif was right, Lenna realized. Albeit unwilling, Lenna too was now a player in this game, and she could not hope to keep her anonymity forever. Aside from Pim, who seemed the most genuine, Lenna had no idea whom to trust, but she was certain that Raif, however important he might think himself, was preferable to a group of Imperial soldiers. She nodded her head twice, silently acquiescing to slipping away.

"Right, this way," Raif said as he took Lenna's hand and deftly guided her through throngs of merchants and tourists.

When was the last time I held hands with a man? Lenna's forays into the realm of romantic interactions were few, and those that did exist were brief; she became tired of the predictable advances of most people and, compared to some of the banal conversations she'd had in pubs in Port Hollish, a good book served as better company to a cold mug of ale than an energetic male companion. Now, in the midst of the largest crisis of her life thus far, she found it ironic Raif's domineering attitude amused her more than annoyed her. It was, after all, difficult to take anyone so smug seriously.

For the young trader, the chaos of Tranum's Landing was his natural habitat. Raif, at a breakneck pace, moved with unparalleled grace between merchants hauling massive shipments of fruits, their faces worn and leathery from exposure to the sun at the high altitudes of the airships. On her own, Lenna could never navigate this fray without colliding into someone, and she secretly held her breath as Raif blazed her past an elegant female merchant from Gallas, resplendent in a flowing white silk dress that practically glowed against her deep brown skin, followed by a trail of underlings hefting reams and reams of cloth.

Before she knew it, Raif had guided the two of them safely out of the crush of people, steering them toward a street leading to the southwest. Here, though there was still the constant hum of the city, the amorphous mass of people had considerably lessened in size, and Lenna breathed a sigh of relief. She slipped her hand out of Raif's grasp and walked in stride with him. While she was secretly thankful for his guidance, she didn't put her gratitude into words.

"This way," Raif said. He strode down the street at a deliberate crawl, seemingly unconcerned.

"Where are we going?" she asked, matching his pace.

"My home," was his casual reply, causing Lenna to blink. "Don't worry; I guarantee your safety."

"Is that wise? You said that the third jewel is in your family's possession."

"That, Lenna, is exactly why I can guarantee your safety. With the power of two jewels at our assumed disposal, no one would dare move openly against you."

Lenna felt a finger of suspicion trace a line down her spine. She did not much care for the term "our assumed disposal," though she could hardly refute Raif's logic. If the Empire or the Brotherhood, or whoever else was interested, thought Lenna was working with the merchant family who possessed a jewel of their own, they would consider it a foolish venture to mount an attack. This protection would not last forever — Lenna was not planning on becoming a member of the Vandever family — but it might buy her some time. And, supposing Raif's clan had influence within the various political circles of Ilya, perhaps she could use it to her advantage to track down her friends.

"I'll go with you, but on two conditions," Lenna said.

"Oh?" Raif turned to face her, visibly amused.

Resisting the urge to scowl, Lenna cleared her throat before continuing with her terms. "First, I'm not going to use the gem for any purpose I disagree with, and second, I need your help finding my friends."

Raif nodded with false solemnity. "Your wishes will be respected, my lady."

"Make the Pact," she said in her broken Ilyan.

The trader's eyebrows rose quickly to peaks of never-before-seen loftiness. After a moment he schooled his expression and stated, "I didn't expect to be asked that by someone who wasn't Ilyan."

"I like to read," Lenna replied flippantly. "Now, the Pact, or I'll head off on my own. And I'll know if you change the words."

In delightful, lilting Ilyan, Raif said in a hushed but resolute voice, "To every corner of the land, I vow to fulfill my duties. By our Pact, if I fail, my soul will never be able to sail the wind."

Lenna nodded with approval. The Ilyans were a fascinating people; they emphasized the importance of maintaining strong familial bonds and encouraged explorers and traders in families to spread throughout the Continent so that the family might spread, like a great tree casting out roots. Because this concept of family was ingrained in them since birth, Ilyans handled social responsibilities with extreme seriousness.

They believed that when they died their souls, lifted by the spreading branches of their families and supported by the strength of good dealings in life, would "sail the wind" for eternity, circling the world and spreading from horizon to horizon, like leaves riding a breeze. If an Ilyan swore the Pact, it could be taken on good faith that he would keep his promise.

"Thank you," said Lenna, a bit tantalized in spite of herself. It was her first time hearing the Pact spoken aloud.

"I trust that's sufficient?"

"It is, in fact." She adjusted her spectacles once again. *Very well*, Lenna thought to herself, *let's make the most of this opportunity*. With any luck, she could be reunited with Pim within hours. Luc might take a little longer, but if Raif's family had the influence she assumed it had, she was certain they would find him more easily than she would. In the meantime, Lenna merely needed to lie low and hide from anyone pursuing her. "Shall we be off?"

Raif laughed and guided her down the sunny street, past well-dressed women who wore gauzy, sequined scarves and elaborate bejeweled hairpins and gentlemen in proper waistcoats. Wherever Raif was taking her, Lenna realized she would look horribly inappropriate; her skin was grubby with dust, and even her coffee-covered skirt would be a happy alternative to the grimy trousers she was wearing. Lenna longed for a bath, some soap, and a nap before meeting anyone important.

"My father will want to be introduced," Raif explained, "but I think you could use a moment to rest."

"You mean, wash my face."

"That too."

Lenna sighed. She was as dirty as a street urchin, and Raif was taking her to the home of one of the wealthiest families on the Continent. She supposed that she had bigger problems to worry about than the social approval of rich Ilyans, but as Raif nudged Lenna down the tree-lined road, matters of the gem, Luc, and everything else were drowned out by a phobia of appearing dirty. She wondered how Raif could stand to walk with her.

But Raif did not seem to mind, and he chatted amiably, humming when any silence fell. If he was bothered by her appearance, Lenna thought, he certainly hid it well. Dutifully placing one foot after the other, the disheveled librarian marched on, hoping the rest of the Vandevers were as accepting as Raif.

As the pair drew closer to the Vandever residence, Lenna became acutely aware of the gradual increase of delicately coiffured trees and manicured flowers. The few people that did walk along the sides of the street were dressed plainly but in fabrics of sturdy construction; servants, Lenna thought. Those that passed Raif tipped their hats or bowed their heads politely as they scurried along. Where on earth was Lenna going?

Eventually the street ended at a wide, arched gate more than twice as tall as Lenna. Although open for the moment, glancing from side to side revealed powerfully wrought iron bars, free from rust, glistening in the sun. Should it come to a matter of defense, Lenna had no doubt the gate would shut quickly and remain steadfast throughout all but the most vigorous of assaults. To one side of the arch stood a particularly tanned, bald man leaning casually against the yellowed stone of the building, a curved blade strapped to his hip. He nodded his head at Raif before his eyes, twinkling with curiosity, fell on Lenna.

The bald man, in a voice that sounded like he was chewing on gravel, said something quick and coarse to Raif in Ilyan. The trader responded by rolling his eyes and spouting off a quick, chiding remark completely incomprehensible to Lenna. She realized that she would need to spend a great deal more time practicing her foreign languages when this was all over. If it was ever over.

Raif, at Lenna's side, protectively placed his hand at the small of her back and hurried her past the bald man and into the courtyard. Walled in at all sides, the courtyard was a tribute to landscaping. A cobbled pathway traced the sides of the rectangular building, and surrounding a large, decorative marble fountain were carefully pruned flowers of every color, artfully arranged into patterns. Topiaries in the shapes of animals were home to scores of butterflies that took to the air in silent pilgrimage at the pair's approach. A unique mixture of scents prodded at Lenna's nose; it reminded her of the perfumed haze from the flower sellers on particularly hot days in Port Hollish's market district. Raif, arm still braced behind Lenna, carefully led her down the left path.

"What was that about?" Lenna asked.

"That's one of the family's hired guards," Raif explained, smirking. "He was inquiring as to whether or not I picked up anything interesting on my latest trade run."

"Ah." Lenna quirked an eyebrow knowingly. So it appeared that her hunch about her appearance was correct. Either that, or Raif had a penchant for bringing home women of varied circumstances. "What do you trade in, anyway?"

Raif looked toward the open sky and answered vaguely. "Bits of everything, really. Curiosities. Rare artifacts. That sort of thing. I mostly do it for the flying."

"I've never been on an airship before," Lenna said.

"It's exhilarating, Lenna. There's nothing like it in the world. When I'm up there, the wind whipping through my hair and the land so far below, it makes all of life seem so insignificant in the great design of things."

"Huh. You didn't strike me as a romantic."

"Maybe I just like the feeling of my hair in the breeze." Raif stopped to point out a particularly unusual flower. The seeds, he said, were imported from the southern cape of Gallas, so far away that until airships had become more commonplace, it had been a grueling, dangerous journey. "You have to soar over the peaks surrounding the cape to get there. It's an amazing feeling to view the mountains from the deck of an airship; you should come along sometime."

"I'm afraid of heights," Lenna said curtly.

"Well. Maybe not, then." Raif shrugged indifferently and removed his arm and scuttled on ahead, his blonde ponytail bobbing with the lightness of his step. Numerous archways and doors led from the courtyard, but the main paths around the rectangular pavilion converged at what was obviously the main entrance to the Vandever residence. Two pristine marble staircases wound their way up from the left and right paths, gently arcing to the main doors: two deep-set mahogany masterpieces, intricately carved with images of birds in flight and trees. It was truly exquisite craftsmanship, and Lenna's stomach dropped in a bout of homesickness. Her father would be even more fascinated with the woodwork.

"Don't worry; we're not going to make a grand entrance. I want to be discreet."

Raif shuffled her through a door in the corner of the courtyard that resembled a servants' entrance and led her down a series of narrow corridors. As they progressed, Lenna futilely attempted to keep track of the twists and turns and spiraling claustrophobic stairways, but the deeper they delved into the house, the more she was convinced that the Vandevers had merely appropriated a maze and were passing it off as a mansion. Eventually, one last staircase, whitewashed so effectively that Lenna felt queer as she ascended the spiral, led to a small but solid wooden door that opened out upon a wide hallway. The space was well lit, with the entire wall before Raif and Lenna plastered with wide glass windows.

Taking a quick glance in both directions, Lenna noticed the paintings anointing the stone Ilyan walls; while she did not have much interest in art, she could certainly recognize masterpieces when she saw them. Under her feet, a plush carpet from Gallas felt spongy. Although a steadfast weariness crept upon Lenna, she felt her very presence might sully the immaculately clean corridor. Wherever Raif was leading her, Lenna hoped the final destination was the bath.

"This floor is for family residence," Raif explained, escorting the goggling librarian down the hall. He stopped before an undecorated but well-polished door with a brass and ivory doorknob. He rapped three times in succession.

After a moment, the knob turned and the door revealed a girl, probably not much older than sixteen, dressed in an extremely elaborate rose frock that fell effortlessly to her knees. Her pale blue eyes widened at the sight of Lenna, who in response turned a shade of red comparable to that of the girl's dress. The likeness to Raif was stunning; when the girl turned something in her profile told Lenna immediately she was Raif's sister.

Raif and the girl conversed briefly in Ilyan, her eyes darting to Lenna, then back to her brother for a split second. Lenna, for her part, stood fidgeting, rocking a little on her ankles and taking in the splendor of the corridor. She could not see much into the girl's room, however; her blonde hair was piled intricately up about her head and secured with several decorative combs. Its mass, like a cloud covering the moon, obscured anything behind her. Lenna imagined that particular style was not very comfortable or healthy for one's hair.

The conversation came to a halt, Lenna having picked up only a word or two along the way, and Raif turned to her. "Lenna, this is my sister, Briet. She's going to help you... clean up a bit."

Briet turned to Lenna and, in perfectly accented Continental, said, "Nice to meet you, Lenna. Apparently Raif has made the Pact with you, which means you're someone worth helping." Her eyes traveled up and down the dusty librarian. "All right, let's get started. You," she said to her brother, "go away."

The elder Vandever laughed merrily and shrugged. "Good luck, Lenna. You'll need it." He turned and started to walk off, but paused after a few steps. "Lenna, I appreciate your coming here. I'll do everything in my power to find your friends."

Lenna nodded and thanked Raif genuinely. Though she had only just met him, and thought he was a bit of a dandy and too self-confident, something about Raif seemed trustworthy. Despite the differences in attitude, he reminded Lenna of Gilbert. Though she would rather be active in the search for her friends, Lenna decided that right now, both physically and mentally, she'd be better served with a little rest. Two jewels were safe, though for how long, she did not know. That just left Pim and Bahl. And Luc. Lenna sighed.

Briet obviously intended to leave Lenna no time to change her mind about being cleaned up. The young girl whisked her startled guest into her spacious room, the entirety of which was covered in a downy, cream-colored carpet. Her bed, larger than any girl would ever need outside of a brothel, would probably not have fit in Lenna's kitchen, let alone her bedroom. Delicate perfumes drifted through the decadent space.

The blonde girl rang a bell and, as if by magic, a servant promptly appeared to answer the call. Lenna marveled at the efficiency of the household as she was passed from caretaker to caretaker until, suddenly, she had arrived in another chamber that appeared to be dedicated solely to housing a bathtub the size of her father's clock shop. All the while, Briet flitted alongside Lenna, chirping conversationally about Raif and current trends in Tranum.

"And you're not from Ilya, am I correct?" she asked with what seemed to be genuine interest.

"Yes, I'm from Fallowfields," Lenna responded, somewhat gruffly. A servant snatched her spectacles away and was now tugging on her muddy boots. "Port Hollish, to be exact."

"Port Hollish!" Briet gushed. "I was there not six months ago! The sea is lovely!"

Lenna was actually surprised. She had been expecting Briet to call it "quaint" compared to an epicenter of culture and trade like Tranum. She took her second boot off and happily handed it over to the servant, finally rid of those ghastly things.

"The people in Port Hollish dressed quite normally, I thought," the blonde girl added. "You must have been through a great ordeal to turn into this!"

Ah, there it is, thought Lenna. *Quota fulfilled.* "Well, yes, it hasn't been the best of times... um, excuse me, may I help you?" After Lenna had shrugged off the oversized vest, the servant immediately began to tug at the once-white shirt Lenna was wearing underneath.

Abashed, the servant took a step back, a look of confusion clear on her face. Briet stepped forward and explained, "Ah, Neeran was just helping you undress before assisting you with bathing. She did not mean any offense."

Lenna blushed fiercely. "It's just that I prefer to, most of the time, undress and wash myself." She

LIBRARIAN

was aware that Ilyan culture encouraged public bathing, and it was a powerful bonding experience between family members and friends. In normal circumstances Lenna would have been intrigued but hesitant to try, but to have someone practically rip her clothes off was, given her current mood, a little too much.

"And," she added, "I'm so grubby from everything I've been through, I'd be too embarrassed to have your staff wash the ravages of the street off me."

There was a tangible sigh of relief from both Briet and Neeran. Briet, mollified, resumed gushing, "What a selfless, thoughtful act! For you to understand Ilyan customs so well, it is no wonder that Raif entered the Pact with you! Neeran, while our guest is bathing, let us see what sort of arrangements we can make for proper attire."

Both mistress and servant swept out of the bath chamber, leaving Lenna alone in a vast pearly blueness. She tucked the leather pouch containing the Godjewel in between two towels in an alcove. Peeling off her clothes, which were soiled with dirt and her own sweat, Lenna splashed some hot water from a bucket on herself and then fastidiously attacked her skin with soap that smelled of peppermint. She repeated this process twice and washed her hair three times with some sort of herbal concoction with a label she couldn't read without glasses. Her skin was red and a little raw, and her scalp tingled, but Lenna felt decidedly more human for it all. Now clean, she sank into the opaque waters of the bath, which exuded a unique, pine-like scent that both burned and cooled her aching muscles. Lenna closed her eyes and enjoyed this brief moment of respite she was afforded.

Lenna must have dozed off in the bathtub, head resting gently against the wall. She was called back to the world of the living by Briet, who from the doorway softly spoke her name. Blinking, Lenna gave a mighty yawn and sat upright, still modestly covered by the frothy bubbles of the bath. For a brief time, at least, she had been unfettered from her burdens; it was remarkable, she mused, that a bath had such restorative properties. It was as though not only her skin but her mind as well felt washed clean of a great weight.

"It is time to get you dressed, Lenna," Briet said. "My father and brother are expecting you within the hour."

Lenna paddled over to the side of the tub nearest the door. "This is just an introduction, right?"

"I haven't been told the specifics, as I'm not involved in the business side of the family."

Neither am I, thought Lenna dryly. She took hold of a great mass of her wet mane and wrung some of the excess bathwater out before piling it atop her head in a great, curly mess. Briet, meanwhile, primly stepped over to the alcove where Lenna had placed her towels and like a good hostess, reached for the top two. Before the dripping librarian could call out, Briet lifted both towels and, to Lenna's chagrin, the pouch containing the Godjewel slipped out and fell to the floor with a solid thunk, sounding distinctly heavier than it should have. The blue stone rolled lazily out onto the floor.

"Well, shit," said Lenna coolly. Briet stared at the gem on the floor, clutching the towels to her breast.

"So that is why you have come," she murmured.

"Believe me, it's not by choice."

Briet nodded and placed the towels on the lip of the tub, all the while eying the jewel on the tiled floor of the vast bath chamber. "You might think me rude, but I should not touch it. I will be waiting outside; Neeran has already laid out some underclothes for you." She indicated a pile of fresh clothing folded on a small table off to the left.

"Thank you, Briet."

Cool air blasted Lenna as she rose from the steaming bath, letting the water trickle off her body for a moment before stepping out onto a plush, round mat with fibers that tickled her feet. After quickly toweling herself off and bundling her wild hair into the smaller cloth, Lenna peered down at the eerily humming jewel on the floor. Even without her spectacles, she could make out strangely ordered patterns in its deep cerulean core. The shapes seemed to pulse in a regular rhythm, as though it were alive. It was unnerving, but for better or for worse (most likely the latter), Lenna was attached to this strange artifact.

Grumbling, she scooped up the gem and placed it on the table near the fresh linens. The cotton shift was simple but smelled of clean air and lemon, and was incredibly soft and well-made. Selfishly, Lenna wondered if, when this was all over, she'd be expected to return the garments. Toweling the majority of the moisture from her hair, she placed the used towels in a wicker basket to the side, took the jewel and satchel, and tiptoed back into Briet's room, where her hostess and the servant were poised expectantly.

What happened afterward was definitely an unforgettable experience for Lenna. Her father was of no meager means, the Faircloth business being quite renowned, but between a modest father and a Freewoman mother, Lenna had been raised to do things herself. Here, however, she was treated like a doll: as Neeran dressed, undressed, tightened, and squeezed Lenna, Briet issued orders and suggestions in such rapid Ilyan Lenna started to feel dizzy. At one point in the disastrous encounter, somewhere between the canary yellow chiffon dress with puffed sleeves and a tight-fitting red and black outfit resembling a riding ensemble, Lenna must have said something regarding the selected attire, because suddenly Neeran had disappeared.

"Where did she go?" asked Lenna, eyes still whirling.

"I think you are right, Lenna," Briet replied. "You need something more practical. Something for business, am I correct?"

Lenna was not exactly sure what proper business attire was for a young woman in Ilya, but she imagined that anything had to be better than an ensemble designed for cutting-edge equestrians. True to her words, within moments Neeran returned with yet another neatly folded assortment of clothes, this time, Lenna thankfully noted, in colors far more muted than the previous selection. From what she could tell, the primary fabric was a soft shade of peach, with a tinge of pink, but light enough that it could easily be said to be cream.

"These were my mother's," Briet said softly. "She always dressed very respectably." Lenna, who was currently in front of a full-length, brightly polished mirror trimmed in gold, noticed a familiar glint in the eyes of the girl standing behind her.

"I lost my mother too." She patted Briet on the hand, giving the only comfort she could: acknowledgment and unvoiced understanding.

Briet nodded and gave a meek smile, much more pleasant and natural than her normal, forced expression. "Let us see how this works out, shall we? And then Neeran can attend to your hair."

"Good luck to her for that!"

Some twenty minutes later, after Lenna had successfully changed into what she deemed more appropriate garments, she actually found herself relaxing under the gentle touch of Neeran's fingers in her hair. It had been years since anyone had arranged it for her, and though Lenna hardly knew the older servant, under the subtle caress of her hand as she loosely pinned up Lenna's wavy locks and wove a pale ribbon through some curls, a warm calm embraced her.

Smiling meekly again, Briet placed a carefully manicured hand on Lenna's shoulder. "You must have Ilyan blood in you; you wear the clothes well."

Lenna had the grace to blush as she was led from the comfortable salon chair to stand once more in front of the mirror. Replacing her spectacles, she was surprised by the girl... no, woman who stood before her in the looking glass. She had not worn her hair up in years, due to both laziness and lack of skill; Neeran had arranged it in such an effortless fashion, with wisps and curls floating about and framing her ears, that Lenna looked at once youthful and mature. The ribbon complemented the dress wonderfully, though until today she would have eschewed the very notion of it.

Raif and Briet's mother had a fashionable, yet extremely sensible, taste in clothing. The peach jacket, fitting snugly but too tightly, was waist-length and worn atop a milky-white, ruffled blouse that blossomed just at the neckline. The sleeves flowed out from the half-length sleeves of the jacket, and while it was a bit elaborate for Lenna's normal tastes, the ruffling effect was not so dramatic that it looked comical or restricted movement. She did not at all object to the polished and supple padded leather boots that just barely reached the hemline of her skirt. After adding a leather belt to hold her satchel (and the Godjewel) and tucking her mother's knife into the inner jacket pocket, Lenna felt complete, clean, and respectable.

Briet seemed genuinely relieved when Lenna offered her sincerest thanks, as though she was not used to being in a position to receive gratitude. In her horrid Ilyan, Lenna thanked Neeran as well, and the woman simply smiled and gave a courteous nod before exiting Briet's spacious apartment as quietly as she had entered.

"Now, my father and brother will be expecting you," Briet said. "It is best to not keep them waiting."

Nodding, Lenna took a deep breath and mentally steeled herself to meet the patriarch of what must be one of the wealthiest organizations outside of the Krevlum Empire. Once again the weight of the Godjewel at her thigh was obnoxiously present. Briet seemed to notice her apprehension.

"I am sorry that you are tied to the stone. It is a terrible fate."

"If you don't mind my asking, Briet, how did your family come across one of the Godjewels?"

"It has been passed down in my mother's family for generations," she explained. "And, by rights, should pass to me."

"Should? Why wouldn't it?"

"Since the — what did you call it — Godjewel, yes, has become active again, my father has been very intent on utilizing the opportunities it provides."

So Raif hasn't been completely upfront about the gems, thought Lenna. Father Vandever, then, was obviously looking to increase his political or economic leverage by adding a second Godjewel to his arsenal. If he was interested in gaining that sort of power, it would not be prudent for Lenna to stay here. If she could pull Raif aside, away from his father, and explain the situation more clearly, perhaps she could still obtain his aid in finding Pim and Luc.

A thought suddenly struck Lenna. "Briet, you just said that the Godjewel had 'become active again.' When was the last time it was active, as you say?" As far as Lenna knew, the Godjewels had only recently become active, or else they would have been unearthed and made their presence known years ago, sparing Lenna and her companions from the current debacle.

"It was twelve years ago," she answered.

"Twelve years ago? Surely you'd have been too young to clearly remember it."

"I remember it well enough, Lenna," Briet said. "Because it was the day my mother died."

CHAPTER FOURTEEN

When Lenna entered Master Vandever's private study, she was immediately awestruck. The first thing her eyes shot to was the sky-high bookshelves crammed with ancient and, as an authority on things bookish, Lenna believed rare manuscripts. It was a treasure trove for the librarian, and she longed to reach out and trace her fingers along the spines of the books with a passionate hunger she hadn't felt in days. The fully stocked shelves were of such lofty distraction — Lenna estimated about two stories in height — that she failed to notice the equally stunned expressions decorating the faces of Raif and his father.

It was, of course, because she was dressed as the late Mistress Vandever, and seeing a stranger wearing something that was a reminder of her death must be startling. Raif, standing beside his seated father, had quirked his eyebrows in a peculiar and almost comical half-arch; Master Vandever, a pockmarked, rotund man with a flatly cropped mane of sandy blonde hair, reddened to the color of a ripe apple, his eyes wide. Lenna quickly dropped into what could best be described as a feeble attempt at a curtsy. Being the sudden center of attention left her at a complete loss as to proper etiquette before a well-established family with considerable social standing. Raif's confused expression shifted to one of amusement, and he delicately swerved around his father's ornately carved — and ornately expensive — desk and strode up to Lenna.

"No need for that," he said, placing his hand at Lenna's elbow and urging her back into an upright position. "Father, may I present to you Miss Lenna Faircloth? Lenna, this is my father, and the head of the vast Vandever trading fleet, Klem Vandever."

"How do you do, Miss Faircloth?" asked Master Vandever. Both he and Raif were speaking in Continental, obviously out of courtesy for Lenna. "Please, sit down." He waved one sausage-like hand, studded with rings, in the general direction of two beautifully fashioned wooden chairs designed more for aesthetics than comfort. The odd curvature of the back dug into Lenna's spine, and she wondered if Klem Vandever enjoyed making his guests sit in painful positions. It was probably why Raif was still standing.

Lenna answered amiably, though in light of recent developments, she was not doing very well indeed. There was a strange film over Klem Vandever's voice, almost like an oily residue, that caused Lenna a great degree of unease. Two great dark patches sagged beneath both eyes and gave him the air of one that was either very ill or very sinister. Lenna could not decide which was the case and settled on it probably being a little bit of both. Raif and Briet must have favored their mother in terms of appearance.

"Raif," Klem Vandever continued. "You've done well to bring her here. Leave us."

Both Raif and Lenna blinked. She had not considered the possibility that Raif would be absent for her meeting with his father, and from Raif's demeanor, he was equally surprised. Despite having some command of magic and a devastatingly powerful arcane artifact humming in her leather satchel, Lenna knew she did not want to be alone with the man seated across from her. She became queasy and distant as Raif and his father engaged in a heated, fast-paced debate in Ilyan; though she picked out her name a few times, Lenna could not follow the argument and instead focused on the walls of books, trying to calm her nerves and stomach.

Abruptly, the conversation ended and Lenna turned to watch Raif retreat. She managed to catch his eye, and he mouthed something that sounded like an apology as he left. Lenna resigned herself; she was doing this to find Pim and Luc and sort out this terrible kerfuffle with the Godjewels. She sat back and, with what she hoped was an expression of cool confidence, focused her attention on Raif's father.

"Now," he said, switching back to the Continental tongue. "I know you are a young lady of some intellect, so I do not see much point meandering about the issue at hand or treating you like anything but an informed business partner."

"I appreciate your directness," Lenna said warily.

"It has recently been made known to many interested parties that all three of the long-forgotten 'Godjewels' have been found. I possess one, locked away in a secret place; the Emperor of Krevlum has another and has bonded with it; the last one, which had long been the Blue Crescent Brotherhood's secret, has serendipitously fallen into the hands of a young woman from Port Hollish. I am sure you are aware of the difference in positions."

"The thought might have come to my mind, Master Vandever."

"Then I shall make a proposal. I am well-connected and, more importantly, well-protected here. The gemstone would be safer here under my vigilant eyes," he gestured again, "than in the hands of someone with no reliable defenses. Those with magical talents will always be able to find you, wherever you are, as long as you possess it."

Lenna knew that Klem Vandever's statement was not entirely true. Having a bond with this Godjewel allowed the librarian to feel it tugging away at her core, like a kite tugging at the end of a bit of string. Up until now, however, it had been Lenna's experience that the magical signal flares of the gemstones only struck when a person attempted to harness the power of the artifact. She could not positively sense the location of the other two jewels at the moment.

"Correct me if I'm wrong, Master Vandever, but these parties of tremendous influence — yourself included — are seeking the Godjewels because of their immense potential."

"Yes, that is correct."

"So possessing even two of the gems, let alone all three, would unleash a very potent and probably dangerous force into the world."

Klem Vandever flashed a knowing smile, full of yellowed teeth. "You think I will use these jewels for my own personal gain or worse, to conquer."

Not wanting to dignify the answer with a response, Lenna held her tongue. Klem Vandever heaved a hefty sigh as he pulled himself up from a large seat cushioned with soft, plush material. He wandered over to a bookshelf at random and fingered the spine of a leather-bound volume with his thumb. Lenna cringed, but composed herself before the large man turned around, having tipped the book out into his meaty hand.

"This is the only copy of this document in existence," he explained. "Its subject matter is irrelevant — there is only one, and it is mine." He placed the book lightly on the desk before Lenna, and she found herself resisting the urge to flip through its pages. "My family has been trading for generations and is well respected for it, but it was I who revolutionized the business. My father before me insisted we stick to the old ways of caravans, but I knew steam power — airships and railways — would change things."

Lenna nodded, waiting for the old man's diatribe to end.

"But I still like the acquisition of rare treasures. One of the reasons I joined with my children's mother was because she herself was an object of beauty, and I felt compelled to possess her."

The objectification of his late wife and obsession with material acquisition left Lenna with a peculiar, unpleasant taste in her mouth. "If you'll excuse me for being blunt, Master Vandever, you're saying that you want me to give up the Godjewel because you simply desire to add it to your collection of rare and unique artifacts." Something did not quite make sense to Lenna, and she recalled the subtle hints Briet had mentioned in regard to her father's view on the stone.

"You are astute," Vandever continued. "But I assure you, I can work no magic and cannot manipulate the Godjewels." His hand had fallen to his waist, fiddling with some decorative band sewn to the sash that secured the bulge of his belly. Lenna glanced at it curiously, unfortunately drawing his attention.

"This?" he said, patting the band. "Are you not familiar with the custom?" Vandever scooted a few paces further toward the desk, and Lenna could see that the band was actually a length of plaited hair, with a ribbon sewn through it and then bound to the material of his sash. The hair was a pale blonde, similar to Briet's and Raif's. "This is my wife's hair. When a man takes a wife, it is our tradition to preserve a braid of her hair and keep it with us always, even after her death. It proves our faithfulness."

Lenna had indeed read of the Ilyan marriage bands, though this was the first she had seen in actuality. Slightly squeamish, the librarian wasn't sure she'd be capable of walking around with someone's hair tied to her, marriage or not. The whole process seemed overtly foreign to her, despite her country's close proximity to Ilya.

"I will be honest, Miss Faircloth," Vandever broke out suddenly as he stared off into space. "My wife was... attached to the Godjewel, and something happened to it twelve years ago that took her life. I do not want that for anyone, especially not my daughter, and I imagine your father would want to protect you from such a fate as well." He paused to cough, and then gave a meek smile. "I am not well, and Raif will soon inherit the industry I have spent my life establishing. The jewels will offer him protection politically, financially, and, if need be, militarily. It is no great secret that the Krevlum Empire is pursuing war."

Perhaps Lenna was too quick to judge the elder Vandever; he was, in effect, pursuing the jewels to protect his family and his life's work. That he was ill Lenna had no doubt, but something about the way he phrased his sentences and Raif and Briet's obvious hesitation set the librarian's brain on edge. No one would want two Godjewels to just sit around collecting dust, and Vandever himself had practically admitted to trying to access his gem's power.

"Master Vandever," Lenna asked. "Can Raif use magic? Does he know enough to use the jewels effectively?"

"Yes," said Vandever simply. "There were arrangements made for that."

Lenna frowned. What Vandever was asking was for her to give a young man she barely knew an almost incomprehensible amount of power. Who wouldn't try and use it? Lenna could imagine herself, in different circumstances, wielding the jewels to prevent massacres like Junction from ever happening again. But who knew what kind of spiral that would lead to? Would she, or Raif, seek the third jewel and effectively become a deity? Would that temptation lead to more violence and death?

"I know what you are thinking, Miss Faircloth. And I have heard some of what you have experienced this past week. You are my guest for the evening, so please rest and consider my offer. I would compensate you greatly and guarantee your safety in addition to that of your friends."

Lenna rose to leave, nodding absentmindedly. She did not think giving away the stone was what Gilbert would have wanted, but the prospect of peace returning to her life and of going home, never to be troubled by the matter again, was very tempting. What would Luc or Pim do in her position? Did they have a price? Did Lenna? Vandever coughed and muttered as there was a sudden pounding on the door to his study. Lenna turned toward it, distracted from her overactive brain.

The door swung open and an enviably tall woman with rigid features and long, impossibly straight hair marched in officially; Raif, cursing mightily in Ilyan, followed like a raging storm. The woman was clad in the white military dress of the Empire, and the quality and tailoring of the garment were pristine. Lenna was not very familiar with military uniforms or their markings, but judging from the distinctive fabric and cut of the overcoat, which tightly fit the woman's upper body and blossomed out in a swath of material, and the numerous pins decorating her left breast, whoever this Imperial soldier was, she ranked above any other member of the Imperial service Lenna had thus far encountered.

"I told her you were occupied," Raif snarled. Lenna thought she detected the faintest hint of a smirk on the woman's pale, stark face.

Klem Vandever covered his mouth politely as he cleared his throat. "General Valant, I was not expecting you. Please forgive my son's foul temper and even fouler mouth."

Raif, scowling, scuttled back to a corner by the door and folded his arms. Lenna thought it was a good thing indeed the young trader didn't have access to the Godjewels, or he might use them to explode his father. "My apologies," Raif said unconvincingly.

The general tugged off her unsullied white leather gloves and smiled icily at Vandever. "I apologize for coming without notice," she said in one long, cool breath. "And interrupting." She smiled at Lenna, who felt like she was being stared down by a wolf.

"No concern there," Vandever said. "We were just finishing." He turned to face his younger guest and gestured toward her. "Allow me to present a guest in my house this evening, General Valant."

"Lenna Faircloth, if I am right?" The general smiled and extended an ungloved hand in Lenna's direction. "I am General Khareen Valant."

Shivers running up her spine, Lenna, with as much grace as she could muster, took the extended hand and shook it, the general's hard, cold flesh feeling like a talon. "Pleased to meet you, General Valant."

"Poor child, you are as pale as a sheet. Sit down; we all have much to discuss."

Lenna suddenly found herself seated once again, this time not just with the head of a prestigious family but also with a high-ranking member of the Krevlum Empire's military. What General Valant knew about Lenna — not that there was much to know, in her opinion — was a mystery, but she supposed that it was easy enough for families and nations to uncover details about Lenna's life in Port Hollish. Master Vandever poured some strong-smelling topaz liquor into three glass tumblers and set two before the general and the librarian, taking one for himself. Lenna noted that Vandever had pointedly excluded Raif, who was still sulking in the corner.

The general delicately sipped at the liquor as Vandever swallowed his in one hefty gulp. Lenna, in an effort to be polite, experimentally took the tiniest bit of the liquid into her mouth and immediately regretted it. Though she was no stranger to alcohol, to Lenna Klem Vandever's special concoction blazed like liquid fire. She sputtered and coughed as she swallowed. Vandever and General Valant mercifully looked away as Lenna regained composure.

"So," said Klem Vandever. "What brings such a high dignitary to my door at this hour? I am no ambassador and have no authority in the Ilyan government, so political and military matters are of no interest to me."

Khareen Valant gently rested her crystal tumbler on the desk. "Master Vandever, let's not play games with each other, shall we? I invest enough of my time in political banter; much like you, I find the direct approach much more preferable to pomp and circumstance."

Lenna heard a distinct snort from behind her, and Vandever shot a piercing glare over her head. If General Valant had noticed Raif's behavior, she gave no indication; she simply continued speaking as though there were no interruption. "Let me be frank, Master Vandever, Miss Faircloth." Valant turned her head and acknowledged the librarian with a curt nod.

"Of course," said Vandever.

"It is no secret as to who is in possession of each of the three Godjewels. One is here, locked away by you, Klem Vandever, and one is presumably on your person, Lenna Faircloth. My lord, Emperor Alderic Sonnet, keeps his close to his side at all times. It is a fire that fuels his fervor for advancement; it moves him faster than any steamtrain.

"We had originally thought to parley with the Blue Crescent Brotherhood, but we knew they would never relinquish their gem; to secure it for ourselves would have taken a substantial military presence throughout the entire Continent and more time than my lord wishes to invest. But, thanks to some traitors from the Brotherhood and Master Vandever's penchant for collecting rare and beautiful treasures, we in the Empire are presented with a unique opportunity: both gems are now held by private parties."

"And that is where I intend on keeping mine, General," Vandever said. He poured himself a second glass of Ilyan Hell Water, as Lenna began to think of it, and tossed it back with resolve.

Valant's smile was tight and forced when she turned to look at Lenna. It was the librarian's first opportunity to gain a proper look at the general's face. Her skin was taut, as though it was being pulled back from her face, giving her a constantly pinched, almost painful expression; still, to wax poetical, Lenna would definitely describe the complexion as alabaster and flawless. But it was Khareen Valant's eyes that paralyzed Lenna: they were two whorls of darkness, midnight eyes that drew you in and never let you escape.

Hell Water seemed like a more enjoyable experience, so Lenna, breaking her gaze, hastily took a larger-than-anticipated swig from the tumbler. Though the liquid burned her throat and left her stomach a painfully warm cauldron, she managed to get a fair amount of the alcohol down without gagging. Apparently the key to drinking this beverage was to have an intimidating, downright creepy woman with bottomless pits for eyes stare at you.

"What about you, Lenna?" Valant asked flatly. "Do you plan on maintaining possession of that heavy blue stone you carry? It's quite a burden for someone not properly trained."

Lenna polished off the last of her fiery drink, feeling its flame color her cheeks. She allowed her liquid courage to choose her words for her. "It's true that I never asked for this. Half of me resents Gilbert for getting me into this situation at all, and the other half, having seen what people are willing to do for these things and knowing Gilbert was ready to die for it, won't let me just give it away." And certainly not to an ever-growing militaristic nation like the Krevlum Empire. Lenna shuddered as she recalled the massacre at Junction.

"I see," Valant replied. "You must realize that I, unlike Master Vandever, am at least telling you the truth. Give up the jewel willingly or we will hunt you down and take it; nowhere will you be safe from the Empire's all-reaching arms. You know we already maintain a presence in Fallowfields; you've seen what destruction our magical technology can bring. He," she cocked her head toward Vandever, "wants the Godjewel just as much, and do not for one second think he won't resort to hasty, dirtier means if he thinks you will not cooperate."

Valant, in Lenna's mind, did have something of a point, though Lenna sensed some kind of important information was being held back and said "point" was not a particularly pleasant one. It was highly strange that two powerful entities — three, if you counted the Brotherhood — would attempt to parley with her, negotiate the gem away, rather than just take it by force. Lenna was, after all, nothing more than a librarian, and though her command of magic had increased over the past few days, she had by no means mastered the Godjewel and doubted she would be able to put up much of a fight. Certainly not against the resources behind the Empire and Klem Vandever's trading company.

Could it have to do with what Jaice and Sebastien described as the bond between Lenna and the jewel? Though she had been chased, no one had attempted to take the jewel from Lenna by force. The only time it had been out of her possession since Gilbert died was when Luc took it, and even then, it appeared as though he couldn't use the Godjewel correctly, and Lenna had still felt its presence long after Luc had left.

"You need me to give up the gem willingly, don't you?" she asked.

Both Vandever and Khareen Valant looked at each other before the general turned back to Lenna. "'Need' is not quite the word I would use. We would... prefer you parted with it willingly."

"Care to tell me why?"

A silence fell over the room so complete that all Lenna could hear was a slight buzzing from the vibrations of the Godjewel at her side. The general's lips were pursed, as though she had bitten into something distasteful but was too polite to comment; Master Vandever was thoroughly occupied in examining the emptiness of his tumbler. Raif coughed loudly and stepped forward.

"It's because it's bonded to you, Lenna. If they take it by force, they won't be able to use it to its full potential." Klem Vandever barked an order at his son in Ilyan and Raif, red-faced, stepped back, but only by a pace or two.

Lenna's mind processed this, but something was still lacking. She could feel the fiery alcohol encouraging her to press on. "Not that this is an option I'd like to explore, but why not just kill me from the get-go?"

To everyone's surprise, General Valant tossed back her head and let out a clipped gurgle of laughter. Her hair fell back and exposed a gnarled, scar-encrusted lump where the general's left ear had once been. Lenna tried desperately not to stare. Regaining her composure, and seemingly oblivious to Lenna's startled gaze, the general flipped her hair back over her shoulder with one hand.

"Killing you would be equally problematic. If we decided to have you murdered, it would take some time to erase the remnants of your bond because it would not be a clean separation. Imagine moving into a widower's house and finding his dead wife's furniture and clothing everywhere." Lenna thought she detected a faint smirk on the general's lips as Valant took in the librarian's attire.

The knuckles on Vandever's hand whitened as he gripped the crystal tightly. Having a widowed father too, Lenna couldn't help feeling a pang of sympathy for the man, despite her distrust of him. Valant was calculating each remark to have the maximum impact on her given target.

"Not to harp on the issue of me dying, but if you're going to kill me anyway if I refuse, why not just get it over with and start the cleansing process? Unless there's something you aren't telling me."

"I never said we'd kill you," the general responded calmly. "I said we'd hunt you down. Torture you, have you raped; perhaps kill a loved one or two — think of it as our way of encouraging you to give up the Godjewel. I'm not against that method, but I like to think of myself as quite an efficient individual. You handing over the gem is the quickest way; torturing you will be slow and painful. If you happen to die from it, well, we'll deal with it then."

Another silence fell over the room. General Valant took this as an invitation to continue. She cocked her head to one side. "Do not expect different treatment from other interested parties, Miss Faircloth. Particularly the Brotherhood: I believe you have firsthand experience of the methods they employ against those they perceive as enemies."

"You are safe here," Klem Vandever interrupted.

General Valant stood up as a lower-ranking soldier raced through the study's door and formally saluted her. She excused herself and went out into the hall to speak with the messenger in private. Lenna strained to hear, but Raif had swooped down like a bird of prey into the general's newly vacated chair and glared at his father.

"I don't like this," he said accusingly at his father. "Allowing the Empire to parley! And threaten a guest in our house!"

Having poured three more glasses of the violent liquor, this time including one for Raif, Klem Vandever sat down in his plush chair. By now, Lenna's back was aching, though through the wondrous effects of the alcohol, which was growing more palatable by the minute, she found that she did not care as much. Her head was swimming and overtaxed. It was almost comical that a timid shrew of a librarian was now a crux in an international power play for a magical gem.

"The Krevlum Empire is too powerful to ignore," Vandever said, gesticulating with his glass. "We do well to stay on their good side. You know they have designs to move in on Ilya and Fallowfields."

"They're just going to come after our jewel as well, you know," Raif said. "Becoming the Emperor's best friend wouldn't stop them."

"That is why Lenna is so important. Lenna, you mustn't believe what General Valant has told you. I would not have you harmed under any circumstance."

Lenna was fairly certain she couldn't trust a bunny rabbit these days, yet here she was, calmly drinking some potent spirit with a man who might possibly have her killed for possessing a stupid gemstone. At least, Lenna thought gruesomely, Valant had been upfront about the torture, rape, and murder; at least Lenna knew what to expect.

Within moments, General Valant swept back into Vandever's study, her straight hair a wave of luster behind her. Her schooled expression gave little insight as to whether the message she received contained good news or bad. Where Lenna was concerned, good news for the Empire more than likely meant bad news for her.

"My apologies for the sudden interruption, but it appears I'm needed on a pressing matter. Some of my soldiers apparently captured one of the Brotherhood traitors a few hours ago, thinking he might be in possession of the Godjewel."

"Luc!" Lenna exclaimed, then inwardly cursed herself. Alcohol always did loosen her tongue.

"Is that his name? Luc?" Valant smiled falsely. "Well, Miss Faircloth, it's a pity he wasn't in possession of the jewel; we might have been able to make a deal with him."

"What will you do with him?"

The general shrugged. "I suppose we'll just send him back to the Brotherhood for execution. It would be very diplomatic of us. In any case, Miss Faircloth, consider our offer. I will find you again in the morning. I hope you choose the correct side with which to align yourself. Master Vandever, we can discuss our options another time."

Giving Master Vandever a terse nod and completely ignoring Lenna and Raif, the general and her messenger simply walked out of the study, presumably to show themselves out. Beside her, Lenna could feel Raif seething with bottled rage. Vandever sat in silence. If the Empire had Luc, would they really just send him back to Crescent Island? He would surely be executed. Lenna wondered where Sebastien was, and if he would do anything for his fellow rogue.

"Miss Faircloth," Vandever said, startling Lenna. "I know that there must be a great deal on your mind. Please rest here for the night. I make the Pact with you that no harm shall come to you while you are my guest."

Both body and brain numb, Lenna looked at Raif, who nodded as if to confirm his father's statement. She supposed she had little choice: outside would be the bustling city of Tranum, Imperial soldiers, and probably agents from the Brotherhood; right now, in the house of Klem Vandever, she had the protection of two Godjewels and friends in Raif and Briet. Who was she to find Luc?

"Yes, thank you, Master Vandever. I think I will accept your hospitality for tonight." Lenna stood up, immediately followed by Raif.

"I'll take you to your room," he offered.

"Have Briet take care of that, Raif. You and I are going to have a talk about your behavior."

"I'll escort her to Briet, then," Raif grimaced.

As Lenna turned and started to follow Raif out of the door to the study, Klem Vandever called to her.

"Lenna," he said, "you must not trust the Empire."

What about you? she thought, and followed Raif up the grand staircase without responding.

Lenna let out a large sigh as she fell backwards onto the bed, her hair, loose now, spread like a fan across the fluffy white pillow of one of Vandever estate's many guest rooms. As with the bath, Briet proved herself an excellent hostess. The room was not nearly as spacious as the family's apartment, but still, it was by far the most extravagant room in which Lenna had ever slept. Either Briet or her late mother had gone to great lengths to ensure their guests possessed a certain level of comfort, and it was evident in the lush carpet that covered the entire room, and the deep satiny cloud of a bed. The apartment radiated calm.

It was a paradise of slumber, or it would be, if Lenna did not have all of the Continent's political powers weighing down her brain like a stack of encyclopedias. She dug her knuckles into her temples, twisting them as though the action would exorcise all her worries. At her side rested the Godjewel, its soft blue light casting strange shapes against the pale walls of the bedroom.

Lenna shifted, propping her head up on one elbow. Glancing down at the flickering gemstone, she wondered if this was what a nervous mother would do: lie awake, looking at a treasure too valuable and improbable to be entrusted to someone so irresponsible. Motherhood, assuming Lenna survived the terrible mess her life had become, would certainly not be in her future any time soon.

Despair was beginning to drag the librarian down. Lenna wondered where Pim was and if Bahl had survived that terrible blast of magic. And Luc, where would the Empire be holding him? Was he safe? Since they did not have a politically established military presence in Tranum, or even in Ilya at all, Lenna reckoned that the soldiers likely used various hideouts and safe houses to conduct their "business." At this rate, Lenna would never be able to fulfill her promise to Gilbert to watch over his lover.

"But did such a promise really deserve honoring?" she said out loud, then immediately hated herself for it, despite Luc's treachery. And though it was almost certain that Gilbert had withheld information concerning the Godjewels, Lenna had to believe he meant no malice. He had died to protect her; she had no right to question his loyalties. Yet here she was, doubting away and lying uselessly on a cloud-like bed while her friends could be lost, or hurt, or worse.

She sat up in bed and looked down at the jewel once more. Back in Brest, Gilbert had attempted to use the stone's power to amplify some kind of communication spell to contact Sebastien. It had led to the group's discovery, but as everyone had told Lenna in no uncertain terms, her location was already well-known. The silver chain bound to the gem was warm to the touch, something to which Lenna had yet to become accustomed, and she ran one finger around the sphere's surface.

Uncertain of how to begin, Lenna slid her fingers up the dome of the gem and let her eyelids slowly shut. Underneath the gentle pressure of her touch, something inside the Godjewel responded, and though Lenna could not physically see it, with her mind's eye she envisioned tendrils of energy intertwining and spiraling beneath her fingers, spinning into a tiny cyclone of power. Her other hand instinctively clenched a fist against her left breast, her heart beating in rhythm to the pulsing of the gem. Synchronized, Lenna dipped her consciousness into that vast pool of life that she called her magic.

She called up an image of the cocksure man, with his dangling earring and exquisitely tailored clothes, whom she had met on the steamtrain to Tranum.

She let that thought and some of her magic float out through her fingers and drift into the whirling vortex within the Godjewel. With her added power, the tornado grew, stronger yet still controlled, and without opening her eyes Lenna saw each tendril arcing and whirling as part of a giant, ever-reaching network. On each line were hundreds — no, thousands — of pinpricks of light.

These are people's minds, she thought. The energy within the jewel increased and funneled outward, and more and more of those sparkling stars of consciousness appeared. Lenna's concentration wavered and a bead of cold sweat dropped from her forehead. Her mind was quickly overwhelmed in her search for Sebastien, and the vortex of magic funneled around her and carried her into the vast reaches of the astral world. There were too many minds for her to discern the one she sought, and she was lost.

And then, in the eye of this tempest she had created, a presence brushed up against her own. A familiar scent enveloped Lenna, like a mother's embrace, and gave her mind a gentle nudge in the right direction. Her focus restored, Lenna channeled the growing energy and propelled her will toward that one particular point of light on one particular string interlaced in a vast web of collective thought.

Sebastien, she thought, and she was there, their minds united. In every way she felt him present in her; there was no magical block between them, not like the one she experienced on the steamtrain. He was initially surprised, but then welcoming; his particular scent — rich with orange and clove — mingled with her own, filling the room around her. Their union was short but powerful, and in a rush of images and feeling Lenna relayed her grief for Gilbert and desire for Sebastien to find a way to save Luc.

Sebastien accepted this burden, and it felt like some of the heavy weight Lenna was shouldering had been lifted away. He gently separated their minds, urging Lenna back into reality, and after a moment the storm raging inside the Godjewel quieted, leaving Lenna, covered in sweat and panting, keenly alone in the room.

She flopped backwards onto the bed, exhausted but highly satisfied. Drowsiness quickly overcame her, taking Lenna to the twilight place between waking and slumber, where dreams and reality are one. Two steps more, she thought, and the sweet oblivion of sleep would take her where Empires and Brotherhoods and Vandevers couldn't disturb her.

"Lenna," a voice called softly, accompanied by three quick raps at the door. "Lenna!"

Groaning, Lenna sat upright once again and felt about for her spectacles, only to realize she had left them on. She slipped off the bed and into the dressing gown Briet had provided, her bare feet noiseless as she shuffled across the carpet. Half-asleep and euphoric from magic, she opened the

BRIAN FENCE

door without much thought to a jittery, anxious Raif.

"Lenna, what was that working you just did?" He had not even changed his clothes yet.

"I was trying a communication spell of sorts, using the stone," she replied with a yawn. "I think it worked."

"I'll bet it did! Half the city probably felt that. Really tingly stuff, Lenna." Raif walked past her into her room, ignoring any sense of propriety. He started pacing back and forth at the foot of her bed.

Unconcerned, Lenna shut the guest room door and went and sat back down on the bed, scooping up the Godjewel and dropping it into the dressing gown's pocket in the process. "Um, Raif?"

Raif stopped pacing and looked at her, wringing his hands. "Oh, right. Sorry — I've had lots of coffee. Lenna, I've found your friend, the Freewoman."

"Pim!" Lenna's focus immediately sharpened. "Where is she?"

"The incident in the city earlier today, when someone magically attacked a foreigner — it's on everybody's lips. It wasn't hard to track down the girl who took the injured man to a clinic."

"So she's at a clinic? I've got to go to her. And is the injured man all right?"

Raif spread his hands out, palms up. "I didn't get any information about the man, but your friend isn't at the clinic any longer. According to my network —

which is pretty accurate, if you don't mind me saying — the Freewoman went out making inquiries all over Tranum, looking for her Freewoman companion and an apprentice from the Brotherhood. It seems she was less than tactful about it."

"That's Pim, all right. Subtlety isn't a quality she's known for."

"Lenna, you don't understand. The Empire was on alert for a Freewoman fitting your description and the apprentice you call Luc. They've got her, and I'm sure you're aware they're not too gentle with uncooperative prisoners."

Stony resolve flooded Lenna. First Luc, and now Pim — and all because of Lenna and the stupid rock in her pocket and her own lack of resolve. "What can we do?"

Raif's face shifted to one of concern. "Valant will expect your answer in the morning, and unless it's favorable I don't think you — or your friends — will stand much of a chance."

"Do you know where they are?"

He nodded.

"Will you come with me?" she asked.

Raif looked at Lenna funnily for a moment, and then his mouth widened into a grin. "Of course. I wouldn't miss out on the fun."

"Don't worry; I've called in some reinforcements." Lenna hurriedly began preparing her rucksack, the contents of which she had unceremoniously dumped out onto a mirrored vanity earlier in the evening.

"You know," Raif said, leaning against a corner post of the guest bed. "I didn't peg you for an adventurer."

"I'm not," she retorted over her shoulder. "I'm just a tired, cranky librarian." Lenna gathered up a bundle of clothes and turned to look at Raif. "Mind letting me get dressed?"

Laughing, Raif headed toward the door. "Wear what you wore earlier," he said with a wave of his hand. "And remind me never to make you angry."

As the door closed, Lenna threw off the dressing gown and took a deep breath. *Keep being angry,* she told herself, *so no one knows how desperately scared you finally are.*

CHAPTER FIFTEEN

Tranum at night was a different city. Bustling crowds of merchants were replaced with much smaller groups of inebriated Ilyans, out to enjoy the city's numerous eateries, smokehouses, and drinking holes. Ilya, and Tranum in particular, was famous for its superior, well-aged wines, and local culture encouraged a healthy consumption of it; in the city, there were unique and delicious vintages sold at half what they would cost in other trading towns, including Port Hollish. Lenna secretly regretted not being able to join in the festivities.

Raif kept up a brisk pace, though not conspicuous enough to draw attention. He insisted to Lenna that it would be far easier and faster to take the main thoroughfares and blend in with the young crowds; once the sun fell in Tranum, its intricate web of alleys and hidden pathways in some

349

places would fill with what Raif described as "spies, pickled thugs, cutpurse hookers, and hooker cutpurses." A couple such as themselves guaranteed unsolicited advances if they wandered into the wrong section of the city.

For her part, Lenna was keen to allow Raif to lead her from group to group, her arm casually resting in the crook of his. He chatted amiably and loudly, acting the role of a cocky young lover out to impress his lady, though Lenna seldom offered any more than a nod or forced tinkle of laughter where appropriate. Her mind was on Pim, and though she played along with Raif's guise, inside Lenna was silently seething. *Stay angry*, she thought.

The clinking of wine glasses, the sweet scent of opium, and the tumultuous laughter from numerous establishments floated on the air around them, dressing Lenna and Raif like characters in the nonsensical romantic pamphlets Lenna abhorred.

Before long the pair closed in on the airship port, where Lenna had met Raif earlier in the day. After darkness fell, save for a few night arrivals and departures of airships, the wide expanse was a lonely space devoid of its trading stalls and merchandise. Barren of people and trade, the port and its outlying environs were easily discerned and made Lenna feel tiny and insignificant.

Around the airfield, the Landing housed numerous warehouses, pubs, and a few of the cheaper inns and brothels, creating a barricade between the city and its hub of transport. Each of the main avenues, and many smaller ones, led to the port and descended down into its vast expanse via large ramps and stairways. It reminded Lenna of a giant arena.

"We're going to make a quick stop," Raif said, and he veered off to the left toward a building at the street corner, overlooking the airfield.

The establishment was of newer construction, built in pine and stone, and was seemingly well-kept in contrast to the ramshackle appearance of some of the neighboring structures. Though the windows were heavily curtained with a dense, crimson material, a soft glow peeking out from the folds of cloth showed that the business was lively with patrons. Lenna's gaze fell on the sign above the door, which bore in both Ilyan and Continental script the words "Midnight Rose."

"Midnight Rose?" she asked. "Are you taking me to a brothel?"

Raif grinned. "I'm taking you for a glass of wine at a very respectable tavern run by a member of my family."

"Is that so?"

"Well, it also happens to be a brothel."

Sighing with impatience, Lenna allowed herself to be escorted through a beaded curtain that draped the frame of the open doorway. On this, her first and hopefully last experience in a whorehouse, the librarian was impressed by the luxurious decor. The main room was a celebration of everything red, from the roses crowning the intimate candlelit tables to the cushions and the countertop of the bar itself. Lenna, naturally curious, was immediately drawn to the counter; after all, she had never seen *red* marble before, and she could only speculate at its cost. The business at this brothel must be lucrative indeed.

Her ponytailed companion led Lenna to a tall, massive-bosomed woman who wore powders and paints so decorously it seemed a crime not to pause to admire her features. As was Ilyan fashion, the lady wore her pale, silvery hair up, though it was styled much more elaborately than Lenna had managed in her hurried preparation. Two curled tendrils gently rested on her ample breasts, which, to the librarian, seemed barely restrained by her corseted silk dress. Garbed in crimson, she was as much a part of the brothel's decor as were the other accoutrements; as Raif introduced her, Lenna realized that the woman strongly gave off the scent of the establishment's namesake.

"Lenna Faircloth," Raif said. "This is my aunt, Ygonne. She is the matron of the Midnight Rose."

Ygonne extended a gloved hand in a most ladylike fashion, palm down, and Lenna shook it sheepishly. The matron exuded a kind of elegance that made being a high-class hooker seem like the only suitable position for a proper lady of society. Luckily, the fiercely independent and academic part of Lenna quickly choked the life out of that thought.

"Pleased to meet you, Miss Faircloth," Ygonne said in an almost theatrical voice. "Raif, the usual?"

"Please."

"Coming right up, then."

Raif escorted a dazzled Lenna across the common room floor to a table in the far back corner, away from other patrons. Not that it would matter, Lenna considered as she took her seat, as most of the men and women were occupied with the starkly beautiful employees of the Midnight Rose, entranced by conversation or by promises of ecstasy beyond the curtained doorway that led to more private places. By the time Raif and Lenna had settled, Ygonne had reappeared with two crystal wine glasses, each filled with a deep, luscious red wine. Lenna inhaled its scent and her tongue began to twitch with excitement as scents of chocolate and plum tickled her nose.

"You've been away for some time, Raif," said the matron, fondly caressing his cheek. "You must make more time for your aunt."

"I'm afraid today's visit will be short as well, Auntie." He said something else quickly in Ilyan, and Ygonne subtly quirked her head. She leaned forward, bosom precarious, and whispered a string of quick, liquid syllables into Raif's ear. He nodded in response.

"Well then," Ygonne said, assuming her normal tone, "for the few moments you have with us, please, enjoy your repose." She turned and addressed Lenna, who was still absorbed in smelling her wine. "And you, Miss Faircloth? Raif informs me you won't be here long, but shall I send someone over to help you relax? A boy? A girl? One of each, perhaps?"

For an instant Lenna's face matched the decor of the Midnight Rose, though she hoped the dim light provided by candles did not betray it. "Um, no. I'm fine, thank you."

Ygonne gave a faint laugh, like a string of chords on a harp, and sauntered off into the shadows to attend to other patrons. Lenna and Raif, for the moment, were alone. In a whorehouse. The librarian shook her head and resumed agitating her wine, letting the blood-red liquid slosh and aerate against the glass. Its color caught the flame of the candle and cast delicious vermilion shadows across the small table. Despite the location and the gravity of the situation, Lenna knew she would be able to relax here, and the wine, upon tasting, was indeed superb.

"So," said Lenna. "Your aunt runs a brothel."

Raif took a long, indulgent sip of his wine. "That's just her cover, though she does enjoy playing up the role a bit. Like I said, my family has quite the information network; it stretches across Ilya and beyond."

"Spies, you mean?"

Raif's face darkened for an instant, indignant. "Yes, I suppose you could use that word, although it has extremely negative undertones. My family," he paused for another sip of wine, "is primarily involved in the occupation of trading. Some deal in goods; others deal in information. Ygonne is affiliated with the latter: I'm sure you can understand how someone in her — position, shall we say — would have access to all sorts of interesting tidbits."

"Which version of the family business are you more involved in, then?" Lenna asked.

"Mostly the import/export side; I like to fly. One of those airships out there is mine, actually."

"You're a captain?"

"The best captain and pilot in Ilya."

"That would make you the best captain and pilot in the world," she commented dryly. Raif merely nodded in response. Lenna rolled her eyes. "So what now?"

"I didn't just stop here for a drink, Lenna," Raif said, and let his voice drop low. "Ygonne is the one who got me the information on where your friend is being kept."

That made sense to Lenna; the Krevlum Empire's military presence in Tranum practically guaranteed that any Imperial soldiers performing covert operations in Ilya were paid well enough to frequent a high-quality establishment such as the Midnight Rose. Lenna wasn't naive enough to underestimate the value of pillow talk. Still, tapping her feet rapidly under the table, she could barely contain her impatience. Lenna wanted, for once, to skip the planning and leap into action.

Suddenly a hand gently placed itself on her knee, and Lenna yelped in surprise, drawing a few glances and giggles from other patrons. "Relax, Lenna. Consider this our base of operations, where we decide our strategy. As much as it's not like me to say this, we really can't afford to just go charging in on this one." He slipped his hand away.

"So what is the plan, exactly?" Lenna said gruffly.

"Ygonne's just given me the exact location of the warehouse General Valant has secured, and it's not too far from here. Since Tranum severely limits, or at least tries to limit, the Empire's military presence within the city, Valant doesn't have a particularly large number of men with her, but still more than we do. There are two squads of six, tasked to various assignments. Valant herself comes and goes, but from what we saw earlier this evening, I imagine she's still there with at least some of the soldiers."

Lenna nodded.

"I wish I could have enlisted some of my father's men or my entire crew, but we need to keep this as quiet as possible, and frankly, I'm not sure Father would approve. The best Ygonne and I could come up with is something of a distraction." He nodded toward a table full of several airship crewmen who were being doted upon by the bar's matron and a few of her lovelier employees. "Anyway, with just the two of us," he continued, "I'm not sure how easily we'll be able to take them out. I'm a pretty competent magician, but I don't have any idea how well the soldiers are trained. And Valant has quite the reputation. Who is this guy you've got coming to help?"

Caught in mid-sip, Lenna choked a bit on her wine. "How did you know it was a man?"

"Aha," Raif said. "So it *is* a guy. You didn't say you had a boyfriend, you cheeky thing."

"He is most certainly, definitely not, and never will be, a partner of mine," Lenna replied firmly.

"Hmm." Raif traced one finger around the rim of his wineglass, and a squeak rang out from the fine glasswork. "Judging by the way you blush, I'm not so sure you're telling me the truth." He ceased fiddling with his glass and took a long, heavy drink from it, sighing when he finished. "Good vintage, this is. So tell me who's coming."

"His name is Sebastien. He's a member of the Brotherhood, and the one who organized the smuggling of the Godjewel off the island. He was Gil... Gilbert's teacher."

Raif raised a blonde eyebrow. "Gilbert?"

A wine of such excellent vintage, as Raif had pointed out, should not be wasted, thought Lenna, so she allowed herself the luxury of letting the velvety liquid caress her tongue before sliding smoothly down her throat. She settled the glass back on the table and looked at the smiling Ilyan squarely.

"Considering all the information your family gathers, and the information the Empire apparently has access to, do I really need to be answering these questions? I'm sure you already know who Gilbert is. Was."

"I do," Raif admitted. "But I wanted to hear who he was to you. He's the reason you're involved in all of this, after all."

"Gilbert was a friend from my childhood; we both were raised in Port Hollish. We spent a lot of time together, he and I. His family life wasn't exactly a happy one, looking back, so he'd spend time at our house as often as not."

Now that Lenna thought back to those years so long ago, she realized just how miserable Gil had been at home. Master Hovey, his father, was a shipwright who had been wounded and turned to drink; Gilbert's mother, who was a tailor by trade but had a substantial income due to an inheritance, had kept the home together through sheer force of will. Unfortunately, Mistress Hovey in her misery grew stony and silent, and young Gilbert was mostly left to his own devices. As he grew older, the boy started spending more and more time at the Faircloth residence. Bitterly, Lenna realized that escaping to the Blue Crescent Brotherhood was probably one of the best decisions Gilbert had ever made.

"Did you love him?"

Lenna considered Raif's question for a moment. "No, I don't think so. Our relationship was unique. It wasn't friendship, and it wasn't family. There was love, but I don't think it was the kind of love to which you're referring." She took another sip of her wine, this time barely able to taste it, and wondered with a strangely relaxed urgency when this plan would go into action. She didn't think she'd be much help exhausted and drunk.

"Good to hear," Raif said cheekily, his smile highlighting his angular Ilyan features. "I'd hate to have to compete with anyone, especially a ghost. Those are the worst."

"I beg your pardon?" Lenna asked, incredulous.

"Well, why else would someone as delightfully handsome and gifted as I put his neck — and future inheritance, I might add — on the line if not for the heart of a lovely lady?"

"I would roll my eyes," Lenna announced loudly, "but to be frank, I've done enough of that over the past few days." In one tremendous swallow, the librarian polished off her wine and replaced the glass on the table with a bit more force than necessary. "I have no interest in cheap banter, idle flirtations, and little girls' romantic adventures. I want to save my friend, save my friend's friend, and get this jewel the hell out of my life."

Raif finished off his glass of wine as well, albeit a bit more gracefully than Lenna. Strangely serious, he did not even bother to toss his ponytail back over his shoulder; instead, he rested one hand on the table and looked Lenna straight in the eyes. To the librarian, it was a very unique, penetrating glance. She'd been the recipient of some strange staring lately, but Raif's eyes were particularly piercing, filled with a depth Lenna didn't quite understand.

After a long minute, Raif nodded. "Good. I'd hate to see you go into this like some naive little schoolgirl with her hair still in braids. Now that I know you're in the proper mindset, it's time to get on with the plan."

Fifteen minutes later, Lenna found herself huddled up against the corner of a yellowed, stony warehouse, shivering in the night air. Raif insisted, quite reasonably, that the two of them avoid any of the four gaslights that illuminated the entrance. Stealth, of course, would be their greatest ally, thought Lenna, and despite a little fear, which she did her best to conceal, the two partners crept into the darkness behind Valant's base of operations.

"Good," said Raif, his voice hushed.

"This darkness should provide us some decent cover, I imagine," Lenna agreed.

"Cover?" Raif asked. "I just didn't want any passersby to think you were a whore."

Lenna resisted the urge to slap him. He grinned and put one finger to his lips, asking for silence. The Ilyan knelt down on the dusty alleyway, despite his fine livery, and cupped his hands as though he were about to drink water from a stream. A slow trickle of words rose from his barely moving lips, and in the cup of his hands a small flickering mote danced about like faerie fire. Lenna tactfully stood in front, masking any faint illumination that might attract unwanted attention.

After a moment, Raif rose to his feet and addressed Lenna in a harried whisper. "We're in luck," he said. "Sort of."

"What does that mean?" Lenna hissed in reply. "And what kind of magic was that?"

"Ilyan spell — we don't like to let many foreigners know about it. Not even the Brotherhood has any knowledge of it. It can detect the body heat of living things, so it gives us a general idea of how many are in the area."

Lenna was surprised; the Ilyans must be quite good at keeping secrets, for the Brotherhood was most efficient at fishing out any and all magical lore, however useless or obscure it might be. This spell, she figured, would fetch a hefty reward for whoever gave its secret to the Brotherhood. She wondered if Raif would teach her, though she intended to have no contact with the Brotherhood whatsoever.

"Well," said Raif, "I'm getting a total count of six people in there."

"What does that mean?"

Raif took a moment to phrase his answer, making Lenna wish she could read his expression in the dark. "Remember how many soldiers I said Valant had under her command?"

"The wine wasn't that strong, Raif," she replied quickly, before realizing what the numbers suggested. "If there are only six people there, it's got to be Valant, Luc, Pim, and three soldiers..." Lenna paused; she did not want to say that, if Raif's spell detected body heat, it could also mean there the occupants of the warehouse could easily be Valant, five soldiers, and two corpses.

Her companion seemed to sense Lenna's fear. "I doubt they'd do anything to your friends, Lenna. At least not yet. They want you to give up the stone freely, and hurting your friends isn't going to make you any more obliging."

Lenna nodded, mostly to herself. She already had little love for the Krevlum Empire, especially after Junction, and if what Valant and Master Vandever had said was true, all parties would protect Lenna in the hope that she would willingly give up the Godjewel and end the damn bond she shared with it.

"What about this Sebastien fellow of yours? Can you contact him again?" asked Raif.

Shaking her head, Lenna said, "I don't think so. We know how noticeable it was when I tried earlier. We'll just have to hope he comes."

Raif shrugged as though he hadn't much faith in Sebastien to begin with. Overhead, the clouds began to part, letting a pale silver ray of moonlight creep up the alley and dimly illuminate the hidden pair. Off in the distance, Lenna could hear a crowd of raucous young men singing, in Ilyan, what she took to be drinking songs. She glanced at Raif curiously.

"And so the countdown begins," he said cryptically. Lenna jabbed him in the ribs. "Even with a bit of wine in you, you are absolutely no fun to tease," Raif mused. "Here comes our distraction; some of my men are going to get into a bit of a drunken scuffle in front of the warehouse. I may not be able to provide us with a platoon, but it's better than nothing." He flashed a smile.

With a somewhat unwelcome familiarity, Raif placed his hands on Lenna's cloaked shoulders and urged her to face the bland stone wall of the warehouse. Annoyed but resigned, she kept herself from elbowing Raif in the side as one of his hands, placed gently under her chin, tilted Lenna's head up to face a higher part of the wall. Set a few feet above their heads was a screened window, with three formidable-looking metal bars spaced evenly across its frame.

"So your big plan is to cause a distraction, blow out the window, and then we hoist each other up?" Lenna wondered wildly if the moonlight revealed the sheer incredulity registering on her face.

Raif's smug self-assurance made the exhausted librarian feel extremely violent at the moment, and she secretly hoped her partner in crime would let her be the one to take a crack at the bars. Still, Lenna had no other options, and if anything, the past few days had — albeit forcefully — helped her embrace a more cavalier attitude. Handling the Godjewels, it seemed, required a certain amount of bravado the librarian hadn't realized she had.

The noisy drunkards passed the dimly lit alleyway, a hodgepodge of airship crewmen in garments ranging from flashy Ilyan evening suits to simple cotton breeches and shirts. Deliberately slurring, or perhaps not so deliberately, Raif's rabble began another round of Ilyan drinking songs, and for once Lenna was content her command of spoken Ilyan was not strong enough to parse the lyrics.

Raif nudged Lenna to draw her attention and then silently began counting down with his fingers. Three, two, one: the boisterous men's singing exploded into a series of what sounded like wild accusations — Lenna definitely picked up a few choice Ilyan swear words — and the sound of bottles smashing against the stone of the warehouse.

"My father would not be pleased with how much coin I paid to get them that thoroughly drunk," Raif chuckled. "Now, it should only be a minute or two, so get ready. Do you know how to shield yourself?"

"Somewhat," Lenna admitted. "But I'm not entirely confident."

"I'll try to cover you as best I can, but fall back if you have to. And here we go!"

Lenna watched as the men at the end of the alley began to aggressively shove each other about, and one or two collided into the wall. Despite their apparent intoxication, they were still capable of following their pilot's orders: although it appeared like natural progression, the men were very deliberately wobbling away from the alley and toward the main entrance of the warehouse. The sound of a heavy door suddenly sliding open and slamming against its frame caused Lenna to jump, and the drunken brawlers' voices were joined by two harsh, commanding ones in strangely accented Ilyan.

Just as the noise reached its crescendo, the soldiers obviously engaged by voracious squabblers, Raif raised his hand toward the barred window above him and sent out a wave of force that twisted and pushed apart the sturdy metal poles and tore through the screen. Had the night been silent, it would most certainly have been noticed, but Raif's drunken sailors muffled the noise. Flabbergasted that a plan so ridiculously melodramatic could ever succeed, Lenna watched as Raif deftly jumped up, grasped the window ledge with both hands and pulled himself through its opening.

"You needn't stand there gaping," Raif said as his head popped out of the window. "Up you come, quickly." He extended his long-fingered hand down to Lenna.

Casting one last glance down the deserted alleyway, Lenna took a deep breath and reached up, grasping Raif's offered hand and planting one leather boot against the coarse stone wall of the warehouse. Her attire wasn't exactly ideal for breaking into private property, but with a minimal amount of grunting and huffing Lenna managed to wiggle her way through the open window. Once inside, Raif, stronger than his lanky frame conveyed, hoisted Lenna to her feet as though she weighed no more than a child, and quickly positioned them both behind a large crate stamped with the insignia of the Empire.

For the moment, they seemed safe; in the dim gaslights of the warehouse, startlingly bright after the darkness of night, Lenna discerned that she and Raif were on a raised platform that extended along the wall through which they entered. The cargo that provided them cover, however, also prevented Lenna from seeing much else except a few more crates lining the catwalk. The row outside seemed to be escalating, with the addition of the sounds of shattering glass and the meaty thud of a fist hitting flesh.

Raif put one finger to his lips before pointing it at Lenna, and subsequently at the platform immediately beneath their feet. The librarian nodded and retreated further in the corner, where the crate's shadow provided even more cover. Raif smirked, and with the grace of an acrobat — or a cat burglar, Lenna thought, amused — he traipsed silently along the catwalk. As he reached the end of the first crate he neatly sank to his haunches, and crept forward felinely until his sandy blonde head peeped out just beyond the cover of the Empire's cargo.

Embracing her new courage, Lenna was eager to move forward herself and see what was occurring; without even realizing it, the librarian had been holding her breath and fingering the softly vibrating jewel in her satchel. To add to her curiosity, a strong female voice Lenna immediately distinguished as General Khareen Valant's began issuing orders in a stark, commanding tone. Raif, several paces away on the catwalk, looked back at Lenna and jerked his head backwards. Nodding, Lenna gingerly tiptoed down the narrow walkway and managed to kneel next to Raif without falling over and getting entangled in her own cloak.

Lenna leaned forward, ignoring Raif's arm as it protectively reached around her back, and peered out at the scene transpiring below. She could not make out Valant, her vantage point allowing only a view of the main entrance to the warehouse. Its door was wide open and filled with a tangle of people, and a few paces into the warehouse itself, a cloaked man stood, watching the brawl.

The roar of the battle below quieted after a rush of air and several thumps echoed throughout the large room. Squinting a little, Lenna realized that the drunken revelers and two Imperial soldiers had all collapsed into a human pile in the threshold of the large door. Valant's orders must have been to silence the lot, her own soldiers included, and the cloaked man did it with magic.

A moment later, the general stiffly approached her accomplice, exchanging a few words that sounded like Krevlum but were unfortunately just too faint for Lenna to hear. She glanced sideways at Raif, who shook his head and shrugged, indicating he was at as much of a loss as Lenna was. General Valant placed a gloved hand on the man's shoulder, and as her cloak shifted with the movement Lenna glimpsed a flash of silver from a long item belted at the woman's waist. The sight of the precariously long sword caused a peculiar tingling sensation in Lenna's stomach, as though fear and excitement had been mixed into a fizzy laboratory concoction. Subconsciously, Lenna's hand shifted from the humming Godjewel to the mother-of-pearl handle of her dagger in her jacket pocket.

Valant pointed at the pile of bodies and mouthed something to her companion before turning and walking out of Lenna's line of sight. Without so much as a nod, the man began to drag the prone bodies of the two downed Imperial soldiers back into the warehouse. With the fight ended, Lenna could make out Valant's voice softly discussing something with someone almost directly below their place on the catwalk; the response that came was that of an angry but feeble man, and definitely not Gilbert's lover. Whomever else besides Pim and Luc

General Valant had captured, they were being held against the back wall of the warehouse.

While Lenna's attention had shifted to the voices below her, Raif continued to keep vigilant watch over the cloaked individual. He tapped Lenna gently on the shoulder three times to get her attention and jerked his head toward the cloaked man. He was sliding the heavy metal door of the warehouse shut, leaving Raif's drunken comrades locked outside. Lenna felt remorse for Raif's crew and hoped they wouldn't suffer too much on her behalf, but all thoughts of the unconscious men shattered like a brittle piece of glass when the cloaked man turned back toward General Valant.

"Luc," Lenna said, voice barely a whisper, and clapped a hand over her mouth.

CHAPTER SIXTEEN

Raif immediately noticed Lenna's distress. In retrospect, the librarian would always be thankful for his keen perception and empathy during the events that followed. His arm around her immediately tightened, pulling her body close to his. Normally, Lenna would have probably slapped him; now, she found his embrace comforting and endearing. He smelled lightly of mint and lemon. It was a clean, fresh scent that reminded Lenna of laundry and baths.

Below the catwalk, Luc had presumably rejoined General Valant and the prisoners. Lenna had yet to recognize the one man's voice that she heard, or even to distinguish a female voice other than the general's, which led her to wonder if Pim was here and, if so, if she was unconscious or worse. Lenna's mind raced, but none of its normal functions seemed to process. Over the years she had adapted to living with minimal confrontation, the tidiness and order of her library, and a routine that involved quiet time reserved for reflection. And it kept her grounded and reliable. Now, perched precariously on a catwalk in a foreign warehouse with an airship pilot and trading heir, she was simply at a loss as to what she should do next.

A shaggy ponytail brushed the top of Lenna's hair, and she tilted her head to glance up at Raif. Once again, he gave her one of his stupid, overconfident grins, but rather than feel revulsion, Lenna managed a tame smile back. They were in this together. At this point, there was no way out without being detected, so the only matter that truly concerned them was when, and how, to confront the group below. Moving forward was the only option, so Lenna's fist tightened around the hilt of her mother's dagger. She slid the blade out of its sheath an inch, and Raif nodded in response.

After a moment of silence, the Ilyan sky pirate — Lenna realized that even she, in times of crisis, could romanticize — began muttering a string of lilting syllables, unrecognizable to the librarian. Light began to rise, similar to Gilbert and Luc's magelight, but rather than appear in Raif's hands, particles of light began to condense and form a large white globe in the air directly in front of the heavy metal door of the warehouse. Within seconds, it tripled in size, now almost as large as a melon, and its luminosity shone brighter than Port Hollish's midsummer sun.

Lenna heard Khareen Valant and Luc call out in confusion as the orb continued to grow. Raif, calm as ever, slid one hand casually up over Lenna's head and pushed it down, so that her gaze was averted and she was forced to stare at the shoddy woodwork of the catwalk. A second later Raif's own upper half was leaning over Lenna, shielding her. There was a flash of light so bright and palpable that the librarian could feel it behind her closed eyelids like a sudden sunburst, and cries of outrage rang from below.

Before Lenna could gather her senses, Raif leapt into action, his lithe body skipping down the catwalk and brazenly leaping down into the large main section of the warehouse. With nimble reflexes, he used a crate as a bounding box on his descent. As she raised her head in the receding light, she watched with perverse amusement as Raif deliberately struck a dramatic, roguish pose before the warehouse door. Intentionally or not, his display of bravado roused something in the librarian that caused her, as well, to spring down the catwalk, albeit nowhere near as gracefully.

General Valant and Luc were already about six paces away from Raif as Lenna finally descended and assumed a position next to her comrade. Sometime during her journey, she had unconsciously pulled her mother's dagger from its sheath and let its pommel and hilt delicately slide into her right hand. Raif, for once, was not smiling but stood rigidly beside Lenna as the cool-eyed general and a slightly stunned Luc considered the pair.

As her senses slowly readjusted and the adrenaline faded from her system, Lenna was able to peer behind her opponents and see the people pushed up against the dimly lit back wall. She recognized Pim, who though unconscious looked no worse for wear other than a black eye, and to her right, a bloody-lipped and weary Sebastien. His hands were bound with thick, hemp cord.

"Quite on time," mused General Valant in Continental. "Your family's connections never fail to surprise me, and you're all so terrifically proud. I gambled that your pride would lead you here, young Master Vandever, and I won."

Lenna could feel Raif's muscles tensing. Despite their short acquaintance, she knew the Ilyan heir did not take kindly to those kinds of insults. For the moment, she was still compartmentalizing the shock that Sebastien was already present and captured, and that Luc was a traitor to the cause his lover had died protecting.

"You realize my family won't look kindly on this intrusion on our city," Raif said coolly, "or our hospitality. The authorities are bound to investigate the unconscious group of pummeled young men outside."

Valant's hand shifted to grip the pommel of her blade. "Please, spare me such patronizing threatening. Tranum enforcement will turn a blind eye to this, especially since the rental of local warehouses comes as much from the Empire as it does the Vandever family." Lenna swore she could detect the faintest hint of a smirk in the general's face. "Or didn't you realize?"

Raif, for his part, stood unmoved. "Am I to understand you planned all of this?"

The general, in her quiet cockiness, answered simply: "It has always been my intention to obtain the Godjewel from this foolish girl" — she jerked her head at Lenna — "and return it to my lord Emperor. I never imagined that I'd get such... cooperation from the Blue Crescent Brotherhood." She laughed, a frigid, tinkling sound like ice falling into a glass.

Lenna focused her most piercing glare at Luc. The young man was noticeably averting her eyes. He had traded his sullied blue robes of the Brotherhood for a simple set of leather trousers, a woolly sweater, and a dark cloak. In comparison to his normally rigid attire, Luc looked strangely uncomfortable in such informal clothing.

"We found this young mage running through the streets," the general continued. "Poor thing was half frightened to death. Something about an incident with a Freewoman manservant, a shiny trinket, and two annoying little girls."

To her surprise Lenna found her grip around her knife lightening as she subconsciously shifted it into one of the fighting stances her mother had desperately tried to teach her as a little girl. She let her anger spread out across her like a pool of water, until a haze glossed over her eyes, blurring the shapes of the enemies before her and the prisoners along the back wall.

"Lenna, run," said Sebastien, and spat a wad of blood onto the floor.

Khareen Valant bared her teeth like a tiger, and slowly slid the long steel blade from its scabbard at her hip. It was slightly curved and etched with whorls like leaves blowing in the wind. Lenna gasped. It was of Freewoman design; she could recognize that much.

"This?" Valant sneered. "Good steel, but it was very expensive. The woman who wielded it before me demanded quite a price." With a gloved hand the general tucked back some of her hair to reveal the scarred lump where once was an ear. "But who can turn down Freewoman metalwork? It's rare enough as it is." Lenna shivered a little as the general conspicuously inspected the handiwork of her mother's knife.

Raif, weary of watching the Imperial general pace back and forth, suddenly sprung into action like a coiled cat. Time seemed to halt as Lenna watched, cringing, while Raif leaped unarmed toward General Valant, who, ever at the ready, skipped elegantly backward and backhandedly brought up her blade in a sweeping arc toward Raif's midsection. The seemingly defenseless Ilyan pulled at the ribbon tying his hair back, and it unfurled like a snake before him. All in one instant the tie had stretched and coiled around Valant's blade, and Raif tugged harshly, using his momentum to propel the blade off into the distance. Momentarily aghast, Valant was defenseless and Raif, snarling, tackled the general to the ground.

Paralyzed, Luc watched with a mixture of astonishment and terror as Raif and Valant rolled around on the floor, tussling and engaging each other with crackling, magical strikes that fired so close to both parties, it was obviously damaging them together. Lenna, noticing Luc's moment of hesitation, mustered all the courage she could and blindly hurled a wave of her anger and betrayal at the startled man in one ozone-reeking crack of magic. Taken by surprise, Luc was slammed back against the wall, doubling over as though punched in the stomach. He panted heavily, struggling to get up.

By this time Valant and Raif had parted, both bleeding and now lightly beating at each other's magical shields with arcane blasts. Raif appeared to be holding his own, but Lenna worried that General Valant's training and experience far outweighed the privileged heir's. She knew she had a limited amount of time with which to work and, taking a deep breath, launched herself past the struggling confrontation between Raif and Valant across the crudely cemented warehouse floor toward the prisoners, knife at the ready.

Lenna slid to her knees, feeling the skin tear on the coarse concrete. The knots that bound Sebastien were tied expertly, she realized, and Luc would be upright in seconds. Thankfully, her father had throughout the years kept the blade of her knife well-honed, and after a moment of creative swearing, the fibers of the twine split apart and Sebastien fell forward from his position leaning on the wall, onto Lenna.

"Shield," he croaked.

Hastily, Lenna recalled the drunken night spent with Gilbert learning how to shield and clumsily felt a bubble of power surround herself and the prisoners just as a surge of power smashed into it. Lenna felt her brain go wibbly-wobbly and her concentration on the shield started to slip. She could feel little gaps in the barrier beginning to widen when suddenly Sebastien grabbed her shoulder. He had been beaten badly, Lenna could see, and the gasping for breath and wincing led her to believe a rib or two might be broken.

Despite this, Lenna sensed his magic buffering hers, helping to restore her concentration and shape the magical warding around them. Just in time, because as Lenna turned around to face the chaos, Luc was up and had hurled another bolt, the strike tingling through the shield as it rippled down and was channeled into the chipped, rough floor. Luc had a glassy, crazed look in his eyes, as though he were a mad hunter closing in on his prey. The librarian could do little but focus on keeping her shield up and wonder just how strong Luc's magic actually was.

Across the room, more of Lenna's fears were being confirmed: Valant had risen to her feet and was lording over the prone Raif, and the prisoners watched as the general summoned one great gust of wind, launching Raif clear into the air and slamming him against the heavy metal door. He slid to the floor and lay crumpled into a ball, groaning. General Valant was clearly a veteran fighter, and her face betrayed no sign of emotion, even as she licked a small trickle of blood from her lip. She waved one of her gloved hands at Luc, indicating for him to stop his attack on Lenna, and Lenna was half grateful and half petrified at what General Khareen Valant had in mind for them. Beside Sebastien, Pim was starting to regain consciousness.

"The Ilyan's attack was courageous," the general admitted, her voice a pinnacle of self-control. "As was yours against the traitorous mage." She was addressing Lenna directly now, and the librarian once again longed to avert her eyes from the strange, tunnel-like gaze of the imposing Imperial commander. "Everyone seems to have come here for one purpose," she smiled, revealing exceedingly white teeth that glowed eerily in the dim light of the warehouse.

"The Godjewel, I presume," Lenna said.

"I wonder." The general began pacing about, collecting her sword along the way and restoring it to its sheath with a practiced hand. "Our little warrior princess over there was looking for your bespectacled face. I had to give her a little bit of a headache."

Pim sat up, groaning and rubbing her head. "She didn't fight fair. She just hit me on the head with the butt of her sword."

"The rogue magician required a bit more of a magical bruising, so to speak. But, thanks to my new assistant..." Valant pulled Luc to her side, dragging him by the arm as though he weighed nothing, "...we were able to catch him off guard as he was poking around the city, looking for my new little pet. It was almost serendipitous of him to be investigating the warehouses when we found him."

"And now you have Raif and me," Lenna said. She felt a twinge of guilt at having been part of getting Sebastien caught.

"Exactly, Miss Faircloth," the general delivered grandly. "All the parties are assembled. What will you do? You have my guarantee that no one here will suffer any further harm — though they may need some mental care, the poor dears — if you willingly relinquish the crystal to me, which will sever its bond."

Lenna blinked and, as was her habit, pushed her fallen spectacles up her nose. What did Valant mean that all the parties were assembled? There was Pim, loyal to Jaice, a leader of the Freewomen; Raif, heir to the Vandever family fortune and ultimately another jewel; Sebastien, a mage on the run from his own people, seeking to whisk away the cursed rock to who knows where; and Khareen Valant, direct envoy of the Krevlum Empire. Representatives of major political powers were present, but only if you considered Sebastien and Luc as active members of the Brotherhood.

Frowning, Lenna glanced at Luc, who was struggling to look as impassive as possible, a poor shadow of General Valant's natural calmness. She remembered well enough the young man's mental evisceration at the loss of Gilbert; if he was already considered a traitor by his order, would he be representing their political interests? Surely he would meet the same fate that Gilbert had and Sebastien most certainly would.

"Ah," said the general. "I'd heard you've got a brain on you. So you've made the connection? With young Master Tural's assistance, we were able to gain the upper hand with Brother Sebastien. In exchange, the Empire will parley on his behalf or negotiate with the Tural family directly. They are not without their value, as well."

Lenna considered her options. Adrenaline and anger had poured away from her as though someone had opened a plug in the well of her emotions. The sandy, metallic smell of the warehouse stung her nose, and the sooty gas lamps flickered against the various wooden crates and some barrels, casting strange shadows across the floor. Reality was an oppressive, almost stupefying noose around her neck.

From behind, Sebastien's voice croaked in her ear, a rugged, pained whisper. "Give me the gem. I can defeat her with its power."

Lenna wasn't certain any of her choices were better than another. She felt like that confused little girl standing over her mother's casket as it drifted out into the bay, uncertain if she should cry or be thankful that all of the traumatic incidents leading up to her mother's death were over. If only Gilbert were here, just as he was that day years ago, slipping his tiny hand into hers and squeezing it softly, letting her know she was not alone...

And then it became clear.

As gracefully as she could manage with her badly skinned knees, Lenna rose to her feet. In the dusty, half-lit illumination of this Ilyan warehouse, Lenna the librarian was the focus of attention, the crux of this stupid struggle for power. She closed her eyes and, smiling lightly, tasted and smelled the briny breeze of the sea.

"I'm keeping the Godjewel," she said.

***

The hush that fell over the warehouse was so complete that, in spite of the gravity of the situation, Lenna wanted to giggle like a poorly-bred little girl in the company of polite society. Her hand had slipped into her satchel, feeling for the warmth and now-familiar vibration of the azure gemstone. From the evening this whole fiasco had begun — no, from long before that — Lenna had existed day by day simply because she felt that it was the appropriate thing to do. Deliberately had she ruined her chances of entering University, reconciling herself to being a martyr to keep her father company. She loved her books and her father deeply, but the one person in life whom she trusted implicitly had entrusted her with the Godjewel.

"Sparkle ponies," she whispered, and emptied her mind of the negative thoughts that had all this time oppressed her, even the ones she was never aware of to begin with. Images of her mother thrashing about on her bed, screaming to be put out of her misery; Gilbert's solitary departure to the Brotherhood and his death in the snowy fields; Bahl's disfigurement; everything melted away as though summer had come to her heart and thawed the layer of ice surrounding it. The book inside her, the volume storing all of her magic, flew open, pages whirling in an imaginary breeze. Her mother's dagger in one hand and the humming Godjewel in her satchel, Lenna raised a shield, just as Gilbert had taught her.

Sounds reached her ears as though she were hearing them underwater. Pim called out her name and reached for her, Sebastien tried to stand and groaned, and Luc looked on, stunned. Lenna ignored all of them and focused her concentration on Khareen Valant, who strode toward the librarian with methodical purpose, sword drawn. The general's own magical aura was tangible; Lenna could feel it raging like a terrible blizzard inside Valant's body. Her magic was stronger than that of any of the magicians Lenna had met before, and for an instant Lenna lost her confidence that the Godjewel could protect her.

Valant grinned, a twisted, uncontrolled thing: she relished these moments. With a sweep of her white-gloved hand, as though she were swatting a fly, Lenna felt the general rip through her shielding, leaving her naked and exposed. Lenna had lost before she had even begun. The general, in an uncharacteristic display of emotion, reached out with her free hand and grabbed a fistful of Lenna's wavy hair, curling it into a ball in her fist and yanking forward tightly. The librarian stumbled forward, the much taller, stronger woman almost lifting her off her feet. Tears welled up and Lenna let out an unholy squeal.

Sebastien and Pim called out the librarian's name and struggled to run to her aid, but some foggy tendrils of force curled around their legs and arms, pinning them to the wall. From the corner of her tearing eyes, Lenna saw Luc concentrating and making subtle gestures with his hand. The shackling spell was his doing, then, and thus he had truly betrayed Gilbert's memory.

"You have no idea how much pain I am going to inflict on you, you uppity little bitch," Valant said, pleased with herself. "Before you draw your last breath, you'll see my face, and this Freewoman blade in your belly." To prove her point, the sadistic general raised her intricately forged blade to the librarian's neck, its impossibly precise and honed edge drawing a thin line of red across Lenna's throat. It was all the librarian could do let go of the Godjewel to try to force Valant's gloved fist away, out of her hair.

"Stop!" Raif's voice rang out throughout the warehouse, slightly shrill. Lenna could barely see him for the tears in her eyes. Valant spun around to properly face the Ilyan merchant, swinging Lenna along by the hair like a rag doll. The librarian groaned in pain mournfully and twisted her head to try and see Raif.

The blonde man, hair loose and streaming over his shoulders, had raised one arm toward the ceiling, the loose sleeve of his shirt falling down to bunch around his elbow. Clutched between two fingers and bound to his wrist lightly by a gold chain was a small round globe that shone an unearthly green, like faerie lights in a bog. The Godjewel began to vibrate uncomfortably.

"No!" croaked Sebastien, while at the same time Luc launched himself toward Raif, tackling him even as the blonde man uttered a few words and an explosion of green light engulfed the room. Thankfully, her eyes veiled with tears, Lenna managed to avoid any pain from the flash, but she could hear the cries of anguish from Pim and Valant over the grunting of Luc and Raif wrestling and swearing. Valant, for her part, stumbled before the unexpected flash, and for a brief instance her grip on Lenna lightened.

The librarian could feel the weight of the stone in her satchel, pulling down on her garments heavily. Tugging, urging her: the Godjewel seemed to whisper sweetly to Lenna, seducing away the pain, pleading with her to act. She squinted, ignoring the fact that her glasses were practically falling off her nose, dropped her mother's dagger, and latched onto Valant's hand with both of her own.

A leather glove. It was tanned and supple, but was once flesh. It knew fire. Hair, like flesh burning in Junction, could burn. You couldn't stop it. Pim had said all it needed was encouragement, and the Godjewel provided it in droves.

The moments moved quickly, and at first General Khareen Valant did not notice any sensation of growing warmth in her glove. By the time Lenna's vision cleared, in fact, the Imperial general had shifted her focus to another corner of the room, providing Lenna with more of an opportunity to concentrate. The pulsing gem at her side was filling her with a uniquely addictive form of euphoria that let her ignore the pain. In the air, the bitter, acrid scent of burning hair and lavender began to mingle as Valant shouted at someone off to the side, by the cargo.

"Don't tempt me, chicken pisser," called back the voice.

Valant said, "You would never risk it." Lenna felt her body being swung again but ignored the pain. She could feel a fire burning in both the jewel and her innermost self, and the objects of her focus screamed in response, realizing their own inner flames. By now, Lenna's hair had completely come undone from the hastily styled coif she had attempted earlier, and so she focused on those few inches curled around the fingers of Khareen Valant's tight grasp.

"Sparkle ponies," Lenna whispered again, letting her hands fall to her sides, and the Godjewel hummed happily as the hair entwined in the general's fist and the crisp, white leather glove of Imperial office burst into violent, blue-hot flame.

The general spat a violent curse as the fire traveled up her arm, and in one precise and swift backhanded stroke swung her diamond-sharp blade, slicing through Lenna's smoldering hair as though it were nothing but air. The librarian fell backwards harshly onto the cement of the warehouse floor, the air rushing out of her lungs in one harsh whoosh. Lenna's head collided with the concrete, and everything, in one sharp, jarring instant, went black as the sound of a gunshot rang throughout the warehouse.

Lenna awoke suddenly to the tangy scent of orange and clove. Two hands were pressed to the sides of her head, and the screaming pain in her body gently receded into a dull throbbing. She must be hungover, she thought, and fumbled about for her glasses and accidentally grabbed someone's knee. Confused, she saw two blurry human-shaped figures leaning over her. Lenna also realized, rather awkwardly, that her head was in someone's lap.

"Spectacles, please," she said in a decidedly nasal tone.

Small, bumbling hands carefully slid the cool metal frames onto Lenna's face as delicately as possible, as though embarrassed. Gradually, the ache in her head dulled and Lenna's vision came into focus: leaning over her, both with brows furrowed in identical expressions of worry, were Sebastien and Pim. Sebastien was pale, and his dangling earring gleamed in the lamps of the warehouse; Pim was red-faced and her freckles severe.

"I think I must be unconscious," Lenna intoned.

Pim surprisingly burst into tears and threw her arms around Lenna, which made the situation exceedingly awkward, as the librarian's head was apparently being cradled in Sebastien's lap. He coughed and, to Lenna's bewilderment, blushed and looked away. Lenna groaned and sat up, with hushed murmurs from Sebastien and Pim advising her to take it slowly, as she had apparently suffered quite a blow to the head, in addition to losing over a span of hair. Lenna wasn't quite sure which she was the most irritated about.

As she rose, the world blurred for a second, as if she had just been spun around in a circle twenty times and set free. Lenna shook her head to clear it and sat back down a bit closer to the kneeling Pim and out of Sebastien's embrace. The librarian rested her brow on Pim's shoulder for a moment until the room ceased spinning. Pim, in something like sisterly affection, softly stroked Lenna's head.

"I would have healed you more tidily," Sebastien said softly, his voice still hoarse. "But I'm a bit weak myself."

Lenna turned from Pim's shoulder to see the older mage, bruised and bloody and in dirty clothes, smiling awkwardly at her. It was a sharp contrast to the confident mage the librarian had met on the steamtrain. Earlier, when Lenna had been in close contact with the Godjewel, which now sat complacently in her satchel, she had sensed the lack of magical reserves in Sebastien. What little he had left for the moment had gone into repairing the damage done when Lenna had so ungracefully crashed into the warehouse's cement floor.

"Master Sebastien," Lenna said, her voice surprisingly calm. "I would have thought you'd heal yourself first."

"It's Seb," he replied, sounding slightly put-upon. "And Lenna Faircloth, you are the densest librarian I have ever met."

Lenna realized his pain at Luc's betrayal, and her mind instantly raced to the traitorous mage, the general, and their respective locations. Pushing those thoughts aside for the moment, she leaned forward, placing three fingers of her left hand on the mage's forehead. Lenna could still sense the influence of the Godjewel but knew she did not need its energy. She thought of Gil, of Pim, of Seb and her mother and father, and lavender filled the air as the wounds on Sebastien's face closed up and healed.

The mage whistled, as though he had been holding his breath. His mouth fumbled about awkwardly, as though he could not find the proper things to say, but he managed to nod and form a few polite words of gratitude. Pim, in the background, laughed heartily, a sound that Lenna had not realized she had missed so much. She turned around and embraced her kindred Freewoman.

"Now, now," Pim said, patting Lenna on the back before hurriedly rising to her feet, her face still red as a strawberry. "Enough of that. Let's get you steady."

The curly-haired girl helped Lenna stand, the librarian admittedly grateful as she was still more than a little shaky, and Sebastien smoothly followed suit, Lenna's healing having apparently been more than effective. Pim, surprisingly adept at management, kept Lenna's gaze directed completely on her own eyes.

"It isn't a pretty sight, Lenna," the freckled girl said.

"What happened to General Valant? And Raif? And Luc?"

Pim sighed and scooted aside, allowing Lenna a full view of the warehouse before her. In the center of the wide room, most of the body of what was once General Khareen Valant remained in a red, sticky mess on the floor. The head was a repugnant pile of mush like a rotted, exploded red pumpkin, and all down one arm the Imperial white leather had peeled away and a charred, blackened arm remained. The air hung heavy with the scent of lavender, burning flesh, and gunpowder.

Grimacing and holding back the urge to be ill, Lenna quickly put her hand over her mouth and nose. "By all that is good, what have we done?"

Pim, face devoid of expression, replied flatly, "We won. Your spell shocked her enough to release you, which gave me a clear shot. The stupid guards didn't believe a girl could be so adept and quick at prepping a blunderbuss, so it was stashed over there." She jerked her head toward the side wall.

"Once that Ilyan man performed his razzle-dazzle, I went straight for it."

Lenna grimly noticed a bunch of slightly singed, dirty blonde hair on the ground near the corpse and reached her hand up to her hair, which was, she realized, now almost six inches shorter and breaking off into flakes at the end. Morosely, she reminded herself that she had been thinking of getting her hair trimmed lately, though this seemed a bit extreme.

"Where is Raif?" she asked.

"Here," replied a dismal voice. The door to the warehouse was ajar, and the cool night was starting to purge the place of its perverse stench. The Ilyan trader was leaning against the metallic frame, his untied hair blowing delicately in the wind. Under more normal circumstances, Lenna would have probably laughed at so melodramatic a sight, but something told her Raif was not affecting any sort of role at the moment.

"Raif," Lenna called out to him. "What happened?"

He turned toward the group, the corpse of the Imperial general and the unconscious bodies of several soldiers and drunken crewmen between them, and even from a distance Lenna could see the tears in his eyes. "I lost it, Lenna. I shouldn't have taken it to begin with; I know that. But I wanted to make sure you were safe."

Lenna did not quite comprehend the situation. Her memory was, admittedly, a bit blurry, though the tingling, highly sensual sensation from the use of the Godjewel lingered in her body. She briefly recalled the struggle with the general, and even Seb's healing had not fully alleviated the insistent aching of her scalp, but all she remembered of Raif was that he had raised a shining object to the sky and started using its magic.

And then she realized. "You brought your family's Godjewel."

The wind mussed his blonde hair as he nodded. "It was a last resort."

"But if you had bonded with it…"

"He'd be as trapped as you are now, Lenna," Seb commented.

"Thankfully, that didn't happen," Raif returned bitterly, stamping forward and sidestepping the corpse of the general. "Despite what my father told you, I have no idea how to use the damn thing."

"We have to take it back to your estate at once," Lenna said hurriedly. "Master Vandever…"

"Lenna, hold on a sec," Pim said, putting one hand on the librarian's shoulder. "I'm not sure you get it."

"What?" Lenna replied, looking from Raif, to Pim, to Sebastien, whose face was grim.

"It's gone, Lenna," said Raif. "That little mage friend of yours you wanted to save? He was tougher than I thought. He grabbed it from me, threw open the door, and then got away before I could even get to my feet. The jewel is gone."

Strangely, despite all she had experienced for the past week, this was the first time that real shock registered both on Lenna's face and in her body. She staggered a bit but was promptly propped up by Pim. The Freewoman was surprisingly calm in situations like this, as Lenna vaguely processed memories of Junction and the thought that the second Godjewel, an object of immeasurable power, was now in the hands of a half-crazed, desperate young man.

"What happens now?" Lenna whispered, resenting the wavering in her voice.

"Well," offered Pim, "it smells like we could all do with a bath.

Still sniffling a bit, Raif managed to exchange a smirk with Lenna and Seb, despite the horrible grimness of the situation. Pim took Lenna's hand in her own and pulled her deliberately out of the warehouse, followed by Sebastien. The autumn air felt good after the stuffy warehouse, and Lenna felt exhausted to the point where every burden felt insignificant compared to Pim's suggestion of a bath and, hopefully, a solid day of sleep to follow.

Raif came out last, his scruffy face streaked with tears and his blonde hair tangled, but he walked to the front and led his group proudly back to his manor, where both Master Vandever and Briet were still awake, waiting.

CHAPTER SEVENTEEN

True to his word, Master Vandever honored the Ilyan Pact he made and treated Lenna and her ragtag group of companions as his guests, guaranteeing their safety. Although, frankly, considering the level of exhaustion of her party, Lenna reckoned that they would have slept at the Midnight Rose with the prostitutes if they had to. As long as the sheets were fresh.

Bed itself was still a few hours off for a grief-stricken Raif; Lenna imagined the "discussion" with his father would be epic. Sebastien, surprisingly, accompanied the Ilyan father and son into Vandever's study, to help explain or perhaps even defend Raif's actions, though the loss of a treasure as extraordinary as a Godjewel was probably, in Master Vandever's mind, indefensible. The librarian was glad to be spared whatever would be said.

Briet, still in her dressing gown, gave Lenna and Pim a tired smile and quietly led them up the arcing staircase toward the guest room Lenna had occupied a few hours before. Despite Lenna's pleas that she just be allowed to go to sleep, Pim was resolute that they bathe away the dust from the warehouse and Lenna wash the soot out of her short hair. Briet sided with the Freewoman, and Lenna ultimately acquiesced to sinking once again into the warm depths of the grand marble bath.

Neeran, the servant who had tended to Lenna, entered silently after Pim and Lenna had finished toweling themselves off and slipped into heavy cotton dressing gowns. She brought with her a pair of silvery sharp shears and, without saying a word, escorted the librarian to a chair by the window, where by now the rays of the early morning light were peeking through the clouds. Lenna sighed as Neeran slowly and deftly trimmed the bits of frizzy, seared hair from her head, working diligently until Lenna was left with a bob of steadily curling locks that fell near her chin.

"Now we look like proper kin," Pim said from behind her.

"It'll curl up even more without the weight."

"Better than being dead," the Freewoman replied cheerfully, her wounds magically healed. She headed off for something to fill her grumbling belly.

The older servant helped a mostly numb and tired Lenna into a fresh set of nightclothes and then nestled her into the downy bed with an undeserved kindness. Lenna watched Neeran slowly draw the curtains of the guest bedroom, blocking out the impending morning sun and bringing a calming darkness to the room. Neeran returned to stand over Lenna's bed for a moment, before leaning over, kissing the librarian on the forehead, and squeezing her hand, which held the Godjewel and was faintly trembling.

"Sleep," the servant said.

"Thank you," Lenna said mistily in Ilyan.

The woman nodded and withdrew, and Lenna was already far too deep into the realm of slumber to hear the door of the bedroom close with a gentle click.

Lenna awoke to the setting sun and that horrible sense of discomfort when one's internal clock has been led astray. A set of clean clothing had been laid out for her, folded neatly on a vanity near the window. They were not formal or borrowed; these were purchased just for her. She shrugged out of her nightclothes and into the comfortable cotton shift provided, and dressed fully in the garb of a mature, but not wealthy, Ilyan woman: new boots, a long, deep purple skirt of a heavy material Lenna didn't recognize, a white silk blouse, and a well-tailored long coat dyed to match the skirt. Whoever had chosen these clearly knew what Lenna fancied. Most importantly, Lenna thought with relief, her spectacles had somehow stayed intact despite the previous night's adventure.

Dressed much more comfortably than she had been for the past few days, Lenna tucked the Godjewel into a pocket at her breast and slung her rucksack over her shoulder. She snuck a glance at herself in the elegant mirror hanging over the wooden vanity, and though her hair was a bit shorter and curlier than she preferred, all in all she was pleased with the healthy glow in her cheeks. The gentle throbbing of the stone in her pocket seemed to fill her with vitality, beating like a second heart.

Attire properly sorted, Lenna opened the door to the guest room, expecting to find the grand hallway empty. Leaning against the wall opposite the door, as stiff as the portraits to either side of him, was a stone-faced Raif. He had changed into clean clothes and combed his hair back into its usual ponytail. When he saw Lenna, his eyes widened and he practically jumped the length of the hallway to her side.

"Awake at last, I see," he grinned.

"Good morning."

"Good evening is more like it."

"Why were you waiting for me?"

"Would you believe it was because I wanted to see your new hairstyle?"

Lenna rolled her eyes. "Strangely, with you, I can imagine that might be the case." The librarian checked her temper; she might have slept the day away in the feathery cloud of the guest bed, but she doubted that Raif had had that luxury. "How did things go," she said quietly, "with your father? Where does everything stand?"

The smile dropped from Raif's face, but he took Lenna's arm all the same and began escorting her down the hallway, toward the grand staircase that would eventually lead them to the dining room. His pace was slow and deliberate, and his voice low. "I suppose it's fair to say my father was less than pleased at the loss of his Godjewel," he said carefully. "I am currently out of favor with the family."

"What does that entail?"

Raif shrugged and clicked his tongue. "It ties up a little bit of my income and cuts off some valuable contacts, but it's not that bad. I never spend much time here in the estate to begin with."

"Does your father still expect me to give him my Godjewel?" Lenna asked bluntly.

"'Your' Godjewel now, eh?" Raif replied brashly. "No, don't worry — your mage boyfriend convinced him that considering the Krevlum Empire will be curious about what happened to one of its high-ranking generals and about the loss of the Vandever Godjewel, it's best to maintain cordial ties and not get further steeped in any kind of mess. Let the blame lie with the rogue Brother, Luc, who somehow managed to thwart our defenses under guise of your friendship and make off with our precious treasure."

It was not an outright lie, but even though she felt betrayed by Luc, Lenna did not much like the idea of making him the scapegoat for all of the events of the previous night. Seb, Raif's father, Raif, Pim, and even Lenna herself had all played their parts in what occurred in that warehouse by the airship dock. Now, the Empire would not only double its efforts to pursue Luc for possession of one of three unique magical artifacts, but also seek his head for the death of one of their prized officers.

"What will you do now, Lenna?" Raif asked quietly.

She had deliberately ignored that question up until now, focusing on the immediacy of events: first a bath, then sleep, then get dressed. But as the vibrating stone against her breast reminded her, she was still a target of the Empire and the Blue Crescent Brotherhood as long as she was in possession of the gemstone. And there was still the problem of her promise to Gil, though in Lenna's mind Luc had completely betrayed Gilbert's memory.

Raif took Lenna's silence as an answer and continued speaking after a moment. They already stood perched at the top landing of the delicately curved marble stairway that led down to the grand foyer. "As for me, I'm going after that little bastard who knocked me down. Not just to get back into the family's good graces: I don't like the idea of a crazy kid with that kind of power running around Tranum."

"And I'm sure pride has nothing to do with this?" Lenna asked suspiciously.

Grinning wider than Ilyanly possible, Raif began to guide the librarian down the steps. "Pride has *everything* to do with this. But what do you say? You, me, that fancy blue stone of yours? I've still got my airship."

Before Lenna could even process an appropriate reply, the pair had reached the foot of the stairs. A servant bowed as he passed Raif and Lenna, and indicated that dinner was ready. Raif, with a nonchalant nod of the head, swerved Lenna past what she imagined to be the entrance to the dining hall and down a narrower corridor, lined with decorative plants and some vases. Off to the left was a set of elegantly carved double doors, much less grand than a proper dining room of a manor house of this magnitude.

"Where are we going?" Lenna asked.

Saying nothing, Raif threw open the doors and bowed grandly, his actions just bordering on mockery. The room beyond was still far more spacious than most people would use for dining, but from the used look of the table and less-artful decorations, such as papers, drawings, and even a few family photographs, that lined the walls and various shelves, Lenna saw that this was where the

Vandever clan most likely took their meals when not formally entertaining.

The large table was spread with warm breads, cheeses, fruits, and a huge haunch of mutton. Around it sat a freshly scrubbed but ever-freckled Pim; Sebastien, who had tidied himself up so that not one hair on his head was out of place; and a man in simple dress with bandaging covering the right side of his head and some of his shoulder.

"Bahl!" exclaimed Lenna.

"About time you got up; I could have taken a cow to market four times over by now for all your snoring," Pim said, her mouth full of warm bread.

The hunter, from his place next to Pim, knuckled her lightly on her curly brow before standing up and coughing. He addressed Lenna directly: "I'm sorry to have caused you trouble, Freewoman Faircloth."

Lenna entered the room, followed by Raif, who quietly closed the doors behind him. She was elated to see that Bahl had survived the horrific gout of magefire that Luc had unleashed, but at the same time she was exceedingly confused as to why the hunter, normally gruff, was addressing her so politely. Slightly taken off guard by his sudden change in demeanor, she replied, "No apologies are necessary, Bahl. I'm just glad to see you alive and well."

"Yes, Freewoman. Pim here was fortunate enough to find a healer in the city, and now Master

Vandever has sent for his personal healer to come and see if he can reverse some of the nastier scarring. Thank you."

"Oh, sit down, Bahl," said Pim. "You too, Lenna."

Lenna settled into a seat beside Sebastien and Raif took the head of the table. The mage nodded as the librarian sat down. He was, of course, very primly cutting his share of mutton with perfect table manners. Lenna, for a moment, considered asking him to give Pim some etiquette lessons.

Before he sat down, Bahl walked to stand beside Lenna's place at the table, and she looked up at him curiously. "What is it, Bahl?"

With an almost affected solemnity, he handed Lenna her mother's dagger, which she realized with a gasp she had dropped the night before in the warehouse. It had been polished to the sheen of a mirror, and in the firelight it sparkled almost as brightly as the Godjewels or Sebastien's earring. "Thank you, Bahl!" Lenna was truly touched, and if she could have hugged the dagger without being pierced, she probably would have.

Across the table, Pim snorted. "I'm the one who remembered to bring it back. Grabbed Valant's sword too; it's ours by right."

"Thank you, Pim," Lenna said in earnest, before looking back to Bahl. "Er, Bahl, was there something else?"

"Freewoman Faircloth..." the hunter began.

"Oh, my ears are going to grow corn before he finishes his story!" said Pim, standing up and walking over to the hunter and pushing him aside, a bold move against someone as strong as Bahl, even if he was suffering from serious injuries. "Listen, Lenna, you're not just kin. You're the daughter of the sister of a Freewoman leader. You've got rank to join a council or be the mayor of a village if it struck your fancy."

Lenna choked on her bread, and Pim pounded her back with such force Lenna wondered if it might not be more comfortable to suffocate. Eventually, though, with the aid of a glass of water poured by Sebastien, she swallowed down the last morsel and stopped coughing. "I beg your pardon?"

Raif whistled; Seb looked nonchalant, as though this information was nothing new. Next to a giggling Pim, however, Bahl looked furious at the young warrior, as though he might clock her over the head for speaking out of turn. "Apparently," Pim continued, "Jaice didn't want to worry about the politics beforehand, but Bahl blurted the news to me and the boys here while under the effects of some wine and happy vibes from Sebastien."

"My magic reserves haven't recovered enough for a proper healing yet. I was simply helping ease the residual pain from his wounds," Seb replied. "In any case, I already knew."

"Me too," Raif chimed in.

"So does your dad, I think," said Pim merrily.

Bahl's face was redder than she had ever seen Pim's, which was no easy feat, and Lenna furtively glared at every single person in the room. "Why has no one bothered to inform me of this until now?"

"I just met you yesterday," Raif said.

"Didn't know 'til now." Pim shrugged.

"Jaice is going to kill me," Bahl groaned.

"Politics," said Sebastien.

Lenna was about three seconds away from throwing a chunk of bread at each and every one of them, but instead she burst out into hysterical laughter. Appalled, Bahl backed up, but the other three, even Sebastien, snickered or smirked until Lenna finished. The librarian-turned-Freewoman-noble helped herself to a slice of mutton, followed by a huge slug of the red wine that Raif, minutes earlier, had happily poured into her empty glass.

"Ah," she sighed, and leaned back in her chair. "So, in addition to this..." Lenna plucked the Godjewel out of her pocket and dangled it over the dining table, where it cast pale blue shards of light that circled the walls like stars, "I now appear to be some kind of politician."

"What will you do next?" Raif asked hopefully.

"Of course, she's coming back with Bahl and me to Granemere Settlement. The Empire's gonna be after her, but we can keep her safe there!" Pim sat back down forcefully.

Having regained his composure, Bahl slowly lowered himself into his dining chair. "For once, I agree with Pim." He took a pull at his wine. "The wards around the village will protect Lenna from detection."

"The Empire and the Brotherhood will still find her," Raif argued. "She and that stone need to stay on the run. And we have to find the other one that little brat stole."

Sebastien, sipping at his wine, said in a monotone voice, "My original plan was to get the gem to the south. The Emperor and the Brotherhood both want another God War and need all three gems to start it." He turned his head to the woman sitting next to him. "Lenna, come with me. Your link with the jewel is strong, but Gallas is far from the Empire. I can teach you to control your power and, more importantly, keep you safe."

"She should come with me," Raif interrupted. "She'll be able to use the power of the jewel to help me catch that renegade mage."

"She belongs with her people!" Pim said aggressively.

The conversation quickly dissolved into a heated shouting match between Bahl, Pim, Raif, and even Sebastien. Lenna, with a strange mixture of resignation and amusement, polished off her glass of wine and stealthily poured herself another. She was unsure what these people meant to her, and even more unsure of where she should take the bloody gem that fate had decided to drop in her lap. War was coming, war between Ilya and the Empire

— and if Junction was any indication, involving Fallowfields as well — but it wasn't coming tonight, she thought. Not for her.

She slid her hand into her rucksack and fished about for a moment before finding the item she was looking for. Its oily leather felt familiar to her skin, and the moment she pulled it from the satchel she could already hear her mother's voice and smell her delicately floral and astringent scent. Wine in one hand and open book in the other, Lenna began to read.

Some time later, when the argument had died down without Lenna's input, the crowd around the table stopped and regarded the wavy-haired woman, already on her third glass of wine and halfway through a book she'd read numerous times before.

"How can you read through all the shouting?" Pim asked incredulously.

Lenna took a sip of the Ilyan wine; the Vandever family certainly did possess an impressive selection of exquisite vintages. "I'm a librarian. I can read through anything." And she let the other four characters resume their conversation, sinking back into the curling pages of her book.

Fleeing Tranum proved a less complicated task than had entering it stealthily. With Raif's connections, however tenuous at the moment, Lenna, Pim, and Bahl quickly obtained passage on a steamtrain for the following morning; its destination was Lenna's beloved Fallowfields. The airship captain was still determined to follow the trail of Luc's treachery and recover his family's lost treasure, but he seemed strangely reluctant to depart as the group massed before the platform of Tranum's railway.

"What is it?" asked Lenna.

"I just wish you'd reconsider," Raif admitted. "Stick around and help me find that rogue mage. That's all."

Pim, her personality making up for the inches her height lacked, stepped between Lenna and Raif before either could speak up. Her mop of brown curls bounced menacingly toward her companions, and she had folded her arms in a pose of rigid determination. She looked like a miniature lioness.

"We've been over this about two thousand times," she said, "and nothing has changed. We all agree the safest place for Lenna is with the Freewomen."

Agree might be a bit of a stretch, Lenna mused. Eventually, the arguing had died off and the librarian, a bit tipsy on both wine and the gratuity of a full night's (day's) rest, had in one sweeping, heavy-tongued statement declared that she had had enough of romping about the wilds in the company of strange men. That had rewarded Lenna with a matching pair of puzzled expressions from Raif and Sebastien, while Bahl looked on approvingly. Besides, Lenna had added, the Freewoman homestead was closer to Port Hollish, and she thought that she had best contact her father before making any more serious decisions regarding the jewel.

Displeased but placated, Raif made hasty arrangements for not three but four, as Sebastien insisted on seeing Lenna and the Godjewel safely to the border of her mother's settlement. Too weary to argue further, the group eventually retired for the evening. Having slept the day away, Lenna was concerned that she would be able to find no rest that night, but in fact she nodded off quite quickly: with her decision made, the softly throbbing stone didn't seem to carry the same weight it did before.

Now, at the station, the brisk autumn wind rushed around Lenna's feet and ruffled the loose curls of her shortened hair; she would have to get used to that, though it would grow out before long. Raif continued to shuffle his feet, looking between Pim and Lenna with an expression that suggested there was more he wanted to say, but the Ilyan nobleman was probably not used to being at a loss for words before a crowd.

Sebastien's well-manicured hand clapped Raif on the shoulder with a kind of male camaraderie. Lenna could not discern whether it was expressive of compassion or condescension, but the muscles in the taller Ilyan's neck tensed and he glared down into the dispassionate face of Sebastien. His wounds healed and properly bathed, the former wizard of the Blue Crescent Brotherhood had once again assumed his stance of haughty aloofness.

"Don't worry, Master Vandever," Sebastien said. "I'll make certain to see Lenna to the borders of her people."

Lenna blinked at the thick, sticky silence that fell between the two men and was about to comment when Bahl pushed his way between them and tugged Pim — and subsequently Lenna — toward the stairs that led to the train platform.

"Come, ladies," he grunted. "Let's let the two boys settle their quarrel in private."

The Freewomen found themselves shuffled from stationmaster to ticket collector to the queue leading to a private car near the front of the train. Lenna was amazed at Bahl's expert navigation of the throngs of commuting people. All the other passengers, it seemed, naturally avoided the solid, brooding man.

A moment after the three had settled in their seats — the car of similar design to the one Lenna and Pim used to enter Tranum — a high-pitched shriek cut through the air. The stationmaster had blown his whistle, and from the seat beneath her, Lenna felt a soft but powerful rumbling as the train began to move like a great behemoth along the tracks. The librarian exhaled heavily, not realizing she had been holding her breath.

With a thunk, the door to the party's compartment slid open and Sebastien dumped himself into the seat beside Bahl with none of his former ceremony. Pim scowled at him from across the way. "You look like the cat that got the cream," she commented. Sebastien, for all his schooling, still blushed.

"What do you mean?" asked Lenna, curious. She was unaware of any disagreement between Raif and Seb, but even though she'd experienced little of life compared to her three companions, the librarian had read enough to dread that the quarrel stemmed from problems of the heart.

"Exactly what you think it means," answered Bahl gruffly, and Sebastien, his face still tinted pink, harrumphed and looked away.

Lenna rolled her eyes and gazed out the window to the platform as the train picked up speed and began to leave the station behind. Raif was there, his flaxen hair blazing in the early morning sun, waving a hand awkwardly in farewell. Before she realized it, Lenna's own had returned the gesture, and Raif nodded before turning back and disappearing into the queues forming for the next train. It was Lenna's turn to blush.

I will not turn into one of those stupid, useless females in adventures, she repeated to herself. Lenna focused so resolutely on repeating this incantation that she barely felt the thrumming of the Godjewel around her neck against the regular knocking and clacking of the steamtrain.

***

In a rocky ravine on the outskirts of the city of Tranum, where the stenches of refuse and raw sewage mixed savagely, a young man leaned against the craggy wall alongside the riverbed. His dark hair stuck in heavy, sweaty locks against his forehead, and his breathing was shallow, forced. A viridian light pulsed faintly in even intervals from the cracks between his fingers.

Luc lowered a vacant gaze down toward his hand, as if he felt the pressure of the Godjewel for the first time. It was an aggressive weight, and its persistent prodding at his mind forced the young mage to recall a tortured childhood in the Brotherhood, where the other members of his house — the groups novice mages joined, separated by year of entrance — harassed and cajoled Luc to perform acts of humiliation. Until another young mage had rescued him, that is.

Balling his other hand into a fist, Luc attempted to stifle himself before an anguished cry had a chance to escape his lips. When had he felt such oppressive misery? Gravel and sand scratched as his feet gave way and his body slowly sank down the ravine wall and he sat, blankly staring out across the murky, shallow stream.

Recent events were hazy, and Luc recalled them as though he were seeing his memories at the bottom of the ocean: everything was dark, blurry, and marred. The only clear image his mind presented was of Gilbert, the man who saved him, falling prone against the wintry night, steam escaping his dying body. And then a great arc cut through the crisp air: Lenna's hand colliding against his cheek.

What was worse? To be betrayed by Gilbert when he chose to die protecting Lenna, or to be accused of being unworthy by the woman Luc's lover had sought to protect? The young mage had no answer; his despair was unlike anything he had ever before experienced. He felt he had fallen into a well of such depth that he would never again see the light.

Once more the Godjewel pulsed in Luc's clutched hand, insistently, like a writhing snake struggling to free itself. He unclenched his fist and looked at the green stone curiously. Tiny and perfectly smooth, the rock looked puny even in Luc's small hand. It was hard for him to fathom that such a peculiar object could be a harbinger of death, a destroyer of nations. And that the cursed blue one had chosen Lenna over Luc.

The jewel thumped again. Luc had been called by this one; it had guided him through the twisting maze of Tranum and toward Gilbert's master, Sebastien. It was sheer chance that he had stumbled on General Valant and her soldiers; his willingness to cooperate with the Empire had been a surprise to the icy woman.

Had it really been chance, then? Could it be that the Vandever family jewel that had brought him this far? Did the jewels manipulate the powers of time and space around themselves to fall into hands with which to bond? And, once bonded, would they stay attuned to the host's soul until the soul willingly escaped the gem's clutches?

It didn't matter to Luc, one way or the other. He knew that with his magical training, he would surely be superior to Lenna if this Godjewel was truly his, had truly chosen him. Perhaps then death itself could bend to Luc's will, and Gilbert...

Yes, Gilbert. He had taken away the pain of Luc's sister's death and had protected a young, quivering boy from the torments of peers who covered him in their excrement and forced him out into the rain for nights on end without shoes. And if Lenna and the blue Godjewel could take Gilbert away from him, then, this world be damned, Luc could use the same power to bring his lover back.

Yes, Gilbert, thumped the jewel. Yes, Lenna, thumped the jewel. Luc's glassy eyes reflected the green strobe light from the gemstone eerily, in turn catching the fine spray of the fetid river where it lapped against his boots. The mage stood up, his garments shedding a layer of dust and grit, and he slipped the humming bauble into the pocket of his trousers.

And if he could bring back Gilbert, why not his sister, Clarie? Why not stop the terrible pain inflicted upon helpless humans once and for all? To stop all grief, all suffering, all the emotional bleeding... yes, Luc could do that. But would two jewels be enough? No. Three. Three and all the pain would stop, forever. Or rather, it would never have been.

Luc smiled despite himself, barely noticing the stench of the sewer anymore. Patting his pocket reassuringly, he let out a little whistle as he started down the dusty riverbank toward the fields of Ilya. He knew he would be seeing Gilbert soon.

Far off to the north, where powdery crystals of snow blanketed the grand forests of Krevlum, a man with smooth, ice-blonde hair rang a delicate porcelain bell. Its faint chime echoed down a pristine marble hall, and within moments a servant appeared in the gentleman's study, a tall room with stack upon stack of precisely ordered books, archaic maps, and, in some corners, remnants of mechanisms and other tinkerings.

The butler, dressed in crisp court livery of deep gold, placed a tray stacked with small sandwiches and a teapot on a low table near a large marble-topped desk. The gentlemen, in gold-framed spectacles and a smart suit tailored to his slight frame, nodded at the servant, who then began to pour a cup of tea.

"Is it true," asked the gentleman, stirring his tea before taking a sip, "that Valant has been killed while in Ilyan territory?" He adjusted his almost blindingly white waistcoat.

"Yes, my lord," replied the nondescript servant. "We recovered her corpse late this morning and disposed of it as per your instructions."

The gentleman gave an affected sigh. "It's such a nuisance to lose a good soldier. Still," he added, "this grants us the perfect opportunity to be more open in our movements in Ilya. Inform the Commander to proceed with the next stage. I trust our lightning wagons have stirred up the countryside in Fallowfields?"

"Yes, my lord. Junction has been destroyed, which should limit foot traffic from the south for some time. We've established a small but strong presence to the north of the country, several leagues south of our border, as you requested. Fallowfieldian military is no threat without backing from Ilya."

"Excellent. The second Godjewel will most likely be headed back to the owner's homeland."

"Indeed, my lord."

The gentleman stood in thought for a few moments before finishing off his tea. He placed the teacup on the desk with the faintest of sounds and began flipping through a large, leather-bound journal off to the side. About halfway through the massive volume he stopped and nodded approvingly. He selected a sheet of paper and a fountain pen from the corner of his desk.

"Very well; you are dismissed. I have work to do."

Silently, the butler exited, off to deliver his master's orders. The gentleman began in a brisk, efficient script to ink a series of circular symbols and single strokes, referring back to the volume every so often. One circle, two strokes, one circle, one stroke, one circle, two strokes. He continued to fill a few lines of the paper with these uniform symbols, alternating their order now and then. About halfway down the page, a sudden tingling sensation overtook him, and he dropped the pen to the desk, halfway through a stroke.

"Well, well," said the gentleman. He unbuttoned the first few buttons of his crisply starched muslin shirt and tugged out a glowing golden gemstone fastened to a chain around his neck. The gentleman cupped the jewel in his hand and peered at it with an impassive expression on his face. After a moment, the light from the stone dulled and faded away, until the pale yellow Godjewel was quiet once more. The gentleman tucked it back into his shirt and fastened the stiff, mother-of-pearl buttons.

"It appears the last of the jewels has found its soulmate," he said dryly. "A bit faster than usual, but I doubt it will do much to accelerate the plan." He checked a golden pocket watch fastened to the belt of his trousers, and frowned. A small scratch had appeared, marring the glistening glass faceplate of the delicate instrument. "What a pity. I was rather fond of this one; I suppose it must be time for me to acquire a new timepiece."

With an uncharacteristic shrug, the Emperor of Krevlum, Alderic Sonnet, picked up the fountain pen once more and resumed his strange task. Circle, three strokes, circle, two strokes, circle — he continued until the page was nearly full with this strange code. Nodding in satisfaction, he picked up the sheet of paper, flipped closed the leather volume to his left, and walked out of his personal study.

And somewhere, deep within the Imperial palace, a small patch of reality began to waver, and a soul stirred with a mournful wail.

Lenna's adventures continue in book two,
Apprentice.

ABOUT THE AUTHOR

Brian grew up in the small town of Whiting, NJ, a magical realm near the sea where pine trees grow in the sand. Aside from deer, his primary company was his imagination. He obtained his BA in East Asian Studies (Japanese) and Creative Writing from Bucknell University, and spent a great deal of time studying, living, and working in Japan before moving to the United Kingdom to pursue a Master's Degree in Sociology at the University of Oxford. He wrote his dissertation in a pub, and proudly continues that tradition by pumping out novels at any bar with good grub and good drink. When he isn't writing, Brian hops around the world tasting wine, collecting My Little Ponies, and cooking a hell of a lot of nomtastic food.

http://www.brianfence.com

CPSIA information can be obtained at www.ICGtesting.com
Printed in the USA
LVOW10s0958130813

347647LV00001B/21/P